# Dauntless

Lea A. Henze

Dauntless: A WWII Novel

ISBN-13: 978-0692374252
ISBN-10: 0692374256

Dedicated to my grandparents

&

In honor of the men and women who
served, lived, and died during World War II.

*"The time will come, when though shalt lift thine eyes*
*To watch a long-drawn battle in the skies,*
*While aged peasants, too amazed for words,*
*Stare at the flying fleets of wond'rous birds,*
*England, so long the mistress of the sea,*
*Where wind and waves confess her sovereignty,*
*Her ancient triumphs yet on high shall bear,*
*And reign the sovereign of the conquered air."*
*-Gray's Luna Habitabilis*

# Part 1

# Chapter 1

Hurrying along the cobblestone path, Margaret spared a glance upward and squinted into the sunshine that was, for once, shining down on London. A plane droned by overhead. Without a moment to lose, she trotted up to the church's large, wooden double doors and slipped inside. The sound of the congregation singing greeted her as she left the din of the plane and the noise of the outdoors behind.

*"Be Thou my Vision, O Lord of my heart;*
*Naught be all else to me, save that Thou art.*
*Thou my best thought, by day or by night,*
*Waking or sleeping, Thy presence my light."*

Margaret bit her lip. She was late. A few people turned their heads to glance her way in curiosity. Wordlessly, Margaret started along the side of the church to the front row where she sat beside her friend.

"Where were you?" the side of Harry's mouth turned up in a smile as he asked her quietly.

"Sh!" Someone behind them, most likely Harry's father, hushed them before Margaret could reply.

She merely grinned and tried to avoid Bess, their housekeeper's, look of disapproval from where she sat behind the piano playing the chords to the well-known hymn. Margaret finished singing the song with all the others and once they concluded, Reverend Sutton arose and took his place by the altar to tell his congregation that they could be seated. The muffled sounds of shoes scuffing the cold, stone floor followed. Harry smiled kindly to Margaret as he gave her his hymnal to put away in the side compartment of the pew.

"So, where were you?" Harry whispered, keeping quiet as the reverend started the sermon.

"What's it to you?" Margaret playfully responded, rubbing her hands together to warm them up.

"Were you lost in a daydream?" He asked in his lilting English accent. Though his family had moved from Australia to London many years ago, they were British through and through.

"It was the ducks' fault. They were hungry. I had bread." She replied with a shrug.

Every so often, she would take a Sunday morning stroll through the park down the street before the service. There were a pair of Shelducks that frequented the duck pond there and Margaret loved watching them and bringing them scraps from the kitchen when she could.

"I see..." Harry shook his head in mock disapproval, but before he could say another word, his father cuffed him on the head from behind, a warning to tell them to be quiet.

The sermon continued and at eleven, the reverend prayed for them and dismissed the congregation. Everyone dispersed rather slowly, lingering around to talk and wish each other a good day. Margaret went up to the reverend and gave him a tight hug around his middle.

"I'm sorry I was late,"

"All is well, my girl." He hugged her back. "Were the ducks back?"

"Yes, they were," she smiled and looked up at him.

"Are you hungry for lunch?"

"I'm starving!"

Together, they moseyed through the church, saying hello to all their friends and neighbors. It was a quiet, sunny, cold day... peaceful and idyllic for the first month of 1939.


In the small stone chapel and rectory nestled cozily between the sea of houses in London, the father and the daughter sat quietly late in the evening. Bess, their housekeeper, had left quite some time ago to return to her own home. Margaret sat on the couch and looked out into the cold street. She had been reading a book for school, but it had started to bore her and daydreams were much more fun. The light from the rectory's windows spilled out into the street and reflected off the cars that rumbled by. She wondered where they were going and who was in them.

Her father was watching her in amusement. He peered over his thick-rimmed glasses and the corners of his mouth turned up in a smile. Folding his paper and setting it on the end table, he reached over and clicked on the brown square radio. Margaret listened as the news crackled out through the speakers and pulled her out of her musings. She played with her brown curly hair and smiled to herself. Their routine, their precious day-to-day life together, was very dear to her. Glancing over at her father, she watched him as he went back to reading the paper, now deep in concentration, the lines on his forehead forming dark shadows.

About an hour passed and Reverend Sutton stood from his place in his chair and stretched. He was a tall, thin man with a nice, friendly face and warm, wise eyes.

"Isn't it time you were in bed?" He looked down to Margaret and outstretched his hand. She took it and bounced onto her feet.

"I'll go to bed... if you promise to take me to the concert tomorrow night." Margaret smiled playfully and looked up to her father with pleading eyes.

She loved going to the London Symphony Orchestra's concerts with him and secretly, he loved it as well. A few moments of suspense passed before he replied.

"Alright, we can go." Reverend Sutton gave in to his daughter's wishes, for she had been pestering him for the past week about going.

"Thank you, Dad! Thank you, thank you!" She hugged him and he kissed her head.

"Goodnight, my girl."

"Goodnight!" With a squeal, she dashed up the stairs that led to her room and got ready for bed, hardly able to contain her excitement for the next day.

Later the next day, the kitchen smelled of many things baking as Margaret sat at the table finishing her homework. Bess was busy fixing an early dinner for them before they left.

"They're playing Franz Schubert tonight." Margaret informed the housekeeper, who was much like a mother to her.

"Is that so?" Bess raised her eyebrows and kept whisking the gravy on the stove.

"Yes," Margaret worked a math problem and began humming the 'Ave Maria.' "I remember when they premiered 'Serenade to Music' by Vaughan Williams." She continued. "It was so lovely!" Margaret exclaimed with youthful zeal.

"How you keep all those songs in your head baffles me, girl. I can scarcely remember the hymns your father sings in church." Bess shook her head and took the pot off the stove.

Margaret looked up and smiled despite the homework. "Dad says I was born to it. Like a duck to water."

Bess chuckled. "I'd have to agree... I'd certainly have to agree. Well, I say it's very generous of him to take you to those concerts. Heaven knows, they're not cheap." She put the gravy boat on the table and asked Margaret to clear it as soon as she could. "But I'd wager..." Bess pulled a meat pie out of the oven, "your father enjoys them as much, if not more, than you do."

With her pretty knee-length red dress on and her black coat over that, Margaret stepped into her fancy shoes and fastened them on over her starch-white socks. Her hair was curled and put up and she even wore a touch of lipstick given to her by Bess, much to the reverend's displeasure.

Margaret and her father said goodbye to Bess and trotted out to their car, trying to spend as little time in the cold as possible. The black boxy car rumbled as it started. Margaret slid into the front seat and felt like a royal. She smoothed her dress as her father steered the car onto the road. It was such a luxury to drive and not have to walk.

"Alright, we had a deal." The reverend stated, for they had agreed that Margaret could wear the lipstick only while they were in the car.

"But we haven't gotten there yet!" Margaret pleaded. "And it'll look awful if I wipe it off." It made her feel grown up and she thought she looked like the ladies that attended the concerts with their glimmering dresses and fashionable makeup.

The reverend sighed. He gave her half a smile and turned onto a busy road.

She took it as his acquiescence and felt she would burst with excitement. Her father had gotten two tickets for the balcony in the Royal Albert Hall. She knew it was something they could scarcely afford, and she felt guilty about it, but the joy she felt when she listened to the music was always enough to make her forget her remorse.

"One day people will drive and pay money to see me play." She wistfully dreamt out loud. "One day I'll be part of the LSO and I'll be a famous musician."

Her father cast her a sidelong glance and let her dream. "I have no doubt you will." He kept his concerns to himself and felt guilt creep over him.

His daughter was gifted... truly gifted. He felt as though he could not provide what was necessary for her to excel and study at university. He could hardly afford the funds to pay for advanced lessons, let alone what it would cost to send her to any of the universities that focused on music. He also thought it strange that his daughter would take such a liking to the LSO, for reasons he dare not dwell on. Turning onto another street, he thought back to a time long ago... A time almost lost that seemed so far away, like the sun sinking behind the horizon to rise on the other side of the world. He thought of his wife. *She was so beautiful and so gentle. To have such a talent and for it to be so misused... My dear, poor Gabriella... Gone... gone from us forever...*

The reverend could not help but think such thoughts. His mind drifted back to the present and away from the painful memories that forever haunted his thoughts.

"Here we are." Reverend Sutton steered the automobile onto Kensington Road.

Margaret looked out the window and admired the streetlights that shone through the bare branches of the trees in Kensington Park. Benches lined the paths, and a quiet atmosphere seemed to drift over the dark, empty park. Ahead, cars were busy driving back and forth in front of the salmon-colored Royal Albert Hall, named after the husband of Queen Victoria, Prince Albert of Saxe-Coburg and Gotha.

*"Thine O Lord is the greatness and the power and the glory and the victory and the majesty."* Margaret spoke the biblical reference that was inscribed in terracotta letters above the high frieze that ran along the circumference of the hall. She continued, *"for all that is in the heaven and in the earth is Thine. The wise and their works are in the hand of God. Glory be to God on high and on earth peace."*

"Amen!" Reverend Sutton exclaimed.

Looking out, her breath fogging up the window, Margaret spied men in fine black suits entering the hall and ladies in beautiful, exquisite gowns that sparkled and shimmered like diamonds. They passed the sight as the reverend found a suitable parking space. Margaret dabbed the lipstick from her lips regretfully and the red gloss tinted her handkerchief. Her father winked at her as she reluctantly gave up, wanting to respect her father's wishes. Coming from Prince Consort Road, father and daughter walked with the growing crowd up the South Steps to the 12th door. Margaret linked arms with her father, and they ascended the steps along with the other music lovers. She couldn't help but feel like she belonged here.

It felt like home to them both.

They slowly made their way through the crowds to their seats. Up on the balcony, Margaret could see all. It was there that Margaret waited for the performance to start. She smoothed her red dress she was so proud of and patted her curly hair to make sure it had stayed in place. Bess had fashioned it especially for the occasion. Leaning back in her seat, Margaret took her father's hand.

"Thank you,." She smiled at him and noticed that his attention was elsewhere. "What is it?" She furrowed her eyebrows.

Bringing his attention back, the reverend looked back down to his daughter and took a deep breath. "I was just looking around." He smiled. "And you are most welcome. I would do this and much more." He patted her hand reassuringly. "Look! It's starting!" He pointed to the stage where the orchestra was preparing to play the wonderful masterpieces of Franz Schubert.

First, the orchestra played the 'Piano Sonata in B♭.' It was a slower piece and took a few minutes to get to the crescendo. The piano was a grand Steinway and Margaret looked at it longingly. She wondered if she would ever play on such a beautiful piano. Mainly, she only played on the small upright they had at the church. But that wasn't her preferred instrument... She scanned the rest of the orchestra. The piano was to the left as were the violins and harps. In the back were the woodwinds, the brass, and the timpani. But to the right were the basses and then Margaret saw them... the cellos.

The beautiful composition that rang out through the hall was 'Ave Maria' on the strings. The cellos could not be more beautiful. Margaret wished she was with them on stage. Ever since she had started playing the cello several years ago, it had become her favorite instrument. And she was good at it. She had taken some lessons from a local music store after Bess taught her to read sheet music. After a year's worth of sporadic lessons, she started teaching herself. She knew the lessons had been expensive and her father had joyously paid for them and her own cello. But after learning the basics, she believed she could take it from there. However, in the last year or so, Margaret had taken a lesson once a month by one of the music shop owners nearby. He was a professional with the instrument and she was glad of his expert tutelage. Her talent had only blossomed more with each lesson.

The song ended quietly, and Margaret breathed deeply. She watched as the grey-haired conductor brought out the next composition of music.

He clicked his wand on his stand and out came the beginning notes of the First Movement of Schubert's '8th *Unfinished Symphony.'* The conductor kept time with his movements and punctuated the correct notes. The bows of the violins moved in synchronization and the cellists, all in black suits, lifted their bows and plucked the strings with their fingers. Margaret imagined what it would be like to play with them. She would be center stage playing a solo with the power of the orchestra behind her. She heard a sniffling as the composition moved into tense pulses. Looking up to her father, she saw that he had a tear in his eye.

She offered him her handkerchief. He smiled weakly and waved it away. Margaret turned back to the orchestra as the song ended. The reverend dabbed the tear from his eye and obviously tried to compose himself.

*Perhaps he feels the same way about music as I do.* Margaret decided that must be the case and sat forward in her chair, eager for more melodies.

Song after song played, waltzes, movements, and solos. When the last song of the night started, Margaret's pulse quickened in excitement. Perhaps the greatest of Schubert's works was that of Schubert's '*Ständchen*,' or Serenade. Hauntingly, the piano started the love song. The strings picked up after about four measures and the song continued. Margaret listened to the music and the feelings that it brought. It reminded her of a pond in the pouring rain; raindrops making ripples and sunshine beaming in from the west underneath the thick clouds and magically illuminating the scene in an iridescent gold and shimmering yellow. It ended and Margaret opened her mind back to the world in which she lived. Everyone applauded and gave the phenomenal orchestra a standing ovation. A wide smile was on the young prodigy's face and the thrill of music pulsed in her veins. It was a passion that was not foreign to the Sutton family, yet the young, lively girl did not yet know it.

The next day was dreary and bleak. However, in the parish no one would have known. Bess was baking loaves of bread for the next week, the reverend was writing his next sermon at his desk, immersed in his Bible. Margaret was hopping down the stairs, having just changed out of her school uniform and still reeling from the concert. She entered the heavenly-smelling kitchen and sat at the table.

"Oh, Bess, that smells wonderful!" She enthusiastically greeted the ginger maid as she took a piece of warm buttered bread that was waiting for her.

"Thank you, dear. So... how did it go?" Her round cheeks were red from the kitchen work.

"Oh, it was wonderful!" Margaret exclaimed.

"Good, I'm glad to hear it. I know you were worried about that test." Bess grabbed a hot pad.

"Test?" Margaret grimaced. "I thought you meant about the concert."

Bess laughed and pulled a loaf out of the oven, shaking her head in mock displeasure.

"The test was fine. I think I did alright with it." Margaret shrugged.

"You have to learn to love your schooling as much as your music." Bess gently scolded her.

A knock sounded on the door and Margaret jumped up. "I'll get it!" She leapt up and sprinted to the door before her father could get to it.

"I'm coming!" She shouted out without opening the door. Margaret grabbed her coat, threw on her shoes, and met Harry outside, having previously discussed on their walk home from school they'd go explore Regent's after their homework was done.

Bess and the reverend watched Margaret go and the housekeeper couldn't help but chuckle. "Reverend, that neighbor boy sure does carry a torch for our little Meg!" She said as she wiped her floury hands on her white apron.

It took a moment for the comment to register with the reverend. "Oh dear! Bess, you're not serious, are you?" He looked up, quite forgetting about his sermon-writing.

"No doubt about it." Bess replied as she washed her hands. "Mark my words; you'll have some trouble from him in the future... that is if Meg ever notices he likes her so."

"Well," the reverend looked off into the distance, deep in thought. "Harry's a good lad. I'm sure no trouble of that sort will come of it." He shook his head to clear his mind and went back to writing his sermon.

The two friends crossed the street and made their way to Regent's Park. From there, they walked around the Inner Circle and chatted. Harry was bundled up in his grey pants, loafers, and heavy brown corduroy coat. He listened intently as Margaret theatrically described the enchanting concert again, but this time in more detail. Though Harry was not musical, he was always interested in what Margaret was playing and listening to, for music was her life. He had even gotten quite handy at knowing what composers had written what.

"Didn't Schubert write the *Ave Maria*?" Harry asked and scratched his head.

"Yes, he wrote so many beautiful songs. I don't know why so many people haven't heard of him. I'm going to learn the Ständchen on my cello. Would you like to come and watch?" Margaret asked.

"No, I can't. Evan is taking me to his school for a speech, or lecture, or something of the sort tonight. It sounds rather dull." Harry scrunched up his face.

"I'm sorry..." Margaret shrugged but understood. Harry was rather close with his brothers and did things often with them.

The two friends finished their walk around the Inner Circle and entered the winding paths of the park. There were waterfalls that were frozen over from the cold, and ponds with grebes and ducks swimming around the ice floes that threatened to freeze the ponds completely. Fog drifted everywhere and no one trod on the quiet paths in the late afternoon hour. Margaret shivered and pulled her coat closer around herself.

"How *are* your brothers?" She inquired. Harry had two older brothers and both were at university in Oxford; one at St. John's and the other at Trinity. "Any other news from them?" She walked over to the railing that overlooked one of the ponds; the ducks were quacking and started to swim over to them.

Harry joined her and watched the ducks. "Rich did well on his latest test *and* he has a girlfriend now." Harry told Margaret about his eldest brother who was studying to become a doctor. "And Evan said one of his professors is being unreasonably unfair. I don't think he has much to complain about, he doesn't have to sit in Mrs. Harris' class and do her history assignments. Harry chuckled and joked about their shared teacher.

Margaret laughed in response. "You couldn't be more right."

The ducks were now swimming in circles before them.

"I wish I had some bread..." She put her hands in her pockets to make sure there weren't any leftovers from the other day.

When she came up empty, she saw that Harry was already holding out two pieces for her, the ends of a stale loaf.

Margaret grinned and took them. "Thank you,"

They stood there in silence for a few moments while Margaret tossed the ducks small pieces she broke off.

"When do you go to your grandparents?" She asked him.

The question elicited a sigh from Harry. "In April; I'm afraid we'll be gone during your birthday."

"It's no matter," Margaret replied.

A small piece of her wondered why her birthday was significant to Harry... Margaret and the Cavanaughs only used to celebrate each other's birthdays when they were younger. The past few years had been slightly different with Harry's brothers moving away.

"Come on, I'm freezing standing here." Harry rubbed his mittened hands together as Margaret tossed the ducks the rest of the bread, dusting the last of the crumbs from her gloves.

They finished their walk and made their way back to their home street. The Cavanaugh's house was two stories and, in the summer, it was beautifully decorated with colorful flowers in the flowerboxes Harry's mother planted. Margaret waved Harry off and looked up to the bleak, grey sky. The fog was beginning to clear, yet the clouds promised rain or snow. Margaret ducked inside and shivered as she took off her coat and hung it up.

Inside their small home, Reverend Sutton was sitting in his chair, deep in thought, with a concerned look on his face.

"What is it?" Margaret asked as she kicked her shoes off and joined him in the living room.

"Just thinking, my girl." Reverend Sutton looked weary. "You read all kinds of things in the papers and hear even more news of the world from the congregation. So many terrible things are happening in Europe. It's... God help the poor souls."

Margaret was perplexed and yet was not surprised. She had heard rumors circulating around the adults' conversations in the church that a war was on the way with the Germans. Already, they had invaded Austria and Czechoslovakia. Margaret remembered reading about the horrors of something called Kristallnacht in a newspaper column.

"Is it true?" Margaret asked, clasping her hands in front of her nervously.

Her father ran his finger thoughtfully across his mouth as he clicked on the radio. He looked up at her with uncertainty. Margaret couldn't pinpoint what she felt. However, she had never seen fear in her father's eyes before. It scared her. If he thought their country was standing on the edge of something terrible, then it must be true...

Suddenly, she couldn't help but feel that she, too, was overlooking a wide, black canyon that was sure to swallow her, and all those she loved, whole.

# Chapter 2

The next few months passed by in a flurry. Margaret and Harry studied relentlessly in school and were rewarded with wonderful grades. However, none of that mattered to Margaret. She was head over heels in her music and every day she learned something new.

Margaret sat alone in their drawing room and looked out the window to enjoy the view of the late March twilight. The tan, plaid curtains were parted and let in the scant amount of evening light. She sat in a wooden chair with her cello resting on one knee. Her fingers gently touched the strings on the fingerboard and her right hand held the bow loosely but firmly. She breathed deeply and played a clear open note on the D string. It resonated deep within her, and she placed her first finger a whole step up. The note changed from D to E. Quickly, she continued up the scale until her forefinger was as high as it could go on the black fingerboard. The A string's highest note sounded more like a violin than a cello. Finishing the scale and removing her bow from the strings, Margaret turned to her music stand that was to her left. She flipped through the music book her father had given her for her latest birthday and stopped on the *'Cello Sonata'* for piano and cello by Beethoven. If Bess hadn't taken the day off to visit her sister in Leeds, Margaret would have asked her to play the piano part. But seeing as she was alone and her father had left to visit some members of the congregation for a few hours that evening, she resigned herself to a solo.

The first note was deep and clear and as she moved through the beautiful melody, she thought it sounded like a royal garden party in St. James's Park. The lovely strain continued, and Margaret read the notes quickly and effortlessly. She hardly had to use sheet music, for she had played the piece many times. The bow rocked back and forth above the decorated, carved bridge of the cello and her fingers worked quickly on the fingerboard. When the song finally ran out, she flipped through the music book and stopped on Bach's *'Cello Suite No. 1 in G Major.'* The tune was familiar to her. She didn't glance at the first note or the hundreds after it. Starting on the G string she began the fast tune. Her fingers instinctively went to the correct places as she played quickly, accurately, and beautifully.

Imagining she was on stage at the Royal Albert Hall, she closed her eyes and pictured hundreds of people watching her. She imagined her father in the front row next to Bess. She dreamt of Harry in the front row too with his brothers and parents. Everything she would ever need was right in front of her. As the song grew and became higher after a minute, she was overcome with mixed feelings. The one that prevailed above all, unexpectedly, was sadness. At two minutes, the song grew even higher and she felt despondent for the one person who wasn't in her dreams... her mother.

People walked by Lily's End Church and often heard the incredible music radiating from the house. Perhaps they thought it was a gramophone. However, it was not. It was Margaret. That evening was no exception. Harry was walking by the parish and stopped. He listened as the music radiated from the stone cottage. He dared not disturb his friend. He leaned on the stone wall and listened for many long moments. People walked by and gave him curious looks and yet they looked extremely confused as to where the classical music was coming from. Harry wondered how Margaret did it. He knew no one so accomplished with music. He recognized the fast, wholesome tune Margaret was playing. Margaret had never let him forget it, for it was one of her favorites. She played it as well as a professional. *How does she do it?* He wondered again to himself. The musical notes cascaded around the street and rose up into the English evening air.

A hearty applause came from the doorway behind Margaret once she finished playing The Swan Sant-Saens.

Margaret was taken aback. She had thought she was alone.

"Dad! When did you get here?" She asked as she closed her music book.

"Just a few minutes ago." He had already hung up his coat.

Margaret looked out the windows, not realizing it had gotten dark so quickly. Her father turned on a lamp. Margaret looked up to him and noticed that his usual happy and easy-going demeanor was gone. Something was up.

"How was your visit with Mr. Haddington?" she asked.

"We had a nice visit. Talked about many things."

"What sorts of things?" Margaret asked, knowing there was more to the story.

"Oh, all sorts. We talked about the church and our families. Oddly enough, he was talking about sending Lucy and Ben to stay in the countryside..." He sat down with a sigh in his favorite chair. "I'm afraid he assumes the worst when it comes to the unrest in Europe. He believes Chamberlain isn't handling Hitler's aggression the way he ought. He's not the only one to think such." The reverend was looking at the radio, as if lost in thought. He propped up his chin with his thumb, his elbow resting on the armrest.

"And what do you think?" Margaret held onto her cello and absent-mindedly plucked a string with her thumb.

"I try not to worry. But Mr. Haddington is certain war is on the way and if that's the case..." Reverend Sutton let the statement hang. "I just pray that it won't lead to war again. King George will steer us right. We can only pray for our country, Meg. Pray that our leaders will be wise and keep us on the straight and narrow." Reverend Frank Sutton gazed at his daughter, and she smiled.

"I will, Dad." She nodded, feeling the tension the ill news had brought.

*What would happen if England went to war?* She thought as she put her chair back in the kitchen, put the cello away, and went upstairs to finish her homework. She knew that war, if it came, would change everything.

The breeze was warmer than it had been weeks ago. Margaret and Harry traversed in silence, lapsing into the quiet comfort they usually found together ever since they became friends when Harry's family moved in next door years ago. Together, they made their way down the long road that was bordered by houses on either side. Their small community in the northern part of London was quiet, as it was in an older district. It was full of mature trees in front of the small two-story homes that were packed tightly together with small plots for yards. The quiet road crossed a busier one and it was at this junction that Margaret and Harry turned up the street. Car engines rumbled by, yet the traffic was half of what it had been years ago. Times were hard and people were forced to be frugal. Most, it seemed, chose to walk or bicycle anyway.

The school appeared ahead and even before she stepped inside, she wished the day was over. It was an old brick building that was full to the brim and bursting with students. Harry held open the door for her and she ducked inside. They were a little bit late, so they hurried along even quicker. Walking through the hallways lined with lockers, they reached their room door, No. 12, home of Mrs. Harris. She was the uptight sort and the most jaded teacher whose hair was always put up in the tightest bun.

Margaret slid into her desk chair and pulled out her literature book. She and Harry were the last to take their seats and Mrs. Harris looked at them from over her round, rimless glasses.

"I hope you two have a good excuse for being late." She stood up from her desk. "Shall we begin, Mr. Cavanaugh?" Mrs. Harris tested him.

"Yes, Mrs. Harris, of course." He smiled pleasantly to her as she tapped his desk.

"Then where is your book?"

Caught off guard, Harry quickly pulled out the book from his bag.

The other students laughed.

She walked to the blackboard and began her lessons. Margaret threw Harry a sympathetic look, and he only rolled his eyes in response. The kids behind them chuckled. Mrs. Harris whipped around, and they were silent again. She turned slowly and finished writing in chalk. Margaret rested her elbow on the table and her head on her palm, already getting lost in a daydream that, of course, revolved around music.

March rolled into April and flowers started blooming all along Regent's Park and the boating lake's weeping willows started to show their green leaves and yellow, pink, white, and red tulips opened their beautiful petals. Margaret watched London become busy as if it were a hive of bees that had just woken from a long slumber.

On a cloudy, warm Sunday, Margaret sat lazily on one of the pews in the church and read her literature assignment. The Sunday morning sermon would start in about an hour, so she wanted to finish her schoolwork early. She had been practicing Chopin's *'Nocturnes for Piano'* and the melody refused to leave her head.

The door to the chapel was opened and Margaret looked up from her spot on the first pew.

"Morning!" Harry stuck his head in and then entered the church with his parents close behind.

Mr. and Mrs. Cavanaugh smiled and greeted Margaret. They both had blonde hair and kind features like Harry. He sat next to Margaret, and they discussed the book they were assigned to read.

"It's not all bad if you don't mind a toad being locked away in a dark prison." Margaret remarked. "It's a little depressing."

"I think we're a little old for talking animals." Harry remarked.

Even though he was older, he had been held back in school several years after they had moved from Australia to London. Therefore, he was in the same class as Margaret and the other fourteen-year-olds.

"I disagree," Margaret smirked. "I don't think I'll ever be too old for talking animals. And I would like to be Mr. Rat and have a little house by a river with the freedom to sail anywhere I wanted to." Margaret closed her book with a thud and set it in the compartment that held the hymnals on the side of the pew.

More people started to enter the church and Margaret wondered where her father was. Curious, she got up from her spot beside Harry and went through the side door that led to their house. She walked down the long hallway and emerged into the kitchen. Her father was looking intently at something on the table. It looked like a flyer.

"Dad?" Margaret broke him from his intent look.

"Yes?" He turned around and put the flyer in his coat pocket.

Taken aback by his secrecy, she tried to smile. "Everyone's waiting." She said plainly.

"Of course, I'm coming. I was just thinking." The reverend started to walk past her. "Come on, we best not be late." He kissed her forehead.

Margaret followed him as he led them back into the chapel.

The congregation received a lively sermon about the love of Christ and the importance of Easter, as it was coming up soon on the ninth. She always loved the holiday and the joy and renewal it brought. However, sitting in the front pew tapping her toe impatiently, she did not feel so excited for the spring holiday or her birthday that was nearing. She only wanted to know what was on her father's mind.

"What's bothering you?" Harry whispered to her.

Margaret stopped tapping her foot. She glanced at him and their eyes met. He looked concerned.

"I'll tell you later," she tried to turn her mind back to the sermon, but it was no use.

Luncheon was served by Bess in the dining room and when they finished, the reverend leaned back in his chair and pulled out the flyer from his pocket and set it on the table. It was a flyer published by the Ministry of Health about London Evacuations. Margaret bit her lip and knew what was coming. A pit formed in her stomach and every second her dread increased. *Surely, he won't send me away like Lucy and Ben! I can't leave London!*

"I've been praying and thinking," he started out slowly.

His thin features looked drawn and tired. For being a relatively young man in his late thirties, he looked older than other fathers his age. *But he's gone through what most fathers haven't...* Margaret thought to herself as the delicate subject she tried never to think about surfaced for a moment.

"If war does come, I want you far away from any danger. Our leaders are trying their best to keep war from happening. However, the more people I talk to, the more they are certain war is coming. This flyer is an example and a testament to the government's assurance of the very-likely possibility of being in danger here." He paused.

Margaret had nothing to say, but her dread grew and grew until it was almost too great of a burden to bear. She felt as though she would burst if another moment passed.

Staring at the flyer as if it determined the fate of England, the reverend continued. "We cannot pretend this will not affect us as well. Families are starting to send their children away to the countryside... They're *evacuating* children from London, Margaret." He looked to his daughter and waited for her to say something... to realize what he was saying.

"Where will I go?" She asked honestly.

Her father's parents lived in Lancashire, a long journey north, and her mother did not have any living relatives Margaret knew of. She hardly knew her father's parents and he was an only child, so she had no aunts, uncles, or cousins. Going to the countryside of England didn't sound so bad. Perhaps she could stay with Harry's grandmother. Perhaps he'd even go too, and they could stay with each other.

He closed his eyes, as if collecting his thoughts. Margaret found herself holding her breath in suspense.

"You'll go to America, my girl."

*America!*

She chuckled, thinking it was a joke. "America?" A few heartbeats passed. Her face fell as realization dawned on her. Her father wasn't joking. "Why America? I don't want to go *there.*"

Two words silenced her. "Your mother." Reverend Sutton took his daughter's cold hand. "I don't like it either, but you'll..."

"No," Maragret shook her head ever so slightly. The person they had hardly ever spoken of was suddenly brought to the present and reality like Margaret had never known. "I can't,"

"I know, I-"

"She *left.*"

The reverend swallowed hard, seemingly having to compose himself, too. "Your mother moved to New York City. You will live with her there. She's not a monster, Margaret, and it's about time you-"

"No!" Margaret had had enough. First, she was being forced to leave London and everything she knew. Now, she was being forced to meet her mother whom she had never met and never wished to meet. "I can't." She choked out, tears starting to form. She got up from her place at the dining table in frustration and hopelessness. Her father stood too.

"I'm sorry, my girl. I'm doing this to protect you. I couldn't bear it if you were in harm's way. And, I don't deny it; you need to meet your mother. You'll be safe in New York... safer than you could be anywhere else. It pains me greatly... but she's your *mother.*" He collected himself again. "She's already written back and said you are welcome in her home." Reverend Sutton tried to comfort her, but she would not hear another word.

"No! No, I won't go, and you can't make me!" Margaret released her outburst, dashed up the stairs, and slammed her door behind her.

Margaret covered her face with her hands and couldn't believe what her father had just said. She glanced out her small square window and noticed that rain was tapping on the four-paned glass. As the rain picked up outside, she lay down on her bed and cried. *I don't need a mum. I don't want a mum!* Thoughts swirled through her mind as she cried. The road before her was uncertain when all she had ever known was Lily's End. It was her life, and she could not imagine living without her father or her friends. She couldn't leave London. She would never leave her home.

As the rain poured down outside, tears rolled down Margaret's face. Uncertainty clawed at her and her heart hurt from the pain of the thought of leaving. The only thing she could do was pray that her father would change his mind, and she would be able to persuade him to let her stay. She would face anything if it only meant she could stay.

Some time after, a soft knock sounded on her door and her father entered.

He sat next to her on the bed and Margaret wiped her eyes with the back of her hand. He passed her his hanky.

"What about the countryside?" Margaret started. "Couldn't I just go live outside of London with another family? If that's what the other children are doing? Or with Harry's grandparents? Then I could still come home to visit and I wouldn't be so far away. Please, Dad... America..." she paused.

The reverend thought for a moment. "My girl... this is an opportunity for you. You must leave London; that is a fact and a decision I will stick to. And since you must go, it makes the most sense to go and stay with family. I wish your mother lived in England; I do. But America will be safest for you. It's the perfect opportunity for you to meet her and spend some time with her. I always wished you could. You would love her... you *will* love her. Please trust me. It may seem frightening and like a hundred other options would be better, but this *is* the best for you. I don't want you to grow up never having met her." He finished kindly.

"Can't you come, too?" She sat nearer him.

"It's not as simple for an adult to move to another country as it is for a child with a parent already there and a citizen. And it won't be for long."

"How long would it be for?" she asked.

"I don't know exactly. Maybe a year or two?"

"Surely not forever?" Margaret bit her lip.

The reverend smiled. "Of course, not forever. A few years, I'd say, give or take some."

Margaret nodded, thinking he didn't look convinced, yet he gave her a reassuring smile.

"Alright?" He asked, wiping a tear from her face.

Margaret couldn't say yes, but she could say no either. She sighed and shrugged.

"We'll talk about it more. Goodnight, my darling. Sleep tight." He gave her a hug and kiss goodnight before closing the door behind him and shutting off the lights.

Margaret lay in her bed and clutched her blankets. Her mind was racing and she did not feel like sleeping. She got up and looked out her window. The streets were quiet and there was not a sound to be had. Margaret sat in front of the low window and the lampposts from the streets shone on her face. *What is mum like?* She found contentment in a verse that arose in her head. *"Therefore do not worry about tomorrow, for tomorrow will worry about its own things."* She had no choice but to crawl back in bed and try to sleep, for the verse was true, she just had a hard time accepting it.

About an hour passed and Margaret still could not fall asleep. She figured it was about eleven at night, so she threw on her shawl and left her room, unable to fall into her dreams. She knocked on her father's door and then entered. He was sitting up in bed reading, glasses perched on the tip of his nose, his neat flannel pajamas on.

"I couldn't sleep." Margaret shrugged.

Reverend Sutton patted the side of his bed, and she sat beside him.

Putting his book down, he replied, "I'm sorry if my words upset you." The reverend took off his reading glasses.

Margaret itched her nose. "No, that wasn't it. I was just thinking..." She looked down in partial embarrassment. "What was mum like?" Margaret had hardly ever asked the question and when she did, her father always avoided answering it.

A somber look came over his face, but surprisingly, he replied. "She was just like you." The love and regret in her father's eyes almost made Margaret choke up.

"Where did you meet?" Margaret asked again. The reverend held her gaze and seemed to be debating whether to tell her.

"We met here, in London. She was playing in several concerts, and I was studying to become a minister. I knew the minute I saw her in the orchestra that I loved her. I had gone with a group of lads to the Royal Albert Hall and when I saw her... I just *knew*... She was the youngest musician, you know." The reverend almost seemed to forget his daughter was sitting in front of him. He was lost in memories. "Only eighteen and the LSO took her in."

"The London Symphony?" She could hardly believe her ears as she looked at her father in shock.

*My mother was part of the LSO!? The London Symphony Orchestra?!*

"Yes," he composed himself. "Gabriella was their main pianist."

Margaret tried to take it all in. So many things were clicking into place. She felt like she had gained a huge part of herself, but so much felt empty, too. The loss of not knowing her mother started to weigh on her. Father and daughter were silent for several moments before Margaret asked another question, one that she was sure her father would avoid answering.

Looking up to her father with tears forming in her eyes, Margaret asked, "why did she leave?" A few seconds ticked by and the reverend searched for words. "Was it me? Dad, I need to know! If I'm to live with her..." Tears trickled down her face. "Did she leave because of me?"

"No, no!" He swung out of bed and kneeled in front of his daughter. "It wasn't you." He dried her eyes and looked intently at her. "Margaret, she loved you. Very much. You are perfect." He said the words slowly and they warmed Margaret's heart. He wiped the tears from her eyes. "There are thousands of girls out there, but you are uniquely beautiful. God created you and He has a plan for you. Your mother's leaving was not your fault, nor a reflection of your worth. Do not *ever* think that."

Margaret whimpered and nodded. She took a shaky breath. Surprised, she listened to her father continue.

"You were only a week old. I was at home making sure everything was in order for you and your mother to come home from the hospital. When I returned to the hospital though..." He paused. "She was gone." He looked up to his daughter and she saw the sadness in his eyes. He was crying as well. "My world changed that day. I was heartbroken that she left without even a goodbye. I questioned the nurses and all they said was that Gabriella had told them she was going out for some fresh air. She didn't return. Oh, Margaret, I wish I could have given you the perfect family. I wish I could have spared you all of this. But God knows..." He nodded his head as though he was trying to convince himself as well. "He knows our future and the way things happen the way they do." He returned to the story. "She left a note, Gabriella did." The reverend stared into the distance.

"What did she say?" She asked, still crying.

Looking back to his daughter, he replied, "She said she was scared." His voice cracked. "Scared of being a mother. Scared of somehow not being the perfect mum for such a perfect child as you. We were young; so young."

Margaret was still trying to take it all in. She sighed and studied her father's face. It was a mixture of concern that she understood, and grief that it had happened.

"I understand." Margaret simply said. "But I don't necessarily forgive her." She said bluntly, her heart was not only broken for herself, but for her hurting father as well. Anyone who hurt him, hurt her.

Reverend Sutton nodded. "I know how you feel. But do not hold a grudge and do not view your mother as though she owes you something." He tucked a brown curl behind her ear and stood up. "What she owes you, she can never give back. She cannot give you a childhood together or take away the pain that she has inflicted. Forgive her. We must both forgive her." He paused when she didn't say anything else. "Do you have any other questions, my dear girl?"

"No, at least not yet. Thank you for telling me." Margaret looked away and sighed.

She closed her eyes and thought for several moments before she said goodnight. Then she went back to her room to try and fall asleep again, the thoughts and feelings reeling through her mind. And that night, she cried herself to sleep.

# Chapter 3

A knock sounded on the front door. The reverend arose from reading his morning paper and answered it, for Margaret and Bess were in the kitchen busy putting away dishes.

"Ah, Harry. Good to see you," he let the young man in.

"Good morning, reverend." Harry took off his flat cap and dipped his head in greeting. "I just came to see Margaret and wish her a happy birthday since we'll miss it."

"That's kind of you. She's in the kitchen with Bess." The reverend noted that Harry had a small box in his hand wrapped with a blue ribbon. "Is your family leaving today?"

"We are, sir." Harry nodded. "Unfortunately, we were delayed a few days. But we're off to Cumbria this morning. I'm sorry we'll miss the service on Sunday."

"You'll be missed," the reverend responded just as Margaret came through to the living room.

"Harry!"

"Happy almost birthday, Meg!"

Harry explained that he and his family were leaving soon for his grandparents' place, but he wanted to stop by and give Margaret her present before they left. It was a small necklace with a cross, a cello, and a musical note attached to the thin golden chain. Margaret put it on and was touched by her friend's generosity and kindness. The reverend was somewhat skeptical of a young man giving his daughter jewelry, but he knew Harry was a good, honorable lad. However, it still didn't sit well with him.

The two left together to take a quick stroll through the park before Harry had to go. Margaret wanted to tell him about possibly moving to America. She had tried not to think of it much, but she couldn't ignore it forever. Sooner or later, she *would* go. When she did relay the news, Harry couldn't believe it.

"Surely your father wouldn't send you *that* far away? Most everyone's just talked about going north into the countryside."

"He's adamant, Harry." Margaret responded as they passed their favorite duck pond. All was quiet today and there were no ducks swimming about.

Harry looked troubled and thought about the news. He didn't seem pleased. "When do you think you'll go?"

"I don't know." Margaret shrugged. "Father thinks the earlier the better."

They were both silent as they circled back around towards home.

"Will you be sent away?" She asked, thinking it would be wonderful but too good to be true to be sent away together.

"No, I won't. I'm too old and Mum and Dad don't want to interrupt my schooling. If anything, I may go stay with Evan for the summer, but we'll see."

Margaret nodded, wishing she was a little older, too, and wasn't being sent away like a child.

"Promise you'll write as soon as you know when you'll leave?" Harry asked. "We won't be at my grandparent's for long, so I'll see you before you leave."

"I promise." Margaret didn't know what else to tell him, she was so uncertain.


Before long, it was Margaret's birthday. While she was still reeling from the sudden decision over her life, she tried to put it aside and enjoy the day. Bess persuaded her to go for a walk that morning.

"They'll be practicing in Westminster, I'll bet." Bess remarked as they walked briskly through the cool morning.

"For their next service?" Margaret asked, keeping up with Bess.

"Of course. The choir is remarkable. You've never heard them before, have you?"

Margaret shook her head.

"Well, today's your lucky day! That is, if you want to go? It's your birthday, the day is yours."

Margaret took Bess's arm with a smile. "It sounds wonderful."

Coming off Horse Guards Road, Bess and Margaret quickly crossed Great George Street and walked down the road with the H.M. Treasury on their left and Big Ben straight ahead. The pointed clock tower could be seen over all the other buildings. The streets were quite busy, so Margaret stayed close to Bess. Together, they traversed the crowded walks and through Parliament Square. It was less busy in the green and as soon as they crossed it, Margaret caught sight of the impressive abbey right in front of her. She could feel the weight of history that surrounded her.

The tall statues in Parliament Square would not let her soon forget that queens and kings had ridden through these streets to the grand abbey either on coronation days or weddings. There were cloaked figures and likenesses of powerful and famous men. Sir Robert Peel stood proudly on a podium, and the 14th Earl of Derby stood with a long cloak falling from his broad shoulders. The statues were intimidating, even the newest statue which depicted a president of the United States, Abraham Lincoln, who stood before a chair and looked dispassionately down on all who passed by underneath. Margaret hurried along behind Bess as they turned onto St. Margaret's Street. The house of Commons was to their left along with the Palace of Westminster, Victoria Tower, and the House of Lords.

The massive buildings made Margaret feel small as she gazed up at their white-columned fronts and many tall windows. They came upon Westminster Abbey and even from a distance Margaret could hear the deep sopranos of the choir inside the cathedral.

Entering the north entrance, several other people had joined them in the north transept. Gathering closely, they listened to the choir. Several men and many boys all sang together beautifully, richly, and deeply. Margaret thought they were like angels singing in heaven. Standing next to several other people, they moved into the abbey and were given a better view of the choir. They wore long white robes and high red collars. Margaret admired their dignity and ability. She wished she could sing as well as them.

"I could listen to this all day." Margaret whispered.

"I know, I know. So could I." She smiled and looked back to the choir. She clutched her purse and had a contented smile on her face as she watched them sing and listen to their lovely voices.

They sang several hymns all with the rejoicing emotion that Christ had risen. Margaret was awed by the grandeur of the church. She thought of all the ceremonies that had been held there and the prospect of grand coronations and marriages that would transpire in the future. Two years ago, England's current king, King George the VI's, coronation had taken place in the very same building. Taking a deep breath, Margaret thought of how many monarchs had graced the hallowed halls. She looked up to the high, ribbed ceiling that was bathed in a glowing, golden light. She imagined Queen Victoria looking up at the same sight. The thought gave her goosebumps.

When the rehearsal was over, Bess and Margaret reluctantly left. The other people who had been watching left as well and they all exited out through the Nave. It was still early and once outside; Margaret looked up to the tal bell towers that peeled loudly. She believed she truly lived in the most beautiful city.

"Meg, come along. You're holding up the line." Bess scolded gently.

Sure enough, Margaret was holding up the crowd and the adults gave her amused smiles. She grinned back at them and excused herself, feeling slightly embarrassed.

"Don't you love London?" Margaret joined Bess who was starting the long walk home.

Bess didn't need to respond... who could not love London on a beautiful spring morning?

They walked through the less crowded streets and Margaret stopped in front of a store that had a violin symbol etched on the front door's glass.

"May we stop in and say hello?" Margaret asked.

The Corner Music Store was home to Mr. Burdelik, the store manager and teacher. Margaret had bought her cello and had learned how to play it from him. He was the one currently giving her lessons once a month.

"I suppose." Bess gave in and they entered the music store that smelled clean... like polish and rosin.

"Good morning, Margaret, Bess!" Mr. Burdelik was sitting in front of a Steinway, working on tuning the beautiful grand piano. "I hope you both are enjoying your day!" The man who was about Margaret's father's age stood up from the piano and shook their hands. "I saw you two pass on Orange Street and thought to myself, *'I bet they're making their way to Westminster to hear the choir.'* Now tell me, was I right?"

"You *are* right," Margaret smiled. "You know us too well." She ran her fingers along the Steinway's ivory keys and longed to play it.

"Since it's your birthday, why don't you pick out your favorite music book and take it home with you?" Mr. Burdelik offered generously.

"Really, Mr. Burdelik..." Bess started to protest, but the music teacher insisted.

"Please, take a book off my hands. You're doing me a favor."

Margaret eagerly made her way over to the wall of sheet music books. She bit her lip and tried to find just one.

As she was looking, the storekeeper asked, "how is your cello treating you?"

"It's wonderful." Margaret cast him a dreamy expression. "I play it every day and the sound is perfect." She elaborated as she searched the rows and rows of sheet music. It was hard to just pick one.

"Good, I'm glad to hear it." He grinned.

Margaret picked out her music book; it was a collection of Vivaldi's Four Seasons. She had heard of them and wanted to learn them.

"I'll take this one." She handed him the book and he wrote it down in his accounting book. "Are you sure I cannot pay you?"

He peered at her. "I'll tell you what... you can let me come to one of your concerts in the Royal Albert Hall when you're the first-chair cellist of the London Symphony." He winked at her as he passed her the book.

Margaret grinned. "I will! Thank you!" She tucked the book underneath her arm and held it close. "You'll receive the first invitation."

They said their goodbyes and Bess led the way back home.

"That was terribly nice of him to give you a free music book." Bess commented.

"It was... He's so very kind." She looked down to the book and flipped through the pages of advanced sheet music. *Someday I'll play in an orchestra... Someday I will.*

Margaret was sitting on her bed when her father entered her room. They had celebrated her birthday, April 21st, late into the evening on Primrose Hill and only returned home when Bess had admitted to being chilled. They had played games and enjoyed a picnic and sandwiches. When they had returned, they had opened presents. Margaret received a book of sheet music from Bess that was full of works from several composers. And she had been completely surprised when her father had gifted her a violin.

Now, sitting on her bed, she looked down to the violin with its beautifully polished wood and it soft, red satin case. She felt so incredibly fortunate.

"Happy birthday, my girl." Her father sat down next to her and he put his arm around her.

"Thank you. The violin is..." She couldn't even find the words. With disbelief, she touched the strings that were new and glossy. "I'll play it every day." She closed and locked the case and put it on her nightstand. She ducked under her covers and her father said goodnight. He lingered for a moment, and she wondered what he wanted to say.

"I don't mean to spoil your birthday. But have you thought any more about New York?" He stood in her doorway and fingered the trim.

Margaret looked down and then back up to him. "I have. And I understand..." She paused. "And I will do what you think's best for me." It hurt her to say it, for she did not want to leave London, let alone England.

"Good girl, we'll talk about it more tomorrow." He was about to leave when Margaret continued.

"Dad?" Margaret started.

He paused.

"Do you think she'll like me?"

Silence hung in the air between them and the reverend looked touched. "How could she not? She will love you, of that I have absolutely no doubts."


The Sunday service ended around noon, the bells of churches all over London ringing joyfully. Flowers bloomed in the parks, people walked here and there in their Sunday best. But the sound of the bells trumped any other spring delights. London was alive with the sound of them.

Margaret stood in the drawing room in front of the window with the brown and off-white plaid drapes. She had her violin on her left shoulder and had Mozart's 'Violin Concerto No. 3' circling in her mind. Without an orchestra, it would sound less grand, but she was determined to do Wolfgang justice. She played the quick, happy, lively tune and was absorbed in her music. It had been a few years since she had picked up a violin, but all the notes, strings, and scales instantly came back to her. God Does Amazing Events. She recited the string order to herself. G, D, A, E. The song flowed from her mind to her heart, to her fingers. Her bow rocked back and forth on the strings. With only a few mistakes, she finished the song.

*Not bad too bad...* Margaret smiled to herself.

That night at dinner the reverend and Margaret discussed their plans more fully.

"So," The reverend leaned back in his chair, obviously very full. "New York."

"New York." Margaret mimicked him and was determined to put on a brave face. "What's it like?"

"I'm not sure." The reverend replied honestly. "But I've heard it's a splendid, vibrant city... so much to do and see." He trailed off as Bess entered the dining room.

"I'll say goodnight." She smiled to both of them.

"Goodnight, Bess." Margaret said farewell.

"Goodnight, Bess. We'll see you in the morning." Reverend Sutton nodded his head goodbye.

She left through the back door and the reverend turned back to his daughter.

"I wrote to your mother yesterday to finalize the plans. I should hear back soon." He looked to his daughter for some sort of reply.

"What-what are our plans?" She asked, feeling unconfident.

"There's a liner that sails from Southampton. I'll purchase the ticket soon. It will arrive in New York on the 30th." He explained.

"Of April?" She could hardly believe her ears.

"Of April," he replied.

A lump formed in Margaret's throat. "But that's so soon!" She felt panic rise inside of her. "Please, Dad, don't make me go alone!"

"I would if I could. Believe me. I can't leave the church, Meg. And I'd have no way to provide for you if I came to America. We'd have so many loose ends to tie up here; we'd have to give up our home, our church, all our things... everything. You will be safe with your mum. I'll hold things down on the Homefront. Trust me, times will get hard here, I'm sure of it. And you'll be safe and well taken care of. And not to worry, you won't be traveling alone. I spoke to my good friend, Casey O'Leary the other day." The reverend stated.

Margaret recognized the name and the man. He was an Irishman who worked in Southampton and had set up a small dockside chapel for the sailors and poor laborers in the city. He had visited them often when Margaret was a child, and she remembered his hefty presence and his thick, brown beard.

"O'Leary will be on the same voyage as you. He's going to New York to stay with his younger sister and her husband who just had their first child." He continued to explain. "He'll make sure you get on and off alright and your mum will pick you up." The reverend finished.

Margaret looked down and studied her hands for several moments. "Alright." She let the plan sink in as this slowly became her new reality.

The reverend took her hand. "We'll be alright. It will be hard, but it will also be good."

And she believed him.

That night, she wrote Harry a letter.

*'Dear Harry,*

*I hope the hills and lakes of Cumbria are most enjoyable and you are having a lovely time with your grandparents. I can assure you, you haven't missed anything here. Mrs. Harris assigned us a terrible science project that will take up all my music time. My cello will miss me this week.*

*I have some news.*

*I leave very early on the 27th for America. It is all very frightening. I'm not sure I can be brave enough.*

*So, I wanted to let you know. I couldn't bear to leave without saying goodbye. We should still be able to see each other before. Just don't let your grandparents talk your parents into staying any longer.*

*Hope that you have safe travels home.*

*Your friend,*
*Margaret.'*

Late one night after school, Margaret sat in the kitchen at the little wooden table that Bess always ate her lunch at. She was doing her schoolwork and was forcing herself to finish it. She felt cross from not being able to even touch a piano, cello, or her violin at all that day. Scribbling on her pieces of paper, she watched Bess linger about, helping here and there.

"I was looking for a suitcase for you, but it seems as though we don't have any. No one's ever done any traveling in this family..." Bess said the last sentence under her breath and to herself, but Margaret could still hear her. Bess had always had poor hearing even though she was only in her forties and the things she thought no one could hear, Margaret could.

"Dad came to school today to tell Mrs. Harris I'll be leaving. I'll have to get some things done before I leave, but they worked it all out. I guess this really is happening then."

"It's happening whether we like it or not..." Bess stated without sympathy.

Margaret furrowed her brow thoughtfully. "But what do *you* think about it? Do you think Dad's idea is a good one?"

"If I were in his shoes, which I'm not," Bess turned around. "I would..." She paused and wrinkled her nose. "I expect I would do the same thing. War's a nasty business and he only wants what's best and safest for you." Bess went back to cleaning up.

"You saw the war years, didn't you?" Margaret paused her homework to listen. She didn't often ask Bess about the past, as she was rather mum on it, but every now and then the housekeeper would open up.

"I did."

Obviously, it was not one of the times she'd open up. Margaret knew from what her father had told her that Bess had been engaged to an officer who had unfortunately died during the war. Margaret couldn't imagine what she had gone through.

"But what about Mum? What do you think about me living with her?" She changed subjects.

Abruptly, Bess replied, "it's about time you met your mum." She didn't turn around or offer any more sympathy.

"Why are you staying so late, Bess?" She inquired gently. Usually she left while Margaret and her father were eating. But it was at least nine o'clock and she was still busy.

"So many questions today." Bess huffed. "Because there're things to do! That's why!" She retorted.

Margaret stopped writing and looked to the kind lady she knew and loved so much. Her frizzy red hair stuck out underneath a light blue handkerchief that was tied about her head.

Bess stopped and let her shoulders relax, taking a deep breath. She put the towel down and slowly walked over to the little table. She sat across from Margaret and sighed. Waiting for Bess to start speaking, Margaret realized how many times she had counted on Bess to dry her eyes and act as a mother would. Now that she would be without her, her person to lean on, she didn't know what she would do.

"I... I'm sorry. That was unkind." Bess trailed off and studied the tabletop. "I'm afraid for you." She admitted. "I'm going to *miss* you." She reached across the table and squeezed Margaret's hand. "Oh, I wish the reverend hadn't insisted on sending you off!" Bess exclaimed. "I'm going to *miss* you *so*."

"I'll write every day, Bess, truly I will." Margaret clasped her rough and calloused hands.

"Letters aren't the same as holding you in my arms, or you being here; bursting into the kitchen humming one of your sweet songs." Bess looked at Margaret with tears in her eyes.

Margaret started to get choked up too.

"You're the closest thing to a daughter I've ever had." Bess shrugged. "Your family is my family and..." She couldn't finish her sentence and started gently crying.

Margaret stood up as did Bess and they hugged each other.

"I'll come back, Bess, and everything will be as it was." Margaret doubted the words even as she said them, but she stepped back and looked up to the kind face that she had known as long as she had been alive. "I'll think of you every day."

Bess wiped a tear from Margaret's cheek.

"My dear girl. My dear, dear Meg." Bess pulled her closer and continued, "I'll think of you every day too. Now," Bess stepped back and took Margaret's shoulders firmly. "You must solemnly swear to keep your values, young lady." She wiped tears from her eyes as she stopped crying and put on a brave face. "No gallivanting or cavorting with strangers in that big city. You mustn't go out after dark alone and don't be in the company of any *young men* until I've had a say with 'em. You understand?" She laughed through her sadness.

Margaret nodded and smiled slightly.

"My heavens, you're not a little girl anymore." She touched her cheek with fond compassion. "You're practically... well you *are* a woman now. Just don't forget where you've come from, or the gift God has given you. Use it wisely. And don't ever forget me." Bess kissed Margaret on the forehead and hugged her again. "I love you, my Meg."

"I love you too, Bess. I love you, too." Maragret hugged her tight and never wanted to let go.

# Chapter 4

The day before Margaret was to leave rushed by in a flurry. Bess helped Margaret pack nearly all her clothes. She had two small suitcases that her father had bought, and they had a hard time packing everything in the rigid, leather cases.

Exhausted, Margaret sat on her bed next to her suitcases. Thankfully, they were able to fit nearly everything.

"I'm so tired..." Margaret breathed out and Bess wiped her forehead that was slightly glistening with sweat.

"What about these?" Bess held up an extra pair of Mary Janes that hadn't been packed.

"Those are too small." Margaret replied.

"And these?" She was looking through the drawers one last time and held up one of Margaret's school uniforms.

"I don't think I'll need those."

"Alright," She looked around the room. "Ah, what about this blouse?"

"I have two. I packed the other."

"Right..." Bess nodded, looking around the room to see if anything else needed packing.

"I have everything I need." Margaret said, realizing it herself.

They both grew quiet for a moment.

"So many things to do today and not nearly enough time," Bess left Margaret in her room and went downstairs to fix dinner.

Margaret sat on her bed and looked around at her room. She was taken aback by how empty it felt. Several of her books were packed and a few of her favorite knickknacks. Her dresser was nearly empty, the necklace from Harry and her traveling clothes for the next day were the only things on top. *I hope he gets back in time...* Margaret thought to herself. She fingered the golden charms on her necklace, the little cello, the tiny musical note and the cross that meant more to her than anything. *He has to get back in time; I can't leave without saying goodbye.*

She looked around forlornly at her room and sighed. She would miss it. She would miss this little cottage more than she dare imagine.

Margaret could hardly sleep that night. She and her father had

had a lengthy conversation when he was saying goodnight. He had told her what she had to do in New York, what she couldn't do, and what her mother would be like. Margaret replayed the words over and over in her mind. *'Keep the Word close to your heart. Write often. Love your mother. Forgive her.'* Margaret wanted so hard to obey his words and not let him down. *'Be strong and of good courage, do not fear nor be afraid of them; for the LORD your God, He is the One who goes with you. He will not leave you nor forsake you.'* She repeated the verse he had told her in her head.

"I will be good. I will be brave." She whispered to the darkness and closed her eyes, wiping away the tears.

The next morning was warm and balmy. At six o'clock everyone awoke and Bess arrived at Lily's End not long after. Suitcases were double-checked and the usual busy atmosphere that is present when one is leaving for a long trip descended heavily upon the family. Lists were checked and Margaret ran here and there, stuffing last-minute things into her suitcases to see if they would fit. Harry, who had returned from his journey late the night before with his family, helped out where he could. Breakfast was scarfed down. And at 7 o'clock, the Austin 10/4 rolled out of the driveway of Lily's End Church.

Margaret watched out the back car window as they turned down a road and her home disappeared from sight. She wondered when or if she'd ever see her beloved home again.

"So, how was beautiful Keswick in Cumbria?" Margaret asked Harry as they sat together in the back seat.

"It was fine. Rich, Evan, and I went hiking in the woods and around the hills. We rowed in the lake and tended Grandmum's garden for her. Rich also brought his girlfriend to Gran's cottage. Her name's Sarah. She's nice. Evan was a bit jealous... I guess he can't find a girl in Oxford that shares his passion for history." Harry chuckled at his middle brother. "Ah well, he'll have a girlfriend soon enough, I'm sure."

Margaret smiled and sighed, content to be with her friend before she had to leave.

"Now..." Harry leaned forward. "Are you excited? I would be. Honestly, I'm a little jealous you get to go to America and I don't."

"Do you want to trade?" She joked and got a look from her father in the rearview mirror. "I don't really know if I'm nervous or excited... or a little of both." Margaret confessed. "But you have to promise to write to me and I'll write to you. I want to know what's happening here... You also must promise to..." Margaret lowered her voice to a whisper so that her father wouldn't hear. "Keep an eye on Bess and Dad. Make sure they're safe."

"Neither are ones to do anything brash or unsafe. If anything, they'll keep me in line." Harry leaned back. "What about your music?" He changed the subject.

"I'm taking my violin with me, but my cello's too big, so I had to leave it behind. I'd gladly leave my suitcases and take just my cello. But no one seemed to like that idea much." Margaret's sensible side took over her whimsical side that wanted her beloved instrument with her. "Besides, it will give me time to practice my violin. By the time I come home, I'll be a professional!" She joked.

"You already are."

"And what about you? What are your plans?"

"My plans?" Harry furrowed his brow. "I didn't know I had plans." He said amusedly.

"Well, if there's a war..." She shrugged her shoulders.

"You know, I hadn't really thought about it. I guess I'll figure it out when or if the time comes."

London was left behind soon after 8 o'clock. Halfway into the drive, Margaret was curled up on her side of the back seat trying to sleep. It would take them a while to get to Southampton and she was completely spent. Harry looked like he was dozing off now too, so the reverend and Bess kept quiet. The adrenaline of the morning was wearing off and soon they would get to the hard part of the journey, saying goodbye.

They passed Farnborough, Basingstoke, and skirted Winchester, home of one of the largest cathedrals in all of Europe. Margaret was more awake now as they approached Southampton, driving south, southeast. The reverend drove the noisy car through Eastleigh and the next stop was Southampton. *Here we go...* Margaret couldn't help but think as her heart started to pound faster and faster.

The next hour was full of activity and bustle. The car was parked and the quartet made their way to the docks where Casey O'Leary was waiting for them. Margaret was introduced to him again and she liked him. On the docks, the grand liner rose up before Margaret and it was a marvel that such a large ship could float. She tried not to look at it much or be intimidated by the giant ship that loomed over her as though it held her fate. She started to get anxious.

"Alright, we should get on board." Mr. O'Leary counseled.

Maragret hugged Bess and kissed her on the cheek as they started their goodbyes.

"Be a good girl, Meg." Bess said as she squeezed Margaret ever so tightly.

Margaret hugged Harry next and told him to write.

"I'll miss you, Margaret." He said as he gave her another squeeze.

If they both had known what would happen between that morning and when they would be reunited, neither of them would have had the courage to say their goodbyes. Oceans would separate them and the scale and scope of what they were about to face was too much to even fathom. But they didn't know. So, innocently, they said their goodbyes as dear friends.

"I'll miss you too, Harry." She replied and stepped back, joining her father and Mr. O'Leary who would board the ship with her to get her settled.

Emotion welled inside of Margaret as she boarded the massive *R.M.S. Aquitania* and was set up in a small cabin. Everything happened so quickly.

"Be strong, my darling girl," the reverend and his daughter stood in a busy hallway that led out to the gangway and it was there they said their goodbyes.

Margaret started to cry. This could be the last time they ever saw each other. Margaret was overwhelmed and scared and terrified of the future. What if she never returned to London? What if the war ravaged England and nothing would ever be the same? Would there even be an England? Would she have a home to return to? Would her father still be alive? And yet the reverend tried to comfort her.

"Everything will be alright," he cupped her head in his hands as her lip trembled. "Promise me you'll be strong, Meg. We *will* see each other again, I promise. I promise with everything that is in me, that we will be reunited soon. I love you with all my heart." He embraced her. "Be brave."

Margaret threw her arms around his neck and held on so tight, hoping to never have to let go. "I promise, Dad." She breathed in deeply and let the tears fall down her face. "I love you." She buried her head in his shoulder that smelled of home; vanilla soap, warm, clean laundry, and a smell so familiar she couldn't even describe it.

The great horn blew out from the *Aquitania* and Reverend Sutton eventually stepped back.

"I love you." He kissed her forehead and then stood up straight. He shook hands with Mr. O'Leary and nodded his head to him. "Godspeed and many thanks, my friend."

"She'll be well looked after." Mr. O'Leary assured him.

The reverend then turned, and he cast one final glance at Margaret. He was framed by the ship's doorway hatch. His brown eyes were full of sadness and regret. He dipped his head. Margaret waved weakly. Then he disappeared into the crowd of people, departing down the gangway.

"Come on up to the top deck." He gently led her the opposite way and finally to some stairs that were quite crowded.

Finally, they emerged into the open air of the top deck and Margaret caught sight of the railing where people were waving goodbye.

Another horn sounded.

Margaret had to squeeze in between many people, pushing her way through so she could get a view of the docks where she might be able to catch one last glimpse of her family. Finally, she burst through the crowd that had gathered, waving handkerchiefs, and made it to the white pipe railing.

Standing on the main deck, looking far below her, she saw everyone that she loved and held dear. Her father was just joining Bess and Harry. That memory she kept with her forever. Her heart raced faster and faster as the horn blew again from somewhere above her. She waved to her family who waved back. Hundreds of others were doing the same and waving goodbye to their loved ones. Several minutes passed as the ship slowly moved out from the dock.

"Goodbye!" Margaret yelled and saw Harry waving wildly and her father and Bess waving their hands in high arcs.

"Your family loves you a great deal." Casey O'Leary stated and waved back to his friend as he stood beside the young lady who was setting off for the new world.

"I'm going to miss them so much..." was all Margaret could say in reply.

The people that she couldn't imagine her life without were staying in England and she was going to New York.

A new world.

A new life.

A new family.

The four smokestacks behind Margaret billowed out white steam as the ship gained in speed. Margaret still stood at her place by the railing as they started to travel through Southampton. The dock could still be seen where her father, Harry, and Bess were still standing. However, it was fading in the distance. Margaret waved to them, clinging to the last view of them. *What will I do without them?* She thought to herself. Suddenly, a verse came to mind. *Be still, and know that I am God.* She started down towards the back deck. Mr. O'Leary followed her and asked her what she was doing. She wasn't about to let her father out of her sight while he was still watching the ship pull away from the harbor. She ran down a flight of steps and continued to jog past the vast number of people on deck. Mr. O'Leary tried to catch up, but he was stuck in between a thick group of people.

Margaret came to an abrupt halt at the back railing. The massive ocean liner left the mouth of the harbor. Her father faded into the distance, and she breathed heavily, quite out of breath. The shores of England were growing smaller and smaller. There was nothing she could do; she was on her way to New York City now whether she liked it or not. For many long minutes she stood on the back deck, savoring the last glimpse of England as it faded away.

"Lass, why not come inside and get some lunch?" Mr. O'Leary suggested.

The sun was high in the sky, and it was warming up outside. However, a cool breeze lifted the perfect brown curls off Margaret's face. She looked to Mr. O'Leary who was smiling kindly down to her. His great brown beard covered much of his mouth and face, yet his brown eyes shone through with a twinkle of adventure and kindness.

"Thank you, Mr. O'Leary. But I'd rather stay here... just for now." Margaret watched England become a thin slip of land on the horizon, then fade from view entirely.

Margaret took a deep breath. Who knew how long she would be

gone for... *Will I ever set eyes on my home or my family again?*

"I can give you a tour, miss. There's not much to see now that we're out on open water."

Margaret reluctantly gave in and followed him below decks.

"The finest of the Cunard Line, at least I think so." Mr. O'Leary remarked as they entered the ship. It was finer than Margaret had expected, and she felt humbled to arrive in New York in such luxury. "It was built by the John Brown and Company shipyard near the town of Clydebank, Scotland." Mr. O'Leary continued to lead Margaret back to the main deck. "She was launched fifteen years ago and made her maiden voyage in May of 1914. Interesting, isn't it?" He asked in his Irish accent that Margaret thought quite interesting. "The Ship Beautiful, as it's called. I'm lucky to be on her, she's a fine ole girl." Mr. O'Leary said. "Follow me." He led her down several hallways. "She's commanded by J. C. Townley." He explained and continued to say they were going to sail across the English Channel and stop in Cherbourg, France for a brief time. Then they would continue to New York City.

"It won't be a very long delay." He assured her and then paused to open a door for her. "Sh... this part of the ship's for A-Class only. But I won't tell anyone if you won't." He opened the door and Margaret emerged onto the A Deck staircase.

It was beautiful. Margaret let out a gasp and stepped onto the white-tiled floor. Several fashionable people were walking to and fro with gorgeous dresses and fine suits. Margaret and Mr. O'Leary stayed in the corner and tried not to be noticed. In the ceiling was a circular glass skylight that let in the sunlight. Ferns grew in pots and the intricate iron railing was curly and spiraled every which way with grace and beauty.

"It's beautiful!" Margaret exclaimed and Mr. O'Leary herded her back the way they had come.

"Very fine and it can hold up to 2,000 passengers. I wish I could show you the lounges, especially the garden lounge and the smoking rooms. They're a sight!" He pulled at his beard and opened another door for Margaret; he was obviously leading her back to her room.

"Thank you for being so kind, Mr. O'Leary. I don't know how I'd cope with all this alone." Margaret stated.

"Not to worry, lass. I don't think your father would have let you board alone. He loves you very much." Mr. O'Leary opened her door for her and she entered her small room. It was larger than the lower-class cabins, at least Mr. O'Leary had told her so, and it was smaller than the upper-class suites. Margaret was content. As long as she had a bed and room to put her suitcases, which were already stacked neatly in a corner, she was happy.

"Shall I fetch you some lunch? I have a cousin who works in the kitchen. She could whip you up anything you like." He asked from outside of her room.

"Do you think I could just have a sandwich? Doesn't matter what's on it. I don't want to eat too much and be seasick." Margaret forced herself to smile.

"What?" He laughed and pounded on her wall. "This liner's as sturdy as a rock." He joked.

"Yes, but rocks sink." Margaret pointed out and sat down on the white blanket that was on her bed.

Mr. O'Leary raised an eyebrow and nodded. "I'll see what I can do." He closed the door behind him and Margaret locked it.

That was one thing her father made her promise she would do, always lock her door.

About twenty minutes passed and while Margaret was waiting for Mr. O'Leary, she organized her suitcases and took her violin out of its case. She perched it on her shoulder and held it with her chin. She played a few notes and even attempted a song, but her heart was not in it. It felt torn in two and she had no way to mend it. She didn't want a mother and she believed she didn't need a mother. Here she was, on her way to meet the woman who had given birth to her and was still married, by law, to her father. Margaret closed her eyes and tried to imagine what she looked like. Suddenly, there was a knock on the door.

Margaret jumped in surprise. "Who is it?" She asked as she went to the door.

"Your waiter," the reply came through the thick wooden door. Margaret opened it for Mr. O'Leary, and he came in carrying a tray with tea and three different kinds of sandwiches.

"In case you get hungrier." He replied after Margaret gave him an amused look. "I didn't know what you liked, and I thought maybe you'd get your appetite." He laughed. "Your father asked me to take care of you and even if he hadn't asked me, I would still want to make sure my best friend's daughter is well looked after. So, eat." he playfully tried to make her laugh.

"Thank you, I really do appreciate it." Margaret sat down at the little circular table along a wall in her room. "Would you like to join me?" She offered.

"No thank you, I have work to do. But I will be back to check on you this evening. If you need anything, make your way to the main deck, I have a friend in the wheel room, and he'll have his eyes peeled for you. He can ring for me down in the engine rooms if there seems to be something amiss." Mr. O'Leary bade her farewell, and Margaret ate one of the sandwiches that had ham and cheese on rye bread.

It was well past noon and she realized she hadn't eaten since 7 that morning. She ate her lunch and drank her tea and covered the sandwiches for later. Next she would explore her room and make it home, since she would be there for the next four days.

The walls were paneled in a rich chestnut and navy curtains adorned the windows that overlooked the ocean. Margaret looked out her small window and sighed. She was high above the waves and towards the middle of the ship. She took in a deep breath and looked back to her room. Her bed was along one wall and pushed in the corner while a small table and two chairs were along the other wall. There was a small dresser that was at knee height and in the other corner was a tiny wash sink with faucets and a mirror above it. There was a small and thin brick of soap by the sink. A sturdy desk was at the foot of Margaret's bed and a stool was pushed under it, but other than that, the room was quite empty. Margaret didn't mind, at least she had a bed and desk and sink. She busied herself by looking through all the drawers, but didn't find anything interesting. There was a beautiful painting of the *RMS Aquitania* above her bed. She gazed at it and felt her adrenaline begin to subside.

The afternoon passed by quickly. Margaret sat on her bed and played her violin here and there. She was in the middle of Vivaldi's Spring when a knock sounded on her door. She put down her violin with a start. Mr. O'Leary wasn't supposed to come until the evening, and it was only late afternoon. She jumped off her bed and approached the door.

"Who is it?" Margaret called out tentatively, thankful she had locked her door.

"Was that you playing the violin?" A female voice asked.

Margaret, taken aback, thought for a moment on how to respond.

"Yes." Margaret replied slowly. "Was I bothering you?" She asked respectfully.

"No, in fact it was awfully good." The female voice continued, and Margaret realized it was an American. "Could you open the door, please?" The American asked.

Slowly, Margaret opened the door a crack and was surprised to see a beautiful blonde woman standing in the hallway. She wore a smile and her lips were painted ruby red. The rest of the hallway that stretched far in either direction was quiet and empty.

"You thought it was good?" Margaret asked, opening the door wider. The lady looked trustworthy and nice enough, apart from being indescribably beautiful. She reminded Margaret of a model.

"Remarkable, more like it." The lady smiled again. "I was just walking by and happened to hear it. Vivaldi's Spring?" She inquired.

"Yes, just so..." Margaret leaned against the door and opened it a bit wider. Anyone who knew Vivaldi by ear was trustworthy enough. "My name's Margaret Sutton." She held out her hand.

The lady shook it and stated, "Miss Dorothy Archer, pleased to meet you, Margaret. You have quite the gift." She tossed her glamorous white-blonde hair over her shoulder. Dorothy gave her one more thoughtful smile, a curt nod, an amused look, and then left. Margaret furrowed her eyebrows and watched the lady leave.

*That was odd...* Margaret closed the door behind her, locked it, and continued playing where she had left off.

As the stars came out one by one, Mr. Casey O'Leary checked in on Margaret. She assured him she didn't need any more food, just tea. He was happy to oblige and even brought her a slice of cake he had smuggled out of the kitchens. The Irishman also informed her they would be stopping at Cherbourg within the hour.

"You don't want to miss the French city. Quite beautiful it is, even from the harbor." Mr. O'Leary closed the door behind him and left Margaret to eat her dinner.

Beneath all the apprehension and nervousness, Margaret was quite excited. She had never been away from England and had never seen a foreign country, let alone France. She gulped down the cheese sandwich that was still fresh from the late afternoon lunch and she decided to leave the piece of cake for dessert. As soon as Margaret was done eating, she realized she hadn't told Mr. O'Leary about the lady who had stopped by, Dorothy Archer. Reminding herself to tell the Irishman next time she saw him, Margaret left her room.

The halls were quiet, and the starch-white walls echoed as Margaret slowly walked through them. Her Mary Jane's hardly made a sound on the wooden floor. She came upon a wide staircase and started up the steps to find the main deck. She went through another hallway and accidentally entered the A Deck staircase. Even though she probably wasn't allowed there, she ducked through unnoticed. *One of the perks,* Margaret thought mischievously, *of still being young... you never get in too much trouble when you're caught somewhere you're not supposed to be.* She exited onto the main deck.

Once outside, goosebumps formed on Margaret's arm. A chilly breeze blew through the crisp, spring, ocean air and Margaret was glad she had put her grey knit sweater on over her blouse. She walked from the main deck to the railing and looked south to where the *Aquitania* was headed. A city full of golden light was due south and they were heading straight for it. Margaret felt a shiver of delight course through her. She leaned on the rail and looked down. The dark water rushed by and the massive steel ship cut through the deep blue waves with ferocity. She breathed deep, smelling the briny sea breeze that wafted about her, and leaned on the rail, letting the wind blow through her hair. It was truly one of the greatest moments Margaret had ever known.

She stayed out of the way as people were busy docking the ship. With no idea why they were stopping in Cherbourg, Margaret watched curiously. She sat on a crate that was to the side of the ship and no one seemed to pay any attention to her. Margaret watched for over an hour as new passengers boarded the ship and walked around the deck with fascination. There were people of all types coming and going. She thought she even heard some French words drift her way. Finally, once she started getting chilled, Margaret decided to head back to her room. They would disembark from Cherbourg soon. *Next stop... New York!* Margaret thought with nervous excitement.

# Chapter 5

The next day was dreary and bleak. It was raining heavily and thunder rumbled occasionally. They had set off from Cherbourg the previous night and when Margaret awoke and looked out her window, they were far out to sea. *Sailing in the Atlantic Ocean!* Margaret didn't know whether to be thrilled or terrified. *I feel like I've stepped into a dream.* She thought as she walked over to her small dresser that had her suitcases stacked on top. Opening the first one, Margaret saw the little necklace Harry had given her in the top compartment. She put it around her neck and pulled out a clean change of clothes. Choosing a khaki skirt and a light blue shirt, Margaret took a quick shower in the women's bathrooms and changed for the day.

She spent her time reading and exploring, getting breakfast, lunch, and dinner at the dining rooms with Mr. O'Leary. She said a silent prayer of thanks that she didn't get seasick at all.

The rain stopped around 8 o'clock in the evening and Margaret was bored out of her mind. She had watched the moon's reflection on the waves from her window for about as long as she could. Grabbing her grey sweater and her violin, Margaret took a deep breath, raised her resolve, and exited her room.

Once on the main deck towards the prow of the ship, Margaret lifted her violin onto her shoulder and gently brought her bow down onto the strings. There was no one around and the night was silent. It was just her, the sky that had cleared, the stars, the wind, the moon, and the salty sea breeze. Margaret played Agnus Dei. The comforting melody warmed Margaret's heart and reminded her of home. She took her time with the piece and stretched it into several long minutes. She breathed in the briny air. Closing her eyes, she let the song pour forth. Margaret felt so small standing at the prow of the ship. The stars were reflected on the ocean waves and their crests. It was as though she was sailing through her dreams into uncharted waters. The music filled her soul and made her feel like she was part of something bigger... something more important. Those in the wheel room looked out of their windows curiously; listening into the ocean breeze, for a sweet sound was carried on the westerly winds.

Margaret finished and let her arm and her bow lower to her side.

She stared out at the ocean that stretched on endlessly. Somewhere out there, her future waited.

The next day came and went uneventfully. Margaret and Mr. O'Leary ate their meals in the Aquitania's dining room and spent their free time reading, writing to their loved ones so they could send off their letters once they landed, and exploring. Mr. O'Leary showed Margaret a few of the A Class public rooms and the swimming pool.

The two of them walked through the hallways and to the dining room for the second-class ticket holders. It was a large, fine room and workmen, middle class families, and traveling individuals were seated in wicker chairs at the chestnut tables. Margaret and Mr. O'Leary took a seat against a wall back in a corner and a menu was brought for them. They ate their breakfast in the hustle and noise of the two-story dining hall then they made their way to the decks.

Many people were clustered together pointing at different sights and admiring the blue ocean. The skies were overcast and Margaret even felt a few drops of rain. She walked to the railing and looked over it. Far, far below the ocean churned by and the white waves crested and foamed, yet she could hardly feel the ship rocking. Mr. O'Leary joined her looking out to sea and she could tell that he felt peaceful, just as she did.

"My bonnie niece is sure to be a beauty." He sighed. "I am so very eager to see my sister and her husband. No finer folk, I daresay." Mr. O'Leary looked out to sea and seemed lost in thought. "I wish I could introduce you all. Maybe sometime we will, once you're settled in."

Margaret relished the peace, something that she hadn't felt since setting foot on the Ship Beautiful. *What can father and Harry and Bess be doing right now?* She voiced her thoughts with the Irishman.

"No doubt they're thinking the same thing, 'What can our little Meg be doing right now?' They will be saying to each other." Mr. O'Leary put in. "You will have a great deal to write to them about." He mused.

"Oh! That reminds me!" Margaret turned to Mr. O'Leary. "A lady stopped by my room. She said she heard me playing my violin and thought that it was good. Her name was Miss Dorothy Archer. Do you happen to know her?" Margaret asked as she turned around and leaned against the railing.

"Miss Archer..." He thought for a moment and pulled at his beard.

"Can't say I do, what did she want?"

"She just commented on my playing." Margaret shrugged and turned her mind from the encounter. Raindrops started to fall and she chuckled. "I guess we'd better head inside!"

Margaret and Mr. O'Leary sat in the promenade and watched the rain pour down outside. Thunder rumbled and lightning struck the endless ocean waves. The promenade had a half-wall running along its broadside and the top was open to let the sea breeze in. Windows were along the wall parallel to the open air. If one looked into them, they would see thick curtains to the side of the intricately paneled windows, and the interior of the first class smoke room. Margaret had her back up against the wall with the windows and had a stack of her only three books on her lap. She was flipping through her Beethoven and Schubert music books and Mr. O'Leary had borrowed her Bible to read and pass the time.

All the songs Margaret knew. Just when she looked at the notes, she could picture being part of a grand orchestra sitting behind her cello, letting the music pour forth. From the smoking room behind them, Mr. O'Leary and Margaret could hear the song *'I've Got a Pocket Full of Dreams'* by Bing Crosby through the windows. The scratchy gramophone records muffled the song and yet it was still a catchy tune that made Margaret want to dance. Mr. O'Leary was tapping his foot and whistling along to the tune. The trumpets and trombones were blaring and Margaret's mind kept switching from Beethoven's *'Sonata Mvt. 3'* to the Crosby tune. She closed her book and sighed. *I can't concentrate here.* She thought comically. Mr. O'Leary looked at her with a smile as the song ended. The next song the gramophone played was *'Roll 'Em Pete'* sung by Big Joe Turner with Pete Johnson at the piano. Margaret growled and Mr. O'Leary stood up. The piano, no doubt an upright, was being hammered mercilessly and one side of Margaret wanted to throw it out the window and the other side of her wanted to dance to it. She laughed as Mr. O'Leary held out his hand.

"Do you know much about dance?"

She shrugged. "A little." Margaret took his hand and danced, swing style. She wasn't much of a dancer, but she had seen couples dancing before and knew a little bit.

Mr. O'Leary laughed and smiled as the fast tune progressed. The Irishman was quick on his feet even though he was such a large man. Margaret twirled and her khaki shirt billowed out as she did. Suddenly, someone appeared on the promenade, and they quickly stopped dancing and came to a halt with many a laugh. The sailor walked briskly by to a flight of stairs and disappeared. Once the sailor had left, the song had already changed to something Margaret couldn't quite hear. She and Mr. O'Leary laughed, caught their breath, and went back to reading.

Thursday afternoon turned into evening and Margaret was thrilled that it was her last night on board the ship. She had been sleeping well, but she couldn't wait for firm land. The wooden floorboards and carpet underfoot did not make up for the feel of the cobblestone and paved streets that covered the face of London. *London! How I miss it!* Margaret sighed as she took a stroll on the main deck. The sun was setting and the sky was painted a beautiful orange, pink, blue, and purple color. Margaret was towards the back part of the ship, the stern, and was walking slowly along the rail. They were sailing into the sunset; therefore, night was fast approaching from the east. Margaret watched as the purple and violet hues of twilight overcame the orange sun and the vibrant colors.

Suddenly, a voice penetrated her thoughts.

"I'm glad I found you again," The voice was that of a woman.

She spun around and saw Miss Archer walking gracefully towards her. For some reason, Margaret instinctively trusted the lady.

"What are you doing out here?" She was dressed in a long red evening dress that was made of satin with a red shawl that was bordered in white fur. Margaret watched as she came closer, realizing she must be very wealthy.

"Just watching the sun set... Were you looking for me?" Margaret asked and put her hand on the railing.

The lady joined her, looking out over the waves. Her white gloves ran along the railing, and she nodded.

"It's not every day I run into a young woman who has the talent you do. What is your business in New York? Will you be staying in the city?" Dorothy asked, repositioning her pearl bracelets.

"I'll be staying with my mum. I left London because... Well because of the unrest in Europe. My father was afraid for me." Margaret explained. Dorothy nodded for her to continue. "So, yes, I'll be staying in the city. Why?" Margaret was curious why the lady took an interest in her. True, she could play music well, but there was something else Margaret couldn't quite figure out.

"I see. Then perhaps our paths will cross again in the future. You see, I live in New York City, too, and have my finger on the pulse of the music scene." The lady straightened up. "I hope I see you again soon. Goodbye, Margaret," the lady held out her hand and Margaret shook it. Then Dorothy Archer leaned in and smiled. "Keep playing, you never know where your talents will take you. Until we meet again..." With that, she left Margaret at the stern deck and gracefully sauntered out of sight.

Back in her room, Margaret jumped into her bed and leaned against the wall it ran alongside. She had showered, gotten into her blue flower-print pajamas, and was ready for her last night on the *Aquitania*. She bowed her head, folded her hands, and prayed to God that she would have enough strength, courage, and forgiveness for the next day. She turned off her lights, slipped under the covers and fell fast asleep.

An urgent knocking made Margaret leap out of bed. She opened the door and saw Mr. O'Leary standing in the hallway.

"It's time, lass. Pack your things. We dock in less than two hours." He nodded his leave and left her to change and get ready.

She couldn't believe it was morning already. Picking out a new outfit and stuffing her pajamas back in the suitcase, Margaret thought, *Mum will see me in this.* She looked at her blue and white polka dot dress with the crisp white collar. She and Bess had packed her things to what day she would wear them. Bess had crooned over the polka dot dress, saying she had worn one just like it when she was young. Margaret buttoned up the front and itched at the stiff white collar. Quickly, she brushed her hair and put it up in her usual style. The front part of her curls was pulled back and the back part hung down. She thought she looked rather nice.

About half an hour passed before Mr. O'Leary returned. He knocked and Margaret opened the door.

"I'm ready." She said with resolve and handed him the largest suitcase as she took the smaller one and her violin case.

She glanced over her room one more time to make sure she had gotten everything. Her letters were in her little, brown leather purse Bess had loaned to her. She had her clothes, her books, her violin in its case... Sighing, she nodded to the Irishman.

"Let me take one of those," He reached for her other suitcase so she could carry her violin safely.

"Thank you," Margaret gladly gave it to him, and they slowly made their way to the main deck.

Everything was a flurry and Margaret's heart was pounding. Today she would meet her mother and see what kind of a life she had led since leaving her and her father.

As the time ticked by, Margaret sat on her suitcases Mr. O'Leary had stacked up. The Irishman was busy somewhere else, no doubt getting his own luggage together. Suddenly, the large horn sounded, and Margaret jumped. They were in the harbor! She ran to the railing, not caring that she had left her luggage behind. There, about a half a mile away, was the Statue of Liberty. Margaret's could hardly believe her eyes as she watched the famous landmark come closer. The great green lady was holding a torch high above her head and held a plaque in her other hand. It was one of the most beautiful things Margaret had ever seen. And to her right she saw a massive city with huge skyscrapers and towering buildings.

*Manhattan!* She smiled with nervous excitement. Butterflies fluttered in her stomach.

A strong hand was placed on Margaret's shoulder, and she looked up to see Mr. O'Leary looking at the sight with her.

"Look! It's the Statue of Liberty!" Margaret pointed his attention to the monument on their left.

"Oh yes, isn't she a beauty?" He nodded in admiration.

As the city drew closer and closer, small boats sailed alongside the massive Cunard Liner and escorted her towards the docks. The ship was expertly sailed parallel to a long dock and the passengers waited for the gangways to be lowered and stretched out so they could depart. Seagulls cried overhead, above the noise of the crowds.

"Thank you so much, Mr. O'Leary." Margaret looked up to the tall man.

"My pleasure, lass. I'll see you to your ma, but I won't say goodbye until then." He smiled and scratched his beard, deep in thought.

Margaret smiled and surprised him by hugging him. "I don't know if I could have crossed the Atlantic without you." She had grown to appreciate the kind Irishman. She stepped back and he grinned.

"It was my pleasure," he assured her.

The gangways stretched out to the docks and the first-class passengers departed first. Crowds were waiting to receive the passengers and Margaret's heart skipped when she thought that her mother would be down there waiting for her.

The verse her father had told her repeated itself over and over. *'Be strong and of good courage, do not fear nor be afraid of them; for the LORD your God, He is the One who goes with you. He will not leave you nor forsake you'*

Margaret clutched her suitcase, and Mr. O'Leary took her back to the decks below where they would depart. Margaret was so thankful to have him leading the way. She didn't know where to go or what to do, but thankfully, he knew.

The pair joined a large crowd below decks that was waiting to leave. They carefully shuffled, one by one, out to the gangway and crossed the little stretch of water that separated them and New York City. Margaret and Mr. O'Leary advanced in line and finally it was their turn. They stepped out onto the narrow walkway that was lined by ropes on either side. Margaret carried her violin case and watched her step. She scanned the crowds, wondering if her mother looked anything like her. Soon, she and Mr. O'Leary stepped onto the concrete and made their way to the back of the crowd where Gabriella would most likely be waiting for them. Margaret looked around everywhere and didn't see anyone who was looking for her. She gulped and looked to Mr. O'Leary.

"Where is she?" Margaret asked, knowing that he wouldn't know either. "How will we know it's her?"

"I don't know lass; we'll stay around here for a few minutes and then go to another spot. Your father told her you would be with me, correct?" He looked to Margaret, and she nodded in reply.

*Where is she?* A lump formed in Margaret's throat as anxiety clawed at her savagely. Any minute now...

The blistering heat was intense on the concrete and Margaret wiped her brow with her handkerchief and scratched at her collar. People were busy and moving every which way and suddenly, out of the throng, someone came jogging towards them. Margaret's heart skipped a beat as she saw a lady in a khaki dress and royal blue blouse, with dark brown, almost black, hair come towards them. She had a brown hat on with a red rose tucked in the band.

"Oh, my! I'm so sorry to have kept you both waiting, I'm so scatter-brained today!" The lady spoke with an American accent as she stopped in front of them. She outstretched her hand and shook Mr. O'Leary's.

*This can't be my mother.* Margaret couldn't help but think. They looked nothing alike and surely Gabriella would have an English accent.

"No trouble at all, miss." Mr. Casey O'Leary assured her. "We were only waiting for a few minutes. You must be Gabriella Sutton."

The woman furrowed her eyebrows and shook her head. "Heavens, no, I'm sorry. I'm not Gabriella... I'm Betty Shea, her friend." She shook Margaret's hand. "Your mom is really looking forward to seeing you." She looked down to Margaret and gave her a friendly smile.

*Yet again, my mother isn't here... Will I ever get to meet her or is this just a bad dream that I won't wake up from...* Margaret sighed and let her shoulders sag. She was exhausted and she didn't know if she would have enough strength for another disappointment and letdown.

"Do I owe you anything?" She looked to Mr. O'Leary.

"No, miss. Not a bob." Mr. O'Leary held up his hands. "Well, lass," he turned to Margaret and took her hands, smiling fondly down to her. "It has been a pleasure escorting you to New York City."

"Thank you for all you've done." Margaret hugged him again and stepped back.

"It's been a joy. Now, New York is full of amazing adventures for you. I know you're nervous... but try to have fun," He winked at Margaret as he handed the suitcases to Betty. "Take good care of her." He addressed the American woman.

"Don't worry, I will. I'd get a whipping from Gabriella if I didn't." Betty laughed and took the heavy suitcases. "Taxi's this way, sweetheart." She inclined her head away from the ship.

As Margaret started to follow her, she cast a glance over her shoulder. The *Aquitania* towered far above the docks and the people were starting to disperse. Amongst the crowd, she saw Mr. Casey O'Leary disappear into a group of people. Taking a deep breath, Margaret turned to follow Betty. Another chapter of her journey began.

The New York City streets were extremely crowded. Betty and Margaret, with help from the taxi driver, put the luggage in the trunk and slid into the back seat of the yellow cab. They were sitting in the parking space for over ten minutes trying to pull out into the street. The driver eventually found an opening and they started down West Street. Margaret opened her window, letting in the warm city breeze and poked her head out to see the sights. They passed huge skyscrapers, drove under railways, and through many, many long streets. Margaret had never seen so many people in one place, not even at King's Cross in London.

"Is it always so busy?" Margaret asked as she eagerly took in the sights from the taxi's window.

"Not usually." Betty said. "The World's Fair starts tomorrow, so that's why there are so many people around today." Betty explained as the driver turned multiple times. Margaret looked up to admire a beautiful building that looked like a church. She sat back in her seat, yet could not quench her awe.

"So, did you have a good trip?" Betty asked her.

"I did," Margaret replied. "I'm pretty tired."

"Oh, I'm sure you are. I don't envy you making that long trip. But you'll have a great space at the house and can rest up all you want." Betty assured her and Margaret felt herself relax a little.

The driver turned onto a road called 7th Avenue and Betty spoke up, "Times Square's up ahead!" Even she looked out her window enthusiastically.

Margaret now leaned fully out her window as the driver moved slowly with the heavy traffic. The billboards, the buses, the lights, the people! Margaret smiled widely and took it all in. Men in suits walked here and there, walking their commute. Women in fashionable dresses went into the eye-catching stores. Cars packed the streets and buses moved slowly like large bugs through the masses. Margaret couldn't imagine how people could live in such a busy, noisy, flashy place. She smiled at the impressive sights.

The taxi driver drove past the southern end of Central Park and Margaret still looked intently out her window. though she now sat in her seat. She admired the greenery in such a huge city. They drove past Central Park, and the traffic subsided substantially. Margaret could feel they were getting close and her anxiety started to build.

"I'm sorry Gabriella couldn't meet you at the docks." Betty spoke up. "She wanted to, but I convinced her it might be better if you met at home... Not on some busy dockside."

Margaret thought for a moment. She could see the wisdom in that, but the fact that her mother hadn't shown up still stung. "I understand." That was all she could muster up as a reply.

They turned left onto Park Avenue, and then right. The driver slowed down, and Betty got out her purse.

*We're here.* Margaret thought as the taxi slowed and then stopped in front of a row of six-story brownstone houses.

There were different colors too, white, grey, brown, dark brown, light brown, but all were the same style, and all were squeezed tightly together. They were beautiful. Trees grew in front of them and the small squares of grass were sectioned off by metal fences. Margaret stepped out of the taxi and looked up. Birds sang in the trees that reached up to the brownstone's topmost floors. All was quiet. A few stray cars rumbled far away. Heat radiated up from the warm concrete underfoot. The shade from the trees was cool in the breeze. All was still. Margaret would always remember that moment. It smelt of freshly cut grass and sunbaked pavement; it reminded her of summer.

*Welcome home, Margaret.* She thought to herself and managed to smile.

# Chapter 6

Betty led the way up the steps and opened the door. As soon as they stepped into the foyer with white tiles and off-white walls, a dog's bark could be heard. Margaret spotted a little corgi running from the large archway to their left.

"Hello, Louis." Betty said as she put down the suitcases in the foyer. "Don't mind him, he's harmless," she chuckled.

Margaret reached down and petted his white and golden fur, thankful for a distraction and hoping her heart would stop racing. The house was cool, opposed to the warm outside temperatures. There was a hush over the house, save for a record playing on a gramophone in the foyer. Margaret recognized the song; it was Mozart's *'Violin Concerto No. 4.'* It played quietly and the needle scratched the record occasionally. She smiled to herself and then looked back to Betty.

"I'll whip something up for lunch, why don't you go and see your mom? She'll be on fourth floor in the studio." Betty smiled and motioned for Margaret to start up the stairs that climbed up the middle of the house.

Uneasily, Margaret started up the stairs and took her time. The sound of the gramophone faded the further she climbed. She admired the pictures on the wall; mostly pianos, orchestras, and children playing various instruments.

Forcing herself to continue, Margaret emerged onto the second floor and saw a long hallway that obviously led to different rooms, for there were many doors along the walls. She went up to another floor and saw the same type of rooms. Everything was soundless and cool, the opposite of what Margaret felt. Her cheeks were hot and her heart thudded loudly in her chest.

Margaret reached the fourth floor and heard something unusual as a stair squeaked under her weight. Someone was playing a piano with incredible talent. Margaret took a deep breath, for in a moment when she climbed the last of the stairs, she would see her mother. Pausing and unable to take another step, Margaret listened. The song was Mozart's *'Concerto No. 26 Coronation'*, and it was played flawlessly.

*One step and I'll see the person who broke father's heart, the person who caused me to cry myself to sleep so many times, the person who brought me into this world... My mother.* Margaret's mind raced and she could feel her palms sweating. *One step and there's no going back. Be strong and of good courage.* Margaret thought to herself and took the step. What she saw took her a moment to take in. Sitting at the piano was a woman in a yellow day dress. Her brown curls fell in cascades to her shoulders, and she was beautiful. Sun was streaming in from the windows at the back of the studio and illuminated her, so it appeared as though she was glowing. The entire studio room was empty, save for the grand piano and the woman playing it.

Unable to move, Margaret cleared her throat and watched in awe. The woman looked up and the flawless piano concerto ceased abruptly. Margaret felt like she was looking in a mirror, seeing a grown-up version of herself. Her mother stood up. For a few seconds they just stared; motionless, looking at each other. Finally, Gabriella Sutton walked forward slowly, her cheeks were red, and she looked just as nervous as Margaret.

"You must be Margaret." She said in an accent that sounded like home.

"Yes," Margaret didn't know what to say. "You must be..." She could hardly get the words out as tears started to form.

Gabriella had tears in her eyes as well. Her fair hands brushed away the tears and by unspoken consent, the two rushed into each other's arms. Margaret let the tears run down her face as she embraced her mother. She held her tight and thought that she smelled of springtime in Regent's Park, crisp, sweet, and fresh... a hint of lavender and pear.

Margaret stepped back after several moments and she wiped tears from her face. Gabriella looked down at her daughter and took a deep breath.

"Welcome home, Margaret." Gabriella touched her daughter's brown curls that matched hers almost perfectly. "My goodness, look at you. You're beautiful."

"Thank you," Margaret took a deep breath as well and gazed up at her mother. "You are, too."

Gabriella's face was beautiful and the wrinkles that usually came with age were invisible. She looked young and beautiful and flawless. Margaret smiled and yet felt a pain inside of her. She didn't know what to think. Her mother stood before her now and she could not tell if she was incredibly glad or incredibly sad. For so many years she had dreamt about what her mother would be like and now here she was, standing before her, perfect in every way.

"Well!" Pulling herself out of her stare, Gabriella clasped her hands together. "Are you hungry? Betty will be making lunch. Would you prefer to eat and then unpack? I shall help you, if you wish."

"I don't mind." Margaret said. "Could we eat first?" she asked.

Gabriella agreed and walked with Margaret down the stairs all the way to the main floor where Betty was getting lunch around and where Margaret's suitcases were stacked neatly in the foyer. Margaret was glad that nothing deeper was spoken between them. She did not trust herself, for she was tired, and she didn't want to say anything she didn't mean. They did not speak of the past, and for that she was thankful.

"Your trip wasn't too hard or long, I hope?" Gabriella asked as they entered the kitchen.

The appliances were squished together, and all were a robin's egg blue. The white cupboards were clean and crisp. An archway led to a long dining room that had a large dark-wood rectangular table in it. About ten chairs stretched down the sides and Margaret wondered why there were so many.

"It was a good trip," Margaret replied and turned back to the two ladies in the kitchen, suddenly remembering something. She hurried back to her purse and withdrew the letters, eight in all; four to her father and four to Harry. "I just remembered," she entered the kitchen again. "Do you think we could send these off today? I wrote them while I was on the ship." Margaret held them in her hands with care.

Betty looked at the letters and nodded. "I can take them down to the post office after we eat." She motioned for them to gather at the long table that had a vase of tulips on it.

They were about to start eating, when Margaret quickly put in, "should we not pray first?" She knew they probably didn't normally pray at lunch, but she and her father always prayed over a meal.

"Of course," Gabriella started after folding her hands. "Dear Lord," Betty and Margaret bowed their heads and folded their hands. "Thank You for bringing Margaret to New York safely, and I pray we can all be friends and love one another. Thank You for the abilities You have given us and let us use them according to Your will. Amen." Gabriella finished.

"Amen," Margaret looked up.

"Amen," Betty nodded.

"Amen!" Surprisingly, a third voice accompanied them.

The three ladies looked up quickly and it was Gabriella who spoke first. "Joe! We weren't expecting you until later." She smiled. "Margaret, this is Mr. Ackerman, he is... another teacher here."

Margaret looked over the man who had grey hair and round spectacles. He had a stern, old face, but he looked kind and sincere. He wore a brown plaid shooting jacket that looked like it was very old. Margaret could not imagine wearing a suit when it was so hot out, but the old man looked unaffected by it.

"Hello, Miss Margaret. It is a pleasure to meet you." He bowed to her and took off his tawny fedora.

"It's a pleasure to meet you, too," Margaret inclined her head towards him and offered him a friendly smile.

"Can we eat, I'm hungry?" Betty asked and caused everyone to chuckle.

All four of them dove into their grilled cheese sandwiches and sliced apples. Margaret ate the meal thankfully and as soon as they were done, Betty left with the letters and Mr. Ackerman retreated to the studio. Minutes later, as mother and daughter hauled the suitcases upstairs, they could hear piano music floating down from the fourth floor. Obviously, it was Mr. Ackerman. Gabriella led Margaret past the studio and to the fifth floor, the attic.

"This is where I sleep. It's quieter and more private in these two rooms." She stated and led her across a small landing at the top of the stairs to a door.

She opened the whitewashed wooden door and Margaret caught sight of her room. It had slanted ceilings that stooped low to about the height of Margaret's waist. Window openings were carved out of the slanted ceiling and dark blue drapes hung to the sides of the floor-to-ceiling windows. There was a big bed jutting out into the middle of the room, but there was still plenty of space. The room was huge and had everything Margaret could have wished for. A large dresser with a mirror, a substantial desk that reminded her of her father's, shelves lined an entire wall and in the middle of the empty shelves was an alcove where one could sit and read.

"I hope you'll like it here." Gabriella drew Margaret out of her thoughts. "I'll be right next door, so if you need anything, I'll be close by."

"Thank you, it's lovely." Margaret walked slowly in a circle, admiring everything.

"It gets a bit hot up here during the summer, but both windows open, so you'll get a nice breeze through here. It'll be quieter, too, than the rooms downstairs." Gabriella explained.

Margaret set her suitcases down on her bed and her mother added the other two as well.

"I heard you mention... teachers?" Margaret was curious as to what she had got herself into as she opened one of her suitcases.

"We run a music school." Gabriella replied. "We give lessons and perform small concerts. Some of the children live here, too. We're a bit of a halfway house, too, but that we didn't plan. We have some associations with Juilliard and the New York Philharmonic, so that helps us out a great deal." Gabriella explained.

"That sounds interesting. Dad told me you were a concert pianist." Margaret thought back to when they had talked about her mum as she continued to unpack.

"Yes, well that was a long time ago. That was the first time I had played anything, in years..." Gabriella changed the subject quickly and gently asked her daughter, "would you like help unpacking?" not wanting to overstep the boundaries that had been formed between them for the past fifteen years.

"Thank you for offering, but I think I can manage." Margaret shrugged her shoulders lightheartedly and watched as her mother nodded and went to leave.

"I should tell you before you run into them..." Gabriella turned back around. "The other children will be home from school, soon. I'll introduce you to them then."

Margaret nodded, thinking. "How many other children?" She asked quietly.

"Well, there's seven currently. But this is a big house; we have more than enough space." She tried to soften the news. "Our oldest is about your age and our youngest are... oh I think they're seven now."

Margaret nodded, not sure what to say.

A few moments of awkward silence elapsed before her mother continued. "I'll leave you to it, then." Gabriella took her leave.

Margaret took a deep breath and flopped onto the big bed. "What a day." She breathed out and then set to work unpacking her things, not thinking too much about the news her mother had delivered.

She didn't know how she felt about living with seven other children. She wasn't used to a big family and enjoyed her time alone, which was why she probably got along so well with Harry, because he was a lone wolf as well.

She turned her mind back to unpacking. Her winter clothes, the ones that were in the largest suitcase, she put in the bottom drawer of her dresser. Next, she put in her dresses and skirts, and lastly, she put in her other miscellaneous things. Margaret walked to one of the three windows that jutted out from the slanted ceiling. Her view overlooked the street. Trees grew in front of the close houses and taxis and cars drove by slowly far below. Margaret looked at herself in her mirror and straightened her hair. *One step at a time...* She left her room and went back downstairs. She saw old Mr. Ackerman in the studio who looked busy at work writing things down.

He paused when she passed by the doorway.

"Ah, Miss Margaret! How goes the unpacking?" He smiled at her warmly.

She joined him in the studio and looked over his shoulder at the paper in front of him. Half of the blank sheet music was filled out, the other half still waiting for him to write.

"Almost done." She shrugged shyly.

"Well, good. I want you to know how happy we are to have you here, Gabriella, Betty, and I. It's a terrible business, this unrest in Europe. Good on your father to want to keep you safe." He nodded his affirmation.

Margaret agreed, but at the mention of her father, she felt a pang of homesickness. "I miss him already."

"Ah," his bushy white eyebrows worked up and down. "To be expected, I'm sure. My own family lives in Chicago, if you would believe it. I miss them very much, too. But it's something we must shoulder as we age; sometimes situations arise that separate us from the ones we love most. I'd say you're doing a mighty fine job of it." He gave her a wink and a smile and went back to writing notes.

Margaret couldn't help but feel her spirits lift slightly. "Thank you, sir."

"Ah, please, dearie, just call me Mr. Ackerman."

Margaret assured him she would, then left the cheery studio behind. She emerged onto the main floor and went into the kitchen to see her mother washing the dishes. The corgi ran up to Margaret as she entered the room, and his nails clicked across the wooden floorboards. Gabriella turned around.

"All finished?" She asked with a reserved smile on her face.

"Yes," Margaret knelt and petted the sweet dog. "Why did you name him Louis?" she asked.

"King Louis... he rather looks like a little King Louis, doesn't he?" Gabriella looked over her shoulder and watched the puppy lay on his back.

"He does," Margaret nodded and rubbed his belly. "Just like Princess Elizabeth and Princess Margaret. They have corgis too." She added amusedly.

"Indeed." Gabriella turned off the water and looked back to her daughter as she dried her hands. "Do you have any pets at home?"

"No." Margaret replied. Her father had never liked pets, especially dogs. Cats, however, he enjoyed, but Margaret was allergic to them. Therefore, they had never had pets before besides the occasional goldfish or rabbit. "But I have Harry." Margaret grinned with amusement. "He's close enough to a pet... he comes around occasionally and we have to feed him and take him for walks."

"And who is Harry?" Gabriella inquired, thinking it was a stray animal.

"He's my friend who lives down the street." She looked up to her mother.

Gabriella laughed sweetly. Margaret didn't know whether to love the sound of her mother's laugh or despise it. She felt so many things at once, it was overwhelming.

"Would you like to go for a walk around the city? Or just stay here? The children will be back soon and then you'll be able to meet them." The unsure mother voiced all options, her tone still reserved.

"We can stay; I'd like to meet the others. How did this place get started?"

"Mr. Ackerman founded this place. Poor man; he was a well-off professor at Juilliard. He taught orchestra. But he fell on hard times and lost everything. So, he started teaching lessons out of his home and it grew into this." She motioned to the house around them. "He has our building classified as a halfway house for children, that way they can stay here and not have to worry about being sent to live in an orphanage or placed in foster homes." Gabriella explained and hung the towel up to dry.

"Why? Are some of the children orphans?" Margaret sat on the floor and played with the puppy.

"A few of them are... They all have quite different stories."

"What about Betty? What's her story?" Margaret took the opportunity to learn about the spunky lady who had picked her up.

Gabriella sighed. "Betty was a student of Mr. Ackerman's. She was learning from him, but she couldn't afford tuition anymore. So, he agreed to teach her after he was let go so she could keep learning. Mr. Ackerman's somewhat of a genius." Gabriella raised her eyebrows playfully. "We're lucky to have him. But we're quite the mix-matched group." She mused as she leaned against the cabinets.

"It sounds nice," Margaret replied. However, several thoughts ran through her mind, not all of them positive.

*How can she consent to raising other people's children and not her own daughter? So now I must share her with seven other children – why can't this nightmare end and when will I be able to return to London? Why does she want these children, but not me?*

Suddenly, the front door flew open, demanding everyone's attention.

The first child that ran into the house was a short boy who looked to be about seven. He was followed by another who looked exactly like him. They must have been racing, for they were out of breath and their blond hair was matted to one side with sweat and their cheeks were red.

"Margaret, may I introduce the Moser twins, Frankie and Tony." Gabriella introduced the two boys, unfazed by the cacophony that was pouring into the house that had been almost silent a few seconds ago.

The next person who entered was a tall boy with dark skin who looked to be about thirteen. His brown eyes were dark, and he looked reserved and shy.

"This is Samuel." She continued the introductions.

The boy dipped his head to her in greeting.

Two girls came in together and one looked bright-eyed and energetic, while the other held the first girl's hand and had a sweet expression.

"Meet Rachel Dunning and Hannah Bishop." Gabriella announced each one. "And this is Pitcher and Andrew," She continued as two boys who looked a little older than the twins squeezed through the doorway together. One was rotund and short, and the other was as thin as a twig.

"His name's Grubbs." One of the twins said as he crossed his arms.

"Call him what you will; us adults will call Andrew by his Christian name." She responded. "Now, children, this is Margaret," She introduced Margaret who had since stood up to meet everyone. Louis was long gone, running around the legs of the gathered children, looking for attention and, of course, food.

"I want you all to give her a warm welcome; she's traveled a long way." Gabriella continued.

Margaret could feel the eyes of all seven kids looking to her. They all said various welcoming phrases, all except Samuel, who remained as quiet as a ghost.

"Alright, why don't you all go out back and play?" Gabriella clapped her hands and most of the kids rushed outside.

Rachel and Hannah stayed behind and ushered Margaret into the living room to sit and talk. Samuel disappeared up the stairs. Margaret sat across from the two girls who had seated themselves on the sofa. They looked nice and kind and welcoming.

"So, you came from London? Miss Gabriella told us." Rachel asked and leaned forward. Her light brown bob was pin-straight. "What's it like?"

"It's very busy, sort of like New York City, but not quite as loud." Margaret leaned into the comfortable chair and forced herself to relax. "Have you always lived in New York?" Margaret tried to make polite conversation.

Rachel, completely at ease, brought her feet up onto the sofa and leaned deep into its cushions. "My parents lived in upstate New York, and I grew up there. But when they both died in an accident, I was sent to an orphanage when I was four. I don't remember much, except getting sent from home to home. Finally, when one family couldn't stand my music and my chattering, they sent me here when I was seven. I've lived here ever since. Miss Betty, Miss Gabriella, and Mr. A. bring out the best in all of us." She smiled and tucked her hair behind her ears. She turned to Hannah who sat quietly beside her, looking at something behind Margaret.

"Why don't you tell her your story, Hannah?" Rachel looked to the girl with a pretty white bow in her hair and a white sundress on.

"Mine's not as impressive as yours." Hannah shrugged. "Mr. A. is my grandpa. My parents live in Chicago and figured I'd be better off here. I guess they've lost everything during these past few years, and they just want what's best for me. But I still miss them." Hannah looked down. Margaret could tell there was something different about Hannah, but she couldn't put her finger on it.

Rachel must have noticed, for she put in rather bluntly, "Hannah's blind." She put an arm around the girl. "But we'll forgive her for it."

Hannah scowled playfully in her direction. "And yet I still somehow play better than you."

Rachel rolled her eyes. "Ouch."

Margaret didn't know what to say, but thankfully she didn't have to say anything, for Hannah continued.

"I suppose it's odd to see a blind musician, especially one that plays the violin." She shrugged.

"Well, you don't particularly need to see to play." Margaret smiled with friendliness. These girls were very nice to her, and she was thankful for their kindness. "I think it's lovely you still play."

"Exactly!" Hannah nodded enthusiastically.

"What do you play, Rachel?" Margaret asked the brown-haired girl.

"I play the flute. The other kids all play instruments too." Rachel pointed out.

"What about you, Margaret? You play the cello?" Hannah gently asked.

"Yes, I do,"

"Well, that's wonderful." Hannah exclaimed.

"We've been needing a cellist!" Rachel added.

"We might have a chance after all!"

The girls' conversation ricocheted off one another. Margaret thought she might be dizzy. Rachel jumped up from the sofa and Hannah followed suit and took her friend's arm.

"A chance at what?" Margaret stood up as well.

"To have an orchestra of course! We need more musicians if we're to be *famous!*" Rachel tossed her hair like an actress. Margaret chuckled and Hannah giggled. "Come on, we'll show you the ins and outs of this place."

The two girls showed Margaret their rooms. There were several small rooms on the second and third floors and they were almost all occupied. Besides the bedrooms that the kids shared, there was also an office and a room for Betty. Some of the rooms had two beds, and some had one. But all were simply decorated and had minimal furniture, a wardrobe, a shelf, a desk, and a bed. However, Margaret's interest peaked when the girls showed her the studio's hidden room. A tall shelf was in the corner of the room that was full of music books and when the girls slid it out of the way, for it was on rollers, there was a long room behind it that stretched the entire length of the studio. It was full of musical instruments.

Margaret's eyes grew wide. There were a dozen violins, all neatly lined up on a shelf. There were two cellos, resting on their stands and covered in dust. Two violas were shelved next to the violins. There were cymbals and drums and flutes in their velvet-lined cases. Oboes hung on the long walls next to the clarinets and bassoons. French horn cases were lined up on another shelf and below them were black trumpet cases. A single trombone was leaning in the corner, and a glockenspiel and guitar were on a table beside it.

"Incredible!" Margaret walked farther into the room and turned to the two girls who looked delighted to show off their prizes. "How did you get all of these?" Margaret asked, touching the scroll of the cello and wiping the dust off the tuning pegs.

"The teachers bought most of them from old orchestras in the city." Rachel explained.

"Some were donated to us as well. They're old, but at least they play and that's all that matters." Hannah added.

"So, what instruments does everyone play? Do you truly have an orchestra?" Margaret was amazed.

"Well, I play violin, Rachel on the flute, Cassie on the piano, Miss Betty plays the violin too... That's it for the girls." Hannah replied with a slight shrug.

"Yeah, and the boys like the loud instruments." Rachel added. "The Moser twins both play the brass, French horn and trumpet, and are always competing to outplay each other. Samuel conducts us. Grubbs plays the oboe and Pitcher's on the drums."

"What about Mr. A. and... my mother?" Margaret turned back to her friends slowly after forcing herself to take her eyes off the collection of orchestra instruments.

"Mr. A. teaches and plays everything, but he never plays in public. Miss Gabriella... well she's never touched an instrument unless she's teaching." Rachel wrinkled her nose with curiosity.

"I don't think I've actually ever heard her sit down and play a song." Hannah added.

"Although sometimes..." Rachel leaned in and whispered secretively, "I hear music coming from the studio late at night. Piano music." She raised her eyebrows playfully and giggled.

Margaret pushed her feelings aside and smiled in reply. She could explain her mother's reluctance to play, it was the same reason her father grew teary-eyed when they had sat in the Royal Albert Hall in January; the London Symphony Orchestra... and a thousand old memories.

That evening, after a crowded, loud dinner around the long table in the dining room, Margaret retreated to her room. She was exhausted and wanted nothing more than silence. She had gotten a pen, paper, and envelope from the office and sat down at her desk. Slowly, she began a letter to her father about her first day and about meeting her mother.

*'Dear Dad,*

*I arrived in New York just fine. Mr. O'Leary was such a gentleman, and he took such good care of me. Next time you see him, please thank him for me.*

*And, well, I met my mother.*

*Did she ever tell you she was part of a half-way house for musical children? I'm not quite sure how I feel about it. There are seven children living here and they have formed an orchestra. I don't know anything else, but I did hear one kid called 'Grubbs' talk about playing in Central Park.*

*I have no idea what tomorrow will bring. How am I ever going to get used to life here? It all feels so foreign. This house is so big and there are so many people living under its roof. I'm feeling so many things at once; I don't know what to do. Do you think I'll ever be able to forgive her? Right now, it seems impossible. She left. She missed my childhood and for what; to help other children? What about me?*

*I'm sorry, I'm trying to be optimistic, but I have no one to talk to here. I feel more alone than I ever have before. I guess this is when I need God more than ever, but it feels like I left Him at Lily's End.*

*How are you and Bess? Please send my love to Bess; I miss her terribly. How is Harry? I sent him a stack of letters. I can't wait to hear from you both. I'm running out of space on my piece of paper (why do they make paper so small in NYC?). I miss you terribly and I love you very much.*

*Sending all my love, Margaret.'*

Margaret crammed in the last bit in the last inch of writing space. She folded the letter and put it in an envelope. Setting it on her desk, she got up and grabbed her books she had unpacked from her suitcase. It made her sad to think she had left behind the book Mr. Burdelik had given her for her birthday. She felt like she needed more reminders of home. She plopped onto her bed and read a few verses of Proverbs. Once she had finished, she sat on the edge of her large bed and tried to pray. The words didn't come, and she ended up just sitting there feeling sorry for herself instead.

# Chapter 7

Margaret awoke to the sound of many feet trudging up and down the stairs from the studio down to the main floor. She opened her eyes and noticed that it was bright and early. Margaret changed into a white and blue day dress, ran a brush through her curls, and slipped on her low, white socks. After bouncing down the stairs, she emerged into the studio and saw that several of the children were carrying their instruments from the back room to the main floor.

"What's going on?" She asked the boy whose name was Samuel.

The young man just looked at her and passed her by. She stopped one of the Moser twins whose name she had forgotten and asked him the same question.

His blonde hair was neatly combed, and he was wearing grey trousers with black suspenders over his dark green shirt.

"We're going to the park. Aren't you coming?" He was carrying a trumpet case and scurried past Margaret and down the stairs.

With confusion, Margaret followed him and suddenly felt left out. *Were they even going to tell me they were leaving?* As she descended the two flights of stairs, she saw all the boys waiting in the foyer with their instruments.

"Remember, everyone must be on their best behavior." Gabriella had a light blue hat on and a robin's egg, plain dress.

She opened the door, and they filed out. Miss Betty was the one, at the back of the group, who noticed Margaret still waiting on the stairs.

"Margaret!" She approached her. "Don't worry; we weren't going to leave you here alone. We were going to let you sleep in. Yesterday must have tired you out."

Margaret shrugged.

"We're going to the park to play. We do every Saturday morning and today is a big day. The World's Fair opens tomorrow and the park's going to be busy. Lots of tourists. Do you want to come and watch?" Betty motioned for her to join them, and Margaret grinned at the kind lady.

*At least someone cares.*

After Margaret made a quick few pieces of toast to take with her, they all set off together for Central Park. Betty was right; the park *was* busy. It was four blocks away from the students' house and it took them about ten minutes to get there. The streets were crammed and people who were still suffering from the terrible economy lounged here and there on the benches, blowing clouds of smoke from their cigarettes; homeless, just watching the world go by and waiting for their fortune to change. Margaret walked with Betty as they brought up the rear of the procession. Onlookers gawked at the sight of seven children carrying instruments in their cases. They came into the very heart of the park. The shade of the mature trees was gratifying and the lush green lawns continued as far as the eye could see. The only reminders that they were in the middle of New York City and not the countryside were the honking taxi cabs and the skyscrapers that surrounded them, towering higher than the steeples in London.

Mr. Ackerman was talking to a police officer and as the children approached, the officer left. Margaret could see her mother and the old professor talking and they smiled and talked, so she guessed all was well.

"Alright!" Gabriella turned back to the group. "Everyone to positions!" The children scampered.

The Moser twins went to the back middle with their trumpet and French horn, Hannah went to the left with her violin, Rachel went to the middle, flute in hand. Grubbs grasped his oboe with his short, stubby fingers; Pitcher went to the back right, snare drum in tow; and Samuel stood in the front, baton in hand. Margaret and Betty sat on a bench and Mr. Ackerman stood to the side, waiting for the song to start.

Gabriella approached the bench after she finished helping Hannah tune her violin.

"Did you get some sleep last night?" She asked Margaret.

She nodded that she had.

"Good, I'm glad. I'm sorry all was a rush this morning. Saturday mornings are early and quite hectic, so..." she trailed off. "Anyway, I'm glad you wanted to come too."

Margaret mumbled a response just as the orchestra composed itself to play. Samuel stood up tall and was at least a head higher than the other children. He cleared his throat, set the timing of the song like a human metronome, and then the music started.

Johann Sebastian Bach's 'Ciaccona' poured forth from Hannah's violin. The orchestra quietly accented the rise and fall of the song that was shortened slightly. Hannah's eyes were closed, but her face showed incredible emotion. As the song ended, people started to gather. They talked with Mr. Ackerman and Gabriella, praising the talent of the children.

Hannah again led them into another song. This time it was Pachelbel's *'Canon in D'*. Margaret closed her eyes and wanted nothing more than to jump in and join them. Samuel conducted them beautifully and the horns, the drum, the flute... The song was tailored to the small mix-matched orchestra perfectly. Margaret only wished that there was more to it. More strings. A cello. A double bass. She had grown used to the London Symphony's utter brilliance and anything less sounded odd to her.

They played four other songs and with every note, more people joined to watch the small orchestra that was situated on a small, hilly rise. The crowd grew to about seventy-five as the sun climbed to its full height in the sky.

It was lunchtime and after the children put away their instruments, Gabriella brought out a picnic basket.

There were plenty of sandwiches for everyone and as they lounged on the cool green grass, they talked and chatted and played. Pitcher, living up to his nickname, was playing baseball with the identical Moser twins. Grubbs was trying to play too, but he could not run quite as fast as the other boys.

The girls sat underneath a large tree and Margaret stayed close to Betty. She seemed like the only person who gave Margaret much thought. However, eating with Hannah and Rachel, Margaret caught her mother looking at her more than once. *What does she think of me? Does she despise me for showing up in her life? Am I what she expected?* Margaret sighed and took a sip of her water. Hannah was listening to the sounds of the park with her eyes closed. She was leaning up against the tree's trunk and looked perfectly content.

"So, the orchestra needs a cellist?" Margaret turned to Rachel and Hannah with a sparkle in her eyes.

Hannah sat up to reply. "Yes! Will you play with us?" Her face looked eager and excited.

After holding them in suspense for a few moments, Margaret nodded and said she would.

"That's great, Meg! Thank you!" Rachel hugged her friend. "We'll be the grandest orchestra that ever graced New York!" She threw her arms up in the air triumphantly and dramatically.

The orchestra played more after lunch and Betty and Margaret returned to the house to fetch the cello. Betty and Margaret secured the dusty instrument in its case along with the bow and extra rosin. They started back to Central Park and on their way, they dropped off Margaret's letter she had written the night before. Margaret was at first reluctant to send it off, for she was forcing herself to be happy and content with where she was, and she felt as though she had complained in her letter. But she didn't have time to write another one and she still wanted her father's advice.

It was a hot day, hotter than it usually was in April, but the tourists were still taking carriage rides in the horse-drawn carriages and window shopping on 5th Avenue, taking in all the sights New York City had to offer. Once back with the group in the park, Margaret sat next to Hannah and tuned the ancient cello. It didn't sound as deep and smooth as the one she had left behind in London, but it was a cello. And it was now hers.

"I didn't know you played, Margaret." Gabriella said as she walked through the orchestra, telling them what song was next.

"You weren't to know; you hadn't asked yet." Margaret bit back and later regretted sounding so harsh.

"I suppose I haven't," Gabriella sounded remorseful.

Margaret continued tuning her cello as her mother told Hannah they would play Elgar's Symphony No. 1. Gabriella asked if Margaret knew it and she only nodded in reply. Even if she didn't know it by heart, she knew it would come to her, as most compositions did.

Samuel counted off again, his eyes bright and alert. The song was slow and meaningful. Margaret put her whole heart into it and could feel the emotion radiating from Hannah. They were kindred spirits; bound together by the love of music and the transformation it brought to their souls. The other children, besides the Moser twins, looked just as lost in their music and thoughts. Yet the song poured forth and ended gently, everyone in harmony. The audience clapped whole-heartedly, and Margaret realized this was her first time ever playing in an orchestra. *And what an orchestra it is!* She looked at her fellow musicians and saw the joy on their faces she knew was also painted on hers.

As they were breaking up, for the day was waning, Hannah touched Margaret on the shoulder. "Play your favorite song."

"Pardon me?" Margaret hadn't heard her, for her voice was quiet.

"Play. Play the song that's your favorite... more than any of the others. I know you have it in you. I can feel it." Hannah grasped her violin case and sat down in front of Margaret.

Margaret thought for a moment and her mind reeled through the thousands of songs she knew. Her mind was on Elgar from playing the first orchestra piece, yet she knew it would be a challenge to play the cello concerto. She hadn't played it for months and it was an extremely challenging piece. Nonetheless, she tried it.

The first two notes radiated from the cello and then the next two were tied so closely together. The despairing melody required her to put forth all her passion, sadness, guilt, and misery... and it required all her concentration. Margaret could hear the orchestra parts in her head, even though the rest of the instruments were packed away and she was playing alone. Margaret played for several minutes and then stopped. She opened her eyes and noticed everyone was watching, including the audience. She blushed deeply, knowing that her face was no doubt as red as a rose now. The audience of tourists clapped and out of the sea of faces, Margaret saw her mother standing far out to the side.

She had tears in her eyes.


Around the table, the children boasted of their feat in Central Park. They said it had been one of their most outstanding performances and had drawn in the largest crowd to date.

"Soon we'll be famous musicians!" One of the Moser twins exclaimed.

"And we'll play for the president!" The other twin called out. "Who doesn't love a good trumpet?!"

"Tony's blowing his own horn again!" Pitcher retorted and the twin stuck his tongue out rebelliously.

Margaret sat in the middle of the table between Hannah and Rachel. They were smiling and laughing and relishing the moment. They passed the dishes of potatoes, green beans, and chicken around so all could fill up their plates. Margaret was quiet, yet she smiled and laughed with everyone else. Out of the corner of her eye, she saw her mother sitting silently at the end of the table, eating quietly and demurely. Mr. Ackerman sat at the head of the table, watching as the children enjoyed themselves.

Betty leaned back in her chair that was to the right of Gabriella. They all finished the meal and thanked Gabriella who had cooked it. Then they trailed up to their rooms and spent the evening mulling about, reading and practicing. There was always an instrument playing in the great big old brownstone to the east of Central Park.

---

'My dearest Margaret,

How dull life seems without you, my girl. Just today I was giving a sermon, and I looked to the front pew to find it empty. I could barely finish the message. Harry was sitting with his parents for the first time in a long time and no one dared to sit in your previous post. How I miss you.

I thank the Lord you and your mother are well. The news you told me of her being part of a half-way house makes me glad. I had prayed for a way for you two to connect and God has provided... perhaps you and the other children will form close friendships.

Bess is well, as is Harry. I am sure he has written to you to announce that he's finished his schooling for the year and yet is taking up summer school to move ahead a grade. As I said, Bess is well. She hardly knows what to do with herself. The house is always clean, I don't eat much, so there's hardly anyone to cook for, and the laundry is at a minimum... However, I believe she enjoys having a break. She's visited her sister in Leeds several times, sometimes once a week.

The changes in London are coming. Posters are being put up in the underground railways about evacuations and preparing for the worst. I know in my heart that it will come.

Forgive me for such a long letter, I must now write on the back...

My girl, I am at a loss for words because of your bravery and courage. You have far exceeded my wildest expectations and hopes and prayers. Do not fall prey to self-doubt. You have come this far. Don't turn back now. Your mother always loved you and loves you still. Talk to her. I know it is hard, but Christ has forgiven her, and therefore, you must as well. She does love you, my dear. But if things are tense between you two, I can only assume she doesn't know how to have a relationship with you yet.

It is so much harder said than done. But I know my Meg, and once she is faced with a challenge, she does not back down easily.

I know you can do it... you can forgive her and have a good

*relationship with her. I believe in you.*
  *Much love,*
  *Your father.'*


It was the 4<sup>th</sup> of July. Margaret sat in her room and looked out the window that overlooked the street. She finished reading that first letter from her father she had gotten back in April. It had been three months since the transatlantic journey. She had gotten several letters, almost two a week from Harry and her father. Margaret kept them all in her desk's drawer and pulled them out whenever she was feeling down. She had reread this first letter over and over again. In it he had told her to be open to her mother, to forgive her, and to talk to her. All three she hadn't yet tried. And he was right; it was much easier said than done. Every day she fought her emotions and thoughts towards her mother. Every day she tried to do better, but she never found the strength to love and forgive. She desperately wanted to talk about the past, but she could never find the words. Despite her shortcomings, Margaret prayed every morning and every night. She wanted to do better, and she had come a long way from those first couple days in the house.

Every day had almost been the same. Once school was over for the children in May, Monday through Thursday students from outside the house came and learned from the professor, who taught several of the instruments. They also took lessons from Betty who taught violin, and Gabriella who taught piano. There was Cassie, the piano student who arrived in a shining Rolls Royce; Cecil, the quiet boy who walked to his piano lessons with his mother; Bradley, the fifteen year old who already drove his father's car to his trombone lessons with the old professor; Simone, a pretty girl with black hair who played a violin beautifully; and lastly there was Grace, Simone's younger sister who was seven and played the violin as well. There were about a dozen other children that came and went about once every month. Margaret didn't learn their names but was always friendly and kind when they arrived for their lessons with the teachers.

On Saturdays, the group of seven would march into Central Park and play for the crowds. They always chose the same hill and sometimes, if they went there often enough, Margaret could find the same hole in the ground where the endpin of her cello would rest. The other students that took lessons never joined them; therefore, they could not show off their full potential as a larger orchestra. However, the talent of each was enough to compensate for the lack of members.

The 4th of July landed on a warm Tuesday, and it was raining on and off. Margaret sat before her window and hoped that the rain would hold off for the fireworks. Although, it was not the fireworks she was looking forward to the most. The teachers were treating the students to a concert in Carnegie Hall by the New York Philharmonic. They were putting on a special 4th of July celebratory performance and all the children were looking forward to it. The boys would put on their best clothes and the girls would get dolled up, and they would all head out early to walk to the concert hall. Margaret was beyond excited. It had been many months since she had seen the LSO in the Royal Albert Hall and she was dying for some quality music.

The sun was starting to set in the sky and Margaret dashed from her spot and excitedly ran into the bathroom that her and her mother shared in the attic. She took a shower, curled her hair in her mother's curlers, and picked out her best dress, the blue polka-dotted one she had worn during her arrival in New York. As Margaret finished, she looked in the mirror and remembered the time when Bess had fussed over her before her outings to concerts with her father. *It seems like it was just yesterday.* She pushed the thought out of her mind as she bounded down the multiple flights of stairs to the main floor.

The boys were all sitting around the table, eating a quick meal of soup before they headed out. They were dressed in clean, pressed pants, and nice-looking dress shirts of various colors. Frank dripped some soup on his clean shirt. The other twin, Tony, laughed and pointed.

"Look at what Frankie did!"

Margaret chuckled. She could never tell the twins apart.

"He's gone and spilled soup all over his shirt!" Tony laughed hysterically.

"Hush, Tony," Margaret said to him and wiped the broth from Frank's shirt with a damp rag she had grabbed from the kitchen. "There, all better." Margaret stepped back and admired her work. The shirt was a little damp in the area of the spill, but it would not stain.

"Thanks, Meg!" Frank slurped his soup and Margaret ruffled his hair and returned to the kitchen.

She spooned out a bowl of soup for herself and Rachel and Hannah; the girls had just slowly come down the stairs. Rachel held Hannah's arm and guided her.

"Aren't you both a picture!" Margaret exclaimed.

Hannah wore a white and yellow striped dress that had a very high neckline, while Rachel had on a khaki skirt and purple blouse. They looked very pretty for the summer occasion.

"Thanks Meg!" Hannah piped up. "I'm sure you're beautiful as well. Is she, Rachel?"

"She's a regular Bette Davis!" Rachel replied and led her friend to the table.

Margaret brought the soup for her friends and then took hers to the table as well. She said a quiet prayer and began eating. The other girls did the same, for when the teachers were away, they unanimously decided to pray separately. The three teachers were all off doing their separate duties. Betty had to make an emergency run for groceries, they were out of milk and the boys drank about a gallon every other day. Mr. Ackerman was off on an appointment with the director of the New York Philharmonic to see if the kids could play in one of Carnegie's smaller halls for practice. Gabriella was also away to a doctor's appointment. She had a cold that she couldn't shake and needed some more prescriptions.

However, the mix-matched family would soon be together for the concert and the fireworks over the Hudson River. Margaret was looking forward to it immensely. Finally, she felt like she was settling into a new routine.

Margaret walked arm in arm with Hannah. She and Rachel sandwiched Hannah in as they walked down the sidewalks to Carnegie Hall. The boys strode boisterously in front of them. Mr. Ackerman led the way as Betty and Gabriella brought up the rear to make sure no one fell behind. People they passed gave them odd stares, wondering why such a group would be together while the rest of the kids in Manhattan schools were on summer break.

Margaret couldn't help but giggle when a little boy pointed to them and said, "Mommy! Those are the music kids that play in the park!"

The group continued on, and it wasn't long before they reached the esteemed hall. To Margaret, it looked so different than the Royal Albert

Hall. It was a red stone building that looked more like a factory. She pressed her lips together and remembered not to judge a book by its cover. She smiled to cover her surprise and focused on keeping Hannah in a safe place.

The group entered along with several other New Yorkers who were going to see the Independence Day concert. Margaret had never celebrated the holiday but was eager to take part in it. The place was quiet, and they walked through several rooms and antechambers before they entered the large hall. The stage was high off the ground and white walls encircled the entire hall. Gold paint accented several columns and features on the three walls that bordered the stage. On the platform there were many instruments just waiting for their musicians to pick them up and play them. Margaret sat beside Rachel at the end of the long row of bright red seats on the main floor. The group of eleven waited eagerly for the concert to start.

Once everyone was seated, the musicians entered the stage. Everyone clapped as they took their seats, and the conductor arrived. *The New York Philharmonic!* Margaret's excitement peaked. *Will they be as good as the LSO, I wonder?* She scooted to the edge of her seat. From somewhere high above them, someone spoke on a loudspeaker.

"Ladies and gentlemen, please stand for the *National Anthem.*" The official voice sounded and everyone stood up.

A few seconds ticked by in suspense before the orchestra started up the recognizable tune. Even Margaret had heard it before. The men and women in the concert hall put their hands over their hearts and took off their hats if they were wearing one as the song started.

The French horns, trumpets, and trombones belted out the melody while the strings and woodwinds played the higher notes. Everyone in the audience sang the song wholeheartedly. Margaret pretended to sing it, for she did not know the words. As the song progressed, the American flag was raised on the back wall of the stage behind the orchestra. When the song ended, everyone clapped. Margaret felt like she was an American as well, for the beauty of the song faultlessly conveyed freedom, liberty, and bravery. These Americans, they were indeed proud of their country and they had every right to be.

The audience sat and Margaret nestled back into her seat. After the last of the fading notes of the '*Star Spangled Banner*' echoed throughout Carnegie Hall, they started up another patriotic song. 'My Country Tis of Thee' was played by a string quartet and following that they played several other patriotic, American songs.

As the next song started, *The Battle Hymn of the Republic,'* Margaret looked across Rachel on her left and saw Hannah leaning forward with her eyes closed, listening to the music intently. She smiled to herself and gave Rachel an excited grin.

"This one is my favorite." Rachel whispered. "I love the lyrics." Rachel turned back to the orchestra and watched them with awe.

Margaret felt the same thing. Even though she did not belong to the history of America and the freedom they fought for against the British, she still felt the meaning of the words and the pride that the Americans felt in their freedom and individuality. The next song the grand orchestra played was the *'Stars and Stripes Forever.'* The powerful and energetic song made everyone in the audience want to stand and clap along with beat. Stand they did not, clap they did. No one could keep back the patriotism of the crowd.

About a minute passed before the next song started up. *'God Bless America'* echoed throughout the halls of Carnegie. The audience was quiet and silently played the lyrics through their heads, yet no one verbally sang. Margaret's eyes were on one of the cellists who was playing with emotion and grace. She wished it was her. She closed her eyes and mindfully went through the notes they were playing as though she was on stage herself.

The song ended and the voice of the loudspeaker spoke again. "Please stand and sing along with us to the final song of the evening, *'America the Beautiful.'"*

The graceful composition of *'America the Beautiful'* was awe-inspiring. The woodwinds were calm, the strings added feeling, the brass brought forth majesty, and the drums brought power. The song commanded reverence. Margaret did not know the words, but she hummed along.

> *"America! America! God shed his grace on thee!*
> *And crown thy good with brotherhood*
> *From sea to shining sea!"*

The audience sang.

The key of the song changed and Margaret's arms were covered in goosebumps. The song continued.

> *"O beautiful for patriot dream*
> *That sees beyond the years*
> *Thine alabaster cities gleam*
> *Undimmed by human tears*
> *America! America! God shed His grace on thee!*
> *And crown thy good with brotherhood*
> *From sea to shining sea!"*

The audience sang with pride.

The song ended regally, and the entire audience applauded. The sound was deafening as the orchestra stood up and bowed and clapped all at the same time. The musicians did not feel worthy of the applause; instead, they owed it all to their beautiful America and the people who gave their lives to defend it.

Independence Day ended with a bang. The group went home and climbed all the flights of stairs out onto the rooftop where they could watch the fireworks. Other people were on their roofs as well and were watching the fireworks explode over the Hudson River. Margaret could not remember such a uniquely exciting night. She was surrounded by her friends and the warm July breeze wafted about them. Sitting on a small bench on the rooftop space with King Louis at her feet, she looked up to the sky and saw the wondrous colors bursting in the night. The Statue of Liberty stood tall over the Hudson as the fireworks burst behind her. She held her torch high over Ellis Island and symbolized free America like nothing else ever could. Margaret knew, deep down, that she was very blessed and that things could only improve between herself and her mother. Her heart was mending, but more importantly, she was learning to forgive.

# Chapter 8

After church, Harry lay on his stomach in his room with his schoolwork spread out all around him on the floor. He could hear a radio chattering downstairs, and it annoyed him. *How can I get school done with that racket?* He gritted his teeth. The last few months had been terribly trying. He had just turned seventeen two days ago, and he was reminded of it every time he looked at his desk to see a birthday card from Margaret that had arrived on September 1st, right on his birthday. According to the school system, he should have been graduating this year. But because of their move from Australia to Britain and being held back, he had two more years to go. But all that had changed over the summer. He had worked extra hard in summer school and now he just had one year left. *One year to go.* Harry was almost as frustrated with school as Margaret and wanted to do everything he could to finish early. *By spring, I'll be free. Just two more seasons. I can do this.*

Harry wanted to get out in the world and start a profession like his older brothers were doing. What he would do, he hadn't the faintest idea. But he would do something... that was certain.

Suddenly, breaking into Harry's thoughts, there was a call from his mother.

"Harry! Come down here!" She called him and Harry rolled his eyes.

"What?!" He yelled back and waited when he didn't hear a reply.

"Now!" His father yelled.

Harry knew he was wanted downstairs, for his father never raised his voice. Harry jumped up and dashed down the stairs of their little cottage. He entered the living room and saw his parents huddling around the radio. They looked anxious as though something was wrong.

"What is it?" Harry asked quietly as he approached them.

They didn't say a word, yet his mother motioned for him to come closer quickly. Walking forward a few more steps, Harry heard the radio.

It garbled out a melancholy voice, *"in this grave hour, perhaps the most fateful in our history, I send to every household of my peoples both at home and overseas, this message."*

Harry listened intently as he put his hand on the mantle of the fireplace the radio was next to. He knew the person who was speaking was the king.

A cold chill ran down his spine... why, he did not know.

The speech continued. *"Spoken with the same depth of feeling for each one of you as if I were able to cross your threshold and speak to you myself. For the second time in the lives of most of us, we are at war."*

The words caused his mother to gasp. She stifled a sob and Mr. Cavanaugh put an arm around her shoulder for comfort.

Harry continued to listen in breathless silence. *What will this mean?* He hung on every word the king said.

The speech continued. *"It is to this high purpose that I now call my people at home, and my peoples across the seas, who will make our cause their own. I ask them to stand calm and firm and united in this time of trial. The task will be hard. There may be dark days ahead, and war can no longer be confined to the battlefield, but we can only do the right as we see the right and reverently commit our cause to God. If one and all we keep resolutely faithful to it, ready for whatever service or sacrifice it may demand, then with God's help, we shall prevail. May He bless and keep us all."* The radio broadcast clicked off.

The announcer said things Harry did not even remember hearing. He looked to his parents' faces and saw the same worry in their eyes that was no doubt a reflection of his own.

It was 11 o'clock in the morning of September 3rd, 1939.

The clock's ticking was all Harry could hear.

The room felt colder, as though a shadow had passed over.

England was at war.

It was a day Harry would never forget.


Not a half an hour later, sirens began to wail. Harry was sitting in the living room with his family talking and worrying about what would change in their family. No doubt Richard and Evan would be enlisted... But all their thoughts were put on hold as they jumped up and responded to the siren. There had been other air raid tests over the weeks. However, this one was real.

Staying in the safety of their home, Harry peered out the back window and saw planes flying overhead. They were traveling from northwest to southeast, so he guessed it meant they were theirs. Still, the sight made him shiver and his blood run cold.

The Germans had invaded Poland, as the Prime Minister Neville Chamberlain, had said just that morning before the king's address, *"we and France are today, in fulfillment of our obligations, going to the aid of Poland, who is so bravely resisting this wicked and unprovoked attack on her people. We have a clear conscience. We have done all that any country could do to establish peace. And now that we have resolved to finish it, I know that you will all play your part with calmness and courage."*

Harry sighed as he looked out the window and the sound of the planes overhead dissipated. *How will I play my part?*

"Harry, come and give me a hand with this," Harry's father called him over from the living room and broke him out of his musings.

He joined his family in the main room and saw his mother sewing together the blackout curtains. His father was tacking the black-painted liner onto a frame that could be lifted into place to black out the windows. Harry went to his knees at his father's side and grabbed a hammer and tacks. He helped his father wordlessly, no one really felt like talking, for all of London had turned grim that day.

---

Margaret walked Louis on the busy sidewalk with Rachel and Hannah by her side. The waning evening sun shone down as they headed to Central Park, not to play instruments, but to exercise the pup that was driving everyone out of their minds with his barking. Louis bounced along before Margaret, and she laughed. His pink tongue lolled out and he yipped.

"Sh!" Hannah gently scolded him.

"Or you'll bring the bobbies down on us!" Margaret chuckled.

Rachel walked ahead of them and playfully skipped. "What a beautiful day!" She called out and nearly ran into a businessman who gave her a stern look.

Rachel shied away and took Hannah's arm again. Margaret smiled, for it truly had been a beautiful day. The September sun was shining and there was just a hint of fall in the air. The next day, they were going to go to the World's Fair with Gabriella. It was a special outing the girls were looking forward to.

Margaret unhooked Louis' leash, and he dashed away into Central Park. Margaret called after him and he went running back to her at a dizzying speed. She threw a stick, and he chased after it, running back to her and dropping it at her feet. His docked tail wiggled, which caused his whole rump to wiggle. She chuckled and threw it again and again. Rachel and Hannah were sitting on a bench in the sun and were talking. Margaret joined them as Louis went running back, dropped the stick and barked. Rachel picked it up and threw it for the pup.

"I can't wait to go to the fair!" Rachel said as she threw the stick as far as she could. "It's all about the future! There's even a television that's called the *Smell-O-Vision!* You smell things as it plays a motion picture." Rachel laughed as Louis fell over from running too fast, his short legs unable to keep up with his energy.

"A *Smell-O-Vision?*" Hannah asked with contempt and surprise. "What a ridiculous idea!"

"Mum says the Magna Carta's there." Margaret put in as she got up and threw the stick, happy to see the corgi exercising.

"Of course, *you* would be interested in something boring like that..." Rachel tilted her head to one side. "You're so smart and proper. Are all the English girls proper?" She leaned back on the bench and played with her straight brown hair, twirling it around her finger.

"Some of them are. What about you, Hannah? What do you want to see?" Margaret picked up the corgi that was huffing and puffing. He squirmed, but she held him close to settle him down.

"I want to see the bands that are playing there." Hannah brought her knees up to her chest. "I love music..." Hannah sighed and hugged her knees.

Margaret smiled and put the squirming corgi down. He looked at her with bright brown eyes and wagged his rump. Margaret threw the stick countless times and was surprised when she saw her mother hurrying towards them. She had her khaki trench coat on, and her heels clacked on the ground. As soon as the girls saw her, she motioned them over to her. Margaret hooked the leash on Louis and walked quickly with Hannah and Rachel to her mother.

"What is it?" Margaret jogged the rest of the way when she saw her mother's anxious face.

"Oh, Margaret, it's happened. I received a telegram from your

father. It was announced on the radio and everyone's talking about it..."
She started to walk with them back to the house. "England is at war with
Germany." She declared.

Margaret's breath caught in her throat. *Can this really be
happening?* She had known it would come... but now that it was finally
happening, she didn't know how to handle it.

"What else did father say?" She asked as she handed the leash to
Rachel who was following them with Hannah at her side.

"Yes. He said war was declared at 11 o'clock in London. He says
he won't be enlisted, surely, but he wants to help." Gabriella responded.
"Oh, Margaret," she stopped and hugged her tight. "Our dear England..."

Margaret squeezed her eyes closed, trying not to cry, somewhat
surprised at her mother's show of emotion.

"Yes, Dad mentioned something about helping out with the war
effort." Margaret stated as she stepped back and they continued on their
way. "But did he say anything about Harry or his brothers? Will they be
enlisted? In the army?" Margaret cast a glance at her friends.

Rachel gave her an encouraging smile and Hannah's face looked
sympathetic.

"He did not say," Gabriella replied.

"What about us?" Rachel asked as they were nearing the house.
"Will America go to war?"

"No, I don't believe we will." Gabriella replied and held the door
open for the three girls. "We'll just have to wait and see though, I suppose. I
heard President Roosevelt will be addressing us this evening on the radio."

The studio was full of boys banging on their instruments and
practicing. Margaret ran up the stairs, trying to hide the tears that were
starting to come. She closed the door behind her and went to her window.
She sat in front of it and quietly cried. She buried her face in her hands
and wished she was home. She despaired and cried for several minutes.
She wanted nothing more than to be home, safe in her father's arms. *What
will the next few years bring?* She could hardly comprehend the question.
*What about Harry?* Margaret burst into another fit of cries. When a knock
sounded on her door, she tried to dry her eyes.

Gabriella entered and made her way across the room quickly. She
sat beside her daughter and wrapped her arms around her.

"There, there, Margaret. It will be alright. Sh..." She tried to comfort her.

Margaret held onto her tightly, trying to quiet her sobs. Her home... would she have a home to go back to? Most of all, Margaret knew this meant she would not be returning to England this year... and most likely the next, too... So long to be away from home and her father and Bess and Harry... It was that which troubled her most of all.

When Margaret's tears finally stopped, she sat up and looked to her mother. "Thank you," she knew she hadn't said the words often enough.

"Oh, my dear." Gabriella cradled her head in her hands. "My sweet one... I'm so sorry." They lapsed into silence. Gabriella fetched a handkerchief for each of them. "We can only wait and see what happens. But I *am* truly sorry. I know how much you miss your father and your home. It'll be alright. I know it isn't home here yet, but your safe." She tucked a strand of hair behind Margaret's ear.

"I know," Margaret sniffed and took a deep, shaky breath. "I'm just... I'm scared." Margaret hugged her mother and did not see the tears in her own mother's eyes.

"I know, my dear. I am too."

Both were afraid for their country. Both were afraid for those they loved. And both were afraid of the void Britain was heading into.

———————

'Dear Harry,

I know I only wrote to you less than a week ago for your birthday, but I wanted to know, how are you? How is your family? I learnt that war was declared. What happened? I hope that you and your family are safe. I know this is a short letter, but please, tell me everything that has been happening. Since I can't be there, you must give me all the details. I am so worried for all of you.

Your friend,

Meg'

Margaret heard back from Harry within the week, his letter caused her to worry even more. He had said that gas masks were commonplace and that his mother always carried one in her purse. He had further explained that blackouts were mandatory, and it seemed as though they were waiting for something to happen, but no one quite knew what. Margaret bit her lip as she read the letter. It hurt her to know that her father and Bess were experiencing the same things, and she couldn't be there to go through them as well. It was a short letter and ended with Harry saying that he had to go and start building the Anderson shelter with his father.

Folding the letter back up and placing it in her desk drawer, Margaret sat on the stool and stared blankly at the wall in front of her. It was about a week after war had been declared and she had been worried ever since.

*What good will it do for me to worry? What good will it do Dad and Bess and Harry?* She got up and took a deep breath. She went to her shelves and picked up her violin that was right next to her three books. Margaret played a few notes and let the beauty of the music penetrate her soul and quiet her racing heart.

A knock sounded on her door and without stopping, Margaret said, "come in!" She finished the little song she had played when she saw Rachel's head peek around the corner.

"We're practicing in the studio for the concert tomorrow. Do you want to come?" Rachel asked with a friendly smile.

Margaret nodded, "I'll be right there." She put her violin back in her case and fastened the clasps.

Rachel took a step into her room and waited for her. "Wow! What a great room!" She commented.

"I know, isn't it?" Margaret turned back to her friend and joined her by the doorway. "I feel bad you and Hannah have to sleep in such small rooms downstairs."

"Oh, don't worry about us." Rachel chuckled. "We don't take up too much space, and besides..." The girls started down the stairs to the studio. "We spend more time in the studio than our rooms. And the studio's big enough for everyone. You came from England; you need the extra space for your things!" Rachel jumped from the last step and jogged to her place in the middle of the mix-matched chamber orchestra. Margaret took her seat across from Hannah and slid between the cello and the stool it was resting on.

Samuel stood on a box facing them and turned the sheet music he read like a book.

"We're playing Vivaldi's *Spring.*" Hannah told her and picked up her violin and set it on her shoulder. Margaret thanked her and relaxed, she could play this song quite well, she thought.

Hannah led the orchestra with the lively string intro and Margaret accompanied her. Music was their passion and despite their differences, it united them with an invisible bond.

The next day, they played in the park as usual and this time they included a song by Pitcher's request from the composer Boccherini. They got several ovations from the crowds and Mr. Ackerman received many donations and even a few new pupils. Central Park's trees were starting to turn color; a reminder that fall was fast approaching and school would be starting soon. The breeze was chilly and as they walked home, Margaret pulled her coat closer around her. She and Rachel always walked on either side of Hannah who was thankful for the added safety. They all carried their instruments and followed Mr. Ackerman back to the house. He had his best suit on and his tawny fedora hat that he often wore. They walked past a restaurant that was playing *'Jeepers Creepers.'* A few of the boys stopped and looked inside to see a live band with a trumpet blaring.

"Golly! Look at that!" The twins peered into the place that was full of men and women, some dancing.

Gabriella scooted them along as a lady began singing the song. The boys reluctantly jogged to catch up with their friends.

As they continued their walk back to the house, the Moser twins pretended to dance with each other like they had seen the people do in the café. Margaret and Rachel laughed as they almost ran into a spindly tree. They laughed and continued anyway. Margaret looked over her shoulder and shared a laugh with her mother.

"You can't blame them; it does make you want to dance!" Betty said as the tune played through all their heads.

Late that night, Margaret lay wide awake in her bed. She couldn't stop thinking about home, her father, Bess, Harry, his parents, his brothers, and what might happen to them if they were enlisted. She was glad her father wasn't forced to serve. No doubt, he would want to help. Yet, he wouldn't be risking his life on the front lines. But would being home be any safer than the front lines? *And what about Bess?* Margaret knew she would be glad she was safe, but she missed her and the excursions through London they always shared. Sighing, Margaret turned over in her bed and as all became silent once more, she heard the creak of a floorboard. Margaret sat up, knowing that the house didn't creak on its own... at least not most of the time. She listened for a second and then heard nothing else. Nonetheless, she kept her eyes open, staring at her door in the dark.

Not a minute after, Margaret heard music. She sat upright again and went to her door. She listened to make sure she had really heard something. Sure enough, someone was in the studio playing the piano softly. *Mum?* Margaret grabbed her robe and exited her room. She tip-toed across the landing and silently walked down the stairs. The song was sad and mournful. Margaret stopped at the base of the stairs and listened. It was a simple melody, one that she had never heard before. The rhythm was kept with the left hand and the melody was executed with the right. Margaret peeked around the corner; sure enough, her mother was sitting at the ivories, swaying with feeling and emotion. Margaret had never heard her mother play since the day she had arrived at the brownstone house cramped in New York City's streets.

*I can see how she was the best pianist in the London Symphony Orchestra.* Margaret kept her place by the stairs, not daring to move.

The song continued on, and Margaret knew somehow that her mother was crying. It was a song of loss, hurt, grief, yet strength. Margaret knew not how long she had been standing there when the song finally reached its climax and the great pianist, with her foot on the mute pedal, played with such feeling it was a wonder not all the children in the floor below them woke from the intensity. Margaret was filled with sadness, but she dare not go to her mother for the sake of risking the precious moment she was witness to.

The studio grew quiet once more as the song finished and Gabriella sat at the piano alone. Several minutes ticked by, but the lady did not move from her place before the piano, dressed in an elegant white nightgown.

Margaret slowly walked forward. Gabriella looked up to her daughter who looked exactly like her.

Margaret sat down beside her quietly.

"You remind me so much of your father." She said quietly as she wiped her eyes.

Margaret suddenly had the urge to venture into a conversation she had never dared to enter before. She looked up to her mother and asked the question before she grew afraid and kept the words to herself. "Why did you leave?"

If the question caught her mother off guard, she did not show it. She merely looked at the piano keys and thought for a moment. "You were so tiny and so perfect." She said as she thought of the distant memory. "I was afraid. So young, married, a mother. In that moment, it was all too much. When I looked into your deep, brown eyes and your perfectly delicate face, I knew you deserved better... better than what I could give you. And I couldn't protect you from... well I had so many things I had to sort through, I couldn't risk you getting hurt because of them." Gabriella said the words slowly and quietly. "I left England shortly after. It was the worst mistake of my life." Her voice cracked. "I'm sorry." Gabriella looked at Margaret, who was holding back tears. "Oh, my darling, I'm so sorry."

Margaret looked up to her mother and hugged her. She was glad to finally know the truth straight from her mother's lips. And yet she still wondered *why?* What fear or pain would make a mother leave her child with the chance of never seeing her again? She didn't have the courage to ask, and even if she did, Margaret wasn't sure her mother would ever answer such a question. Maybe there wasn't even an answer to such a question.

"Now," Gabriella straightened up, composing herself. "I have a question for you." She stood up and Margaret followed. "What was your childhood like?" For once, the two spoke openly to each other. "I want to know everything."

Margaret followed her mother into her room, and they sat together on the big bed swapping stories and talking for hours and hours. Margaret finally felt a measure of peace as she told her mother all about what her life had been like growing up. She told her mother what her fears were and what she loved. Gabriella listened intently, soaking up everything.

Old wounds were beginning to heal.

# Chapter 9

Margaret looked out her window and squealed. It was Christmas Eve morning, and their street was covered in snow. Dashing to her dresser and pulling out the bottom drawer that held some of her winter clothes, Margaret threw on a dark blue dress that came just below her knees and thick grey socks. She secured the necklace Harry had given her around her neck, thinking fondly of home. She was ecstatic for the snow and loved it. They never received much snow in London. However, last night it had been a regular blizzard in New York City. She ran down the stairs, combing her hair as she went. That evening they were going to City Hall to see the Christmas tree being lit. Mayor La Guardia was going to give a Christmas address and the city's police department glee club was going to be singing. Downstairs, she was greeted by the wonderful smells of pine from their Christmas tree and breakfast cooking; fried eggs, sausages, rolls, and hashbrowns. The fresh evergreen tree stood tall in the back corner of the house, shining brilliantly. It filled the whole first floor with the delicious smell. When she reached the foyer, the song *'Here we come a Wassailing,'* was coming from the gramophone.

"Oh, Betty! You've outdone yourself!" Margaret exclaimed as she surveyed the breakfast spread Betty was working on.

Rachel and Samuel were already sitting at the table eating.

"Come have some Adam and Eve on a Raft and Wreck Um!" Rachel held up a piece of toast with eggs on top and Margaret joined her at the table.

"Merry Christmas, Rachel!" Margaret said as she filled her plate with eggs, a roll, and a sausage. "Merry Christmas, Samuel!" She said cheerily.

He grinned and dipped his head to her... always a young man of few words.

It was going to be a wonderful day.

"It's only Christmas Eve." Rachel corrected her.

"Oh, what difference does it make?" Margaret shrugged. "Christmas is Christmas."

Slowly, the other children joined them to eat breakfast. They were all taking advantage of sleeping in since they were on Christmas break.

Their small school was just a few blocks away, tucked in between the skyscrapers and massive buildings. Margaret wasn't thrilled about it and wished she could just play her music, but Betty and Gabriella and Mr. Ackerman were adamant about them going to school and getting a good education. She had fit in well there. Rachel and Hannah went to the same school and the girls always walked there every morning together even though they were all in different grades and classes.

The next song that filtered in from the foyer by way of the gramophone was 'Rudolph the Red-Nosed Reindeer.' The Moser twins, Grubbs, and Pitcher all sang along. Gabriella came downstairs looking sleepy-eyed. She grabbed some coffee and sat next to Margaret. Betty, who was bright-eyed and ready to start the day, ate with them and then went back to the foyer to take out the Christmas record that had ended.

*It's clear who the morning person is and who isn't.* Margaret thought with an amused grin.

Louis came trotting into the kitchen with a little red and green bandana tied about his neck. The boys laughed at him and Margaret picked him up and put him on her lap. He wagged his rump and tried to eat some of her scrambled eggs. Of course, she let him have just a bite.

The boys were the first to venture outside, hardly finishing breakfast before they tugged on their winter boots. Gabriella fussed over them as they protested wearing hats and gloves. But finally, they were all dressed and running out the front door.

"Wait, Tony! You forgot your coat!" Gabriella called.

Margaret joined her at the threshold, shrugging on her woolen coat as the cold air billowed into the warm, toasty house.

"I'll take it to him." She offered.

"Thank you," Gabriella sighed. "Getting those boys into their winter clothes is like trying to dress cats."

"You sound like you speak from experience." Margaret chuckled, pulling on her mittens and hat.

Gabriella only eyed her humorously, "you don't want to know."

Margaret laughed as Rachel and Hannah joined them and together, the three girls all ventured out into the winter wonderland.

They trudged through the sidewalks where the snow came up to their shins. They threw snowballs and poor Hannah, she just squealed whenever Rachel and Margaret accidentally hit her. It was all in good fun and she even threw some at Margaret and Rachel. Then the boys came running out behind them and pelted them with as many snowballs as they could make. They ran down the sidewalks and away from the house; Margaret could hear her mother calling after them to be careful. The streets were quiet for once because the snow was still falling and the roads were too deep with snow. The three girls slowly jogged behind the boys, going as fast as Hannah would allow. They finally made it to the park, all ruddy-faced and exhilarated.

Once in Central Park, they threw snowballs, found other children doing the same and before they knew it, there was an army of snowball-throwing children running through the rolling hills and groves of Central Park. They pelted each other and found refuge behind the large hills and stone bridges. Hannah stayed close to Margaret and Rachel who could both successfully hold off the relentless boys. Margaret threw a snowball at one boy who would not leave them alone and it hit him right in the face. He fell backwards dramatically and then his friends jumped on top of him. She laughed from the sight. Margaret slid back down the hill and landed right beside Hannah and Rachel who were hiding and giggling.

"I wish it snowed every day!" She panted and felt like taking off her coat because she was so warm from running about.

The girls laughed and had sly looks on their face. Margaret furrowed her eyebrows and before she had time to question them, Grubbs and Pitcher dumped a load of snow on her from behind. It went down the back of her coat and soaked her hair. She gasped in surprise.

"I'm going to get you two!" She chased after them and threw snowballs at them in retaliation, however all of them missed.

After their excursion in the park, the eight children all returned to the house hungry and wet and tired. They entered the foyer, deposited all of their wet coats and gloves and hats in a pile which Gabriella groaned over. She took the things downstairs in the basement to dry them. Betty had already prepared lunch which was hot, delicious beef stew. They all ate it greedily and happily. The three teachers joined them and they shared stories and victories in the park.

The afternoon was just as grand. The children all played Christmas songs and sang carols to accompany their instruments. Hannah played a pretty version of 'Silent Night.' Grubbs and Rachel played 'Away in a Manger' with their woodwinds. The Moser twins and Pitcher played a foot-stomping, feet-dancing version of *'Rudolph the Red-Nosed Reindeer.'* Lastly, Margaret was asked to play something.

She settled on *'O Holy Night.'* As she started the beautiful song, the children looked dreamy-eyed all around the room, lost in their own thoughts. Gabriella and Betty and Mr. Ackerman joined the children to listen. Margaret finished the song after going through several of the verses. Her last thought as she finished the song was, *I wonder what Dad is doing right now...*

---

The garlands hung from the pews, wreaths were hung on the old wooden doors, and Bess played a Christmas hymn on the organ. The congregation sang and yet the reverend's perspective was grim. The faces of his friends were weary, yet on this Christmas Eve, they had put on their best to make the short journey to Lily's End and greet the reverend with ruddy faces and magic in their eyes. Christmas always bolstered one's spirits. Reverend Sutton finished his sermon and wished everyone a Merry Christmas. He then shook their hands and bid them farewell as they made their way out into the cold night to go home and listen to the king's Christmas address.

The reverend locked up the church and then retired to his cottage. Bess said goodnight and left for home as well.

"Be careful on the roads, Bess." The reverend had cautioned her, for the streets were dangerous with the blackouts enforced. Several had been injured or killed because of the dark streets and the cars that drove without headlights. But the housekeeper assured him she would be safe.

Now, sitting in his chair by the radio, the reverend listened to the king's Christmas address, a tradition that His Majesty upheld.

*"Such unity in aim and in effort has never been seen in the world before."* The king said.

*Indeed!* The reverend nodded his head. Britain was pulled so tightly together by this war. Neighbors took care of neighbors and the reverend was reminded of that every day. He had been helping carry sandbags to the buildings in London and several of the men in the neighborhood had joined him. They set out almost every morning to help where they could. The fathers were happy for the work, for their children were either evacuated or being enlisted in the army.

The reverend continued to listen. *"A new year is at hand. We cannot tell what it will bring."*

"O Lord, bring us through this safely." The reverend prayed and listened.

*"If it brings peace, how thankful we shall all be."*

He sighed and prayed fervently that the former statement would be true. *Please let this year bring peace.* His gaze lingered on the Christmas tree that was in the corner of the living room with no presents underneath its green boughs. The living room in which he sat was chilled and dim and unfilled. The reverend sat, weary of the emptiness, the quiet solitude weighing down his shoulders as he listened to the last few words of the Christmas message.

*"If it brings us continued struggle,"* the king proceeded in his methodical way. *"We shall remain undaunted."*

---

In the afternoon, the phone rang. Margaret, Rachel, Hannah, Betty, and Gabriella were all playing Monopoly at the dining room table. Margaret looked up with surprise. The phone rarely rang. Only about twice a week it would cry out for someone to pick it up... and never on holidays. Gabriella got up and made her way to the telephone that hung in the hallway.

"Who is it?" Hannah asked, but she never got an answer.

Gabriella dropped the earpiece and gasped.

Margaret leaned back in her chair to watch. Gabriella quickly scrambled for the phone earpiece and put it to her ear again. She motioned for Margaret to come quickly. Margaret did, knowing that something was wrong.

"Of course, she's right here." Gabriella handed the old-fashioned telephone earpiece to Margaret who stood in front of the machine awkwardly.

"Hello?" She spoke into the speaker.

"Margaret! Merry Christmas!" The voice made her squeal with delight.

"DAD! It's you!" A huge smile spread across her face. "Merry

Christmas!"

The oh-so familiar voice laughed with delight on the other end. "I hope you like your present, my dear girl. Oh how we miss you here!" He laughed still and Margaret wished she could jump into the telephone and be transported to her home.

"I miss you too, Dad! Oh this is spectacular! It will cost you a fortune! How is Harry? How is Bess? What are you doing? Did you decorate the church?" All her questions poured out at once. No longer were her and her father's thoughts separated by an ocean.

"Bess is fine and Harry is fine. I just saw him this evening in church with his family, Evan and Richard included, for they're both home for the holiday. And Bess left a little while ago. Things are quiet here for once, no sirens. It seems even the Germans stay out of the air during Christmas." The reverend said.

"Dad, I'm so relieve to hear that you and Bess and Harry are alright. I sent you all letters two days ago, they should be arriving soon. What did you do tonight? Are you all alone?"

"Yes, I am alone... but not lonely. I listened to our king give his usual Christmas speech this evening. The only thing I regret is not seeing your shining face in the morning, looking for presents from Santa Claus." He chuckled quietly and Margaret twirled the phone cord around her finger.

She remembered fondly the Christmas morning game they used to play. Her father always hid her presents around the house and she had to find them like a scavenger hunt. It was unusual, but it was their tradition and she loved it.

"I miss you, Dad." Margaret bit her lip.

"I miss you too." His voice sounded sad. "But how is New York and all your friends? What are you doing this evening?"

"We went to the park this morning and played in the snow together. And we're going to City Hall tonight to see the tree being lit. Then I think we're going to stop by Rockefeller Center and see the Christmas tree. Mum says it's beautiful." Margaret paused and knew her father was searching for words.

"How is she?" He finally asked after a few seconds of silence. His voice was soft and quiet.

"She's... she's wonderful, Dad." Margaret didn't know what else to say, especially because the others were in the dining room and could hear every word she said. However, she knew her father understood her perfectly.

Margaret looked to the dining room and saw her mother laughing and laughing as Betty made comical faces and jested about their game in which she was winning intolerably.

"She's everything I've hoped for." Margaret said more to herself than to her father. And she knew in her heart that it was utterly true, now more than ever.

"I'm glad. This is what I've been praying for." He let out a relieved breath. "I'm thankful, so thankful you're there and out of the country. The king said this evening that *'if this New Year brings us continued struggle we shall remain undaunted.'* I want you to stay brave, Margaret... If the worst comes, I pray that we all will have the strength to continue on and face it. For the worst surely will come if peace is not won soon."

"I will. I'll be brave. And I'll pray for your safety as well as Bess' and Harry's and his family's. I wish I was with you all... What else did the king say?" She asked and waited for him to reply.

"*'Go out into the darkness, and put your hand into the Hand of God. That shall be to you better than light, and safer than a known way.'* Wise words. Keep them close to your heart, my girl."

"I will, Dad. I promise I will." Margaret nodded.

"Well... I should let you go; it sounds like there's a jolly party going on." The reverend chuckled and Margaret did too.

"Should I call mum back over?" Margaret looked to where her mother sat beside Betty, waiting for Margaret to rejoin them and continue their game. She had a lovely smile on her face.

"Yes, thank you." He said quietly. Margaret motioned for her mother to come to the phone.

"Alright, goodnight. And Merry Christmas, Dad! Give everyone my love." Margaret said.

"I will." He promised. "I love you."

"I love you, too."

After handing her mother the phone, Margaret left her alone in the hallway and sat back down at the table with a grin she couldn't shake.

"Was it your father?" Rachel asked enthusiastically.

"What did he say?" Betty asked.

Margaret didn't answer; instead she looked to the hallway and saw her mother smiling into the telephone. She didn't know what was said between them, but Margaret felt like the past was mending; a past that could only be healed through the forgiving love of their Almighty God.

Later that night, Margaret sat by her mother on a bench in front of the massive Christmas tree in Rockefeller Center. The other children were mulling about, gazing up at the grand tree that looked magical on Christmas Eve.

Margaret looked up in silence at the tree, her breath coming out in big white puffs. *Even though I'm not in London, I can just imagine what everyone was doing for Christmas.* Margaret thought. *Harry was no doubt happy to be with his brothers again. The church would be all decorated for the service. The garlands are probably hanging on the pews and the wreathes above the altar and the doors...*

"Christmas is the best holiday, I think." Gabriella commented as she sat close beside her daughter. "Your father sounded so pleased to be able to talk with you."

Margaret looked to her mother and smiled up at her. "I miss him. But I know I'm lucky to be out of England." She adjusted her grey beret and watched as Rachel threw snowballs at the Moser twins who had put a handful of snow down the back of her coat. They watched in silence for a few moments before Margaret asked what the twins' story was.

Gabriella sighed before replying. "Frankie and Tony? Unfortunately, their family was affected by the Depression. Their father died most unexpectedly... Then they moved here from Chicago with their mum. A few times every year Mrs. Moser pops in to check on them. She knows they're better off here where they'll be taken care of and fed. She cannot provide them much except a tiny apartment in Queens that she can barely pay for with the wages she earns." Gabriella explained.

Margaret nodded in reply and watched as they played with the others. She thought it encouraging that all the children had challenging pasts, yet it seemed as though their circumstances made them stronger, more resilient, and more determined.

"What about Samuel?" She inclined her head towards the African-American young man who was always quiet and passive.

Gabriella leaned back against the bench and raised her eyebrows.

"We don't really know. Samuel showed up on our doorstep four years ago and has been with us ever since. He has such a talent. I've seen him sitting in his room writing out scores of compositions of his original music. Never has he let anyone see them."

"Has he ever spoken?" Margaret was perplexed by the boy's shyness. "He *can* speak, right?"

Gabriella smiled. "Of course he can. He just chooses not to. He's spoken to me a few times, but no more than yes and no." Her face grew solemn again.

"And what about Pitcher and Grubbs? What's Pitcher's real name? And what of their stories?"

"Pitcher's real name is Potter Watson. He got the nickname, I assume, from playing baseball in the park so often. I don't believe he's fond of his first name, so everyone calls him by his nickname. Their stories..." Gabriella trailed off. "Pitcher was homeless, if you would believe it."

Margaret listened intently.

"I passed by him in the park almost every day for a week. After that, I couldn't take it anymore and asked him why he was there alone. Once I learned the truth, we brought him in. He said his mother left him and won't say more than that. I believe he was abandoned... he was such a young child. In regards to Andrew Grubbs, he does have a father. I don't know the whereabouts of his mother, but his father..." she took a deep breath. "He had some troubles with the law. But when he would bring Andrew to his lessons with a black eye and that started happening more frequently, we had to get involved."

Gabriella didn't have to elaborate, Margaret knew.

"That's awful." She looked to where Pitcher and Grubbs were pelting each other with snowballs.

"His father was deemed unfit to take care of him and the state relinquished him to us; told us he could stay at our halfway house."

"Well, I'm glad they're both here."

"As am I." Gabriella agreed.

Margaret took in her mother's words and turned her attention back to the Christmas tree. It was shining and the lights reflected off the glass of the buildings around it. The hour was growing late. They had gone to see the Christmas tree lighting at City Hall and had heard Mayor La Guardia speak. Then they had gone to St. Patrick's Cathedral for the

Christmas service. The gothic-style church was impressive with its spires that towered into the sky and the great, colored rose-window. It reminded Margaret of London and the countless cathedrals there. After that, they had made the short jaunt to Rockefeller Center and had admired the Christmas decorations. In the morning they would exchange presents and open the gifts Santa Claus left under their tree.

The song *'Here we come a Wassailing'* was being comically sung by the children as they walked back to the house. Margaret joined in on the chorus and realized that even though she was separated from her father by an entire ocean, they could still continue on with their lives and have good times. And even though her friends who were starting to feel more like brothers and sisters had been through rough pasts, there was always joy ahead. There was always a choice; to either be consumed by all the terrible things that had happened or things they wished would happen, or to walk the road that had been laid before them and try to face it as bravely and as undaunted as they could.

*Cinnamon rolls.* Margaret couldn't remember a more divine breakfast. The gooey cinnamon oozed out from the swirls of dough. Margaret ate one and then she ate another while they were opening presents. Each of the children had one gift from Saint Nick, then one from the teachers, and one from another student. Margaret had bought for Rachel. She watched in suspense as Rachel had taken off the red ribbon that held the lid of the box. She gasped as she saw what was inside. It was a lovely necklace with a musical note on it.

"Now we match!" Margaret showed Rachel her necklace that matched it almost perfectly.

"Oh! It's lovely! Thank you so much, Meg!" Rachel hugged Margaret and wished her a Merry Christmas.

Margaret had gotten a new skid-stopper for her cello from Grubbs, a boxful of hair ribbons from Saint Nick, and a Johannes Brahms book of compositions and sheet music from the teachers. She thanked her mother, Betty, and Mr. Ackerman whole-heartedly and watched as the other children finished opening their gifts. On their shopping trip to Macy's the students had put together their small amounts of money and had gotten their teachers a few small things. They gave Mr. Ackerman a new fedora hat; Betty, a new apron; and Gabriella, a silver bracelet. The teachers, who had expected nothing, were very touched by the show of kindness and thoughtfulness of their students.

Once everyone had finished opening their gifts, Mr. Ackerman got up and clapped his hands together. He got their attention and stood tall, his grey hair peeking out from under his new black and grey fedora.

"I have an announcement! This present will be for all of you, yet it's something that I cannot hand over to you." He looked eager.

Anticipation could be felt in the room as everyone wanted to hear what he would say. They all looked up to him from their places on the floor of the living room.

"Tell us! Tell us!" Tony shouted and Pitcher hushed him.

"If you keep asking, he won't tell!" He whined.

"I spoke with the concertmaster of the New York Philharmonic a few days ago. Now, I've been waiting to tell you until this morning. Merry Christmas, children." He looked to the shining faces of the students who looked up at him with expectant eyes. "We are allowed to use the Chamber Music Hall at Carnegie! The head of the philharmonic offered to let us use it every Sunday."

Everyone cheered and thanked Mr. Ackerman. Margaret clapped her hands together and hugged Hannah and Rachel who were sitting next to her. Louis came running into the room, aroused by the shouts and exclamations of joy that the boys and girls were displaying. He barked and wagged his rump, looking for attention. Everyone laughed as he bounded through the wrapping paper and got tangled in the ribbons. Pitcher put a red bow on his head to top off the wrapped-up corgi. Margaret truly felt at home for the first time in months.

Later that night, once everyone had finished their delicious Christmas feast, carols were sung, and the festivities ended, Margaret sat on her bed and wrote a letter to Harry and her father. As she was writing, a knock sounded from her door.

"Come in," she looked up.

Her mother entered with a smile, holding a small box wrapped up in a bow and wrapping paper. "I have something for you." She joined Margaret on her bed and sat down beside her.

"What is it?" Margaret asked as her mother handed her the gift. "You didn't have to get me anything." She suddenly felt terrible for not getting her mother anything else special besides the gifts all the children had pitched in to get.

"I know, but it's our first Christmas together and I wanted it to be special. Go ahead, open it up."

Margaret carefully ripped the paper and removed the ribbons and bows. She let out a small gasp of excitement as she saw what it was. Her mother's gift was a beautiful, ornate wooden box. It was a foot long and six inches wide. It opened up with a small key and smelled wonderful, like freshly cut cedar.

"I thought it would be a good place to store all your letters." Gabriella explained. "You have so many coming and going, you needed somewhere special to keep them. Maybe we can look back on these days with fond memories and forget the worry we felt for our loved ones back across the sea."

Margaret wiped a tear that had escaped her. "Thank you," she set the box down on her bed and threw her arms around her mother in a hug.

Gabrielle held tightly to her. "Oh my dear, Merry Christmas..." She paused. "I know I haven't been there for you in the past. But please let me be here for you now. We need each other. We need family. And I love you very, very much."

Margaret squeezed her tighter. "I love you too."

---

Harry couldn't believe his ears, yet here were his brothers sitting at the table relaying the most terrible news... and on Christmas no less. Harry rubbed his face with exasperation. Mrs. Cavanaugh kept a brave face and Mr. Cavanaugh looked solemn.

"I understand and respect your decisions." Mr. Cavanaugh told his two eldest sons who had just shared the news they had been waiting to impart until the last moment.

Rich had volunteered for the British Red Cross, something that all his fellow university medical students were doing. It meant he would be working in hospitals, usually away from the front lines in relative safety, and doing his part to help win the war. But that was not the worst part. Evan's news was far more distressing.

The middle son had volunteered for the British Expeditionary

Force and after training, would be shipped off to France very soon. His boyish face looked determined, considering he was only nineteen.

"It'll be fine, mum. Really..." he tried to reassure her, yet she stifled a sob. "I don't mind giving up university and I'll still be in England for six months of training. I can't sit by on the sidelines and watch. I'll get recruited eventually anyway." He replied bravely and took his mother's hand from across the table.

Harry looked down to the table and sighed. *If Rich and Evan are doing their part, what must I do? I have to do my part too. I cannot be a coward and hide in the bomb shelters like a child. I'm not a child anymore... I'm seventeen.* He looked up and listened to his oldest brother whom he admired greatly.

"It seems as though I'll be sticking with our teacher, who's also going with to the hospitals. Doctor Wells said he'll keep a close eye on me. We won't be on the front lines, at least not for a while. We'll be setting up with the Joint War Organization where we can accurately record the wounded and missing. But there's still a lot of work ahead and we won't be sent out for a while." Richard, who was always calm and collected and wise, spoke with his father in his usual placid tone.

It seemed to put his mother at ease, but Evan's face was still pale and he looked ashamed of the news he had delivered. He had enlisted. There was nothing any of them could do to change that fact.

Harry lay in bed that night and stared up at the ceiling that could hardly be seen because it was so dark in his room. The lyrics from the Christmas carol played in his mind.

*'We wish you a merry Christmas!*
*And a happy New Year!'*

He shook his head slightly, wondering how the New Year could be happy. *1940. How did I get so old? How did Rich and Evan get so old? Seems like just yesterday we were running around the streets playing conkers or bung the barrel.* Harry knew that the New Year would bring about change, mostly in regards to the war. *It has finally hit home. And I never thought it would hit so hard.*

# Chapter 11

The stage of the Carnegie Chamber Music Hall beheld fifteen children all from the ages of seven to fifteen. A single cello, trombone, piano, harp, oboe, clarinet, several timpani, violins, French horns, trumpets, and flutes were all present as their young prodigies played them. Samuel conducted the chamber orchestra as they played Bach's Orchestral Suite No. 3 vividly and excitedly. Mr. Ackerman sat in the empty theater seats behind Gabriella and Betty. The teachers watched with pride.

Margaret finished playing the orchestral suite and congratulated Hannah, Simone, and Grace, the three girls who were the violinists. They had played wonderfully, their bows rapidly working over the strings and their fingers keeping pace with every note that had to be played.

"You did just as well, Meg!" Grace, the seven year old sister of Simone, sat on Margaret's lap and put the cello in front of her. "I wish I could play the cello!" She plucked the strings of the cello that was much too big for her.

"Maybe someday you will." Margaret replied.

Simone motioned for Grace to get up. She tuned her violin and looked to Samuel who was picking out the next arrangement.

"Didn't we practice Beethoven's 7ᵗʰ Symphony?" Simone walked up to Samuel and pulled out the pages of sheet music that was buried in his music stand. "Can we play that?" She asked as she put her violin under her arm.

"You'll soon learn, Simone, that Samuel picks out the music and we always have to keep up with him." Rachel laughed from her place beside Grubbs.

"You don't mind, do you, Samuel?" Simone, the strong-willed fourteen year old asked.

Samuel shook his head in reply.

"Good," She smiled and put her violin back on her shoulder.

Since all the children, who included the students that didn't live at the house, didn't always have sheet music, they relied on their memory. All the songs, movements, arrangements, and concertos they played, they played from memory or by ear. However, for their Carnegie outings every Sunday, they always practiced, for they wanted to show off to the musicians of the New York Philharmonic that sometimes watched.

Margaret prepared to play the 7<sup>th</sup> Symphony and her gaze wandered to the audience. Betty, Mr. Ackerman, and her mother were all seated there, but there was someone standing in the doorway. Margaret had a hint of recognition, but she couldn't place where she had seen the woman before. Margaret was forced to return her mind to her music when the violins started up without her. They played the slow, moving piece that stretched seven minutes long. Closing her eyes, she focused on nothing else but the music. The same feeling she had known hundreds of times before overtook her as she slipped into the world of her music.

The moon lit up her paper and the little lamp on her desk illuminated Margaret's writing. She started a note to her friend, feeling sorry for him and his family concerning Rich and Evan's latest news.

*'Dear Harry,*

*I hope that you are doing alright. From your last letter you sounded quite put out. I understand why. Know that I am praying for your brothers. God won't leave them.*

*You ask what is new here, but I'm afraid I don't have any news to share. We continue to go to Carnegie every Sunday and I can tell that Mr. A. is happy to have his foot in the door. Not for himself, but for us. He hopes that we can get opportunities from playing there. Some of the students are so talented. I cannot imagine them not getting accepted in the New York Philharmonic or receiving a university scholarship.*

*Enough about me. This New Year seems like it's going to be a long one. It feels like January will never end. What has the New Year brought for London? I am itching for news. Any news! I know you said there are rumors going around about a 'Phony War.' But I'm glad for your sakes there hasn't been much excitement on the Homefront. Father has not written for about a week and I can understand why. We all have to make sacrifices while the war rages, especially when it comes to our time.*

*I miss you all and cannot wait till we see each other again.*

*Your friend,*

*Meg.'*

Margaret swiveled on her stool and looked out her window onto the quiet, moonlit street. Cars still rumbled by on the other busy roads and

Margaret could hear them and the subways rumbling. She thought about the New Yorkers and how they seemed so pleased to not take part in the war. No one thought America would go to war and Margaret had to agree with them. It didn't seem like they'd get involved much at all. The fighting seemed so far away. Sure there were newspaper headlines, magazine articles, and movie reels about the war, the terribly cold fighting, and France being a primary target for Hitler. But in America it all seemed so far away... like it was in another world.

Climbing into bed in her pajamas, Margaret was just glad they were safe. *Maybe the war will end soon and I can go home. Maybe mum will even come with me.* She hopefully thought, but deep down she knew that it would not be over so soon. In the last few weeks, the newspapers had been explicit in describing the attack of several of His Majesty's ships. No, for the time being, she wasn't going anywhere soon.

---

"Oh! No! No! Sod it!" Bess cried out from the kitchen.

She wiped her dirty hands on her apron. She sniffed and cried a little with rage, anger, and disappointment.

"For goodness sake's, Bess!" Reverend Frank Sutton came running into the kitchen to find a pot of stew all over the floor. "Oh dear!" He remarked with surprise and then looked to the housekeeper who was completely disheveled.

"I've ruined your only meal, reverend and now..." She cried and put the back of her hand to her forehead in despair. "Now I've nothing else to make for you! Blimey, you might as well throw me out on the spot!" Bess sank down to the chair by her little table.

"There, there, Bess. I would never throw you out. It was just a mistake." He tried to reassure the sobbing woman.

"This bloody rationing! Sugar! Butter! Bacon! How am I supposed to cook with no butter and sugar?" She cried into her hands that were covered with bits and pieces of food.

"Bess, do try to calm down." The reverend said. "You have enough food on your hands to feed you for a week. Go and wash up, then we'll see about dinner. Did you happen to spill all of the stew? You didn't burn yourself, did you?"

She shook her head and whimpered that she had not.

"Good, now go on. Out of here." He shooed her out of the kitchen and looked back to the floor with a sigh. *What a mess.* He thought to himself.

The reverend grabbed a mop, a pail, and set to work. As he cleaned up, he thought of the rationing. *Only 50 grams of butter... 225 grams of sugar... Hardly enough for a grown adult. At least we'll all lose some weight.* He chuckled to himself. The reverend glanced over to his buff-colored ration book that had the words *'Ministry of Food'* printed on the cover. He shook his head, but was not totally put out by the rationing. Some families were going through much worse and he had to be thankful for the food they did have. *At least Margaret is safe, well-fed, and happy. Which reminds me, I must write back to her! Perhaps on the bottom of a grocery bag...* He smiled, for paper was hard to come by. He continued cleaning up the soup that would have tasted so very good.

Once the mess was cleaned up, the reverend sighed as he sat back down in his chair. Apart from his sermons to bolster the spirits of those on the home front, he had recently applied to become an Air Raid Precaution Warden. Knowing that his job would soon start, he valued his peaceful evenings. He would have to go out during the night and inspect the blackout conditions to make sure everyone was adhering to the ARP's restrictions to protect the citizens from aid raids. He would also deliver Anderson and Morrison shelters, hand out gas masks, some in the shape of Mickey Mouse's for the children, and report bomb damage, if there was any. So far there was hardly any damage or movement on the Homefront. This, the reverend was thankful for. *The less action, the better,* he thought to himself.

He wished he could hold his daughter in his arms and tell her everything would be alright. However, he knew both things were impossible. He could not travel across the ocean, as it had become much too dangerous, nor could he promise his daughter that everything *would* be alright. The only thing he could do was be courageous and support Margaret and the war effort any way he could.

---

Margaret sat in the backyard on the picnic table that had been there for years and years. It was so permanent that its legs were half buried in the sod. Margaret read a letter from Harry as Samuel secretly and protectively wrote one of his compositions. The boy, who was now fourteen, had grown more open to letting the others see his music. He even let them play one of his songs he titled *'Grace Unto Thee.'* Everyone thought he was a natural. Margaret watched him from the corner of her eye and then turned back to reading her letter, the early May sun shone down, warming her back and shoulders.

*'Dear Margaret,*

*I hope all is well with you and you are enjoying the warm weather in New York. London is chaotic. I can't even begin to describe how busy we've been. Dad and I put up the shelter; it was painstaking digging down into the ground. Your dad has been patrolling the streets of London with the iconic 'W' on his metal helmet. He looks very professional; you should be proud of him. He even stopped at our front door and told us to turn off our light that was shining a bit through our curtain. It was rather funny and I couldn't help laughing. Mum and Dad scolded me. I couldn't help it... it was funny to see your father so business-like and professional when he's always been more like a second-father to me.*

*We received a telegram from Evan. He's fighting in France, trying to hold back the Jerry's. No news from Rich though. Last we heard, he was following Dr. Wells and helping him. We have no idea where he is. No word for three months. It makes mother sick and father worries, but what can we do?*

*Running out of grocery bag paper... Please forgive the sloppy writing. It's about one in the morning and I'm writing in the bomb shelter. We have one small torch for light. Sirens went off a little bit ago and we'd rather just sleep here than go back inside and have to come back out again.*

*Your friend,*

*Harry.*

*P.S. Almost done with school! Wish me luck on my tests!'*

Margaret reread the letter and put it in her pocket. She leaned back and placed her hands behind her on the picnic table top.

"It was a letter from Harry in London." She told Samuel, whom she hoped would reply. When he didn't, Margaret continued. "He doesn't know where his oldest brother is and his other brother, Evan, is fighting in

France. I can't even imagine." She shook her head and looked up to the sky that was full of fluffy white clouds.

It was a beautiful Monday, the first Monday of summer break. Margaret couldn't be more relieved. Their school was dusty, cramped, and dirty with irritable teachers and a blue-nosed principle that liked to scold them beyond belief. However, now they were on break. No more half-hour walks to the school and no more cramped, hot days.

Samuel cleared his throat and brought Margaret out of her thoughts. She saw Rachel and Hannah come from the house and descend down the steps that were very steep. Once the two girls joined Margaret, they sat on the picnic table's seats across from Samuel.

"Want to go for a walk?" Rachel asked. "Betty gave us five dollars. We can go to the park and take a carriage ride, get on the subway, with an adult of course, and hop down to Coney Island. Or go to Macy's." Rachel looked up to Margaret.

"What's it to be?" Hannah asked. "Although I'll bet you want to go to the island. You haven't even been there yet!" She exclaimed.

Margaret thought for a moment and nodded. "Coney Island sounds great!" She took out Harry's letter and continued, "Let me just put this in my room."

"Alright, we'll tell Miss Betty and your mom. Maybe one of them will be able to go with us!" Rachel replied.

"Do you want to come, Samuel?" Margaret asked him.

The young man actually grinned and shook his head.

Margaret dipped her head in understanding and ran inside followed by Hannah and Rachel. She bounded up the flights of stairs and finally made it to the attic quite out of breath. The sun was streaming in through her windows and she knew her room would be stifling hot by the time she got home. She never cared, as long as she had a window to let in the breeze. Margaret put the letter in the box her mother had gotten her that was starting to fill up with countless correspondences. She smiled as she saw the one from her birthday peeking out. Harry had gotten clever and had torn off a Vims wrapper and had written on the back of it. He had also sent a little pin in with the letter. It was a golden ARP pin with a crown on the top of it. Harry had said he found it in a street near Regent's Park. Margaret wore it often, for it reminded her of her father who would be wearing the same pin so far away.

Gabriella was busy; she had piano lessons to teach that afternoon. Therefore, Betty offered to take the girls to Coney Island. They got there by way of subway, bus, and taxi. It took them less than an hour and once they arrived, Margaret could smell the salty air and see the endless stretch of beach. There was a cool breeze, but the sun was warm and by noon it would be warm enough to wade into the water. However, the girls were just there to enjoy the sights, sounds, smells, and attractions.

Small amusement rides were starting to go up, but they were not open yet. However, the concession stands were open for beach-goers who were walking along the boardwalk. The three girls walked up onto the boardwalk and saw that a few other people were enjoying the day.

Hannah closed her eyes and smelled the air. "I can almost picture the waves and the sand! Can we go down onto the beach, Miss Betty?" She asked.

"Of course!" Betty, who was always easy-going and carefree, nodded as she joined them.

They walked out onto the sandy beach that stretched far out in front of them. Margaret slipped off her Mary Jane's and wiggled her toes in the sand. The two other girls did the same and Rachel looked ready to run and frolic on the beach. Hannah cold tell and told her to go and run, she could stay with Betty. Rachel and Margaret raced to the surf and splashed into it, the water swirling up to their knees when a waved crashed into them. They laughed and splashed and tried their best not to get their skirts all wet.

"Oh, this is so glorious! I've never been to a beach before!" Margaret kicked a wave and accidentally sprayed Rachel.

They wanted nothing more than to dive headlong into the waves, but there were people watching and they had a half an hour of traveling before them and surely they could not be dripping wet on a subway or taxi. Besides, it was rather chilly still with the wind whipping down the beach.

The two girls joined the others and they decided to get something to eat. It was almost noon and they were all hungry. Betty took orders for the girls, Rachel went along to help carry the food, and they returned to the beach carrying hot dogs for all of them. Margaret, who had never tried one, liked it immediately and asked for a second which she split with Hannah.

The ladies then went back to the boardwalk and surveyed the shops and vendors. They didn't buy anything, they just looked. As they peered into a shop that had swimsuits for sale, they came across a young man leaning against the shop door. He nodded his head to them and smiled, especially at Betty.

"Good morning, ladies. Would you like to buy something?" 'He asked in a thick New York accent.

"No thanks, we're just looking." Betty replied.

"Good, 'cause I don't even work here." He straightened up.

Margaret noticed he couldn't take his eyes off Betty. Rachel giggled and Hannah elbowed her.

"Don't you?" Betty continued to walk and the three girls followed close behind. The young man walked briskly to keep up with Betty.

"Nah, I'm just out enjoyin' the day. With such a pretty, happy face like yours, you seem to be enjoyin' it too." He was pushing his luck and Betty turned to him.

"Would you please leave us alone Mr..." She searched for his name.

"Wallace." He outstretched his hand and Betty shook it carefully. "Ted Wallace. Pleasure to meet you..." He waited for Betty to tell him her name.

When Betty didn't, Rachel piped up, "Her name's Betty Shea." Rachel giggled and Hannah elbowed her again.

"Stop it," she hissed in Rachel's ear.

Margaret smiled and watched to see what Betty would do.

She looked up to the young man who looked to be in his early thirties and suddenly she stomped on his foot. He howled in pain from her hard heel and she marched away. The three girls ran after her in surprise and left the young man named Ted Wallace whimpering in pain.

Rachel asked, "Why'd you stomp on that man's foot, Betty?"

Betty, who was walking with her head held high, replied, "There are two types of men, Rachel dear, princes and toads. Some men are only looking for a pretty face, they're the toads. It's a woman's job to avoid the toads and wait for her prince... someone who will treat her right." Betty plainly replied.

"Doesn't the story go that you have to kiss a toad for him to turn into a prince?" Rachel asked with a mischievous smile on her face.

"Not in this world, ducky." Betty chuckled and the girls grinned in amusement. "Not in this world..."

"I'm finished! I can't believe it!" Harry ran onto a bench and leapt off of it with delight.

He and Robert were walking back from their last day of school. It was the end of May and the two boys were looking forward to their newfound freedom and the lovely prospect of a warm summer.

Robert, the gangly-looking boy who was as thin as a stick and as tall as Harry, laughed. "Now what, Harry? You're going to have a lot of free time what with Miss Carlson off your back." Robert referred to their teacher.

"And I plan to enjoy it." Harry confidently strode down the sidewalk as they walked home.

He was on top of the world. He wondered why Rob didn't seem as excited. They had met each other when they had started school in the autumn and had instantly become friends. Robert was somewhat of a morose young man and was always pessimistic. Perhaps that was why no one else liked him. Harry was simply amused by it.

"What about you, Rob, what are you going to do with your free time?" Harry stuffed his hands deep into the pockets of his faded black trousers. He also wore his white undershirt and a khaki vest on over that. He had a tartan flat-cap on to cover his messy, dirty blonde hair. Soap was a commodity that was now hard to come by. However, he could care less about the shortage of soap.

"I'm getting out of London." Robert stated. Robert's family lived in London and he was very close to them. Harry wondered why he would want to leave.

"Where will you go?" Harry inquired, already guessing at the answer.

"Northolt Air Force Base. I'm joining up with the ADCC." Robert shuffled along the sidewalk with his shoulders sagging. Harry had never seen him walk straight before, he always slouched, as though his spine was permanently crooked.

"ADCC?" Harry raised his eyebrows. He had heard Robert talk about joining the Royal Air Force before, but this was a new development.

"The Air Defense Cadet Corps. I've never flown a plane. I'd be useless to the Royal Air Force if I didn't know how to keep myself in the air. I'll get the training and experience, and then when I'm ready I'll join up with the RAF. I feel so useless and stupid sitting in a classroom reading about history when history is being made out on the front lines. I want to be a part of that, you know?"

"Of course," Harry looked down to the pavement and thought for a moment. He walked on, lost in thought. *When will my turn come to fight in this war? I'm already older than Rob. And Evan and Rich are off doing their part. Am I useless here, like Rob thinks he is?* Anxiety clawed at his stomach. He did not want to run off and save the world like so many of the others lads in his class. He wanted to help, but wisely. *I don't want to rush into things and die...* Harry took a deep breath and looked over to Robert whose jaw was set with determination.

"Well, I'll see you in a few days, Harry." Robert stopped at their intersection. He had to go one way home and Harry had to go the other. "Graduation day will come soon enough." He nodded his head and went down his street.

Harry watched him go, thinking how odd his stride was. He looked like a seventy-year-old man. Shaking his head with subtle amusement, Harry went down his street and jogged the rest of the way home. *The Air Defense Cadet Corps. When I get into the war, I'm going to get in a plane.*

Harry kicked off his shoes as he closed the door behind him. "Afternoon, Mum!" He called out. "I'm home!" He took off his tartan flat-cap and hung it up on the coat rack by the door. Usually his mother said hello, but today there was no answer. He wondered if she had gone out to the shelter. However, he hadn't heard any air raid sirens on his way home.

As Harry took a few steps inside, she called back. "In here, Harry." Her voice came from the kitchen and it sounded quiet.

Harry entered as he started to unbutton his vest. He stopped when he saw his mother's face. She was seated at the table, clutching a letter in her hand, shaking slightly.

"Mum?" His hands fell to his sides. "What is it?"

She didn't answer, instead she held out the letter for Harry. He took it quickly, panicking, and wondering if it was from Margaret. When he saw the typewriter's print, he knew it wasn't.

'Telegram

*05.27.1940*

*IMMEDIATE FROM WAR OFFICE LONDON REGRET TO INFORM YOU THAT YOUR SON SECOND LIEUTENANT EVAN WILLIAM CAVANAUGH IS REPORTED MISSING AS THE RESULT OF INFANTRY OPERATIONS 22ND MAY 1940 ENQUIRIES ARE BEING MADE THROUGH INTERNATIONAL RED CROSS AND ANY FURTHER INFORMATION RECEIVED WILL BE IMMEDIATELY COMMUNICATED TO YOU STOP LETTER CONFIRMING THIS TELEGRAM FOLLOWS STOP*

Ministry of Defense, London

27th May 1940'

'Sir,

*I am commanded by the War Office to confirm the telegram in which we were notified that your son, Second Lieutenant Evan William Cavanaugh, British Expeditionary Force, is missing as the result of infantry operations on 22nd May 1940.*

*Your son was retreating from France with the British forces and was separated from his division near Dunkirk. He has failed to return. This does not essentially mean that he is killed or wounded, and if he is a prisoner of war he should be able to communicate with you in due course. Meanwhile enquiries will be made through the International Red Cross Society and from all possible local sources. As soon as any certain update is acquired, you will be informed at once.*

*The War Office desires me to express their sincere sympathy with you and your family in your present worry.*

*I am, Sir,*

*Your obedient Servant,*

*for War Office.'*

Harry could hardly finish reading. He put the letter on the table and looked to his mother. She was sniffling and dabbing at her eyes with her handkerchief.

"This doesn't mean he's... gone, though." Harry tried to reassure himself and his mother. "Did you tell Dad?"

She shook her head and started to cry harder. Harry walked quickly to their telephone and dialed the number for his father's office in downtown London. He could hardly dial the phone; his hands were starting to shake. The phone rang for what seemed like an awfully long time.

Finally, his father picked up and spoke in his deep, smooth, calm voice.

"Hello, Eugene Cavanaugh's office," the voice said.

"Dad, it's Harry." Harry knew he sounded as panicked as he felt. "We just got a telegram about Evan. He's missing in France. You'd better come home." Numb with shock, he didn't even remember what his father had said.

He put the phone down and sat in the chair next to it, feeling disoriented and grief-stricken. Harry forced himself to calm down. He took deep breaths and wanted to be strong for his mother. He got up and went to her in the kitchen. He sat down beside her and put his arm around her, both silent with shock.

*Dunkirk...* He had heard about evacuations being arranged there and that hundreds of British Infantry were being pulled out of Nazi-overrun France. Harry's mind was buzzing, yet he kept his thoughts to himself until his father stepped into the house and went by his family's side to comfort them.

Harry had thought the air raid sirens and the barrage balloons and the enlistments were bad. He felt a pit form in his stomach, and he knew, deep down, that they had not yet seen the true monstrous power of what this war would do.

Five days passed and there was still no news on Evan's condition. Word had been sent to Richard's Red Cross group base, yet they had not heard anything back from him either, nor did they know where he was. Harry's graduation came and went, no one felt like celebrating. However, as Harry walked along the streets of London, he kept his eyes open and looked at things in a new light. He could have a job now. He could enlist in the war. He could drive. He could do so many things now and his freedom was unlimited, yet his parents had plans for him. They wanted him to take up a job and stay close for the rest of the year. Since he was still seventeen, he would not be conscripted this year. Harry kicked a stone across the sidewalk. *But is that what I want? What would it be like to join Rob in the ADCC? Or what if I just signed up for the Air Force and got all my training out of the way while I'm still young?* Harry bit his lip and stopped in front of a busy street, thinking. He had an idea... and he wasn't sure if it was a good one or not.

# Chapter 12

Feeling like a fish in a bowl, Margaret sat at the picnic table in the small backyard. Inside a twenty-foot square with tall houses on every side, she felt that people were watching her all the time. Her violin was on the table as was a letter from Harry. He had written it on the 28th of May and had told her all about Evan and how he was missing. Margaret was heartbroken for him. She couldn't imagine losing a sibling.

"Meg! Are you coming, or what?" Pitcher called to her from the house's back door.

"You all go on without me," she called back.

Most of the family was going to the park to play. However, Margaret didn't feel up to it after reading about Harry's news. She watched Pitcher disappear from the doorway and folded up the letter. Sitting at the picnic table, she studied the grain of the wood and watched a red lady bug crawl along the edge of one of the boards. She felt a knot of homesickness grow in her stomach. More than anything, she wished she could be home for the Cavanaughs. *What if Evan's been killed?*

Thunder rumbled outside of Margaret's window and lightning flashed brilliantly outside. She couldn't sleep, so she threw on her robe, wrapped a blanket around her, grabbed her pillow, and went down two floors to Rachel's room. She knocked quietly on the door and Rachel opened it for her. Her light was on; obviously she couldn't sleep either.

"Come on in, Hannah's already here." Rachel jumped onto her bed and Hannah was curled up in the corner of the room amongst blankets and pillows.

Margaret joined her and added her blanket and pillow to the pile. She sat next to Hannah and jumped as thunder rumbled nearby.

"I hate thunderstorms," Hannah moaned and pulled a blanket over her head.

Margaret clutched her pillow and nodded. "Me too,"

Rachel was buried under her blankets and reached an arm out to turn off her lamp. She clicked on a flashlight and lit up her face to scare Margaret.

"It was a dark and stormy night!" She teased in a spooky voice.

Hannah whined and shook underneath her blanket. Margaret laughed and threw a pillow at Rachel.

"Cut it out," She laughed and was thankful that there weren't any windows in Rachel's room.

The girls talked and giggled and threw pillows until the storm subsided sometime after midnight. They fell asleep in their blankets with their heads on their pillows. *I wonder what Dad and Harry and Bess are doing right now,* were Margaret's last thoughts as she drifted into her dreams.

---

One early morning, Harry found himself driving through the fog of London's west side. The roads were not busy at 7 o'clock, but Harry drove slowly, nonetheless. The closer he got to his destination, the more nervous he became. Doubts swirled through his mind.

He almost couldn't believe what he had done on Dukes Road several days ago, but here he was. What would his parents say? He hoped they would be proud.

Taking a deep breath, Harry turned into the Northolt RAF base. He was asked for his name; he gave it and told the man his business. They let him through after checking his ID and he parked by one of the office buildings. Harry got out of his parents' car they had let him use and looked around. The base was quiet, silent and shrouded in fog. He looked up to the office building, took a deep breath, and went inside.

A man was seated behind a counter reading the London Gazette with his feet propped up on the desk. Harry approached him and cleared his throat, leaning on the counter.

"Excuse me, sir, could you help me with something?" Harry licked his dry lips and watched as the man gazed up at him with curious and skeptical eyes.

He folded his paper and took his feet off the desk. "What can I help you with, lad?" He asked quickly in a Scottish accent.

"My recruiting officer told me to report here this morning." Harry explained. "They sent me this letter," he took it out of his pocket and handed it to the man behind the desk.

He raised his eyebrows and asked in a curious tone. "How old *are* you?"

"I'm eighteen." Harry replied. In his mind he added, *in three months.*

The man appraised him for a moment, running his hand over his beard thoughtfully.

"What's your name, lad?"

"Harry Cavanaugh."

"You've had your medical exam?"

Harry nodded.

"Well then, you'll get kitted out while you're here, need to sign a few more papers, and you'll start basic training. You have a job in mind? And spare me if you say you want to be a pilot."

"No, sir, I'm going to be a mechanic."

The man laughed, obviously amused at something. "We are in desperate need of another mechanical assistant. Best for you to meet your officer before you sign anything further." He laughed again and gave a playful wink. "Head out back to the warehouse hangar, fourth hangar on your right, and talk to Ed Marwick, he's the lead mechanic. Tell him Fyfe sent you. Report back here after you've spoken with him."

Harry said that he would and thanked the officer before he headed back out into the damp morning air. Letting out a slow breath, Harry straightened his dress shirt and started down the road that ran along the hangars.

There were a few men walking around in navy uniforms and navy caps. Harry started walking away from the office building, not particularly knowing where he was going. He passed a group of boys that were about his age, or a little older. They threw him and his civilian clothing perplexed looks and went back to their business. However, one young man did not turn away. He jogged up behind Harry and joined him.

"You're not from around here, are you? Are you looking for someone?"

Harry nodded. "Ed Marwick."

"I'll show you where his hanger's at." The man led the way past a taller building that looked to be barracks.

Harry followed, happy to have found someone who knew his way around, but also slightly embarrassed.

"I'm Flying Officer Guy Neff of the 600 Squadron." He shook

Harry's hand.

"Harry Cavanaugh; pleased to meet you." Harry replied.

"So, Ole Fyfe sent you out here?"

Harry nodded.

"Achaius Fyfe," Guy said the name to himself. "He's as Scottish as... well, I don't know, haggis maybe." Guy chuckled. "His assistant isn't much better."

Harry kept up with the tall pilot. "I've enlisted. My parents don't know yet, but..." He trailed off.

"You're not the only one. Besides, you'll be fine." He hesitated and pointed to a hangar a little ways away. "Warehouse hangar's there. Good luck, Harry Cavanaugh. Hope to see you around here." He bade him farewell and turned to leave, but stopped short. "Oh, and be careful around Mitch... his assistant can be quite the handful."

Harry furrowed his eyebrows and watched the pilot go. He turned around and looked up at the hangar that was shrouded in the early morning mist. *Please, God, let this work out.* He entered through the side door and the sound of someone welding met his ears. Harry looked up in awe at the large plane. There was a man on the plane's wing who wore a welding mask and was dressed in dirty navy pants that were full of oil spots and petrol. He had a white shirt on that wasn't white anymore and his black suspenders kept his pants on that were much too big.

Harry shuffled his feet, unsure whether he had been seen or not. A few moments of awkwardness passed before the man stopped welding, saw Harry, and flipped up his mask.

"What do you want?" He asked roughly.

"Are you Mr. Marwick?" Harry asked, putting his hands in his pockets.

"Who's asking?" The man took off his mask and climbed down from the wing of the Spitfire.

"Well, Fyfe sent me. He said you were looking for a Mechanic's Assistant. Told me to come meet you." Harry stayed in one place as the man walked to him.

He was surprisingly short and glared up at Harry as if trying to make out his character.

"Fyfe sent you, eh?" He stared at Harry for a few more seconds before running his dirty hands through his black hair. "Why does he always think he can bother me? Do you know I've got six planes to put in the air this morning and not a lick of help or consideration coming my way? Mitch's gone for the day. I have wing commanders breathing down my neck. Deadlines to meet. Quotas to fill. And those bloody pilots are always destroying their planes and expecting me to miraculously fix them by morning. I ain't no fairy godmother with a wand so's I can wave it over those wings and fill all the bullet holes with magic." He growled in thick cockney.

Harry raised his eyebrows. "I don't know about all that, sir, but I'm a quick learner and if you give me some training, I'm sure I could-"

The mechanic cut him off. "I don't need a wimpy London boy who's never fixed an engine or tightened a bolt in my hangar." The mechanic started sauntering away. "Come see me after basic and see if you're still so bright-eyed and..." he waved him off, muttering to himself.

"Wait!" Harry stole his nerve.

The mechanic stopped and half turned to listen.

"I may've never worked on a plane, but I promise, if I do get placed here, you'll have no harder worker. I'll do what you tell me and learn quickly." Harry made his case calmly and the mechanic eyed him silently.

The seconds ticked by and Harry thought that the mechanic was just going to walk away and not respond at all.

"If... IF! You get stationed here for your training and IF you aren't sent Out There, come see me." He considered Harry and looked him head to toe. "Cavanaugh, wasn't it?"

Harry nodded enthusiastically. "Yes sir."

"And wipe that stupid smile off your face. War ain't fun."


Harry drove home. He felt nervous and yet excited at the same time. Finally, he'd be doing his part, just like Evan and Rich. He knew his parents would be proud of him and his decision, even though they, of course, loathed the idea of their sons participating in the war. But there was nothing he could do about that now. The only thing he was nervous about was that he had bent the truth about his age... three months wouldn't make that big of a difference, would it? He shook the thought from his head and forced himself not to worry about it. His parents wouldn't be happy, but again... nothing could be done about it now.

The sense of purpose Harry felt vanished as soon as he went

inside his home and entered the kitchen to see his father holding his mother as she cried.

"Mum? Dad?" Harry held tightly onto the car key until it dug into his palm.

His mother was sobbing.

His father looked at him with tears in his eyes. "It's Evan."

A wave of fear washed over Harry. "Tell me,"

"He died two days ago, Harry." Mr. Cavanaugh's voice trembled.

Harry felt dizzy, as though all the blood was rushing from his head. He grasped onto a chair's back and tried to breathe, but it was hard.

"How? Does Rich know?" Harry choked out.

Mr. Cavanaugh shook his head as his wife buried her head in his shoulder, weeping. He motioned to a letter on the table.

Harry tried not to cry as he read the telegram, but it was no use. Evan had been shot in Dunkirk. He dropped the telegram back onto the table. Black spots swam before his vision. He was aware of his mother hugging him, then he peeled himself away from her and ran upstairs, closing the door behind him in his bedroom. He paced, feeling heat color his face.

Evan was gone.

He took a pillow off his bed and threw it as hard as he could at the wall.

"No!" He yelled, grabbing a jar of pencils on his desk. He threw it as hard as he could and it clattered against the wall, throwing pencils everywhere. "No! No! No!"

Rich was gone.

The day seemed never to end. Mrs. Cavanaugh was completely torn apart and went into the vegetable garden in the back and weeded it. Her tears could not be stopped. Mr. Cavanaugh sent a telegram to Richard, for he was back in England now, arriving from who knew where. Harry sat on the back steps and watched his mother. He wanted to be strong for his mother and he forced himself not to break down again. He thought of Evan. He had always been a headstrong boy and did what he wanted. But he was kind. When they were children, he would always let Harry win their games and he would beat up Richard if the elder brother won too often. Harry ran his fingers through his hair and rubbed the back of his neck. He hadn't told his parents the news yet and was now dreading it more than ever. But he would have to tell them soon, as he was expected for training at the end of the week. He still had to get his kit out of the car before either of them saw it...

Reverend Sutton held the funeral for the Cavanaugh's that weekend. Rich came. But Harry was acutely aware of the empty space that should've been filled by Evan's unmistakable presence. It felt odd. There was no casket... no reminder set before them of why they were there, all dressed in black. It was as though Evan had just vanished. And the grief felt like something was missing; as though he had reached out his hand for something reliable that always had been there only to find it gone. He bit his lip and took a shaky breath as the sound of his mother's sniffling filled the church that was full of the Cavanaugh's family and friends. The congregation sat down when Bess finished playing the hymns and the reverend stood up to give the service. Harry didn't hear anything. He stared at a stone in the floor. The full force of grief had not yet hit him, but he knew it would in the coming weeks and months. Harry could hardly stand it. Just like that, life had been snatched away. It scared him more than he let on.

Afterward, Rich caught up to him outside the church.

"You alright?" He asked.

"Fine." Harry said.

Rich held his shoulder firmly, stopping him. "We'll get by."

Harry nodded, knowing he would never take a day with Richard for granted ever again, and he knew Richard felt the same way.

"We will." Harry replied resolutely, looking into the face that was a mirror of his own, just older and wiser and more mature.

*It's just us now.*

"You and me, Harry." Richard grasped his shoulder, as if he was holding him down to earth... not about to let another brother fade away. "It's just you and me now."

Harry swallowed hard. "I've enlisted, Rich."

His older brother leaned back, surprised. "You've... You haven't told mum or dad yet, have you?"

He shook his head.

Rich took in the news and nodded, looking as though he was slowly processing this development. "Come on,"

The brothers walked up to the house, arms around each other's shoulders... knowing that they were missing a sibling, but they would see him again someday.

And that gave them hope.


Harry still felt like he was in shock, but he had to do the inevitable. That night, he forced himself to tell his parents the unexpected news. Mrs. Cavanaugh was proud but felt sad that he, simply, had lied about his age. Mr. Cavanaugh was quiet and simply listened, only speaking when he agreed to drop Harry off at training. Without meaning to, Harry felt like he had broken their hearts all over again.

---

Margaret read Harry's letter with trembling hands. She had heard about Dunkirk from the papers and how so many men were evacuated from overrun France. It was terrible. But now it had hit home. Evan was dead. She had often played with the Cavanaugh brothers and it always comforted her when Evan was around. He protected her and Harry and had always made them feel like they were important and their presence mattered. Now he was gone. And she wished with all her heart that she could be in England for the memorial service. She felt as though she had to be there for the Cavanaughs. But she couldn't. Margaret sank onto her bed and turned off the light.

She hardly slept that night.

When she awoke the next morning, the sun was streaming in through her windows. *Another hot day...* She groaned and got dressed in a cool summer skirt and light blue shirt. Downstairs, everyone was just as groggy. It was hot in the house and their only respite was going to the park to practice and play. At least there was a breeze there and they could beg the ice cream vendor for free cones if they played for him.

Margaret and Rachel and Hannah walked along the sidewalks together arm in arm. They held their instrument cases and Margaret had decided to take her light violin instead of the heavy cello. No one said anything; they just walked across the streets and didn't relax until they were sitting on a bench in the shade of an elm.

Hannah and Rachel knew about Evan, Margaret had told them

over breakfast. For once, Margaret didn't even feel like playing. It seemed superfluous compared to what the Cavanaugh's must be going through. The boys were playing their trumpets and trombones as Margaret reread the letter. She was glad that Harry had found a job, but she loathed the day when he would be sent to the front lines. Deep down, she hoped it would never happen. However, no matter how much she wished it, she knew that it would.

"Oh, I'm in such a state today..." Margaret leaned back on the bench. "I wish this day would end already." She sighed and wiped her glistening forehead.

"Why don't we go to the beach? We could go swimming at Coney. Maybe it would cheer you up." Hannah offered.

Margaret cast her a glance and shrugged. "We could. But all I want is to go home and be there for Harry and the Cavanaugh's. I wonder what Dad thinks, and what Bess thinks."

"No doubt they are just as concerned as you." Rachel squeezed Margaret's hand.

They stayed underneath the shady trees for some time, watching the boys play their instruments before Margaret got up with a sigh.

"I'm sorry; I'm going to head home. I'll see you both back at the house." Margaret smiled weakly and started back down East 61st Street, the road the house was on. Once she was back, she was greeted by her mother.

"Back so soon?" Gabriella asked gently.

Margaret nodded and started up the stairs.

"Are you all right, Meg? Do you want to talk about it?" Gabriella asked as she came to the stair railing.

"I'm all right, I just want to reply to Harry... let him and his family know I'm thinking about them."

"Of course," Gabriella continued, "let me know if there's anything I can do."

Margaret thanked her and ran up the rest of the stairs and sat down at her desk in her room out of breath. She put her violin down beside her and picked up a pen and paper.

*'Dear Harry,*
*No words can describe my sorrow when I read your letter. I can't*

*imagine how you and your family feel. I truly can't. My prayers are with you and it is a comfort to know that God is always watching us, helping us, and supporting us. I know that those thoughts will relieve your family, for Evan was a man after God's own heart.*

*I wish I was there with you all in your mourning. Evan will be so terribly missed.*

*I can't even find the words. I'm so, so sorry. I love you all and will miss Evan terribly. He was so kind and thoughtful and knew his own mind. I'll never forget all the times we spent together.*

*I'm with you all even though I'm so far away.*

*Meg.'*

Margaret put down her pen and folded up the short note. She put it in an envelope and went downstairs. Putting it on the table with the gramophone, Margaret kneeled down and scratched Louis. He woofed at her and trotted into the kitchen. Sighing, Margaret sat on a stool along the kitchen wall.

Her mother was reading something at the table and put it away when Margaret came back down. "Can I do anything?"

Margaret shook her head. "No, I'll send off my letter this afternoon and hopefully hear back from him soon. Although..." Margaret leaned forward. "Do you think I could call him on the telephone? I know it costs a fortune, but..."

"Of course you can," Gabriella nodded enthusiastically and joined her daughter in the kitchen.

"Here, I'll take this down to the post office and call him when I get back!" Margaret suddenly felt excited.

She hurried down to the post office, said hello to Loretta, the older woman who worked the front desk who liked to believe that Harry and Margaret were sweethearts even though Margaret assured her they were not.

Margaret hustled into the hallway and stood in front of the telephone. She knew Harry's telephone number by heart, for she had forced herself to memorize it when she moved. It rang. And then it rang again. Someone picked it up and Margaret recognized Mr. Cavanaugh's voice.

"Hello? The Cavanaugh residence."

"Hello, Mr. Cavanaugh, this is Margaret."

"Ah, Margaret, it's good to hear from you."

---

*Margaret? On the phone?!* Harry could hardly believe it. He raced from the foyer to the phone in the hallway and took it from his father, ignoring his father's protests and chastisement of Harry's rudeness.

"Meg? Is it you?" He held the phone up and listened.

She was chuckling on the other line. He hadn't realized how much he had missed her.

"Hello, Harry." The garbled, electronic voice of Margaret sounded on the other line.

"Meg! It's so good to hear from you. How are you?" Harry's spirits lifted for the first time in a long time.

"I am well. It so good to talk. I just sent you a letter, but it wasn't the same. I'm so sorry, Harry." Margaret started to get choked up. "God knows, I'm so sorry for you and your parents and Rich. Are you all doing alright?"

"We're holding up. Barely. Your Dad's been grand through all this. He's brought us meals, Bess has helped Mum in the garden, and she's even brought flowers every day from Lily's End. It's helped greatly and it's been good to have Rich back. Who knows where he'll go next. None of us really want to see him go."

There was silence on the line for a moment.

"Meg?" Harry thought he had lost her.

"Oh, Harry..." she was stifling a sob. "Harry, I'm so sorry. We'll all miss him so much."

He bit his lip and took a shaky breath.

"I wish I could be there for you all." Margaret said. "It's killing me that I can't. I'm so sorry." She sounded torn apart.

"Don't apologize, Meg." Harry found himself trying to hold back the tears as he listened to her gentle, quiet sobbing on the other end. His throat was thick, and he knew that if he started crying, he wouldn't stop. "Just knowing you're thinking of us and praying for us makes all the difference in the world. We miss you, though."

"I miss you all too." Her quiet reply came crackling through the receiver. "I miss you all so much." It sounded like she was taking a deep breath. "Give your parents my love and of course Bess and Dad. Tell them I miss them and will try to call again soon."

Harry found himself not wanting to hang up. "Wait, Meg. I have something to tell you."

"Yes?"

He took a deep breath now. "I've enlisted."

A pause.

"I'm going to be a mechanic for the air force. I leave next week for training. I won't be able to write for six weeks. But it'll go by quickly and once I'm done, I'm hoping to get stationed at Northolt so I'm not far from home. Already I have a few connections there, so maybe that will help. I don't know."

"I'm proud of you, Harry. I'm scared, too, but you'll do wonderfully. Thank you for telling me."

"I'll write you with more details before I go."

"I'd like that."

Harry knew he had to hang up soon. "Be safe, Meg. I... I miss you."

"I miss you too, Harry. You be safe as well. We'll talk soon." Her voice faded.

They said their goodbyes and then the buzz in the receiver went silent.

Harry stood there for a moment. For a brief second it felt like she was just on the other side of the wall... just an arm's length away. He hung up the phone and put his cold hand against the wall, as if to still feel some sort of connection to his best friend.

An ocean away, Margaret hung up her end of the line as well and broke down into sobs, bent over, the grief and homesickness weighing her down. Her mother rushed over to her and embraced her tightly, helping to hold her up and give her comfort.

# Chapter 13

Harry didn't know what he had expected for basic training, but he hadn't expected it to go by so quickly. Six weeks flew by as he and his fellow soldiers were taught how to shoot, fight, and survive. He was grateful for this new knowledge and hoped he wouldn't need it, but who knew what the next few years would bring?

Training continued once he was, thankfully, stationed at no other base than Northolt.

On his first day he had to report, Harry woke in a fog. He washed his face with ice cold water, hoping it would wake him up, but it didn't. He jumped into his uniform and left the barracks behind.

Harry made his way to the warehouse hangar and found Mr. Marwick sipping a cup of tea on the wing of a bomber aircraft. Harry didn't know what type of plane it was; it simply looked huge.

"I hope you've brought your wits with you today." The mechanic gulped down the rest of his tea.

"More or less," Harry shrugged, his hands were deep in his pockets.

"What's that supposed to mean?" Mr. Marwick retorted.

Harry didn't have a good excuse other than the fact that he hadn't been able to fall asleep because he had been thinking about Evan.

"I'm sorry, sir, my brother died a few months ago. It's just... it's been hard." Harry said truthfully and Mr. Marwick eyed him for a moment.

He sighed. "I'm sorry to hear that." He climbed down from the wing. "Too many good lads out there dying, there are."

The mechanic went to a table that had a small lamp on it and piles of odds and ends. Papers, tools, pencils, wrenches, rags, you name it. Harry watched him as he picked up a paper. He wondered what he would be doing on his first day. He felt bad Mr. Marwick had to train him, but at least he was here to learn and help. Surely that counted for something, didn't it?"

"You're going to have to work very hard. I'm sure Mitch'll be willing to help you. Then again, maybe not." He shrugged and opened a drawer, withdrawing a manual that was several inches thick. "Read this." He handed the manual to Harry. "That's your homework. Now, whenever you're not working with me or Mitch, you're reading that. Even on the bog, read it. Read it in your sleep, I don't care. Just read it and learn it."

'Aircraft Maintenance' it read. Harry flipped through it.

"Thank you,"

"When we're done here today, be sure you head over to the office and get all the necessary paperwork filled out. They didn't insist on having it right away because I said I needed you *here... today...* and I'd walk if they didn't let you start."

"You said you needed me?" Harry grinned slightly.

Mr. Marwick had changed his tune since their first meeting.

"Oh, come off it. I'll admit to it when I'm wrong. Come on, Cavanaugh, you have a lot to learn." The mechanic walked underneath the plane and slapped its fuselage. "This here's a Blenheim Mk1. This light bomber will blast the snot right out of the Germans. 360 radial piston engines..." He let out a low whistle. "three hotseats, machine gun in the port wing, 450 kilogram max bombload, and a Vickers K gun in the dorsal turret. Hit by flak; almost beyond repair. Crew made it back safely... But you know what the best part is?" Ed turned to Harry who had no clue what the mechanic was talking about.

*I can't imagine...* Harry sarcastically thought to himself.

Ed Marwick grinned. "You're going to help me fix her."

Waking up on the base, well before the sun arose, Harry felt the same determined excitement he always felt when the day began. Harry made his way back to the warehouse hangar, his home away from home. The hot sun beat down on him and he was thankful he didn't have to be out on the tarmac.

Planes came in low and landed on various runways, most of them were Hawker Hurricanes. The engines roared and Harry watched them with awe. They were impressive machines, and he wondered if he would ever fly one. Turning his attention back to his job, he strode up to the hangar, feeling somewhat alone now that Guy had been transferred with his squadron to Manston, in Kent. They had become friends and Harry hoped that he would see the officer in the future.

Harry pulled open the access door to the hangar and heard the usual sounds of welding.

"Morning, Ed!" He called out as he put on his navy mechanic

jumpsuit and zipped up the front.

Harry was starting to get in a routine as he had been working there for a little over a week now. He glanced over to the plane; a Hurricane that had a few minor bumps and bruises and saw the welding mask of the mechanic flip up. But instead of Ed's face, it was a girl's. His mouth gaped open.

"Who are you?" They both said at once.

The girl who was dressed in the same kind of jumpsuit Harry wore set down the welding gear and put her hands on her hips.

"I asked you first." They both said at the same time again.

Harry looked at her in surprise.

"What's the matter? Never seen a girl before? Take this!" She tossed a wrench to him.

Harry caught it in his gut with a grunt.

"I hope you're not as weak as you look... You seem a bit peely wally..." She eyed him over, her green eyes sharp and quick. "Well come on, there's work to do." She flipped down her mask and went back to welding.

Harry stood watching her with a wrench in his hand. *A girl?! Really?*

Ed came in not long after Harry and he smiled when he saw the two working together.

"I see you've met Mitch," Ed zipped up his jumpsuit and put on his dirty hat.

"This is Mitch?" Harry thought it was just some helper, not Ed's assistant

She laughed. "You're working for *me* now." Mitch's voice came from the other side of the plane.

As Harry repainted the roundel, he muttered. "We'll see about that." He was thankful no one heard him. "Is your real name Mitch?" He asked loud enough for her to hear.

"Full name's Michelle Hugal. I like Mitch better, at least around here."

Harry kept on painting and hoped that he could put up with the precocious girl. Ed started working on the plane as well and before lunchtime, they were finished with the Hurricane and it was taxied back out onto the runways, fueled and ready. After lunch, there was not much to do. A faulty hydraulic, a damaged tail piece, Harry relished the opportunity to learn and Mitch was more than eager to show him. She taught him how to fix hydraulics, rewire the cockpit, and what controls did what.

"Where did you learn all this?" Harry asked as he watched their latest repair take off on the runway with its engine roaring.

"Have you ever heard of the Women's Auxiliary Air Force before? I went to pilot training school. I learned with some of the best, but I couldn't be kept in an op's room or a radar station. I would die." She nodded and watched as another plane took off into the sky. She turned to head back inside and Harry watched her go. She looked to be in her twenties, had dark red hair underneath a brown bandana, and was just a little shorter than him.

*What an odd girl...* He thought and put his hands into his pockets. He walked out of the hangar and felt the heat radiating off of the hot tarmac. Mirages floated off the runways in the distance. Harry ducked back inside the hangar and the trio of mechanics spent the rest of the day lounging about. Ed even fell asleep and started snoring as Harry reread the mechanic's manual.

*'Run Rabbit Run'* came in through the little radio on Ed's cluttered desk. Harry tapped his toe and the music reminded him of Margaret. *I wonder where she is right now... what is she doing?* He leaned back in his swivel chair and read.

Mitch stretched her arms wide and yawned. "Would someone *please* turn off that song? The *run, run, run,* won't stop playing through my brain." Mitch tinkered with something.

Harry got up, turned off the radio, and watched her take apart whatever it was she was working on. He couldn't even tell what it was anymore, she had dismembered it so. And then he watched her as she started to put it all back together.

"Are you always so scatterbrained?" He asked her.

"Are you always asking stupid questions?" She glared at him.

Harry sat back down and started humming *'The Blackout Stroll'* by Joe Loss. He watched as Mitch became more and more irritated. Finally, she slapped down her hand and pointed her screwdriver at him menacingly. Harry held up his hand in surrender, stopped humming, and kept reading. As his eyes drifted over a diagram, he heard a frightening wail. He looked up and the wailing grew. *Sirens.* He jumped to his feet and looked out of the hangar's front opening. The sirens that were above the barracks and the office buildings were droning on and on and suddenly, pilots started pouring forth from the Mess and the barracks. The ones that were already in their hangars came running out with their parachute packs strapped onto their backs and flying helmets positioned on their heads. The ground crews ran behind the pilots in a frenzy. Harry was joined by Mitch. Ed joined them as well.

"Just another bloody drill." Ed moaned and started to go back into the hangar. "Curse the *phony war*." He mumbled.

Harry watched with tension, *is this really just a drill?*

"I don't think so, Ed..." Mitch sounded afraid.

Harry followed her gaze. He saw black specks far out of the horizon.

Planes.

"Get to the shelter!" Mitch yelled over the cry of the sirens. "NOW, ED!"

They all ran out of the hangar.

The sound of several planes starting, taking off, and flying off into the sky was enough to almost deafen Harry. He sprinted behind Mitch, surprised at how fast she and Ed could run. They all ran to a bomb shelter surrounded by sandbags. They half fell, half ran down the steps and emerged in total darkness. It took Harry a few minutes to become accustomed to the darkness, but he could hear voices, several of them women's. Once he could see, he saw that the shelter was actually an operations room. Several women, all dressed in the air force blue, were standing around a plotting table. Men were on the outskirts with headphones on their heads and all along the walls were blinking lights and gauges.

"What's going on, corporal?" Mitch stood by a lady's side.

The lady with curly blonde hair said something to Mitch, but Harry couldn't hear. She cautiously glanced Harry and Ed's way and went back to the map and the little triangles they were moving here and there.

Mitch joined them by the stairs and said, "an air raid. Hopefully our aces will be able to intercept them." She stated and sat down out of the way.

Harry watched with fascination. The men and women didn't pay any attention to Ed or Harry, but allowed them to camp out in the underground shelter until danger was past. It had been ten months since war had been declared and it was edging closer and closer. Harry wondered just what dangers lurked ahead. However, he took comfort that his family and Margaret were safe.

———————————

A world away, Margaret was sitting in Central Park by a pond that was alive with frogs croaking and turtles bathing in the sun. She was sitting with her friends, admiring Belvedere Castle that was situated behind the pond. The stone turrets reminded her of England; she could almost imagine she was back at home.

"Quit it, Frankie!" Grubbs whined as Frankie sat on him, pinning him to the ground.

Margaret was pulled out of her thoughts and glanced over at the two boys who were wrestling. She sighed in exasperation.

"Tubs Grubbs can't get up!" Frankie laughed and teased.

Margaret, being one of the oldest, took responsibility to scold them. "Frankie, get off of Andrew," she motioned for him to move.

"*Andrew?* Who's *Andrew*?" Frankie got off his friend.

"That's my name, dummy." The boy sat up and brushed off his trousers that were now covered in grass. "You gave me a bruise." Grubbs whined.

Margaret and Rachel exchanged annoyed glances. The boys were becoming irritable. It was hot, there was no breeze, and they had already played a great deal of songs.

"You gave me a bruise," Frankie mimicked him in a girly voice.

"Really?!" Margaret shot him a warning look and Frankie shrunk back and looked over to the baseball fields where Pitcher and Tony were playing.

Frankie couldn't catch a ball if it hit him in the face, so he always felt left out when his brother played with the other boys on the ball fields. However, he was getting better.

"Go play with the others. You need to burn off some energy." Margaret told the twin.

"Fine," he huffed and got up, sulking as he joined his twin brother and the other boys they occasionally met with to play ball.

With their instruments scattered about them, they sat in the shade of a weeping willow and watched the other New Yorkers lounge about in the cool shade. Everyone seemed to be moving slowly, yet butterflies flew about everywhere and Margaret watched them with entertainment. The children were silent for several minutes. Hannah smelled a flower, Samuel was scribbling on his blank sheet music with a guitar at his side; he had just started playing it and was rather good. Rachel was making a clover necklace, and Grubbs was pulling up handfuls of grass and putting them on Rachel who hadn't yet noticed. Margaret, deciding to lighten the mood, picked up her violin. A melody played in her heart, inspired by the butterflies flying about the pond. She played the first few notes pizzicato, like a butterfly landing on a flower. Then she picked up her bow and played a few playful notes that gave way into the melody. Samuel looked up and watched her for a few moments and then picked up his guitar and started strumming and plucking at the strings to add a rhythm. He knew the notes instinctively.

Then, as though a butterfly had just flown off and escaped the hands of an eager child, Margaret played a fast series of notes all the way up her violin until her fingers were high up on the fingerboard. Hannah, learning the melody with each passing second, took up her violin as well and added a few pizzicato notes to add to the harmony. Samuel quickly and almost effortlessly played the guitar and plucked at the strings. Margaret lowered her bow for a moment and Hannah joined in on the pizzicato. Then, they ended the song together, tying in the melody and adding in a crescendo to finish it off. Margaret lifted her bow and drew it off the strings quickly. Rachel and Grubbs clapped for them.

"Well done!" Rachel congratulated them. "Did you just come up with that now?"

Margaret shrugged. "I suppose so. Thank you both for joining in." She smiled to Samuel and Hannah who grinned in return.

"It's catchy." Hannah admitted. "You should write it down." She held out her hand to Samuel who gave her a reserved look with his eyebrows furrowed. "Come on, Samuel, it's only a few pieces of paper..." She convinced him.

He reluctantly handed over his notebook and Margaret began jotting down the notes that had come from her heart. Once she was finished writing both the violin and guitar chords, she surveyed her work. Rachel watched over her shoulder.

"What are you going to call it?" Rachel asked.

Margaret wrinkled her nose and thought it over. "Well, I was inspired by the butterflies. So, why don't I call it '*A Butterfly's Flight?*'" She looked to her friends who nodded with enthusiasm.

Hannah nodded and picked up her flower and put it in her blonde hair. "It suits it well. I also imagined a butterfly flying about, with radiant wings like an angel's." Hannah lay down in the grass and twirled her hair around her finger.

Margaret chuckled at the wistful dreamer as she ripped out the two pages of sheet music and gave the book back to Samuel. He nodded his thanks and she could see his face relax now that he held his sheet music book again. *Another day away from home, but another day in the company of friends.*

A few days later, the house celebrated the Moser twins' birthday. They were now nine and were starting to grow up. Everyone enjoyed the cake, made by Gabriella, and they gave the twins a few little gifts. The twins were in such good spirits that day; it was as if they had been replaced by little angels.

Late that night, while everyone was down in the basement playing a game of charades, Margaret went up to the studio. She ran her fingers along the grand piano, the sets of three and sets of two black keys felt so familiar to her. Sitting down on the bench, she played the song she had written. *Me? A composer?* She could hardly believe she had written a song. She got out the sheet music that she had folded neatly in her pocket. Spreading the two sheets on the music stand on the piano, she played the song '*A Butterfly's Flight*' in G major. It took her back to the day she had written it. Butterflies everywhere, a hot sun beating down on them, cheers from the small groups of people watching the baseball game... When Margaret opened her eyes, she saw her mother standing along a wall in the studio.

"I saw you leave," She said quietly once the music had faded and the sustain pedal was lifted.

"I wanted to play it on the piano." Margaret took down the sheet music and folded it back up again.

"Hannah told me you had written it." Gabriella made her way to the side of the piano.

"It's just a little song." Margaret shrugged.

"A little song can change the world." Gabriella sat down beside her on the bench and playfully nudged her.

"Mum..." Margaret looked up to her comically.

"Alright, perhaps not the *world*. Have you ever thought about composing?" She peered at her daughter in the dim studio.

"Not at all. I guess not since the other day."

"If you ever want to, you could." Gabriella patted her daughter's back.

"Mum..." Margaret whined and Gabriella chuckled.

"Mum, what?" She tickled her daughter and Margaret laughed.

"Stop! Stop!" Margaret almost fell off the bench. Gabriella stopped and waited until Margaret sat back up. They sat together staring at the keys for a few moments, both were lost in thought.

"You know..." Gabriella touched a key. "That day you came was one of the only times I've played in over fifteen years." She said quietly.

Margaret pressed her lips together and played a note that was two steps higher than the one her mother played.

"You inspire me." Gabriella's voice drifted off. "You make me want to play again."

A few moments of silence elapsed before Margaret asked. "Why don't you play?"

"Memories have a way of not letting go. They surface when you least expect them to and before you know it..." She played a low E loudly, "you're locked up in fear."

The E reverberated in the grand piano before she released it.

"Can't you overcome your fear? God tells us not to be afraid." Margaret replied innocently and truthfully.

Gabriella smiled slightly. "Sometimes it's not as easy as that. Sometimes God isn't clearly heard." Letting her voice drift off, she got up and took on a new tone. "Come, let's go back down and finish the game of charades. I'm sure we can beat Hannah, although she seems to have the cat in the bag."

---

A massive blast went off not far from Harry. He scrambled from the warehouse hangar and saw Mitch running towards him from another hangar. Planes were taking off late and the base was paying the price. The surprise attack from the Luftwaffe couldn't have been worse. The sirens on the fuselage of each Junker JU 88 sent goosebumps up Harry's arm and made his hair stand on end. Another bomb land some ways away. Soon, the pilots wouldn't have enough time to get to the right height and fight them off. The last Spitfire was just leaving the ground.

Harry ran like he had never run before to the Op Room and dove into the darkness. Mitch was on his tail and slammed the door closed, enveloping them in eerie lamplight. The drone of the Junkers could still be heard and the ground reverberated with every bomb blast. Catching his breath, Harry sat on their usual bench and put his hands on his knees. He panted and thought that July would never end.

RAF bases were getting bombed all over England. Northolt was no exception, and the constant chest-reverberating blasts of the bombs would not let Harry soon forget it. Outside, it was pure chaos. The Luftwaffe would shoot at the RAF's grounded planes when they were not engaged in a heated air battle with the furious Spitfires and their pilots. They bombed their airfields and hangars relentlessly. Thankfully, the warehouse hangar hadn't been bombed yet. The enemy bombers and their escorts, the Messerschmitts, were obviously preoccupied with the anti-aircraft guns and the few RAF pilots that managed to get into the air.

The real destruction and terror came at night... when all of London was a target.

Harry gripped the bench with white knuckles.

"Don't flip your wig." Mitch teased him half-heartedly and got up from the bench to see what the WAAFs were talking about.

Harry watched her go and wished he could be as calm as the spunky mechanic. *She's a girl and seems braver than me.* The thought made him mad, but he instantly let it go as another bomb shook the Op Room. The ladies paused and looked up as some silt came down on their table. However, they went back to work and seemed oblivious to all else as they wore their large headphones. *I'm still not used to this.* Harry pressed his back against the dirt wall to try to stop himself from shaking. *I need to get ahold of myself. What would Evan say if he saw me with my knees shaking like a schoolgirl?* He got up and straightened his jumpsuit.

He went by Mitch and asked, "How does it look?"

"The Jerry's are starting to head back." She said over the din of the anti-aircraft guns that were being fired from bunkers out near the runways.

A few minutes elapsed before it was safe to go outside again. Harry emerged into the daylight, squinting against the sun. There were scattered clouds around and in the patches of blue, Harry could see Spits returning. They landed, were taxied to hangars, and a few were parked in the warehouse for repairs.

Harry saw a pilot, probably a squadron or group leader, talking to another pilot. "We got twelve in the air, ten came back. They went down not far from Wembley and both parachuted out in time."

"Yes sir, we'll take care of it." The shorter pilot nodded and hurried back to the dispersal office.

The squadron leader glanced Harry's way and Harry saluted.

"At ease, mechanic," Harry thought he could detect a hint of amusement from the man's exhausted tone.

He strode off towards the barracks and Harry relaxed. He always choked when talking to the superior officers. *I'll do better next time.* Sauntering off back to the warehouse hangar, Harry noticed that several of the runways had large pock marks in them. It would take a while to repair the damage. He entered the hangar and set to work with Mitch. She was already on top of the Spitfire, helping the pilot out. He had on his tan life jacket and thanked her before climbing down from the aircraft. He stiffly stretched his back.

"Rough ride?" Harry asked as he walked past him.

"You have no idea." The pilot laughed back. "Just wait till it's your turn." The pilot limped out of the hangar and Harry thought over his words as he helped Mitch start on the repairs.

*When will it be my turn?*


The bombings and the constant thundering of the Junkers was all that Harry could remember that summer. He spent most of his time repairing the Spitfires that were constantly being blown to smithereens by the German fighters. However, Harry developed an impressive knowledge of the planes. He and Mitch worked day and night on them and she taught him all she knew as he continued his training. When her knowledge ran out, Ed taught them both. It was a small repair crew. Granted, there was another small crew on the other side of the base but there were always more than enough planes for them to fix. Sometimes, Harry stayed late into the night alone in the warehouse hangar. With the doors closed and the windows blacked out, he would dare to light a small work-light to see the machine. With oil and grease all over his hands, he tinkered and fixed and by and by, he became more familiar with the parts of the Spits and how they worked. He was confident in his work and as the weeks passed by, he needed Ed and Mitch's help less and less.

One cool, foggy morning, Harry slid into the cockpit of a Spitfire and surveyed his work. Late the previous night, he had repaired some of the wiring and fixed the rudder and flaps that were sticking. Engaging the flaps, he grinned when he saw that they were all working properly. He checked the fuel gauge, oil pressure, and water temperature. They all read to his satisfaction, and he allowed himself a few more seconds in the fighter seat. The quiet in the cockpit was calming and yet he resisted the urge to start the plane just to hear it roar to life. Suddenly, something clinked on the glass right beside his head. He turned his head and saw Mitch standing with her hands on her hips and shaking her head in the doorway of the hangar. Harry rolled his eyes and opened the hatch and exited the beautiful machine.

"What were you doing?" Mitch went to the cluttered desk and switched on the radio. She zipped up her jumpsuit and put on her ever-present bandana.

"Just checking to make sure everything was working." Harry said as he listened to the chorus of 'A Nightingale Sang in Berkley Square.' "And thinking." He added.

"Thinking about what? Getting shot down? There's no glory in hurtling to the ground 300 kilometres an hour." She retorted and strapped on her work belt that had several tools in it.

Harry sat down in the chair and put his feet up like he had seen Ed do so many times. "You don't think it would be glorious to shoot down enemy planes and see *them* go hurtling to the ground?" He teased.

"You couldn't hit a German plane to save your life." Mitch raised her eyebrows and tossed a tool to Harry, one of her favorite pastimes. "Taxi this Spit over to Hangar No. 3. That should keep you busy." She sauntered off and went to go look at one of the clipboards on the wall.

"You're not joking?" Harry jumped up; he had never taxied a Spitfire by himself.

"I mean it. Just don't crash it into the hangar. Ed would kill us both."

Mitch waved him off and in a matter of seconds, Harry was in the cockpit. He put on the leather pilot's helmet, earphones, oxygen mask he didn't use, with a microphone that fit over his nose, cheek, and chin, on his head. The whole contraption smelled like old rubber, but Harry didn't mind. It wasn't far to Hangar No. 3, so he had to take it slow, but starting up the Spit was enough to excite him. He kept the goggles up on the top of the helmet and took a deep breath. He strapped himself in, straps going over his shoulders and up across his thighs. He pulled them tight, like he had been taught.

The cockpit fit Harry like a glove, almost as though the plane was a part of him. The canopy almost touched his head, the sides brushed his shoulders, he could only move his feet a few inches, but he could move his arms. *I'm going to fly a spitfire!* He checked himself and reined in his enthusiasm. *Well, not fly, just taxi. Just taxi...* He wanted nothing more than to take off at top speed, but that was just his seventeen-year-old restlessness talking. He cranked the rudder and nose to make sure he would go straight, adjusted air pressure, turned the brakes on, turned the fuel cock on, uncovered the starter and booster coil buttons, turned the magneto switches on, and took a deep breath. He had been holding it and forced himself to relax. *Throttle set, idle cut-off, pressure the fuel lines...* Harry tried to remember everything. Outside the cockpit, Mitch was doing her part. She was down by the trolley ground accumulator.

Harry primed the gas and did it about five times. He turned the ignition switches on and started up the Spitfire. The propeller began to turn and Harry's heart hammered in his chest. *I'm actually doing it!* Then another thought crossed his mind. *I hope I don't get in trouble. If I do, it's Mitch's fault.* He chuckled to himself.

He refused to worry, for he had to apply all his wits to operating the plane that was now alive. He checked everything over again while Mitch removed the chocks of the vibrating plane. She wheeled the trolley out of the way and gave Harry a thumbs up. The Rolls-Royce Merlin engine roared and Harry wished the helmet was even more soundproof. His mouth was dry as the roar of the engine penetrated deep into his chest.

"Here goes nothing," He said out loud to himself, not able to hear his voice.

He released the brakes and pushed the throttle forward. He was moving! Part of him wanted to laugh hysterically, part of him wanted to run for his life. However, he turned the plane and left the hangar behind. Not being able to see in front of him, he had to rely on his memory of the taxiing runways along the hangars. He moved slowly past Hangar No. 1 and Hangar No. 2. A pilot who was up before the others, watched Harry go past him with furrowed eyebrows. He came up to the third hangar and slowed down. He went a little past the wide hangar and then pulled back on the reverse. It slowly backed up and he moved his flaps and wheels to back up. Harry was proud of himself as he took various steps to turn off the Spitfire. He let out a breath as the engine quieted down and all that was left of the glory was his beating heart and his dry mouth.

*I did it.* He thought to himself after he undid his harnesses and made the plane ready for its next pilot. Harry opened the canopy and jumped out onto the wing.

"I didn't think you could do it." Mitch shook her head in disbelief.

Harry jumped down beside her and took off his helmet. "Thanks for the vote of confidence."

"Anytime." She shrugged. "In all seriousness," she continued, "well done. We'll make a decent mechanic of you yet."

They walked back to the warehouse hangar, the sun rising through the fog, with another long day ahead.

# Chapter 14

'Dear Dad,

I'm afraid I don't have much to write about. Not much has happened since my last letter.

Mum and Betty took Hannah, Rachel, and I to Coney Island to swim. It's been so hot here and the ocean was so lovely. I hope that we can go more often. There were seagulls all over; on the boardwalk begging for food, down by the waves, on the little shacks and buildings... Maybe one day you can see it.

After we went swimming, we went to the World's Fair over in Queens. It was so busy! There were people everywhere looking at the sights and exhibits. And guess what? I won ten dollars playing a game where you have to throw a ring around a bottle at the fair. There are loads of other exhibits and attractions too, I lost track of the ones we went to see. It's much like the last time we went right after I arrived. Bands were playing outside, people were strolling on the sidewalks, lounging in the shady green lawns, and they swarmed around the large exhibition halls. What a sight! I only wish you were here to share it with me.

Tell me everything that has been going on in London. How is your job as an ARP Warden? How is the church doing? How is Bess? I hope to hear from you soon.

Love,

Your girl, Meg.'

Margaret reread her letter while she sat at her desk. She put it in an envelope and addressed it, setting it down with Harry's she would send off that day as well. She had written him a letter for his birthday which was coming up. In it, she asked him what he was going to do now that he was part of England's armed forces. Would he stay in England and remain a mechanic, or join in the war effort oversees? Would they truly deploy someone his age into active war? Margaret feared the answer, for she knew her friend well...

---

Harry finished reading a letter from Margaret and slumped down in the chair in his room, quite forgetting he was supposed to be helping his mother clean on this rare Saturday off. He scribbled down his reply, describing that many of the young men he had gone through training with were being placed with squadrons now. He had thought about the possibility a great deal and was still trying to decide whether he wanted to keep learning as a mechanic, or transition into something else. Every day he watched the Aces take off in the planes he fixed and wondered what it must be like.

Suddenly, air raid sirens wailed. The sound he had heard many times always made his skin crawl. *Not another one...* He jumped up, ran to the backyard, and saw his mother in the garden. Her face looked worried and Harry told her to get into the shelter. As he started into the dark gloom after her, he gripped onto the sharp metal doorframe and heard something. Turning on his heel, he looked up to the sky. Dive bombers were descending rapidly towards the city. Harry's world stood still and his breath caught in his throat. He had seen dogfights and bombers at Northolt, but these were in London... during the day. The built-in siren on the underbelly of the Junkers could not be mistaken anywhere.

"Harry! Get inside!" Mrs. Cavanaugh yelled over the drone of the planes.

As the planes grew closer and the deafening air raid sirens relentlessly went on, Harry closed the door to their shelter with a bang and hunkered down with his mother by his side. Harry's throat became dry and he stared blindly ahead as the Anderson shelter shook with the reverberation of bombs.

*What house did that bomb fall on? Were the people safe in their shelter?* Harry wondered. Another bomb shook the streets and explosions from gas lines and mains made the damage worse.

"Are you alright, Mum?" He asked over the noises.

She nodded even though her face was pale.

It was September 7th, 1940.

What was once a peaceful city enjoying the early fall weather, had turned into a screaming war zone with the fire and destruction of Hitler's Luftwaffe raining from the London skies.

Harry stood in front of his superiors and officers of the Northolt

Base, including Fyfe, the Scotsman with the large jowls, thick beard, and bald head. They were all dressed in their stately uniforms and on their brassards were the bars of their rank. Nervous and yet excited, Harry saluted them and exited the room. In light of the recent targeted attacks on Lond, they had decided that Harry was not as valuable on the ground in the warehouse as he would be elsewhere in His Majesty's service.

As Harry left the office behind, Fyfe came out and followed him.

"We need all the help we can get." Fyfe said. "That's one of the reasons why they're reassigning you. You have the makings of a good pilot and they have a fresh new wave of recruits to take your place, some, I'm sorry to break it to you, are more qualified." He clasped his hands behind his back.

Harry nodded, understanding.

He motioned for Harry to open the door and they went outside into the chilly September morning. "We'll be in touch as soon as we have your new station. I'd say Hornchurch, if I'm not mistaken, but they'll confirm with you."

"Thank you, sir, I appreciate it,"

"Don't mention it, lad." He shook Harry's hand and left him alone.

Harry took a deep breath, feeling accomplished and like he was finally back on track after Evan's death. *Onto the next thing... Just one step at a time.*

---

A week later, on September 15th, Reverend Sutton was putting up a sign in the church. 'CLOSED DUE TO AIR RAIDS,' it said. It was the first time he had ever been forced to close the doors of Lily's End. With the air raids, it was much too dangerous for large groups to be together in one building. If the church was hit... Well, the reverend could not imagine what that would mean for his flock. Clearing his throat, he sent up a silent prayer that everyone who had been hurt during the bombings would heal and that the families who had lost loved ones would be brave. *Surely the bombing can't last much longer...* He thought back to all the destruction he had seen as an ARP Warden as of late. Children with gasmasks on, adults clutching onto each other with panic and fear as their houses were burnt to the ground. London was in shock. The valor of the firefighters was unmistakable. The volunteers that fed them and gave them water during the long hours of the night so that they could press on putting out the flames that licked the London sky, was unfathomable. Some of the volunteers had lost their lives due to such self-sacrificing acts.

Closing his eyes, he thanked the Lord that none of the bombs had destroyed the church. They had fallen close, closer than he would have liked. Some of the bombs merely blew up parts of roadway, others landed in Londoners' backyards, setting fire to their vegetable gardens, while some incendiary bombs fell into peoples' houses, giving the skyline of London an orange tint that lasted day and night.

The reverend was exhausted. He had given his time, energy, and strength to help those who had been hit. Bess, too, had returned to London with her sister to give water to the firefighters so they could work as long as they physically could.

Sighing and opening his eyes, Reverend Sutton looked up to the sky. Smoke left a strange haze in between the earth the clouds, making it seem darker and gloomier than usual. He could smell the smoke in the air. Occasionally, a stray piece of ash fell from above. The reverend ducked inside to get some much-needed rest. He had been up all night inspecting bomb destruction and reporting it in to the ARP headquarters. Little did the reverend know that more bombers were on the way, this time coming in droves...

When Reverend Sutton awoke at noon to the sound of sirens and the reverberation of aircraft, he knew something was up. He jumped out of his bed, still in his clothes from that night's work, and dashed outside. Looking up, he saw hundreds of planes flying overhead. The reverend had seen many things; dogfights high in the sky, German bombers spiraling out of control with black smoke billowing from their engines, but nothing was quite as impressive as seeing a cloudy sky that had hundreds and hundreds of planes silhouetted against it. They looked like gnats swarming on a humid day.

"Extraordinary formation, is it not, reverend?" The voice of the reverend's neighbor broke into his thoughts.

"That it is, Mr. Radcliffe, it must be the whole Royal Air Force! I wonder what they're up to." He said to his longtime neighbor.

"Aye, the lads want to get out of the shelter and see for themselves. I suppose I ought to join them, Charlotte will begin to worry."

He smiled over the tall fence and disappeared from sight.

The reverend descended into his shelter and closed the door, thankful for a few more minutes' of sleep. However, sleep did not come. Gunfire was relentless; some bombs made the earth shudder and explosions could be heard all around London and the surrounding towns. The drone of the planes was nearly deafening. It was a long day, one that the reverend would not soon forget as he lay on the cot in the dark shelter, thinking of the people who were dying all around the globe as war raged unremittingly.

A thin beam of light streamed in from the top of the door of the shelter. It had been at least three hours since the war in the air had started and it had been quiet for some time. The reverend must have dozed off, for when he ventured back inside, it was 2 o'clock in the afternoon.

He praised God that their street was unharmed. Yet in the distance, he could hear the sirens of fire engines busy putting out the fires the bombings had caused.

He made his way to his desk and reread the letter he was going to send to Margaret. In it, he had described how rationing had further squeezed them. Meat, margarine and tea were rationed, and fruits and vegetables were scarce unless they were homegrown. Petrol had been rationed since the beginning of the war, but he rarely needed it, for he always traveled on foot or bicycle. The reverend had also explained to his daughter how people banded together and were beyond determined to win this war, no matter the cost. They were prospering and holding England up in this uncertain time. He had also included a part of Winston Churchill's speech delivered earlier in the year, *'We shall fight on the beaches, we shall fight on the landing grounds, we shall fight in the fields and in the streets, we shall fight in the hills; we shall never surrender,'* The words comforted him and millions of others. It was plastered on colorful posters in the underground tunnels of London and on lampposts here and there.

Reverend Sutton folded up the letter and put it in an envelope to send off within the hour. Throwing on his black overcoat, he swiftly made his way to the post office where he deposited the letter in a red, cylindrical post office box. The reverend then made his way to the ARP Headquarters where he would receive his orders for the night. A faint hum of airplanes made him hurry up and the blare of an air raid siren directly above his head, made him jog. He covered his ears, for the siren was deafening and he started to run. Too many times he had seen people caught in a bombing in the middle of a street. The reverend passed a few air raid shelters, all surrounded by sandbags he had helped lay. His quick pace did not stop until he was safely in the ARP Headquarters. The day was waning, but his work had just begun.

---

Meanwhile, Harry found himself driving northwest with his father, his suitcase in the back of the car. They had left London yesterday, stayed at an inn in Stokenchurch for the night, and were making their way to the RAF base of Brize Norton. Harry had been assigned to training there and after his training, he would join up with the 600 Squadron.

The car rolled to a stop in front of the dreary base. Rain misted the windshield. Mr. Cavanaugh sighed and turned in the seat of the car.

"Rain's picking up." He remarked quietly. "This if for you," he started and pulled something out from under his seat. It was a small parcel wrapped in grocery bag wrapping paper that he set on his lap. "I want you to know how proud your mum and I are of you. I know it hasn't been easy. I know we were shocked, initially at your decision, but we're proud, son. Rich is proud of you and Evan would be as well." He sounded sad for a moment, and he paused.

Harry thought of his older brother and wondered what he would say about his decision to fly.

"You'll do well, I'm sure of it. Write often. Hopefully we'll see you on leave and on the holidays." Mr. Cavanaugh smiled fondly, yet sadly at his son.

"You and mum be safe, too." Harry smiled weakly and Mr. Cavanaugh handed him the parcel.

"Things have been lean these past few years, and I'm sorry we've put off getting you one, but your mum and I think now is the best time." Mr. Cavanaugh watched as Harry opened the gift.

"Dad, thank you," Harry smiled. It was his very own Bible. It had a dark leather cover and was small enough to keep with him. "Thank you,"

They got out of the car; Harry hugged his father and took out his bag of luggage.

"I'll miss you," Harry said and truly meant it.

"We'll miss you too. Come home. Be safe." His father hugged him one last time and then went around the front of the car and opened the driver's door to get back in.

"Oh!" Harry went after him and put a letter in his father's hand. "It's for Meg. I wrote it last night and meant to send it off before we left London."

"I'll be sure to send it," Mr. Cavanaugh gave him a wink. "You sure there's not more there than you let on?"

Harry shook his head and chuckled. "Have a safe trip home." He changed the subject.

Mr. Cavanaugh slid into the car and Harry waved goodbye with his bag slung over his shoulder.

Men with life-jackets, harnesses, helmets, and goggles ran by every which way. Harry made his way to the main headquarters where he was met by a pretty, young secretary, no doubt a WAAF like Mitch. She had been sad to see him go, even Ed had seemed disappointed, but they all knew war could change everything within an instant and nothing was certain.

"Can I help you?" The blonde asked curiously in her navy outfit.

"Yes, I'm looking for Training Instructor Beal?" Harry leaned on the counter.

The blonde looked amused. "Beal? You might want to rethink that... He's a bit of a tough nut." She chuckled. "He's in the back room, waiting for the rest of the students. Room No. 4." She handed him two forms that he needed to fill out and he did quickly and gave one back to her. "Take this other one with you." She instructed him and Harry walked down a long hallway with his bag still slung over his shoulder.

He made it to Room No. 4 and saw that it was a large, airy room that reminded him of a schoolroom. Chairs were in rows and the trainer was in front of the students that were filing in. Harry took a seat behind a tall, young man who had jet black hair. He put his bag down beside his chair and leaned forward on the desk. The instructor turned around. He had large aviator sunglasses on, a cigar sticking out of his mouth and a stern face. The trainer looked over the group of about twenty-five young men, all looked younger than twenty.

"So, this is it," He pulled the cigar from his mouth and held it between two fingers. "I hope you lads are tougher than you look, because if you're not, you have one rough year ahead of you. The squadron leaders and wing commanders give me six months. Six months to whip you lads into shape, teach you how to fly, not get yourselves killed, and turn you into flying officers." He paced in front of the young men. "If you want a friend, look to the boy beside you because you'll find no sympathy from me. And you'll find no sympathy from the Huns. Out There is war and war has no compassion. Your job as a pilot is to follow orders no matter what, even if it claims your life. The only words you will say from here on out to me are 'yes sir,' and 'no sir.'" The trainer took of his sunglasses, folded them, and put them in the chest pocket of his uniform. "Any questions?" He put his hands on his hips and scoured the faces of the young men. His dark brown eyes raked the group and his greasy brown hair was neatly combed under his hat.

No one said a word, the young men stared at him, not quite sure what they had gotten themselves into.

"I SAID! ... Any questions?"

"NO SIR!" They all replied.

"Good," The trainer started pacing the floor again. "Some of you have experience with planes, you just need finishing off. But I don't want any smugness seen on your faces. Do I make myself clear?" He stopped and turned to them.

"Yes sir!" All the young men replied heartily and sat up straighter in their chairs.

"Good. Now get to your barracks." The trainer turned on his heel.

Harry swallowed nervously. He stood up and surveyed the room as the other young men filed out. Posters of the war machines they were about to fly were plastered on all the walls. Harvards, Spitfires, Hurricanes, Blenheims... A large blackboard was behind the instructor with shelves on either side that held volumes and volumes of books and manuals. Harry swung his bag over his shoulder, wondering what planes they'd be flying first.

"Find something particularly interesting?" Beal's annoyed voice broke Harry out of his thoughts.

"No sir," Harry replied quickly.

"Then I suggest you follow orders." He said icily.

Harry quickly followed the rest of the young men out of the room before the instructor found fault with him on his first day. He trailed the group as they all walked away from the one-story building to the multilevel barracks that held countless RAF pilots. *I've spent too much time with Margaret; I'm starting to pick up on her daydreaming...* he thought with amusement as he and the rest of the pilots entered the old barracks.

# Chapter 15

"Mum! We're home!" Margaret called out as she closed the door behind the others who had all filed in behind her.

Their orchestra had finished their last concert in the park for the year. It was growing much too cold now that autumn was underway. The boys and Hannah and Rachel all trudged upstairs to put their instruments back in the studio.

When her mother didn't reply, Margaret set her cello case down in the foyer and entered the kitchen. She saw her mother at the kitchen table. An African-American lady was sitting down across from her. She looked stern and unhappy. They were talking quietly and stopped their conversation when Margaret entered.

"Meg, would you please bring Samuel in?" Her mother asked.

She nodded that she would, wondering if everything was alright. She went back to the foyer and up the stairs until she met Samuel headed to the boys' floor where their rooms were.

"Samuel, my mum wants to speak with you. She's in the dining room... she has a guest." Margaret wanted to warn him but not speculate about who the lady was.

The reserved young man nodded, "alright, thank you." He went downstairs and Margaret watched him leave, wanting to give him privacy and space.

"I'm starved!" Pitcher said loudly, coming down the stairs towards her.

"No you don't," Margaret blocked the way. "Back upstairs," she told him and Grubbs who was behind him.

"Why? I'm so hungry I could die." Grubbs added.

"Out of my way!" Pitcher tried to push past.

"Upstairs! Now! We'll get something to eat later. You lot are worse than Louis." Margaret succeeded in herding them back to their rooms.

She half-wished she could lock them in, they exasperated her so.

Margaret resolved herself to sitting on the stairs outside of their floor to make sure they didn't interrupt whoever her mother and Samuel were talking with. *I hope Samuel doesn't have to leave. We'd be lost without him conducting us...*

That night, Margaret silently slipped into her mother's room, her stocking feet padded across the floor quietly. Gabriella was sitting in a window seat that overlooked the backyard.

"Mum?" Margaret quietly informed her mother of her presence.

"Yes?" She turned from the window and looked to her daughter.

They were both dressed in their matching floral print two-piece pajamas they had bought together a few weeks back. Margaret joined her mother at the window seat. Gabriella's room was just as big as Margaret's. It had slanted ceilings, tall windows, and wide plank floors.

"What happened with Samuel? Was she his mother?" Margaret pulled her legs up to her chest and was thankful that Samuel hadn't left with the stern-looking woman earlier that day.

Her mother shrugged her shoulders and looked back outside. "Yes, she is Samuel's mother. She asked him to come home, but he refused. Apparently, she saw him playing in the park... it's a long story."

"Did he run away?"

"Yes... I'm afraid he did. She has every right to insist that he returns home. She *was* angry," Gabriella sighed. "What mother wouldn't be angry if one of her children had run away and not returned for years on end? She agreed to let him stay. It sounds as though she has her hands full with her other children. I don't know what will come of it, but things seem settled for now."

Margaret thought for a moment. "I hope he stays."

"So do I, darling." Gabriella stood and hugged and kissed her daughter goodnight.

Margaret said goodnight to her mother, but still couldn't quite get the problem out of her head. She thought about it throughout the night before she finally fell asleep around midnight.

The next morning, a letter came for Margaret. The return address said 'RAF BRIZE NORTON, BRIZE NORTON, OXFORDSHIRE.' She opened it with haste and plopped onto the couch in the living room to read Harry's latest news.

*'Dear Meg,*
*I wish I could tell you everything that's been going on here lately.*

*Unfortunately, I can't give too much detail, 'Loose Lips Sink Ships,' they say, but I'll try my best.*

*I am sitting by a small creek near the base. It reminds me of our walks in Regent's. It's getting so very cold out here. I can imagine New York is just as cold, if not colder. Now that we are both out of London, it feels so odd. Dad's sent me letters saying how the bombing has lessened. You wouldn't know that here. Planes are taking off every second. Just now there's one going over my head. Loud as anything, I tell you.*

*I've met some nice lads though. There's Donald Bailey, a farmer's son from Cheshire; Valentine Woodard, who was a mechanic like me; and there's Jim Murphy, who is perhaps the youngest of the group and was part of the ground crew here at Brize Norton.*

*Training is going well. I'm flying more and more every day. The view is beautiful; I wish you could see it. Maybe someday I'll be able to take you flying. You'd love seeing England from the air.*

*Your friend,*

*Harry.'*

Margaret reread the letter and folded it up. She thought about what he had said and wondered how long it would be until they saw each other. She wondered whether he thought about her as much as she thought about him and the danger he was now in. *He's a pilot!* She marveled at the idea and shook her head, wishing she was back at home.

That Sunday night, Margaret walked into the silent studio. *If walls could talk.* She smiled to herself and thought of the countless hours she had spent in the empty studio that only had a grand piano in it, a stack of chairs along the far wall, and the secret door. Margaret sat down at the piano. The only light came from a sconce along the stairway at the far end. It reflected off of the shiny black and white keys. For some reason, the verse her father had told her came to Margaret's mind. *'Be strong and of good courage, do not fear nor be afraid of them; for the LORD your God, He is the One who goes with you. He will not leave you nor forsake you.'*

Repeating the verse in her mind made her feel close to her father and her home. Touching the keys and letting her feelings pour forth, Margaret played a song unknown to anyone else. It was the song of her heart and she could see the title clearly in her head. *'Good Courage.'* She kept a fast, driving rhythm with her left hand and a moving melody with her right hand. Margaret could picture planes flying in the clouds and feel the fear and exhilaration that a pilot would feel. The melody's crescendo was freeing and made her feel like she was an onlooker to a great sight, a great moment, and a great time in history when courage and hope was all that one lived by and victory was a distant dream.

---

Harry tightened his grip on the Harvard's controls, anticipating the verbal beating that would come. *Three... Two... One...*

"Try that one more time, Cavanaugh, and I'll..." Training Instructor Beal didn't need to finish his threat that came in over Harry's headphones.

"Yes sir," he replied and adjusted his control on the training aircraft.

It was his fifth time flying the Harvard AT-6 training airplane and the same adrenaline rush was still pulsing through him. However, he had to calm down. He had tried a climbing right curve and had gone too fast into it. Hence, his instructor's scolding from the back seat. If he had been alone, he wouldn't have been so nervous. But he needed to pass this test in order to move on with the rest of the young men he had come to respect and cheer for.

Harry leveled out the aircraft and took a deep breath. His instructor barked out orders and Harry executed the maneuvers. *Don't practice making mistakes...* He remembered Beal's constant instructions of do's and don'ts. Harry didn't think they would ever stop rolling through his mind.

The yellow Harvard climbed into a left curve and the sheer force, power, and control of the plane made Harry feel like he was in a rocket going millions of kilometres per hour. Instead, he was just in a training plane going the average speed, with no enemy in the vacant skies of central England. Nonetheless, the drone of the engine and the exhilarating climbs and dives he had to execute made him feel like he was one step closer to being an RAF pilot.

As their training time came to a close, Harry circled twice over Brize Norton and then proceeded to do his best landing to date. It was smooth, perfect, and he could see his fellow pilots cheering from their place by a hangar. Harry let out a relieved breath.

"You passed, Cavanaugh." The emotionless instructor said as Harry taxied the plane successfully over to an E-pen.

He turned off the machine and listened to the last whirr of the engine fade into silence. Harry took off his helmet and thanked the instructor as he opened the canopy and they climbed out. His pilot boots hit the ground and Harry stretched, relieved at being able to move.

"Well done!" Val slapped Harry on the back.

"Thanks," Harry grinned and shook his hand.

The instructor joined them and all manner of celebration died away.

"Congratulations everyone on passing this test. Refuel the Harvard and then you can all have the rest of the afternoon off." He nodded his leave and his huge shape sauntered back towards the hangars.

The young men all looked excited. It was their first day off since joining the training program a month ago.

Jim was the first to speak. "What are we going to do? Where are we going to go?"

"Just enjoy the moment," Don, the tall and lean farmer's son replied.

"I don't know about you lot, but I'm getting something to eat down at the pub." Another boy replied who was a bit older than Jim.

They all set about refueling the Harvard in the E-pen, set up specifically to protect the planes from bombs. There was a Spit in the same pen and all the lads couldn't wait until it was their turn to fly the impressive fighter plane.

That evening, the group descended upon the neighboring town of Carterton. They filled the local pub and all ordered their meals. Harry took a seat in the back with Don and Val and they all placed their orders. Most of them hadn't had good, *good* food since they left home, so they treated themselves to dessert as well. Harry talked and laughed with his friends while the usual pub sounds echoed around him; glasses clinking, dining ware clashing, men laughing, and everyone talking.

"I'll have the cake," Val and Don ordered the same thing.

Harry skipped on the sweets and Val joked, "What are you doing, Cav, trying to watch your weight?" He joked.

"You've eaten enough for both of us," Harry replied jokingly. "I thought I'd leave some for the others." He leaned back in the booth, content to have a full stomach.

Val laughed. "I think I've actually lost twenty pounds since I came here..."

Don scoffed. "Still a bit flabby in the middle, Woodard."

Val swatted at him. "Mind who you're pointing fingers at, *Bailey*, you could hardly run the two kilometer when you got here. Your mum bake you too much cake back in Chippenham? You not used to manual labor?" He joked.

Harry chuckled and put in, "it doesn't take muscles to fly a plane. It takes brains."

"All hail the all-knowing Cavanaugh." Don dug into his cake that had just been set on the table.

"I'd like to hear you tell that to Beal." Val addressed Harry. "Strength is important to him, that's why he makes us run so often and do all those idiotic exercises. If our planes go down over enemy territory, mark my words, we'll be glad for those exercises."

"I can't argue with that." Harry grunted in agreement as everyone finished up and got ready to head back.

The sun was setting as they made their way back to the base in the chilly air. Harry wore his thick Royal Air Force-issued jacket and was thankful for the fleece collar. The streets were dark and quiet except for an owl hooting nearby and a dog barking from the town far away to their left. Harry relished the peace. The trio was joined by Jim who came running up behind them.

"I was nearly flogged!" He was out of breath and had a mischievous tone in his voice.

"What'd you do now?" Harry asked him.

Jim laughed and straightened his jacket. "I was trying to talk to the waitress, but she turned out to be the pub keeper's daughter."

Don lifted his eyebrows. "No girl would be keen to have you as a beau, Murphy. You're practically a kid." Don ruffled Jim's hair and the younger boy hit his arm away.

"Say that to my face, you beardless lank," Jim put up his fists and threw a punch half-heartedly at Don who dodged it easily.

"Can't even reach me, Tiny Temper." Swatted at him, slapping him on the head.

Jim threw him a vulgar hand gesture.

Val laughed and Harry watched in amusement as the two started wrestling and exchanging obscenities.

Harry lay on his top bunk and pulled out a piece of paper. He shared the bunk with Val and he could feel the bed rattle and shake every time he tossed and turned. However, Val was up reading and all the other young men in the barracks were getting ready for bed. Harry pulled out Margaret's letter and started to reply to it. She had described how pretty Central Park was with all the colorful leaves changing and how they were going to surprise Mr. Ackerman with a Thanksgiving feast at his apartment next month. Harry wrote about how training was hard and how he missed being home. But he also added that he wouldn't change anything. Soon he would be helping his country and making a difference.

"Who are you writing to?" Jim's head popped over the side of Harry's bunk.

Startled, Harry jumped and made a face at the younger boy. "Scamper off." Harry waved him away impatiently.

"Meg? Who's Meg?" Jim looked at the heading. "Is she your girlfriend?!"

"I said clear off!" Harry covered up the piece of paper.

Val kicked Jim's legs from his spot on the bottom bunk.

"Go on, Murph, leave him alone." Val's voice was more patient.

"Oi, does she have a sister?!" Jim pushed.

Harry muttered under his breath and rolled his eyes. He kept on writing his letter but couldn't concentrate with Jim right there.

Blessedly, someone called him and his attention was drawn elsewhere.

"Don't listen to him," Val said from the bottom bunk. "He's got no one to write to, I hear."

Harry looked at his writing and then pulled his Bible out from under the piece of paper. The top cover of it was indented with the pen's tip and the countless words he had scribbled on the pieces of paper on top of it. He opened the cover and saw his parents' note on the inside.

*'We love you and are proud of you.*
*Love, Mum and Dad.'*

Harry sighed and remembered how blessed he was to have family and friends who cared for him. He finished his letter as everyone turned in for the night and the lights were turned off. Smiling to himself with amusement, he didn't particularly mind the thought of Meg being called his girlfriend.

# Chapter 16

A thick fog was covering the ground and lay heavily on the tarmac. Snow clung stubbornly to the edges of the runways, unwilling to melt all at once. Harry stood in front of a hangar and watched as a formation of Beaufighters circled around the base. He could barely see them through the fog... But he could hear them.

He peered out from under the brim of his blue service cap and observed the sun's rising through the fog. It painted the world in a hue of orange and turned the mist into what looked like floating fire. He thought back to a verse he had memorized that morning, Isaiah 41:10, *'Fear not for I am with you, be not dismayed for I am your God. I will strength you, yes, I will help you, I will uphold you with My righteous right hand.'* The words comforted Harry.

Thankfully, Harry hadn't been chosen to train that day. He had written a letter to home and explained anything he could; how one of his friends had met a girl in town and they were now going out, how he missed being at home, and how he hoped they were doing alright now that the bombing wasn't so heavy. Nonetheless, he still heard Hurricanes and Spitfires flying overhead to intercept German bombers and their fighter escorts.

He looked out over the tarmac, thinking of the events from the last few weeks. Jim had been transferred to an aerodrome in Wales after running off the runway during a flight test. He had broken the undercarriage of one of the Harvards and had smashed through the fence at the far side of the runway, eventually skidding to a stop in front of a car on the roadway. Beal had been livid, but thankfully Jim hadn't been hurt and the training aircraft could be repaired.

All the other pilots, Harry included, had passed their tests with flying colors. Spring would arrive in no time and they'd all be ready to join up by then.

"Harry," Val's voice broke into Harry's thoughts.

Harry turned slightly to see Val approaching wearing a heavy leather jacket and a pilot's helmet.

He had a paper under his arm and Harry noticed the title of a paragraph, *'RAF Bombs Dusseldorf and Turin.'* Harry was about to comment on the headline when Val continued.

"Beal wants us in the briefing room. I think he wants us to transport some Spits to Benson."

"Really?"

"Beal doesn't joke."

"You have a point there," Harry walked with him back to the small building where their instructor would be waiting.

Beal was sitting at his desk and looked up from a report as the young men entered. He started quickly, "the two Spitfires were force-landed here when one had a petrol leak and the other was hit in the rudder. Both have been repaired and need to be returned to the base at Benson." Beal informed them. "You'll deliver them and then get a ride back by Flight Sergeant Boyce; he's part of the ground crew."

"Yes sir," the two young men replied.

"Good, now see to it," The instructor left the room and went down the stairs to the Op Room as the pair carried out his orders.

"It's a good thing we're both familiar with Spitfires." Val remarked. He had repaired countless Spits and so had Harry.

"Couldn't agree more," Harry replied as they left the office behind.

Taxiing down the runway, Val asked Harry, "So what's the verse today, Harry?"

Val had taken up the habit of asking Harry what verse stood out the most to him when he read his Bible every morning. Harry was happy to oblige, because Val seemed genuinely interested that Harry was a Bible-reader.

"It's in Isaiah, he was a prophet, and it says '*Fear not for I am with you, be not dismayed for I am your God. I will strength you, yes, I will help you, I will uphold you with My righteous right hand.*'" Harry turned onto the runway and would be the first to take off.

"Amen," Val replied over the R/T.

Taking a deep breath, Harry set the controls to their right places and remembered everything their handbooks and manuals had instructed them to do. Sure he had taxied a Supermarine Spitfire, but he'd never taken off in one. '*Easier than it looks...*' Beal had said during one of their classroom days. But it was not so easy to believe when you were in the cockpit of the fastest machine in the world. Harry felt the harness digging into his shoulders and the sharp metal digging into his hindquarters from his dinghy, but he hardly noticed. The Spitfire roared in his ears and the radio static nearly deafened him, but it was all worth it as the glorious power of the machine took off down the runway. He remembered what he had been told about the Spitfire's prop being long, so he couldn't push the stick too far forward. The takeoff slid him backwards in his seat as he went faster and faster. In seconds he was in the air and climbing steadily into the endless sky. He made a circuit and waited for Val to get to the right height. Harry took in the power of the aircraft around him. He had never flown in anything so magnificent. He was infinitely glad of the countless hours of solo flying he had under his wing so far.

Harry altered course, pulled the map out of its compartment to his left and saw that the RAF Base in Benson was only 50 kilometres away. *This'll be easy.* He thought.

"Just a few minutes of flying, it's only 50 kilometres." Harry informed Val.

Harry climbed a bit in height with Val to his side and looked out the plane's canopy to the ground below. Who would've thought he'd be flying a Spitfire over England in December of 1940... He almost couldn't believe it. Not long ago he was still sitting at his desk at school, just a boy, hoping for a chance to fight for his country. Now here he was, a pilot flying around 3,000 metres above the ground, entrusted with one of Britain's most powerful weapons.

*You've come a long way, Harry Cavanaugh, you've come a long way.* He licked his dry lips and turned back to the task at hand.

After about a minute of flying southeast, Harry spotted something on the horizon. "Val, I see a flock at 11 o'clock. Ours or theirs, can you make it out?"

Harry recognized the large silhouette of bombers... big bombers. They had small fighter planes to the front and to the back, escorts.

"By the looks of things-" Val was cut off by Harry's frantic reply.

"Those aren't ours, Val! They're German! Head right. Make for that patch of cloud cover." Harry turned sharply to the right and felt the G-forces escalade.

"Ops would have given us a heads up." Val followed close beside Harry. "This doesn't make sense."

Swiveling his head around, Harry saw that the formation was still far off, at least for now.

"Maybe the radar's jammed; they'll get her loose soon." Heart pounding faster and faster, Harry headed for the clouds quickly and swiveled his head around again.

This time, instead of open air and blue sky, he saw two grey flashes of metal and double turbines pursuing them.

"They're on our tail!" Harry hollered to Val and sped up. "Two ME's at eight o'clock."

His heart started to pound out of his chest. Not a moment too soon they both plunged into the thick clouds as gunfire split the air. Harry relied on his instrumentation more than ever and kept a close eye on his left to make sure Val was still there.

"I think we lost them." Harry stated as they came out the other side of the clouds.

Unfortunately, as he looked behind him, he saw they were still there. Harry knew what he had to do. They both made gut-wrenching tight turns and were able to swiftly get behind the enemy. Harry thanked his training. Looking down at the golden trigger on the Spitfire's yoke, Harry took a deep breath. He had never fired a gun in his life... but this was war. Harry pressed the trigger.

The Spitfire's machine guns raked through the air. The bullets left comet trails through the sky. Harry yelled as he pressed the trigger again, trying to fly the plane and aim at the same time. Two more gunfire bursts sounded and strafed through the air. The Messerschmidt veered, trying to get out of the path of the bullets. Val hadn't hit his plane, but was letting out three-second bursts of gunfire as he came up behind the enemy. Both fighter planes climbed into the sky and out of Harry and Val's range. Harry dove away from the plane as it climbed in height and circled back towards the protection of its formation. Harry followed Val who was nearing the ground, trying to get out of sight of the enemy. Harry pulled up alongside him and checked his map; they had moved too far east.

"Are you alright?" Harry asked and still kept an eye out for more fighters.

"I'm fine. You?" Val sounded shaken.

"Steadying the buffs." Harry commented and felt his heart slow. He had never known such an adrenaline rush and he had never been so afraid in all of his life. "I would go after them, but I'm afraid we're a bit outnumbered. I'll try HQ again." Harry tried getting in touch with Brize Norton's Control Room and found only air static. "Nothing, try yours." Harry told Val while they flew over a stone barn with a wooden roof. The horses in the field went running each way, spooked at their low flight.

"Nothing here," Val replied through Harry's headphones.

"Alright, let's just get to Benson then. I don't want those Jerry's coming back for more." Harry pushed his Spitfire into a faster pace, thankful they could outrun their enemy. Val stayed by Harry's side the entire time.

They reached Benson RAF Base, made a loop, and tried to contact their Control Room. For two circuits there was nothing and then finally radio silence was broken.

"I see you. You have a clear landing." The operator informed them and Harry went in to land first.

He put on the brakes slowly and after he stopped, he followed the ground crew and taxied to a hangar. Val was close behind him.

After climbing down from the wing, a few mechanics looked over the plane and put chocks under her wheels. Harry waited for Val outside of his hangar and gave him a knowing nod.

"Nice flying," Harry shook his hand.

"Likewise." Val shook his head; obviously in disbelief he'd had his first skirmish with the enemy.

Harry felt the same way.

They were led to their transport vehicles after they relayed the news about the formation that had pursued them. Spits were sent up in pursuit not long after. Harry shaded his eyes and watched as the planes took off... slightly jealous. His knees were still shaking, yes, but he had fought in his first air battle. And it felt good to finally be fighting back.

---

Margaret sat in her window seat and watched the snow fall outside her window. The scene was peaceful, but Margaret was unsettled. She held the Times in her hands and read the headline again, 'Roosevelt Calls For Greater Aid To Britain.' She chewed the inside of her lip as her eyes wandered over the front page. How she worried for her family... Harry would soon be launched into the war and her father was putting his life on the line every day as a warden. She had been hearing from Bess occasionally, but hadn't had a letter from her in over two months. Who knew where she was now and what she was doing? No doubt she was helping those in London who couldn't help themselves. She could almost see Bess walking the streets, helping people get to bomb shelters, bringing water to firemen, and scooping up those that were fleeing their destroyed homes as it snowed... snow mingling with ash in the London streets.

Life seemed so peaceful in her little corner of the world. They played their instruments, went for walks in the park, attended school, and went on adventures around the city on the weekends. They had celebrated Christmas joyously without a care in the world. She saw no worry on the faces of the men or women in New York and it bothered her. Did no one care about what was going on in Europe? Did they not know that friends and allies were dying, or that the German war machine wouldn't stop at Europe if they came to victory? Margaret saw signs and posters of anti-war propaganda and she read quotes from politicians and leaders that opposed joining the war. To her, they were refusing to help her friends... her family. Margaret would've helped had she been in London still. She would perhaps have become a nurse, or a WAAF like Harry's friend he used to work with. She would have even helped her father set up sandbags. But what could she do from so far away? She was just a girl... just a girl in a country that wasn't fighting in a war.

---

Harry and Val stood in Training Instructor Beal's office with their hands clasped behind their backs, chins held high, feet close together, and stomachs sucked in. They were expecting a nice verbal beating from their instructor at putting the Spits in danger, or going off course, or doing anything other than what he had instructed them to do.

The instructor slammed the door behind him and walked behind his desk, smoldering cigar clamped between his teeth. He eyed his students who stood in front of him. He put the cigar down. With a stare that could crumble stone, he peered at the two young men who stood like statues.

"I heard about your flight to Benson." He stated without emotion. Beal held them in his gaze for several long minutes. Then he picked up his cigar and his voice changed. "Congratulations on flying in your first dogfight."

The two friends could hardly believe their ears.

"Thank you, sir." They said in unison and blinked in confusion and surprise.

The instructor stifled and chuckle. "You don't have to sound so afraid. We have two things in common, our ties to the RAF and our mutual disdain for the Luftwaffe." He continued slowly. "I'm only glad you didn't get yourselves killed and our planes wrecked. But now I have a proposition for you two..." He sat down and folded his hands on his desk. "At ease, gentlemen," a wry smile formed on his lips.

Harry and Val relaxed their shoulders and listened with interest to what their instructor would say, their past fears forgotten since he had changed his tone.

"Here at Brize Norton, we now have a waiting list of men, young and old, who want to train as pilots. We're sending the youngest lads to the ATC, but there are men your age wanting to help who are too old for the Air Training Corps. I want you to consider this. You gentlemen have the most experience of your group, which was why I asked you to fly the Spitfires over to Benson this morning. And now you've been in a skirmish, one of the things I can't offer the students until they join up with a squadron. Here is my proposition. Join up with the RAF this month. Most of the others will be graduating in February or March, but I'm suggesting you two get out of here and make room for more. You'll gain experience that no amount of classroom or guarded flight time can give you." He sat down and leaned back in his chair. "You've both met your flight hour requirements... but ultimately it's up to you... and as long as my higher ups don't mind. But if I suggest it, they'll do it."

"We've only had twelve weeks of training, sir. Is it enough?"

"How long have you both been aircraft mechanics?"

Harry couldn't reply right away, because he had to think back.

"My point exactly. This is war and we don't have the luxury of time. You've both shown exemplary progress and there's nothing more I can teach you. I'll put you both out on leave for a week and then send you your orders..."

Harry nodded. "Yes sir. I'll do it."

Harry was alright with the news, but he wasn't sure how Val felt about it.

Training Instructor Beal stood up. "Good. I've arranged for your departure tomorrow morning. You both struggled a bit when we practiced, so I thought it best to give you another shot at chuting practice." The instructor had a glimmer of amusement in his eyes and wore an ironic smile that made Harry dread what it was he had planned for them. "You'll be dropped off at Northolt and will take your leave from there." He shook their hands. "It's been a pleasure training you both."

Harry and Val thanked him.

"Now get out of here. And take some Jerry's for me."

The next morning their bags were packed and Harry and Val found themselves cramped into an Airspeed Oxford. The pilot was on his way from Brize Norton with a formation of other bombers to Coastal Command. They would fly right over London, so the pilot was happy to drop Harry and Val off.

"Beal has a strange sense of humor!" Harry yelled over the cacophony of the plane and the wind whipping in through the open hatch.

Val didn't reply.

"Are you ready?" The pilot yelled back at them.

Harry gave a thumb's up. The ground was far away and the thought of jumping into open air made Harry queasy. He had hated when they did parachuting practice during their training. And Beal had been right; he had been shoddy at best. But who could blame him? It would never come natural to Harry to jump out of a plane.

Harry took a deep breath; far below he could see the X-shaped airfield of Northolt. Never had he seen it from the sky. He jumped before he lost his nerve and before he knew it, he was falling through the cold open air. He counted to eight and then released his parachute. Nothing was between him and the ground besides a vast expanse of nothingness. The lofty winds buffeted him about, the cold wind stung his face, but he remained calm. Val was a little ways above him and Harry could hear him hooting and hollering as if this was the greatest thing he had ever done in his life. Harry couldn't help but laugh and tried to calm down. The ground came nearer and nearer and the thunder of the bombers' engines died away. Harry and Val landed in a field to the east of the airfield.

"What a rush!" Val remarked as he unclipped himself from the parachute and proceeded to bundle up the fabric. "I want to do that again."

Harry shook his head.

"You didn't like it?" Val asked incredulously.

"You're insane, Val!" Harry scoffed as he bundled up the fabric of his parachute as well, slightly embarrassed that he felt like he was going to be sick to his stomach.

"I thought it was fun." Val grabbed their bags that had also been dropped out of the Airspeed Oxford. He threw Harry's to him.

"There's loads of words to describe parachuting. Fun isn't one I'd include." Harry slung his bag over his shoulder. He had never seen Val so excited about something. Usually he was the quiet and reserved one, keeping to himself more often than not... never *excitable*.

"Suit yourself." Val shrugged. "Spoil-sport."

They walked across the green field toward the small army car that was coming towards them.

"Enjoy your leave with your family." Harry said.

"You as well, Harry. I hope I'll be seeing you soon."

"Let me know what squadron you end up with. Perhaps our paths will cross again soon." Harry hated the thought of falling out of touch with the friends he had made, but he couldn't complain... there were bigger things to worry about during a war.

At the end of the week, he would be with a squadron and bound for who knew where. The thought was only slightly disconcerting... at least he would be on leave during Christmas and New Year's and get to see his family.

"And Val?" Harry stopped walking as the car came closer. "Merry Christmas." It was strange how foreign holidays felt when they were away from home.

Val grinned. "Merry Christmas, Harry. And Godspeed."

# Chapter 17

1941.

The air was cold in the barracks. Harry wished they could turn the heat up, but no matter how high they turned up the radiators, it didn't take the North Yorkshire dampness out of the air. He rubbed his hands together as he lay on his bed and read a letter from Margaret.

*'Dear Harry,*

*I'm so glad to hear you've joined up with your squadron. Of course, I'll be terribly worried for you now that you'll be joining the fighting, but I know how much it means to you to be fighting for our country.*

*I hope you had a wonderful visit with your parents. Was Richard able to come home for Christmas? Even if he wasn't, I know it must mean the world to your parents to have at least one of you home for the holidays. Were you able to see Dad or Bess at all? I heard from Dad just last week and he said London was being cleaned up rather well, but there were still many streets completely destroyed. For the most part, though, he said things have settled down and you're not being bombed every hour of every day. I'm so glad. I've worried so much for you all.*

*Christmas here was lovely. We've had quite a bit of snow and it's always fun to play in. It's so beautiful. Still, we're playing in Carnegie every Sunday and we just started school again now that winter break is over. I envy that you're done with your schooling. But you'd be surprised to hear I'm actually learning to enjoy it.*

*Now that a new year is upon us, perhaps the end of the war will finally happen. I know it's probably wishful thinking, but I pray it's over soon and everything can return to normal. Nonetheless, we remain undaunted, pray every day, and do what we can.*

*Be safe.*

*Your friend,*

*Margaret.'*

Harry finished her letter and clicked off the torch by his bedside. Staring into the darkness, he thought over what she had said. His visit home had been a welcome respite. However, it had hit him rather hard that both of his brothers weren't there. Harry had often wondered, morbidly, where Evan's unmarked grave was in France. Most likely, he didn't even have one and had been left by the forces fleeing Germany's advance. He turned over on his bunk and sighed, grateful he had joined the 600 Squadron thanks to Fyfe pulling a few strings for him. Upon joining up that day, he had reunited with Guy who had showed him around the base of Catterick in North Yorkshire and was now bunking with the other new recruits that had joined recently.

Staring at the darkness, he thought of what he'd reply to Margaret. She seemed hopeful. How could he tell her that so much of London still lay in ruins? How could he tell her that things were still so bad; rationing was hard on everyone, bombs *were* still falling on English soil, and that the gloom and oppression of the war felt like a thick, heavy presence that hung over all their heads... as though a wave big enough to drown all of England waited just on the horizon and every man and woman lived in fear of when or if it would ever break.

*No,* Harry thought. *I can tell her. She'd want to know. I'd want to know if I'd been sent away because I was too young to join the war.*

The silence was broken by someone entering the room. Harry guessed from the huffing and puffing that it was a recruit struggling with a bag and trying not to wake anyone.

A bang sounded and expletives were murmured by the newcomer. It sounded like he had stubbed his toe or run into one of the bunks. Harry reached for his torch he had put next to his bed. He clicked it on and was surprised by the face that was illuminated in its beam.

"Well, well, well... I should've known. Skulking about in the shadows, Val. You should be ashamed?"

"Turn the bloody thing off, Harry."

The other men in the barracks were complaining at the commotion. Harry pointed the flashlight away from him, amazed that his friend had been put in the same squadron.

"You have Beal to thank for this." Val remarked.

"Well, I'm glad, for the most part." Harry got up and grabbed his pillow.

"What do you mean *the most part?*" Val asked. "And why are you getting up?"

"There's no way I'm sleeping on the bottom bunk below you. Do you have any idea the noises you make when you sleep? You need your own air raid siren."

Val sighed in exasperation. "You're such a pain in the arse."

"Sh!" Someone silenced them.

"Good to see you," Harry said honestly.

Val dipped his head and tossed his things down on the floor. "You too,"

Everyone quieted down and got settled. Harry climbed onto the top bunk and smiled to himself, more relieved than he let on that he had his good friend nearby.

---

January's icy grip loosened and soon flowers were sprouting up all over Central Park. Tulips and violets grew along the sidewalks the children trod on their way to school. New York had transformed from a cocoon to a butterfly overnight. April showers fell on the Big Apple and Margaret's seventeenth birthday was celebrated by going to a philharmonic concert at Carnegie. They had played the works of Mozart and everyone had enjoyed every minute of it. The city slipped back into a warm summer, the children were let out of school for their summer break, and the house grew busy with young musicians coming and going for their lessons... there was always an instrument being played in that old, proud brownstone house.

Late one lazy Sunday afternoon, the group from the house closed up Carnegie's Chamber Music Hall. They had been practicing together all afternoon and after they bid farewell to Simone and Grace and Cassie who left with their parents, they all walked back together to their house in the city that never slept.

Margaret walked with her mother and carried her cello at her side. She fanned herself with her hand as it was still rather warm out. The boys were giving each other piggy-back rides as the familiar sounds of New York surrounded them. Taxis honked, subways rumbled underfoot, sirens wailed in the distance, manhole covers rattled in their grooves, footsteps sounded on concrete; the sounds had all become familiar to Margaret. It had been over two years since she had left London. She could remember all the lovely sights and sounds of her home and the friendly people. She always wanted to go back and hoped that it would be unchanged when she returned.

"What are you thinking about?" Gabriella interjected as they brought up the rear of the group.

"London and how much I miss it." Margaret replied and they walked on in silence for a few steps. "What are you thinking about?" She asked her mother.

"I was thinking that it's been... well, over seventeen years since I've been in England. I can still picture it. No city will ever compare." Gabriella walked with her hands in her pockets.

It was the first time Margaret had heard her mother speak about London and her life there.

"What was it like being part of the LSO?" She ventured to inquire.

Gabriella failed to respond for a few minutes, lost in a sea of memories. "We played every composer's finest; Beethoven, Bach, Brahms, Mozart, Schubert, Debussy, Chopin, Vivaldi, Haydn, we played them all. I knew I was beyond lucky. I was so young and... well, there were so many others more talented than me. But, it was resplendent, I'll give it that." She looked up at the full green trees they walked under as they neared home.

Margaret wondered why it sounded like she hadn't enjoyed it. "Did you like it?

Gabriella smiled slightly. "I loved to play. After some time, I just... I lost the passion I once had."

"Is that why you don't you play anymore?" Margaret asked and adjusted her sweaty grip on her heavy cello.

Gabriella merely shrugged and kept on walking.

Margaret knew she wouldn't get an answer and decided to change the subject. The others were all nearly a block ahead of them. She was grateful she could have this time to spend with her mother alone. Still, Margaret wasn't used to such a full house and having to be around everyone almost constantly.

"I've been thinking..." Margaret paused. "What can *I* do for the war? To help win it? I feel so useless sometimes. I just want to help somehow. Dad and Harry and Bess are putting their lives at risk. I have no right to do any less."

Gabriella listened attentively. "Your father sent you here to keep you out of such danger, Meg. He wants you safe and out of harm's way."

"But surely there must be *something* I can do. If I were home, I'd help carry sandbags or I'd join Dad or Bess in their volunteer efforts. I'd even become a nurse if it meant I could help protect my home and those I love." She felt unsettled and impatient.

Her mother sighed. "My darling, you're only seventeen. If you would like my honest opinion, I think you're wishing to grow up too quickly. You have plenty of time to do all those things. Finish your schooling, plan for what you'd like to do next. Don't wish your childhood away. It'll be over before you know it."

Margaret knew her mother's words were wise; she had a hard time accepting them though. "I guess that's my lot in life," she half-joked, "to always be ready for what's next." She sighed. "I'll try to be patient." She looked to her mother who was gazing at her with pride. "Why does everything have to be so hard, though?"

Gabriella only smiled. "I asked myself the same question once." She put her arm around her daughter's shoulders. "What would life be if it were easy all the time? How would we ever get stronger if all we knew was ease? I know it's hard. Life is, oftentimes, very hard and you'll see as you get older that it doesn't get any easier. But thank goodness we don't have to face it alone, eh?"

Margaret returned her smile.

The summer went by faster than any Margaret could recall. They were starting school again and before they knew it, New York settled into the slow lethargy of winter as the cold temperatures wrapped itself around the city. The first days of December were icy and snowy. In the morning, they would begin decorating for Christmas, something Margaret looked forward to most during winter. She sat up in her room on the first Saturday night of the month and finished writing a reply letter to her father before she went to bed.

She put down her pen and picked up the letter her father had sent her. She read it with such sadness.

*'Dear Meg,*

*Bombs are not falling on London anymore. I am thankful for that. But Hitler's air force has left behind such destruction and desolation... During the bombings, the dense smoke would turn day to night... Whole neighborhoods are reduced to nothing. The British Red Cross has set up places for the Londoners who have lost their homes to stay. I am glad you* are in New York, my girl. At least you are safe. I still cannot believe that poor Mrs. Radcliffe's life was taken by an incendiary bomb just next door. She was only 30 and had little ones to look after... her husband is devastated.

My ARP duties are not as arduous as they were in the spring. In fact, I rather miss my responsibilities and obligations. I have word from Bess; she told me the most distressing news... Her sister was severely injured in an explosion and died just yesterday. My heart goes out to her and I am shocked at this news. Now, Bess is helping in the soup kitchens for the poor souls whose houses were destroyed. She has never given up or lost heart. Many have lost so much.

I'm sorry to write you such sad news. Be praying for the Radcliffe's and Bess.

Tell me some happy news from your corner of the world. I'm in dire need of it.

Love, your father.'

Margaret had written as many happy things as she could in her letter. And she put a 'P.S.' at the bottom and told him that she would call on Christmas Day, for she needed to hear his voice.

Turning off her light, Margaret climbed into bed and pulled the covers up tight to her chin. The chilly attic made her put an extra blanket on as she thought about the horror of some of the things happening across the Atlantic.

*What am I going to do?* The thought still plagued her. She had dwelt on it every night since summer and still she couldn't decide what it was she could do to help her family, her friends, and her country win the war. She wiped a tear from her eye. *I'm just a silly girl. What difference could I possibly make?*

After dinner the next evening, the boys were playing in the living room while Margaret idly chatted with Hannah at the dining table. They were discussing the differences between Bach and Handel, composers who had lived near each other and were born in the same year. Margaret told Hannah about Bess' sister and her neighbor. She almost started to cry and Hannah put a hand on Margaret's. Lately, the two had become rather close. Rachel had been acting like a flirtatious moll lately and it was something Hannah wanted no part in and quite frankly, neither did Margaret. But

Margaret knew Rachel would grow out of it. She was only thirteen after all...

"It will be alright, Meg, you'll see." She smiled and finished her dinner as Mr. Ackerman came hurtling into the foyer.

Louis jumped up from his little bed in the corner of the kitchen and barked at the old professor in surprise.

"Meg, where's your mother?" He caught his breath; the look on his face was shocking, as though he had just been dealt the worst news.

Margaret felt herself grow cold and it had nothing to do with the frigid winter air that had come in through the front door with Mr. Ackerman.

"I believe she went out on an errand. What is it? What happened?" Margaret stood up.

"I need to speak with her or Betty."

Margaret nodded. "Betty's just upstairs. I'll get her." Margaret ascended the stairs quickly and got to the second floor where Betty's room was. Knocking on the door, she called out to Betty. "Mr. Ackerman. just got here; he wants to talk to you."

"I'll be right there, Meg," Betty's replied from behind her door.

"I think something's wrong." Margaret piped up and Betty opened the door with furrowed eyebrows. She had been cleaning out her closet.

"What's wrong?" Betty asked.

"I don't know," Margaret truthfully replied as they went downstairs together.

Mr. Ackerman swiftly led her into the kitchen where the children could not hear them.

"Go on, Meg," Mr. Ackerman shooed her out of the room.

Margaret went to the living room where Tony and Frankie were playing with paper airplanes. She stared blankly ahead and Rachel looked up from her magazine.

"What's the commotion?" She asked.

"I don't know." Margaret shrugged and sat down by Hannah.

The Moser twins played on the floor and made their airplanes fly through the air with different sound effects. Tony crashed his plane into Frankie's and it crumpled.

"Hey!" He whined.

Tony continued to smash his plane into Frankie's. Margaret paid them no mind, for Betty came back into the room just then. The children looked to Betty expectantly as Mr. Ackerman joined them. Betty wrung her handkerchief in her hands and sat down on the couch. She looked shocked.

"Betty? What's wrong?" Rachel asked.

Mr. Ackerman was the one who replied.

"Unfortunately, American forces were attacked this morning in Hawaii."

"Attacked?" Margaret could hardly believe her ears. "By who?"

"By the Japanese." He replied to her.

Margaret put her hands to her mouth and let out a gasp. She knew their enemies were in Europe, but now they were coming from Asia too? Was Britain at war with the Japanese? She had so many questions, but not the courage to ask them.

Betty's face was white.

"What does that mean?" Frankie asked, having forgotten about his ruined toy.

"I believe we will find out soon." Mr. Ackerman looked so very grim. He said more to himself than the children, "the question that has been in the headlines for some time, *'How Long is America Going to Pretend the World is Not at War?'* Well, I believe that question is about to be answered..."

And Mr. Ackerman could not have been more correct.

Everything was put on hold for the evening. They weren't planning on going to Carnegie Hall and the Christmas decorating they were going to start was pushed to the back of their minds. The four younger boys went downstairs and played while the older teenagers stayed upstairs and talked with the adults. It wasn't until the following day did any more news come. School was canceled. Mr. Ackerman came to the house in the afternoon and gave the announcement that the United States was officially at war with Japan. The young boys did not know how to respond to the news, so they did not seem too affected. But to Hannah, Rachel, Margaret, Samuel, and the three adults, they were very somber and grief-stricken. Margaret wrote a note to her father right away and sent it off on that eerie Monday afternoon. The streets were silent and the cars that did drive on the cramped New York City streets were few.

"Terrible news, ain't it?" The postmistress, Loretta, remarked when Margaret had dropped off her letter.

"It is," Margaret didn't know what else to say. "I can't quite believe it."

The old woman tsk-ed. "These are hard times." She said as she took Margaret's letter. "The world is at war." She shook her head, looking out the window of the small office. "What times we live in. God help us all." The words made Margaret shiver.

Loretta waved the next customer forward and Margaret bid her farewell solemnly.

*God help us, indeed.*

When Margaret got back from the post office, she went in her room and sat on her bed numbly. She hadn't avoided the war like her father had planned. Who knew what the future brought now? America was at war. *America is at war!* The immense gravity of the situation made Margaret cry. She buried her face in her pillow and wondered why such hurt had to be brought to those in her life and why God would let such terrible, horrific things happen to His children.

As the household sat around the radio that day, Margaret sat close to Hannah for comfort. The address from the President of the United States started.

*"Yesterday, December 7th, 1941 -- a date which will live in infamy -- the United States of America was suddenly and deliberately attacked by naval and air forces of the Empire of Japan."*

An ocean away, Harry was listening to the same speech next to Val and Guy in their barracks. He hung on every word and could scarcely think of what this would bring. He could only think of how foolish a country would have to be to go up against the might of the United States.

*"The United States was at peace with that nation and, at the solicitation of Japan, was still in conversation with its government and its emperor looking toward the maintenance of peace in the Pacific.*

*"Indeed, one hour after Japanese air squadrons had commenced bombing in the American island of Oahu, the Japanese ambassador to the United States and his colleague delivered to our Secretary of State a formal*

*reply to a recent American message. And while this reply stated that it seemed useless to continue the existing diplomatic negotiations, it contained no threat or hint of war or of armed attack."*

Reverend Frank Sutton stood in his empty kitchen in his empty house and closed his eyes and balled his fists in despair as he listened to President Roosevelt's speech. He thought of his daughter whose home country was now entering into a worldwide war.

*"It will be recorded that the distance of Hawaii from Japan makes it obvious that the attack was deliberately planned many days or even weeks ago. During the intervening time, the Japanese government has deliberately sought to deceive the United States by false statements and expressions of hope for continued peace."*

Poor Bess in a kitchen with her group of Women's Voluntary Service workers cried softly. One of her friends patted her back and soothed her. The soup kitchen had been put on hold to hear the speech.

*"The attack yesterday on the Hawaiian islands has caused severe damage to American naval and military forces. I regret to tell you that very many American lives have been lost. In addition, American ships have been reported torpedoed on the high seas between San Francisco and Honolulu.*

*Yesterday, the Japanese government also launched an attack against Malaya.*

*Last night, Japanese forces attacked Hong Kong.*

*Last night, Japanese forces attacked Guam.*

*Last night, Japanese forces attacked the Philippine Islands.*

*Last night, the Japanese attacked Wake Island.*

*And this morning, the Japanese attacked Midway Island.*

*Japan has, therefore, undertaken a surprise offensive extending throughout the Pacific area. The facts of yesterday and today speak for themselves. The people of the United States have already formed their opinions and well understand the implications to the very life and safety of our nation."*

Margaret bit her lip as Hannah took her hand and gave it a reassuring squeeze.

*"As commander in chief of the Army and Navy, I have directed that all measures be taken for our defence. But always will our whole nation remember the character of the onslaught against us.*

*No matter how long it may take us to overcome this premeditated invasion, the American people in their righteous might will win through to absolute victory."*

Margaret took comfort in those words, for even though she was British through and through, America had become her second home. The presidential speech came to a close.

*"I believe that I interpret the will of the Congress and of the people when I assert that we will not only defend ourselves to the uttermost, but will make it very certain that this form of treachery shall never again endanger us.*

*Hostilities exist. There is no blinking at the fact that our people, our territory, and our interests are in grave danger.*

*With confidence in our armed forces, with the unbounding determination of our people, we will gain the inevitable triumph -- so help us God.*

*I ask that the Congress declare that since the unprovoked and dastardly attack by Japan on Sunday, December 7th, 1941, a state of war has existed between the United States and the Japanese empire."*

Then radio silence.

# Chapter 18

Margaret jogged up the sidewalk that led to her house. She opened the door with her key and shook off the snow that had fallen on her shoulders. She took off her coat, hat, and gloves and hung them up on the coat rack.

"Hello, Louis," She petted the handsome corgi on his head and he woofed quietly. "Merry Christmas, boy." She held his head between her hands gently and gave him a kiss on the forehead.

She had just walked down to the nearest church, St. Vincent Ferrer Church on Lexington Avenue, and had said some Christmas prayers. The quiet cathedral-like church had calmed her immensely. The beautiful stained glassed reminded her of Lily's End and quiet churches always made her feel at ease... especially around Christmastime.

In the kitchen, Betty and Gabriella were cooking dinner. It smelled heavenly as Margaret entered the warm, bustling room.

"What can I help with?" Margaret asked, putting on an apron.

Gabriella looked up, her hair messy and her cheeks rosy from the busy day. "You were going to call your father, weren't you? It'll be nine in London now. It's getting late."

"Go on, Meg," Betty put a great big dish in the oven and closed it with her foot. "I'm sure Gabriella and I can wrangle this pot pie together." She laughed.

Margaret smiled her thanks and went to the hallway where the phone hung. She dialled the number and waited to hear her father's voice.

"Hello? Is this Margaret?" The reverend's voice sounded more beautiful to Margaret than anything in the world.

"Hello Dad! How are you?" Margaret couldn't help but smile.

"Fine, quite fine. I just excused myself from the Cavanaugh's. They invited me over for dinner. It was very good to see Richard and Harry. They looked so happy to be home for the holiday. It was a Christmas miracle they could be home together and on leave at the same time. How fortunate we are!" The reverend exclaimed.

"How is Harry? Did he look well? He wrote to me and told me he was in Cornwall."

"He looked very well! Inquired after you and was quite jealous I was excusing myself to come and talk with you. But tell me about New York; has much changed since war was declared? How is your mother? What are you doing for Christmas Eve?"

Margaret chuckled. "New York is so beautiful during the holidays... The window displays are gorgeous, and people are still out walking in the snow and going on carriage rides in Central Park. Of course, with the 'dim-out,' we can't have outside Christmas lights, but we have garlands everywhere, a wreath on the front door, and the whole inside of the house is decorated. Much has changed... there are enlistment offices being set up everywhere. We see men in uniform here and there. I think Pearl Harbor shook everyone terribly. There aren't any more posters up about keeping out of the war. Everyone's woken up and realized just how bad this war is." Margaret took a deep breath and lapsed into silence for a moment. "But all is well here for now. I just got back from St. Vincent's and will go help Betty and Mum with dinner when we're done talking. And Mum's doing wonderful. She's..." Margaret hesitated. "She's the mum I've always dreamt of and prayed for, Dad."

The reverend's voice was quite when he responded. "I'm glad, my girl. I'm so very glad that you two are there for one another. It's been my sole prayer since you moved there... that you two would have the relationship a mother and daughter should have."

"She still hasn't told me why she won't play any piano and she's rather private, but we're growing closer, I think. Slowly, but surely."

She could almost hear her father smile through the telephone.

"That's how she is. She is rather quiet and pensive; quite like you." He told her. "Give her time. There's more to her than meets the eye. It takes her a little while to open up. I believe she'll tell you when the time is right... she hasn't walked an easy path."

"I will. I understand and know she'll tell me when she can. And Dad?"

"Mm?"

"Thank you for sending me here. I never thought I'd say that. But thank you." She smiled to herself.

"Thank you for being willing to go. You've been so brave. I'm very proud of you."

His words warmed her heart. "Even though war has come, I feel safe. I pray every day that we'll see each other soon."

"I do too, Meg."

There were several seconds of silence.

"Dad?" She needed his counsel and tried to think of the words to say.

"What's troubling you?"

"What can *I* do? I mean for the war... you're a warden, Bess volunteers for nearly everything, Harry's in the Royal Air Force... I feel so useless. We sit around and play our instruments and what's it all for? I love it... you know I do. But I want to be of use and I don't know how."

The reverend thought for a moment. "What you're already doing is very brave, living in New York, helping your mother and Betty take care of the children. I know you're helping them immensely. Besides, you *are* only seventeen, yet you have the fearlessness most adults could only dream of. If you feel like you truly need something else to do..." He paused. "Perhaps look into getting a job. I know you have your schooling now, but you'll be graduating soon. Taking on university may be out of the question for right now, but of that I'm not sure. Think about what you could do... what would you wake up in the morning and be excited for? You can find great purpose in a job; perhaps it would even be in correlation to helping the war effort."

Margaret nodded. "That makes sense. I knew you'd have an idea of what to do."

"And don't take what I said about university to heart; it very well could still be the path you are supposed to take. Just because a war is on, doesn't mean you have to give up on your dreams. I know you've wanted to study music for a long time."

"I have, but there are more important things at stake right now." She responded. "I'll think about it, I promise."

"Stay strong, my girl." The reverend's voice quieted.

"I will." They both paused for a minute. Margaret felt the void between them keenly. Whenever they spoke on the phone, her homesickness came over her like a wave. "Goodnight, Dad. I love you and Merry Christmas."

"I love you too. Merry Christmas."

The phone went quiet.

Putting it back in the cradle, Gabriella joined her in the hallway and leaned up against the entrance.

"He said 'Merry Christmas,' and wished that I was home with

him." Margaret smiled and then sniffed. "I miss him." She wiped a stray tear from her eye.

Her mother took her in her arms and hugged her.

"Oh, my dear, I know you do." She held her tight. "It'll be alright. Wars don't last forever..." Gabriella patted her daughter's back soothingly as she comforted her. "I'm here for you; and I always will be."

---

Rubbing his eyes, Harry walked briskly through the cold night air to the Beaufighters that were just waiting for him and the rest of the squadron. Another night fighter mission was ahead of them. Harry had hardly gotten any sleep for the past few weeks. He was awake on adrenaline, nothing more, as it had been since he had joined the 600 Squadron.

"What's the verse today, Harry?" Val asked as he walked along beside him, their heavy boots clomping on the tarmac.

Harry glanced at his friend and smiled, thinking back and remembering the words he had memorized some hours ago. " 'The wicked flee when no one pursues, but the righteous are bold as a lion,' Proverbs 28:1." Harry spoke the verse and Val nodded.

"Godspeed, Cav. I'll see you in a bit." Val jogged away with his Beaufighter group and Harry followed Guy to the Beaufighter they would fly.

Harry dreaded the chilly dorsal turret he would have to occupy with the 7.7 mm Vickers machine gun. Nonetheless, some warmth from the engine usually would seep into his spot in the plane and keep him warm in the high altitudes. Nonetheless, he put his collar up as the cold January winds blew at his back relentlessly.

*1942, how did that happen? The years go by faster the older I get.* Harry gritted his teeth as he approached the Beaufighter.

It was 0200 hours and he truly felt exhausted. After looking over the plane and inspecting it, the two comrades parted and Harry climbed into the hole in the fuselage that led to his dorsal turret and the small bubble he could look out of. Guy went into the cockpit and they went through the start-up drill they had done so many times. At 0210 hours, chocks away and one by one, the planes flew into the sky and took up formation. The stubby Beaufighters were being heavily relied upon for German night fighter raids. The Predannack RAF Base in Cornwall was a prime location for the raids, so that was where the squadron was located with their new Wing Commander, J. R. Phelps who was leading them now. Costal Command had also taken up stock at Predannack. It was the busiest base Harry had seen since joining up with his squadron.

The 600 had been stationed in Scotland for a little over a month during the spring before moving to Colerne, Wiltshire and then Fairwood Common in Wales. From there, they had gone back to Colerne and then to Predannack in Cornwall, where they were currently. Harry would take Cornwall over Scotland any day. It had been terribly cold there. At least in Cornwall they had a decent amount of fair weather for flying and weren't hemmed in by clouds and fog every day. Harry thought it was perhaps his Australian blood that made him favour the warmer climates.

He shook himself of his thoughts.

The several V formations made their way across the English Channel to Le Touquet where they would drop their bombs, do as much damage as possible, and 'seek and destroy the enemy,' as their orders put it. Guy and Harry were in Wing Commander Phelps' formation of three and were leading the way. Harry had the best view behind his dorsal gun and it was his job to keep the Huns off their tail.

The time passed slowly as they headed west. Harry rubbed his gloved hands together to keep warm and listened to the radio silence. Flying was to pilots as marching was to infantrymen. The minutes lumbered on without any time ever seeming to pass. The duel Hercules engines roared unceasingly and Harry thought he remembered closing his eyes and falling asleep. It wasn't until the radio silence was interrupted that his eyes shot open in alarm. They were now over the western part of the English Channel and were closing in on a German Luftwaffe aerodrome. Reports of the enemy's counter attack and retaliation to the bombing raid were coming in over the R/T and the strength of the defensive was being calculated. Harry shook his head and woke himself up. Finally, the report came that half a dozen Messerschmitts were on their tail. Breaking formation, one section flew upwards, including Guy and Harry in their Beaufighter ten-ton terror. In the opposite direction, the other formation was turning into the enemy that would come up on their tails. Harry repositioned himself behind his gun and breathed out.

*Here we go.* He had gotten used to shooting and being shot at very quickly.

The Huns grew closer and closer, the manoeuvre was executed in a matter of seconds and soon all terror broke loose. It was every man for himself. Harry shot relentlessly at the Messerschmitts with their black crosses and yellow nose. They were like silver fishes darting in and out of the inky blackness of night. He saw two enemy planes hurtling into the sea with smoke billowing out behind them and fire erupting from their engines. Harry aimed at an Me 109 that was flying right for his Beaufighter and he let out a triumphant yell as he aimed and fired. The cockpit burst into flames and dove down, down, down to the Channel.

Harry found himself deafened by the cacophony over the radio, so he tuned it out and relied on his instinct. Guy was busy hammering away at a Me 109 he was chasing, only the flash of metal glinting off the moon's light gave any indication to there being a plane in front of them. Harry moved like a roulette wheel and kept the Huns off their tail. Thankfully, the enemy retreated and climbed into the sky, scurrying off back to their bases with minor injuries.

The fight lasted no more than five minutes and as the last three Messerschmitts flew off, the group got back into formation and proceeded to close the gap between them and Le Touquet.

As they neared the Luftwaffe base, Harry's heart started thudding loudly in his chest. His mouth was dry as he realized they would be in even greater danger soon.

"Flak ahead. Stay sharp. Keep alert." The wing commander said over the radio.

As they came over the base, bombs away. Deafening and chest-rattling explosions went off. The formation dove down to the base where the Nazis were scrambling, some running to the anti-aircraft guns, some trying to get to the grounded Focke-Wulf and Messerschmitt planes. But they had no chance. Guy and Phelps flew side by side and strafed the ground, all. Those in the gun turrets of the Beaufighters shot at anything they could; planes, towers, barracks, hangars, transport vehicles, storage sheds. Anything was a target. Planes were diving bombing from above. There was mayhem all around. The Beaufighters assaulted the enemy that couldn't even hear it coming. The heavy fighter was silent from the front, sending its entire clamour out the back. They aerodrome was obliterated.

Smoke from the bombs billowed everywhere and Guy expertly guided the plane around the columns that rose into the sky. Harry shot at anything he could. Suddenly, anti-aircraft guns were being fired at them. Guy rose up in height to get away from the gunfire and the flak that was starting to pepper the black night. Orange flames burst in the sky everywhere and rocked the plane back and forth.

The offensive was put up too late. The Beaufighters had already done what they'd come for. Mission accomplished, Guy steered the plane back to the relative safety of the channel. *Back to Predannack.* Harry let out a breath and wiped the cold sweat from his forehead as they left the battlefield on the shore behind. It was aglow with orange flames that licked high into the air and the occasional explosion of petrol tanks. Destruction broke the stillness of the night and another win for the RAF was added.

"You good, Cav. Any damage?" Guy asked. "Indicators and gauges look good up here."

"Some damage on the fuselage, we flew through some rough flak."

"Roger that, Cav." Guy commented.

"I see some more Beaus at 7 o'clock, looks like they all got through."

"Good. We don't need a repeat of yesterday."

Harry couldn't have agreed more. The previous day a flight group had gone out to bomb Le Havre and less than half had returned. Apparently, the flak had been terrible. It claimed five Beaufighters and the lives of the ten pilots.

It was an all-too grim reminder that any one of these missions could be their last...

# Chapter 19

Margaret was busy upstairs in the studio when she heard the doorbell ring. *Who could that be?* She thought. Everyone had gone to Carnegie to practice and wouldn't be back until later that afternoon. Margaret had stayed home. Unfortunately, she had a small cold and didn't feel up to practicing.

Descending down the several flights of stairs, Margaret approached the door and opened it. She saw a man and a woman whom she had never met before.

"I'm sorry, can I help you?" Margaret asked through her stuffy nose.

"We were looking for Joe Ackerman," The man stated gruffly. He had dark brown hair and a cap on his head. His grey outfit was slightly dirty and dishevelled.

"And Hannah." The woman put in. She had blonde hair and a red hat on. Her dark brown overcoat had patches where it had torn.

"Mr. Ackerman and Hannah are over at Carnegie, practicing in the Chamber Music Hall." Margaret held the door firmly, determined not to let the strangers in until she knew who they were.

"I see. Do you know when they will be back?" The man asked. He seemed impatient.

"They'll be back later this afternoon, perhaps around 3." Margaret replied.

The man and woman looked to each other and then the lady spoke. "Will you phone them for us? You see, we're Hannah's parents. Joe's my father and what with the outbreak of war, we want our little girl close to us."

Margaret couldn't believe her ears. "I thought Hannah's parents lived in Chicago." She furrowed her eyebrows and sniffed.

"We do, but we've come to pick her up." The man said roughly.

"And what are your names? Mine's Margaret." She held out her hand, and then thought better of it, since she had sneezed into it before the couple had arrived.

"Philip Bishop." The man shook her hand.

*Too late now,* she grimaced, slightly abashed.

"And I'm Myrtle." The lady shook her hand too.

"It's a pleasure. You'd better come in," She didn't like the couple, but if they were Hannah's parents, she had to show them some respect. Perhaps she didn't feel so guilty about shaking their hands.

Margaret showed them into the living room and offered them a cup of tea which they accepted. As the kettle boiled she washed her hands and then rang for the hall.

Margaret asked for Mr. Ackerman and waited a few minutes until he came to the phone in the office of Carnegie. She knew her mother would start worrying once she heard that Margaret had called.

"Meg, what is it?" The old professor asked with concern.

"Mr. Ackerman, a couple has come here asking after you and Hannah. They say they want to take her home and asked me to ring you."

A long pause, and then the professor replied. "I'll be there as soon as possible."

Margaret took the kettle off of the heat and poured two cups of tea for the couple and set out the usual saucers of cream and sugar.

She sat down across from them. "I'm sorry for the wait, Mr. and Mrs. Bishop. It will only be about twenty minutes before they get back." She smiled as they drank the tea thankfully.

"Have you been in New York long?" Margaret asked.

Mrs. Bishop replied. "We just arrived by train this morning. Once we heard that war was declared on Japan, and then on Germany, we wanted our family together again, isn't that right, darling?" She looked to her husband.

"Yes." He sipped his tea.

Fifteen minutes passed awkwardly as Margaret tried to keep the conversation afloat. She was thankful when Mr. Ackerman returned with a pale Hannah on his arm. Rachel was close behind.

"Myrtle, Philip! What a pleasant surprise this is." Mr. Ackerman's face was anything but pleased.

The couple stood. Hannah was standing slightly behind her grandfather as if to hide behind him.

"If you could give us a few minutes, Rachel, Meg..." Mr. Ackerman said to them and they went upstairs silently to leave the family to sort things out. Margaret knew what was coming and didn't want to face it or even consider it.

After twenty minutes, the rest of the children came home and Betty called Rachel and Margaret down. They joined everyone downstairs in the living room as Mr. Ackerman informed them Hannah would be leaving with her parents right away. The younger boys had protested loudly, begging Mr. and Mrs. Bishop for Hannah to stay a little longer. However, she couldn't; her parents had purchased return tickets to Chicago for that afternoon. It wasn't very kind of them, Margaret thought, to spring this on their daughter so suddenly. But there was nothing to be done. Margaret and Rachel started to cry and they embraced their best friend in a hug.

"Oh, Hannah!" It was the only thing Margaret could say.

"You can't be leaving! We need you!" Rachel said desperately.

"Don't be sad. I don't want to go back, but I have to. Chicago isn't too far for letters and I'll just be a phone call away." Hannah gave Margaret another squeeze and stepped back.

"Let's go pack your things." Gabriella took her hand and she, Betty, and the other girls went upstairs.

The room was quiet as the four ladies helped Hannah pack her suitcases. However, as Rachel packed some of Hannah's clothes, she broke the sad silence.

"But *why* do you have to go? Why can't you just stay *here*?" She asked incredulously. "It's not fair! Your parents can't just show up and take you away in the same hour!"

"They're my parents, Rachel." Hannah responded, resolved with her fate.

"They've had every right to come pick up Hannah whenever they wish." Gabriella added. "Until she's eighteen, she must abide by what they say."

"But it's not *fair!*" Rachel retorted.

"It won't be so bad." Hannah tried to cheer up her dear friend.

Margaret realized Rachel was holding back tears. She looked so upset; her face was turning red and her lip quivered. Betty went over to her wordlessly and hugged her tightly. Hannah looked the most composed of all of them.

"Hannah's right," Margaret helped Hannah pack the rest of her things with her mother, putting on a brave face for her friend. "We'll have an excuse to visit Chicago now. We'll still all be friends and keep in touch. Trust me," Margaret took Hannah's shoulders and tried to reassure her, "friendships and families are not broken up no matter how far away you live."

Hannah smiled weakly and embraced Margaret.

"Thank you, Meg. I love you all so dearly."

"We love you too, Hannah. And we'll miss you so much."

Margaret, with the rest of the children and the teachers, said their goodbyes to their dear friend. She bore up well and her parents watched on stoically. Mr. Ackerman carried his granddaughter's suitcases, including her violin case, and escorted her to the waiting taxi. Her parents had gotten into the car already.

Everyone went to the front steps and waved. Hannah waved back and then got into the taxi with her family.

"Bye, Hannah!" The boys all waved, not fighting amongst each other for once.

Rachel and Margaret held hands and still waved as the taxi drove away and out of sight.

Standing on the rooftop, Margaret watched the stars come out one by one. It was cold on the lofty perch and her breath billowed in white puffs. Margaret hugged her arms closer inside of her coat and thought of Hannah and how she would be traveling to Chicago at that very moment.

"I miss her too." Rachel's voice broke into Margaret's thoughts. Turning around, Margaret smiled at her friend.

"I can't imagine her living anywhere else besides here." Margaret watched as Rachel walked across the rooftop.

They stood close together as they watched the sun set below the horizon.

"Now what?" Margaret shivered from the cold, still air.

"Well, I suppose we keep playing. Maybe we can recruit Simone and Grace to come and play with us in the park. They only live a few blocks away." Rachel tossed her light brown hair behind her shoulder and blew into her hands to warm them.

The two girls were silent for a few moments before Rachel asked. "What news from your dad?"

Margaret smiled. His latest letter had contained a 'Dig for Victory' poster that he had found on the street during his ARP Warden round. She had put it up on her wall. Margaret told this to Rachel and she listened intently.

"I'd like to plant a garden this summer. Do you know how?" Rachel asked her.

"I can't imagine it's that hard." Margaret shrugged. "We could plant one out back; maybe even try a small one up here. There's more than enough space."

The girls were silent for some time, lost in thought.

"I miss her," Rachel sniffled.

Margaret put her arm around the younger girl. "I do too," she felt the age gap between her and Rachel keener now that they didn't have Hannah to split the years between them. "But all we can do is 'steady the buffs,' as Harry says, put one foot in front of the other, and take things a day at a time. We'll all miss her... but maybe we can visit sometime and there's always letters."

Rachel sighed and agreed half-heartedly.

The day that started out like any other had turned into a sad day of goodbyes. How quickly things could change. Unfortunately, there would many more moments like that in the days to come... many more farewells as time and life moved steadily, steadily on.

Over the next few months, news trickled in from various sources, the *New York Times*, the *New York Post*, and various magazines Betty and Gabriella brought home. Japan captured the Philippine city of Manila. Japan invaded Burma. Japan invaded the Solomon Islands. The first troops of the United States arrived in Britain. Japan invaded Singapore. Japan invaded Rangoon in Burma. The news was always centred on the war, especially now that America was involved. However, on this special day, no war news was talked about in the house, for it was Margaret's 18th birthday.

Waking up on the sunny, April day, Margaret was greeted by Betty who brought her breakfast in bed, something Margaret found quite odd. Yet she gobbled down the cinnamon rolls thankfully. The treat was growing rarer as the war progressed. Margaret got dressed in her favourite outfit, a dark blue knee-length dress that buttoned to the side and had ¾ sleeves. Margaret slipped on her white socks and her thin house shoes. When she reached the bottom of the stairs, everyone jumped out from behind furniture.

"Happy birthday!" They all exclaimed.

"Oh! Thank you!" Margaret smiled and hugged everyone, thanking them graciously. She hugged her mother and Betty as they asked her what she wanted to do that day. "Shall we go to the park?"

"No!" Tony moaned.

"We go there every day!" Frankie added.

"Hush now. You two have been in such a mood lately." Betty scolded them.

"Meg gets to decide today." Gabriella stated.

Margaret smiled and thought of the perfect alternative. "Well then, how about we all go down to Coney Island and play there?" She had thought up the brilliant plan that night. All the boys grinned wide.

"Yay!" Tony, Grubbs, and Pitcher cheered.

And Frankie echoed, "to the beach!"


The early morning sun shone brightly on the lapping waves. The vendors were setting up their little stores and a few early beach-goers were mulling about. Margaret kicked off her shoes and ran to the shoreline. Rachel ran after her and so did the five boys. Betty and Gabriella, along with Mr. Ackerman, set up blankets for their picnic they would have that afternoon.

All morning and for most of the afternoon they played, ate, ran along the shore, and the boys held races. Samuel and Margaret won, being the oldest there. Samuel was sixteen now and was growing into a fine young man. But he was still just as quiet as ever, only speaking through the music he created.

Seagulls flew overhead and cawed in the lovely April day. It was chilly, but that did not stop everyone from playing in the waves. Margaret splashed Rachel who squealed in surprise.

"Let's go warm up," Margaret said with chattering teeth.

"Good idea," Rachel laughed.

The sun was warm, but getting wet in the strong breeze was enough to turn their lips slightly blue. The girls left the boys who were still playing in the ocean, trying to drown each other.

"Here you go girls," Gabriella tossed them towels as they ran up to the little place they had set up to picnic at.

"Thanks," Margaret wrapped it around herself tightly.

"I'm freezing." Rachel sat down on the blanket as Gabriella handed out sandwiches.

"Where's Mr. Ackerman?" Margaret asked.

"He went to go get some things out of the car. He'll be back shortly." Gabriella assured her.

"Where's Betty?" Rachel spoke up as she took her lunch from Gabriella and passed a sandwich to Margaret as well.

Gabriella only inclined her head towards the boardwalk. The girls looked to where she had gestured.

"Betty's talking to a man!" Rachel gasped.

"Rachel!" Margaret laughed. "It's not a crime."

"But who's she talking to?" Rachel asked again, very curious. She was always enthralled with a little bit of drama.

"Looks like we're going to find out." Margaret remarked as she saw Betty walking back their way with the man beside her.

"He's too short." Rachel quickly said. "Is that a navy uniform? He doesn't look old enough for Betty."

Margaret and her mother exchanged amused looks. Thankfully, Rachel quieted down as the two of them approached. The man looked kind and though he did look young, he probably wasn't as young as he looked. Suddenly, Margaret recognized him. He was the same man whose foot Betty had stomped on during their first visit to Coney Island.

"Gabriella, Meg, Rachel, this is Ted Wallace." Betty introduced them.

"Pleased to meet you, Ted." Gabriella greeted him with a warm smile.

"Pleased to meet you, ma'am," he tugged slightly on the brim of his cap he wore. "And you two as well." He addressed Margaret and Rachel.

"We've met a few times before. Funny how we keep bumping into each other..." Betty glanced at him with quite a look in her eyes.

Margaret called it then and there that something would start between them. She merely smiled and invited the young man to join them for dinner. The boys were all coming back to shore now with chattering teeth and blue-tinged lips. It was time for lunch and what a happy gathering they all made. Margaret could hardly have been happier. However, it hit her out of the blue when she caught a glimpse of the ocean's horizon...

The breath caught in her throat. She hoped no one noticed. No matter how long it had been since she moved to New York, she still missed her father and Bess and Harry... *Oh, Harry.* From her spot on the picnic blanket, she stared into the distance over Rachel's shoulder. It felt like she had taken a blow to the stomach. The homesickness washed over her with such a force. She tore her gaze away from the horizon... the horizon that led to home, and down to her hands that rested in her lap.

"Meg?" Rachel whispered to her.

Everyone was talking and laughing, so no one noticed, except perhaps Gabriella.

"I'm alright." She forced a smile.

The look on Rachel's face seemed to ask, *are you sure?*

"At least I will be." She took her friend's hand. "Don't worry about me."

Rachel gave a weak smile.

Margaret shook herself of her thoughts and turned back to the conversations going on around her. She tried to focus on what people were saying, but she couldn't help but wonder about the feelings stirring inside of her. Usually she only felt this wretched and homesick when she thought of her father and her home and Bess... But this was something else entirely. She realized with a little bit of fear and not a small amount of shock what this was about.

This was about Harry.

---

Harry jogged from a hangar that sheltered a beautiful, deadly Beaufighter, to the barracks that housed the multiple squadrons and scores of pilots.

"Where are you going?" Val called out to him in the dim light of twilight.

"I have something to do! Give me ten minutes?" Harry called back.

Val gave him a mock salute in response. Harry and Val were supposed to be doing checks on the planes, but no one would miss him for a few moments. He made his way to the public phone in the hallway entrance to the barracks. He dialled Margaret's home phone number and listened to the phone ring a few times.

"Hello, this is Betty." The friendly voice of a woman with a New York accent answered the phone.

"Hello Betty, could I speak to the birthday girl, please?" He inquired as he scratched his head, feeling mischievous.

"Who's this?"

"It's Harry."

"Just a minute," the short reply came and then Harry could hear Betty yelling for Margaret.

A few seconds passed before Harry was met with the lovely voice of his dear friend. "Hello? Who's this?" Margaret asked. Her voice seemed so gentle and happy. It was music to Harry's ears.

"Hello, Meg," He smiled as he replied quietly, treasuring her voice.

"Who is this?!" She asked with spunk.

Harry straightened up and furrowed his eyebrows. "I'm thoroughly offended you don't know who'd be calling you on your birthday." He laughed. "Forgotten me already?"

"Harry!" Margaret recognized his teasing. "Your voice has gotten so much deeper!" She exclaimed.

"Has it?"

"Must be because you're turning into an old man." She teased back.

He smiled. "Thanks for that." He chuckled. "Happy birthday!"

"Thank you! How are you? How is your squadron? Fly any exciting missions?" Margaret inquired.

"I'm afraid I can't tell you about our missions, but it *has* been going very well. And I'm fine, same as ever. What did you do for your birthday?" Harry leaned up against the wall and studied the blank white ceiling. As she spoke the next words, he felt loneliness wash over him stronger than ever... he *missed* her... terribly so.

"Well, we all went down to Coney Island and spent the morning and early afternoon there, now I was just opening up presents before we ate dinner. What have you been doing, Harry? It's so good to hear from you."

Harry realized how grown up she sounded.

"Val and I've been doing checks on planes today and looking for any damage." Harry responded. "Nothing nearly as exciting as your day."

"So tell me, are you in a great deal of danger every day? I worry about you." Margaret's voice was quiet.

Harry sighed, for he knew he couldn't tell her the truth; the truth was that he could die any day... they all could. Nothing was certain.

"I'll be alright, Meg, don't worry about me. I have some good pilots around me. They're sure to get me out of any tough spots."

"I'm glad, Harry." Margaret paused. "Please be careful."

Harry nodded, though he knew she couldn't see him. "I'll do my best." He thought for a moment, not wanting to hang up. "How's school? Are you out yet?"

"Finishing up in a few weeks,"

"I'm sure you'll be glad of that. You'll be an official graduate!" He grinned.

"You have no idea," she chuckled. "You know how much I love school." She added sarcastically.

"Any plans for after graduation? University? I know you had mentioned possibly getting a job in your last letter."

"I *have* thought about it... although I'm still not quite sure. I don't really know what direction to go. I supposed I just have to pray for guidance and try to make a good decision soon."

The phone's connection crackled.

"Harry?" Margaret checked to make sure he was still on the line.

"I'm here." He replied.

"I wish we could talk longer." Margaret knew it cost so very much to talk long distance.

"I know, I do too. We'll have to resolve ourselves to letters for the time being. I'm writing up one for you that I'll send off soon." Harry took a deep breath. "Well, I should let you go."

"Alright." Margaret sounded as reluctant as he felt. "Take care of yourself, Harry. Please be safe. God knows," her voice cracked, "I pray for you every day."

"I pray for you, too. And I'll be careful. I promise I will. Happy birthday; hopefully we'll be able to celebrate together one of these days." Harry couldn't quite think of what to say.

"Goodbye, Harry. And thank you for calling." Margaret's voice faded and they hung up simultaneously.

Parts of their conversation had been awkward and Harry had struggled to find questions and the words to say. Such things had never happened before between them. Harry wondered at it. Perhaps it was because they hadn't seen each other in so long, or because they had both grown up and turned into adults.

Sauntering back over to the hangar, Harry opened the access door and walked in to see Val on the wing of an impressive Avro Lancaster bomber.

"Were you talking to your girlfriend?" Val asked as he straddled one of the four engines' turbines to reach the prop.

Harry grinned weakly as he wrote down some things in a log book. "I was just talking to Margaret." He answered, distracted.

"Well, aren't they one in the same?" Val evaluated the yellow-tipped propeller.

Since they had both been mechanics, they were often chosen to look over the bombers, heavy fighters, and medium fighters to make sure they were in top condition and ready at a moment's notice.

Harry started circling the plane to look it over. "What? Think of Margaret as... well... more than a friend?" Harry thought for a moment and paused in his work. When he didn't reply, Val started up again.

"Harry, if there's one thing this bloody war has taught us is that life is short..." He paused to look at the propeller. Deeming it in good condition, he got up and continued. "We have to make the most of the time we have, wouldn't you agree?"

"But," he started to protest.

"If you like Meg, why not tell her?" Val, still high up on the wing, looked down to him. "It's clear to everyone that you do."

Harry, lost in thought, was merely staring at the log book in his hand.

"Eh," Val squatted down and threw a rag at Harry which hit him in the face. "Why not?" He grinned mischievously and then went back to work.

Harry put the rag in his back pocket and thought about what Val had said. *Do I really like Meg more than just as a friend?* A pit forming in his stomach, Harry knew that it was a question he knew the answer to; he just didn't want to face it.

# Chapter 20

"Cav? You awake?" Val asked from his bottom bunk and Harry's eyes fluttered open. For once they were sleeping at night, something that they had only known off and on for the past few months at Predannack.

"Why, you want a bedtime story?"

Silence.

"About the verse you told me this morning..." Val started.

By 'this morning' Val meant at 3 o'clock in the morning when they had gone out for a night bombing over Brest, France to destroy any of the transport ships that would be going into the harbor. They had been successful. Five transport ships had been reduced to burning rubble. The pilots were rewarded with being able to sleep for the entirety of the next night.

"Yeah?" Harry rolled unto his stomach. He had been at that critical moment when one is trying to fall asleep, either he would drift off, or if anything dared to stir him, he probably wouldn't be able to fall asleep at all that night.

"When someone says they have faith without works and vice versa... Does that mean that if someone who does good things but doesn't believe, won't go to heaven?" Val was obviously confused. Harry thought it must have been because of their lack of sleep.

"I believe so." Harry closed his eyes.

"Hmmm..." Val mused. "But what if-"

Harry cut him off unkindly. "Really, Val, I don't know. Just go to bed." Harry rolled over and fell right asleep.

The next morning was chilly, but promised to warm up throughout the day. Harry met Val outside and together they silently watched the other pilots play a rousing game of football to pass the time and keep warm before their mission. Val looked irritated and Harry tried to smooth things over.

"Want to join them?" He asked.

"Go ahead." Val replied.

A moment of awkward silence passed before Harry spoke up. "I'm sorry about being short. I was tired."

Val sighed. "It's alright. I know we've all been short on sleep lately. No one wants to talk theology that late at night anyway." He clearly was accepting of Harry's apology.

"When someone does a lot of good things, but doesn't have faith in God, it still doesn't mean they will go to Heaven. There's no way we can earn our salvation. It's a given gift we accept and because we accept it, it changes our actions. Does that make sense?"

Val nodded and took in the words. "It does, that." He looked like he was pondering the implications of such words. "I never really heard it explained that way, and I grew up in the church." He chuckled.

"What church did you go to?" Harry asked.

"My family's catholic. So we were actually told, it seems, kind of the opposite."

Harry nodded and their conversation lapsed.

"Any more thoughts about you know who?"

Harry glanced at him out of the corner of his eye. "Who?"

Val scoffed. "I don't know what she sees in you. You're clearly not very bright." He shook his head and ran out to the field.

Guy had the ball and kicked it lightly between his feet, running towards their makeshift goal with all the other aces chasing behind him. Their little game wouldn't be kindly looked upon by Wing Commander Millward, their new squadron leader. He was a tough nut and had received extremely prodigious honours years ago. All the men were afraid of him yet greatly respected him.

Harry jogged out to the field. He ran up to Guy and immediately stole the ball from him with a triumphant cry. Running down the field, kicking the ball carefully in front of him, he passed around the other pilots and kicked it into the goal. Cheers went up and Harry raised his arms up in victory. He may not have been adept at facing his feelings, but at least he could still score a goal.

---

Margaret was in the kitchen with Betty learning how to make bread from the zucchini's that had come straight from their garden when the doorbell rang. Betty, with her yellow apron on, went to the door and answered it. Margaret paused from her cooking to look over into the foyer.

Louis was right on Betty's heels and he was headed for the open door. Margaret bolted for the corgi and picked him up in her arms. As she straightened up, she saw the face of someone she never expected to see in her house. Nearly dropping the squirming dog, Margaret's mouth opened in surprise.

"Miss Archer!" Margaret gasped.

"Hello," The lady, who was as pretty as a movie star, smiled.

"This lady says she knows you, Meg?" Betty closed the door behind Dorothy.

"Yes," Margaret put Louis down and furrowed her eyebrows with contemplation. "We met on board the *Aquitania.*" Margaret could remember the lady very well. Lately, she could have sworn she had seen her here and there, but never well enough to know for sure if it was her.

"She has a wonderful ability with the violin." Dorothy recalled.

"Would you like to sit in the living room?" Betty offered and took off her apron. Margaret did as well.

"Thank you," Dorothy smiled pleasantly and revealed shining white teeth.

"Can I get you some coffee or tea?" Betty asked as Margaret led the woman into the living room.

"No, thank you," Dorothy replied and sat down on a chair in the living room.

A terrible cacophony could be heard from the studio several floors up and it made Margaret blush. They were all obviously still trying to learn Samuel's new composition.

"What a musical house!" Dorothy commented.

Margaret sat down across from Dorothy and sat on her hands rigidly. She was a bit nervous and perplexed all at the same time. "Yes, they're always playing."

Dorothy nodded. "I heard you were playing in Carnegie's Chamber Music Hall. Then I had the luck of bumping into the director of the hall while he was talking to Mr. Ackerman. I then asked about where your musical school was located and he gladly told me when he heard how I was part of the New York Phil." As Dorothy finished her account, Betty walked in and sat down by Margaret. "Perhaps we can get down to business..." Dorothy opened her purse and Betty and Margaret exchanged curious glances.

"Excuse me, Miss Archer," Betty furrowed her eyebrows. She wanted to proceed carefully, especially because Gabriella couldn't be there, for she was in the middle of Cassie's piano lesson and everyone knew that Cassie's lessons could never be interrupted. "But what sort of business are we talking about?"

Margaret nodded in agreement.

"Well, I was merely wondering if you would like some lessons from the violinist of the New York Philharmonic?" Dorothy withdrew a pamphlet and handed it to Margaret.

It was a picture of a fashionable woman with a violin on her shoulder. She was smiling at the camera and above the picture were the words, *'Carnegie Hall Welcomes the Esteemed Violinist Henrietta Von Reyna.'*

"Me?" Margaret looked up to Dorothy. She was shocked.

Dorothy nodded. "Your talents with the violin are incredible."

"But..." Betty looked at the pamphlet and handed it back. "Meg plays the cello."

Dorothy looked surprised. "The cello? My goodness! A violinist *and* cellist prodigy! Perhaps I could speak with my colleague then, Professor Seymour. He is an honoured cellist in the philharmonic."

Margaret couldn't believe her ears. "Why are you offering this to me? I mean, all the others are so talented as well and... well I'd just feel strange taking lessons without them." Margaret sank into her chair.

"Your consideration and humility does you credit." Dorothy smiled. "I could pull some strings."

Margaret thought for a moment and glanced at Betty.

"It's quite the opportunity and I don't offer this lightly. I believe your friend, the flutist, is about your age. You two could take lessons together; you from Mr. Seymour and your friend from me. It's not every day I meet young people who have the talent your little orchestra has."

Taking a deep breath, Margaret nodded. "Alright. If Rachel can take lessons with me, I'll do it."

"Wonderful." The woman smiled, her red lips parting to reveal the whitest of teeth.

"And where will this be?" Betty asked about the logistics. "You said this Mr. Seymour's a professor?"

"Yes, that's right. His private studio's at Julliard."

"Julliard?!" Margaret was shocked.

Dorothy smiled again. "Monday's are his lesson days. Even though school's out for the summer, he still works there around four days a week, giving lessons and such. Swing by around noon next Monday and I'll introduce you. Be sure to bring Rachel as well." She stood up.

Margaret and Betty rose to their feet too and shook hands with the flutist.

"Thank you so much, Miss Archer. I truly can't thank you enough. I mean, it's been so long since we met on the Aquitania; this is rather a surprise, but thank you, truly."

"My pleasure, dear. We'll be looking forward to it." Dorothy gave her a friendly wink and bid farewell to them.

Margaret couldn't quite believe it... she was to be taking lessons over the summer at *Julliard!*

Margaret wrote to her father late that night and explained everything to him. She knew he would be proud of her. It had always been his desire to see her go to university and now it had finally happened, although not officially. She would be learning from a master and her self-taught skills would be polished to perfection.

Margaret had also kept her eyes open for a job. However, all the positions she had looked into just hadn't felt right for some reason. Nothing quite fit and she had grown frustrated in her job search. Although she still felt like she needed to do something for her country. She could, like she had thought back during the winter, become a nurse, but the sight of blood always made her queasy. She could be a journalist, but she didn't know how to write well and employers would be looking for someone with more experience. Perhaps she could get a job at Juilliard if she was to be taking lessons there soon. But that wouldn't help the war effort. And so her thoughts went round and round... She had heard Betty talk about applying for a job down at one of the factories. That was her only lead she just might follow up on. But she needed to think about it and she asked for her father's advice in her letter. He always had some insight and wisdom to counsel her in the right direction.

As Margaret finished writing her letter in her quiet room, she heard her mother come in.

"Yes?" Margaret turned around on her little stool.

"You'd better come down... We're all in such a state. Mrs. Moser is here."

*Not again,* Margaret thought as she rolled her eyes. Mrs. Moser had come a few times before to check in on her twins. She was very kind and courteous, but she hated the music and it seemed like she only let her boys stay at the house so they were out of her hair. Margaret followed her mother out of her room.

"What does she say this time?" Margaret asked her.

"Well, that's just it." Margaret's mother led the way down the stairs. "She doesn't say anything in particular... She *wants* something this time. And I'm afraid she wants her twins."

"What?!" Margaret stopped on the stairs. Gabriella looked up to her.

"She's come to get them. She says she has a job at a factory over on Long Island and while she works, there are child care rooms set up now and an apartment to go home to. Mrs. Moser is adamant and the twins are so distraught."

"But she can't!" Margaret trotted down the stairs ahead of her mother.

"I'm afraid she can!" Gabriella called after Margaret.

When Margaret reached the main floor, she saw that Mrs. Moser was standing in the foyer with her arms across her chest. It looked like her patience was being stretched to the limit.

"I tell you, Miss Sutton!" She looked up to Gabriella. "If you don't hurry those boys up, I'll..." She shook her head.

"They will be right down, Mrs. Moser, I assure you. They were just collecting their things. We were very surprised to see you tonight." Gabriella calmly spoke to the lady. "Perhaps coming back in a day or two would suit better. Tony and Frankie would be more ready."

"I'm not waiting. I'm sorry I didn't write, but I just got this job a few days ago and I didn't have the time." Mrs. Moser didn't look very sorry.

Almost as though the twins were being sentenced to jail, they slowly made their way down the stairs with their suitcases at their sides. Rachel followed them with their two instrument cases. Even though their mother didn't like when they played, she had allowed them to bring their instruments home.

As the two crestfallen faces reached the bottom of the stairs, Mrs.

Moser said, "What a sight you two are. Come on, hurry up." She ruffled Tony's hair. "We can come and visit whenever you like, if that'll make you both happy.

They still didn't look too happy.

Pitcher and Grubbs were standing on the stairs behind them.

"Can't they stay another week?" Grubbs begged.

"Yeah, we just got out of school!" Pitcher added.

"Please?" Frankie and Tony both said at once.

"I'm not taking a taxi all the way home and all the way back here in a few days just so you can have more time to play. Say your goodbyes to your friends." The twins grudgingly obliged. "We'll visit soon. Thank you for all you've done with them, Miss Sutton and Miss Shea," She smiled to Betty who had joined everyone in the foyer.

Everyone gave them hugs and well wishes.

"Be good, boys," Margaret said as she gave them both hugs. "Don't worry, we'll visit." She smiled and assured them, wiping a dirt smudge from Frankie's cheek.

"Bye Meg," he smiled sadly.

The twins' mother left first and they followed slowly, waving and saying goodbye over their shoulders.

"Hopefully no more goodbyes for a very long time," Margaret sighed.

Rachel and her mother came up beside her as the boys stood in front of them waving, watching the taxi drive down the road.

---

For the last time, Harry flew the Bristol Beaufighter over the Predannack RAF base. To his left, the English Channel's dark blue waters were rippling with white foam on the crests of waves. The cliffs that he had grown so accustomed to seeing looked even more beautiful in the twilight. The dark boulders rose out of the sea and the waves crashed into them. Grey, black, and green rocks and hills met the onslaught of the channel as white spray shot into the air. Climbing in height, the minor details faded. The orange and purple and pink sky silhouetted the formation of the squadron. They were being transferred to North Yorkshire to a small city east of Leeds. In the village of Church Fenton there was an RAF base waiting for their defence abilities. They would provide protection to the cities of Leeds, Sheffield, Humberside, and Bradford.

Harry looked to Val in his Beaufighter that was right beside him. They gave each other a thumbs-up and continued to fly in formation. It would be a long night, but Harry had become nearly nocturnal over the past few months. He slept during the day and was up all night; it was starting to feel normal. True, it was hardly what he had been used to years ago. But then again, he wasn't the boy he was years ago. He was twenty today, for it was September 1st, 1942. How Harry had lived that long, he didn't know. But he thanked God every day and prayed for his comrades' safety.

The sun set and the brilliant colours of a Cornwall sunset gave way to the dark purples and blues of the night as they flew north. The stars shone and Harry found himself settling into the Beaufighter's seat and relaxing, something he hadn't done in a plane since he flew the Harvard back at Brize Norton. Every time he had sat in a Beau since joining the 600 Squadron, he was being shot at, shooting at something, or dropping bombs. The night wore on and he thought about Margaret. More and more he had been thinking about her. Reminding himself to write to her once he landed, he switched to thinking about Richard. He had finally received a note from his brother a few days ago for his birthday. Richard was going with Dr. Wells, the doctor from Oxford to North Africa. He gave no other information, besides wishing Harry a happy 20th birthday.

He wondered what Evan would be doing if he were still alive. No doubt he'd be fighting with the British Army somewhere; Russia, North Africa, Europe... the ground forces were made of stern stuff. Harry didn't know how they were doing it, as they seemed to have the hardest job out of all the Allied forces, fighting through the mud and carnage of the front lines. It was unimaginable. He knew he hadn't properly mourned his brother's death, but there was always something else to think about. His missions required his full attention and thinking about Evan when he was trying to rest only resulted in him not being able to fall asleep. So, he tucked that piece of himself deep, deep down. Maybe when this was all over, he'd let it sink in that one of his brothers wasn't coming home from this war.

Unintentionally, Harry thought back to Margaret. They still wrote to each other, giving out information and updates to what they had been doing. But an unseen, unwritten tension was between them. Harry knew what it was, and he had no idea how to approach the situation. Thinking back to earlier that day, he smiled. He had reluctantly shown Val one of Margaret's letters and he had said some choice things about her script.

They had been sleeping on and off with the blackout curtains up. Nonetheless, the sun still shone through despite their efforts to block it out and get some rest.

"Is it from Meg?" Val had asked quite out of the blue from his bottom bunk.

Harry supposed he had seen him reading one of her letters.

"Yeah, it is."

"Let me see it."

They had spoken quietly so they wouldn't wake the other pilots, as there were at least twenty-five other bunks in the large room on the first floor of the barracks. Harry hung his arm over the side of his top bunk. Val reached up without moving his head that was plastered against his pillow. He took the letter and started to read. There was just enough light coming in for him to make it out.

A few seconds of silence elapsed before he spoke up. "Clearly she likes you."

Harry furrowed his brow. "How do you come by that?"

"She says, *my dear*, and *please be safe*." He spoke in a girlish voice. "She likes you, no doubt. She may not know it yet, but shouldn't take her long to figure it out. Girls can be fickle though, so don't take my word for it."

Harry looked over his bunk and saw Val reading the letter.

"If you don't tell her, you'll be the death of us all." Val reached his arm back up and Harry took the letter. He tucked it in the pages of his small Bible, his only possession he kept with him. "You're distracted." Val continued. "You haven't been yourself lately. It's dangerous. Tell her for all our sake's."

"Would you shut up?!" A man hissed from across the room.

*Her.* Harry lay back down in his bunk. *Since when did that word suddenly have a name; a face; and have so much weight and meaning?* He had fallen asleep thinking such thoughts.

Harry took a deep breath and blinked away the recollection. He was flying a plane. He couldn't daydream or be distracted by thoughts of her. Putting all his attention back on his controls, gauges, switches, and the like, he tightened his grip on the yoke of the Beaufighter. A few more hours and they would be in North Yorkshire for the start of their next assignment, protecting the skies of Britain.

---

The trees were turning, and the air was crisp. Margaret came alive during the fall. She inhaled the cool air and pulled the collar of her wool coat closer about her neck. Her black heels clacked on the pavement as she made her way through Central Park. Geese could be heard honking some ways off, taking off from a pond that was no doubt steaming in the chilly morning. They reminded her of the ducks she used to feed at Regent's. She loved New York, but her heart would always be in London. *One step at a time, Meg.* She told herself. *Wars don't last forever.*

As she made her morning commute through Central Park, she was not alone. Rachel walked with her, for Dorothy Archer had offered to give Rachel flute lessons while Margaret took lessons from Mr. Seymour. The two girls thought they were the luckiest in the world.

Margaret led the way on the paths she knew so well. Rachel kept up with her brisk pace. They had taken lessons all throughout the summer and had loved every minute of it. Since they had made so much progress, Miss Archer and Mr. Seymour had offered to continue their lessons into the school year. Rachel was excused from morning classes at her school so she could continue her lessons. She was more than thrilled at the opportunity. And Margaret had graduated, so she had more free time on her hands than she knew what to do with until she figured out what she wanted to do in regards to university.

With their cases in tow, they crossed Central Park and made their way to Lincoln Center where the Juilliard School was. Coming upon the school, Margaret admired the fall flowers and shrubs that were still blossoming in the autumnal sun. It was almost as lovely as Christmas... Almost.

There were students everywhere when the two girls entered the school. They quietly made their way through the halls until they reached Mr. Seymour's office and personal small studio room. The other students paid them no attention, for they all had classes to attend and things to practice and study. Margaret couldn't help but feel a little out of place since she and Rachel weren't officially attending any classes or courses. Nonetheless, she opened the office door with resolve and they both entered.

"Good morning, Meg, Rachel." Mr. Seymour, the professor with round spectacles, rotund, full cheeks, and kind eyes, invited the girls in. "Miss Archer will be with us in a jiffy." He motioned for them to sit. Someone else entered the room and Mr. Seymour looked up. "Ah, Arthur, I'm glad to see you."

Mr. Seymour went to his desk as a young blonde man entered the room.

"Here is your paperwork." Mr. Seymour handed Arthur a bunch of papers and then the man left the room. "Mr. Winifred is leaving Juilliard for the US Army, good, brave man he is." Mr. Seymour sighed. "We must all do our part." He clapped his hands together. "Now! To stations!"

Miss Archer and Rachel went in the studio while Mr. Seymour and Margaret stayed in his office.

"Now, we will be looking at chords today and..." Mr. Seymour trailed off when he saw that Margaret was looking out the window. "Meg?" He pulled her attention back. "What is it?"

"Nothing, I'm so sorry, Mr. Seymour." Margaret apologized and repositioned the cello between her knees, embarrassed she had been distracted.

The professor smiled with amusement. "I'll give you something challenging then this week. Play the piece you learned last week, Haydn's Serenade." Mr. Seymour leaned forward and listened to every note Margaret played.

Never had Margaret's work been so scrutinized. Her music had always come from her heart, no matter if she did the vibrato correctly or not. Now, she was being turned from a prodigy to a professional and she was learning to love it.

"Good, good!" Mr. Seymour praised her. He gave her some tips and pointers which made the song sound even better. "Would you please play Vivaldi's Cello Concerto now?"

"Which key, Mr. Seymour?" Margaret asked and the professor chuckled.

"C minor please. Just play the first movement." He smiled.

Margaret thought for a moment and then placed her fingers on the neck of her cello. She played the song flawlessly and Mr. Seymour raised his eyebrows when she was finished.

"And here I thought that was a challenge!" He chuckled. "I should know by now... Three and a half months with the most talented cellist I've ever taught." He shook his head with disbelief.

Margaret looked up to him curiously. "Really, Mr. Seymour?" She was touched by his kind words.

"Really, Miss Margaret Sutton. You are a natural." He got up and went to his desk.

Pulling out a few pieces of paper, he set them on the empty music stand to her left. It was two pieces of sheet music. He took another piece from the collection and sat down at the small upright piano in the corner of his office.

"Now, shall we play that? It is an original composition done by one of the students here at Juilliard."

Margaret scanned the sheets and then nodded. Mr. Seymour sat down at the piano to accompany her. The piano started up and played a few bars before the cello part joined in the duet. Margaret played the first few notes, but she was lost. Something in her mind couldn't connect with the song. Mr. Seymour stopped and then started playing the piano again to let Margaret read the music through once more. However, she still couldn't get it.

Not knowing why, Margaret stopped, as did her teacher. "I'm not quite sure... I don't know the melody I'm supposed to play."

"What is it that you can't understand?" Mr. Seymour asked kindly and got up to stand behind her. The sheet music was not at all difficult. When Margaret didn't reply, the professor added, "I believe I've found your trick." He went back to the piano.

"Trick?"

"Have you ever played Simon Says?" He asked her.

"Of course," Margaret nodded.

"Alright, we're going to play Simon Says with a piano and cello." He played a simple melody of eight notes that Margaret repeated to perfection.

She brought her bow off of the strings as the professor continued. He played another melody, this time it was thirty seconds of Vivaldi's

Spring. Margaret repeated the notes. Lastly, he played the melody that Margaret couldn't grasp. She played it without any hesitation.

"I've got it." He got up from the piano and stood in front of the cellist.

Mr. Seymour pressed his lips together, nodded his head with satisfaction, and clasped his hands together.

"Most of the young prodigies that come here have this habit. They can play any song as long as they hear it." He pointed to his ear. "This ability is wonderful, but sometimes it is not desirable for orchestras or any song that you haven't heard before, such as this melody. Now..." He pointed to the sheet music. "It gives us clues..." Mr. Seymour pointed to the writing above the bars. "Very slowly, with feeling. You don't need to hear a song to feel it, even though it is easier. Close your eyes." He instructed her. Margaret did. "What does a song that goes very slowly and has feeling sound like? What would the composer be thinking?"

Margaret thought for a second and thought about what she felt when she had created A Butterfly's Flight and the piano improvisation. "He or she might feel that they are reminiscing about something, either sad or happy." Margaret replied.

"Good, now look..." Mr. Seymour brought over a Beethoven sheet music book for piano. "Tempo is another key that you can look at to draw feeling from the song. *Presto* means very fast. *Vivace* means lively. *Allegro* means fast. *Andante* means walking tempo. *Adagio* means slow. Do you understand?"

"Yes, I do." Margaret replied.

The professor nodded excitedly. "Wonderful! Now there are more, *moderato, ritardando, accelerando, largo*... I could go on and on. But what you can do is memorize these. It will give you keys along with the feeling of the song. When you are in an orchestra, say with Samuel composing," the friendly composer explained things to Margaret patiently. "Look at his expression. Is he sad? Mad? Contradicting? Happy? Lively? You will learn to grasp the feel from the composer, you don't even need to hear the song before it radiates off your instrument. Also, next week we will study timing more. I believe that's something that's causing you to trip up. We'll look at some more of the complicated measures and timing of certain notes. This will help you immensely when it comes to sight-reading and learning new pieces without ever hearing them. Am I making any sense?" He asked, knowing that when he got excited about music, he could ramble on and on.

"It makes perfect sense. Thank you, Mr. Seymour," Margaret smiled widely and knew that with every lesson her knowledge would grow more and more.

# Chapter 21

"That's the last of 'em." Margaret dumped the massive zucchinis on the counter in the kitchen and Betty shook her head with fascination and amazement that zucchinis could grow so big.

Victory Gardens had sprouted up everywhere that year and now the growing season was over. The zucchinis that had been hiding underneath the massive prickly leaves were now as big as baseball bats. They probably tasted horrible. It took Pitcher everything in him to keep from using one during his friends' baseball games in Central Park. Margaret laughed when she thought of Pitcher swinging a zucchini instead of a wooden bat.

"More bread then..." Betty set to work chopping the five massive vegetables.

Margaret helped as much as she could before her next lesson. Rachel was getting more and more excited with every lesson that passed by. Miss Archer was extremely helpful and Margaret had noticed a change in Rachel. She was trying to be less of a moll and more of a mature musician. Margaret was proud of her.

The fall colors were in full bloom in Central Park as the cold October wind blew down from Canada.

Soon, it would be winter.

---

Harry shivered in his aviator's jacket and wished he had put on a few more layers. Fall in North Yorkshire was almost as cold as winter in Cornwall. Here in the north of England, they flew more night missions and patrols around the densely populated cities. They flew some night sorties out across the North Sea and attacked transport ships and planes that were lurking about. From those missions, Harry had sent several planes hurting to the sea and his successes made him proud. He was now somewhat respected around the older pilots and aces, but he still preferred Val's company and his faithful friendship.

Church Fenton was a small village in the north of England and was very subdued and unassuming. Harry relished the peace, for the night raids he went on frequently were taking their toll. He was tired. More tired than he had ever been in his life. And it was cold. So cold that his teeth chattered audibly every time he went outside. The barracks were fairly new and were clean and comfortable; however, they did little to keep out the drafts that always found a way in under a windowsill or over a door's trim.

Harry woke up one October evening at 1900 hours and got dressed in multiple layers. He didn't know whether they would be called into action that night or not. This past week he had only gone out once and had quietly savoured the small respite. Val silently mirrored Harry's actions and they strode out into the cold night. Harry checked in with Wing Commander Millward and he said they would go out at around 0100 hours for a transport raid in the harbor and surrounding areas of Wilhelmshaven, Germany. There was a formation of Messerschmitt ME 323s that would be delivering supplies to the Germans on the offensive in Rostov, Russia. Near Wilhelmshaven, they would intercept them and 'seek out and destroy the enemy.' Harry was not looking forward to the raid. Many planes had been lost near Wilhelmshaven and the other port cities near Bremerhaven and Cuxhaven. Any bombings over Germany were dangerous and this one proved to be as well. Harry decided to break the news to Val, who had gone to the Mess.

As Harry was walking to the Mess, he spotted another group of men headed for the dark building. No light came from the windows, for they were blacked out, but Harry's attention was caught by one of them. He sauntered like an old man and walked with a hunch.

"Rob?" Harry jogged forward, wondering if it could be his friend he had met during the last years of his schooling in London.

The young man stopped and turned to Harry. "Well, well, well, I never expected to see you here..." Robert shook his hand.

"Rob! It's good to see you in one piece!" Harry slapped him on the back.

"Nice to see you too, Harry." Rob said as they entered the Mess. "What have you been flying?"

"Beaus," Harry replied. "And you? Are you still with the ATC?"

"No, I graduated from the Training Corps a few months ago. Now I'm with the 85th Squadron, flying night patrols, intercepting raiders, that sort of thing."

"We've been doing a bit of the same as well." Harry took his dinner over to the table where he, Guy, and Val always ate.

Introductions were made and Rob sat with them for a bit, recounting stories of sorties over France and how the 85th Squadron had lost seventeen pilots during the air battles there. All the men grew somber when recounts of losses were told. It made them realize that it could be them and they were never promised tomorrow.

Harry's hands were shaking. Oddly enough, it wasn't from the raid he had just gotten back from. Their formation had shot down four enemy ME 323's, and three fighter escorts. Harry boasted one of those victories. The raid had been dangerous, but they had only lost one Beau to the sea and the pilot had parachuted out in time. Coastal Command would be notified and the pilot rescued, for he went down not far from England's shore.

But no, the letter in Harry's hand was what made him nervous. He sat at a table in the Mess at 0600 hours and took a deep breath. The letter was from Reverend Sutton, and it was a reply to his inquiry about Margaret and an acknowledgment of his feelings for her. Harry still couldn't believe that he had written to the reverend at Lily's End and asked if he could speak to Margaret about his love for her. Ripping open the envelope, Harry read the formal, neat handwriting.

'Harry,

I am happy to hear from you. It seems like so long ago you were here with your family last Christmas. In truth, I had become accustomed to your presence and relied on it for a smile or a laugh. Ever since you moved here when you were six, you were like another child to me.

Often, I have wondered what would come about when or if your friendship with Margaret ever grew to anything more. I knew what I would say, and I know how I feel. But seeing as I cannot speak to you and look you in the eye, a letter will have to do and I hope I am clear and understood.

Margaret is still young.'

Harry paused and took a deep breath. *This isn't a good sign...* He kept reading.

'And I hope that you would respect her and honour her as you *honour and love and respect your friends and family. I give you my permission to speak to Margaret about how you feel. But as I said, if she writes to me and is troubled, it will not be pleasant for either of us.*

*My last piece of advice would be not to rush into things. Of course, the war and our peers tell us otherwise, but the Lord says to be anxious for nothing, but in everything by prayer and supplication, with thanksgiving, let your requests be made known to God. Let your desires be made known to Him who comforts. And pray, Harry. Pray that in these dark times we all will seek and find what He wills for us.*

*Reverend Frank Sutton*

*Lily's End Church.'*

Harry smiled wide and rubbed the back of his neck in relief. Not even flying could compare to what he felt. Grabbing the letter, he ran from the Mess, almost bumped into Wing Commander Millward, and ran all the way back to the barracks. Harry ran past Val who looked at him with furrowed eyebrows.

"Harry? S'everything alright?"

He grinned stupidly in reply. "Everything's just grand, Val." He held up the reverend's letter.

Val shook his head in amusement and called after Harry, "It's about bloody time!"

By 0430 hours, Harry had written a thank you to the reverend and a letter to Margaret all at the same time. He sealed both letters and had dropped them into the post bag. No longer would he head into the fray with troubling thoughts... He had spoken from his heart. Now he just had to wait and see what her response would be.

---

"Meg!" Rachel's voice came from the base of the attic's stairs.

Margaret rolled her eyes and shouted back. "What?!"

She was busy setting out her new clothes and moving out the old ones she had brought with from England three and a half years ago. *How time flies...* Margaret couldn't help but think as she looked fondly at the blue and white polka-dotted dress she had worn when she first arrived on the *RMS Aquitania*. It didn't even fit her now.

"It's a letter!" Rachel yelled up. Margaret went to the attic's stairwell and met Rachel halfway.

"Thanks," She smiled and took the letter that was from Harry.

No doubt it was another letter that described how much he wished the war had never happened and how he couldn't tell her what he had been doing, besides the fact they were in North Yorkshire. Margaret set the letter on her bed and went back to moving out her clothes that didn't fit anymore. They were going to Rachel who would still fit in them.

About a half hour passed before Margaret was called down to dinner that evening. They had a hearty stew that satisfied their hungry stomachs and the ever-present zucchini bread they ate as dessert. Later that night, Margaret was working on her homework from Mr. Seymour in her room when Rachel came in and looked at the pile of clothes on Margaret's bed.

"Are those for me?" She asked with a smile. If there was one thing Rachel enjoyed, it was new clothes, even if they were hand-me-downs.

"They're all yours!" Margaret nonchalantly replied, her mind occupied with her homework.

Rachel left with the pile of clothes in her arms as Margaret continued to read about the differences between the baroque composers and the renaissance composers.

The next day was Sunday and all day Margaret was busy. She practiced her cello pieces all morning and then in the afternoon they went to the Carnegie Chamber Music Hall where Mr. Seymour, Miss Archer, and Miss Von Reyna gave them all tips and pointers and watched the performances they had worked so hard to master. Henrietta Von Reyna was in her thirties, had the curliest hair Margaret had ever seen, and was an amazing violinist. She coached Simone and Grace here and there, but mostly just watched the chamber orchestra with a pleased expression on her face. With the Steinway being played by Cassie behind them, the orchestra played Biber's Mystery Sonatas with sentiment and the sacred admiration they merited.

The letter was forgotten in the days that followed and Margaret was unaware of the stress she was causing Harry and even her father. She was completely absorbed in her lessons, her practicing, and the usual dreaminess that came over her when she was immersed in the world of music. Besides, she had gotten a cold as well and felt terribly under the weather. Between practicing and resting, she had little time for anything else. About a week later, Halloween was also almost forgotten as well. Grubbs and Pitcher had made ghost costumes out of sheets and had hidden in dark corners of the house to scare anyone that came near them. Margaret was caught by their pranks and was spooked multiple times. She retaliated by threatening to give them her cold by sneezing on them. They stopped spooking her after that.

      The quartet was taking the night off. Gabriella, Betty, Margaret, and Rachel were all going to see a movie. *Holiday Inn* was supposed to be very good, if anyone believed the critics' raving reviews, and even more so because it was a musical and Bing Crosby's vocal talents graced the stage. The four ladies excitedly entered the movie theatre in downtown Manhattan and sat in the seats, ready for the show to start. Marjorie Reynolds' and Virginia Dale's fashion was something all the women of New York City were trying to emulate. Betty and Gabriella spoke to themselves enthusiastically about what their friends had been saying about the motion picture. Margaret was just eager to hear the music, feel the holiday cheer, and enjoy herself.

      The lights went dark and everyone grew quiet as a few commercials played. However, the most interesting preview was when they played a newsreel. The footage started with planes flying and the announcer talking about the latest news from the war. It showed planes being shot down, crashing into the sea, and bursting into flame. The grainy footage flashed before Margaret's face. It made her hands go numb and cold. *What if that was Harry?* The newsman spoke about how the German offensive was progressing into Russia and explained Stalingrad's fierce fighting. It showed footage of machine gunfire dealing out shells relentlessly. Margaret's breath caught in her throat and she knew that all the people in the theatre felt the same way too. Then the newsman spoke about the Pacific Theater; the Solomon Islands' ground and air force battles, and the battle at Santa Cruz. Then they switched back to showing footage of more planes strafing a city. Margaret could hardly stand it. She remembered Harry's letter she had forgotten about and wanted to rush home and read it even if it was simply repetitive and he couldn't tell her anything...

      Margaret got up and whispered to her mother as she left, "I'll meet you at home. I don't feel very good." And it was the truth.

Gabriella watched her daughter leave with a quizzical look and followed her.

Stepping out into the cold air, Margaret pulled her coat tighter around her shoulders. Her breath came out in giant white puffs.

"Meg?" Gabriella trotted to catch up with her. "What's wrong?" She put her hand on her daughter's shoulder that was almost the same height as her own now.

"Oh mum," it was then that Margaret broke down. She burst into tears and put her head in her hands.

Gabriella hugged her and tried to sooth and comfort her. She had no words; and no words would do. However, she wondered why Margaret was crying. She had been acting strange; almost preoccupied, for the past several weeks and months.

"Why don't we walk home, and you tell me everything, alright?" She knew there was something going on.

Margaret stepped back and wiped the tears from her eyes with her black-gloved hands. "I've been angry..." she confessed quietly. "And confused and I don't know what to do... I almost feel ashamed."

They started walking home, arm in arm.

"Is it about Harry?"

Margaret nodded. "I feel like I love him, Mum. And I haven't read his latest letter because I just can't stand it... not knowing whether he feels the same way." Her voice rose in pitch, and she spoke swiftly. "I can't sleep; I can't eat. It's like there's this silent roar in my ear constantly and I can't get away from all these thoughts about him. I'll see a plane fly over and think of him. I'll see newsreels and wonder if I'll see him in any of them. I'll be playing the cello or walking in the park and wonder what he's doing or if he's safe. It's driving me mad! I can't get him out of my head... and then I wonder if I'm even supposed to. Maybe I'm not supposed to get him out of my head."

Her mother responded after a few moments of silence; letting the heat from Margaret's words die off. "Well... why don't you just ask him?"

"What?" Margaret scoffed.

"Ask him how he feels."

"Mum..."

"This is 1942, dear. We're modern women." She gently teased as they walked under some tall trees that bordered the quiet road they had chosen to take. "In all seriousness," she stopped and looked her daughter in the eyes that matched hers perfectly. "Harry seems like the best of young men. He'll understand. If correspondence between the two of you has felt strange for you, I'm sure he picks up on that and feels it too. Maybe he even feels the same way about you."

"What if he doesn't?" Margaret shrugged. "And what if he does, but he just doesn't have the courage to ask me? I know Harry's brave, but if he isn't bold enough to ask me first, I don't know if it would work between us."

"You worry too much." Gabriella offered her a kind smile, and they kept walking. "Take it from a woman who's learnt from her mistakes... I worried too much about whether or not I could take care of you and that made me miss out on seeing you grow up. If I had simply taken everything in stride, trusted God that He'd see us through, and relied on my husband's support, things would have been very different."

Margaret thought deeply about her mother's advice. It was one of the first times she had asked for it and she was astonished... She looked at her mother, wondering if that's why her father had fallen in love with her. She was wise. He was right, there *was* more to her than met the eye.

"How did you know Dad was the one you would marry?" Margaret asked.

Gabriella smiled; a true smile of a happy memory. "He was wonderful. He was unlike any other man. He drove me crazy." She chuckled. "I hated how he challenged me, but I needed it. I was too stuck in my ways. But over everything, he was kind. What you describe is how I felt, though. I couldn't think of anything else but him. And I know he felt the same way."

Margaret smiled to herself and held her mother's arm tighter. "Thank you."

Gabriella gave her hand a squeeze.

Back at the house, Margaret and her mother searched all around her room, yet they could not find Harry's letter. Margaret started to panic. She searched in her drawers, in her dresser, on her desk, on the floor, under her bed. However, she still couldn't find it. Standing up, Margaret put her hand to her forehead and thought.

"Could it have been tossed in the trash?" Gabriella asked.

"The clothes!" Margaret exclaimed. "Rachel!"

Margaret ran down the steps and didn't even respond to the boys' curious questions, for they were in the studio playing a game of tag. Bursting into Rachel's room, Margaret went to her dresser and started to look through it. Suddenly, she saw it hiding between two shirts.

"I found it!" She called to her mother.

Walking out of Rachel's room and stopping on the stairs at the end of the hallway, Margaret opened the letter that was bent and wrinkled. All Margaret had to do was read the first paragraph and then she stopped breathing. Gasping, she covered her hand with her mouth and sank down to sit on the stairs, tears falling onto Harry's script.

"You found it?" Gabriella was coming down the stairs. "Margaret? Are you alright?"

Margaret couldn't reply. She sat reading the letter again, this time slower. She read it again and again to make sure she understood it correctly.

The letter went like so,

'Dear Meg,

I hope this letter finds you well.

It's 4 in the morning here and my mind is reeling. But how can it not when I just had a letter from your father. He replied to the letter I sent him. You are no doubt asking why I sent him a letter. Well, dear Meg, I asked him permission to tell you about my heart.

The tension between us is entirely my fault and I cannot continue to speak to you without telling you how I feel. My heart has always been yours, Margaret, and if I may say so, you have such a hold of it in this present hour that I find it drives me every second of every hour of every day. Before missions, I pray that I will return and someday see your face again. How I wish I could look you in the eyes right now and see your reaction, your feelings, and your thoughts.

Your father encouraged me to pray and to be anxious for nothing. And yet I am told by this war and my peers to do the opposite. And no matter what, I will be patient, for I know this changes everything for us. Please, just tell me how you feel and tell me whether I have any chance with you. We have been friends for so long and I do not want this to ruin the friendship that we do have.

Harry Cavanaugh.'

"Oh, mum," Margaret broke into a grin through her tears.

Gabriella knew there was only one thing that could make a woman cry and laugh all at the same time. She sat beside her daughter as she told her everything.

Shortly after, Margaret turned on the little lamp on her desk and wrote back to Harry. Her mother left her to write back in peace. She took out a piece of paper and smiled to herself as she started her reply.

'Harry,

She wrote slowly and thoughtfully, trying to harness her emotions into words.

'Thank you for your letter. And thank you for asking Dad if you could ask me. I'm so sorry I took so long to respond. I lost your letter and only just found it.

I'm not quite sure how to even say the things I'm thinking, but I will try my best. I feel the same way for you, Harry. It came on so suddenly. I was sitting on the beach during our outing there for my birthday and it hit me like a wave... out of everyone I knew, I wanted you there the most. Perhaps I had always felt that way and I never knew it, but this feels completely different than what our friendship used to be.

I understand my father's concern about rushing into things. I think if we take things slowly, that would be wise. But my heart is yours as well. I can't imagine it belonging to anyone else. You are so wonderful and kind and protective and caring. I feel like the luckiest person in the world that you would dare to love me.

Please be safe. I pray for you every day.

Yours, Margaret.'

Even though she had to restart her letter several times, throwing the crumpled-up pieces of paper behind her, Margaret finally finished and was content with her reply. She sealed it and wrote a note to her father as well. She sent both off into the mail that afternoon.

The next day, Margaret stayed home while the others went for a stroll around cold Central Park. She had the entire house to herself...

except for Louis. He followed her around, wondering why the house was so quiet. Margaret sat at the piano in her stocking feet and closed her eyes. All the emotions that had coursed through her the previous day left her feeling tired and confused.

Margaret turned her mind to her music. She played an improvisation and simply let her emotions pour off of her. It was a simple, lovely melody that somehow reminded her of Harry. It had four sharps, giving it a cheerful feel. She played the simple chords with her left hand and the slow melody with her right. G sharp, F sharp, A. Her mind drifted and she began thinking of what he was doing far away. Suddenly, she thought of something. Margaret raced upstairs, took out two folded up sheets of paper that were worn and saw her handwriting and the notes she had written for *'A Butterfly's Flight'*. She folded up the pieces of paper again, and wrote a little note on the back of it.

*'I don't know if you'll be able to play this, but I wrote it and I hope it will make you think of home.'*

Margaret sealed the envelope with the sheet music inside and raced back down to the post office for the second time that day. Loretta's dreams were coming true. She teased Margaret's several letters to Harry, but this time Margaret didn't care. Now they were more than friends.

---

Harry let Margaret's delayed reply slide for a few weeks. He was a wreck, but he knew that Margaret might need time to reply or get her thoughts in order. Val thought he was crazy and so did Guy, but Harry took Reverend Sutton's words of wisdom to heart, *'Be anxious for nothing.'* It was hard, but Harry was determined. So determined was he that even when his squadron moved from Church Fenton back to Cornwall, Harry still didn't send any word to Margaret. The RAF base in Portreath was a stopover for USAAF, RAF, and RCAF planes bound to and from the Middle East and North Africa. It was just a matter of time before the 600 Squadron would be transferred out of England, bound for distant shores.

Harry prayed. Harry waited. And early in November, his patience was rewarded.

Harry was aglow. He felt such relief that Margaret had gotten back to him and she felt the same way he did. What their future held, he had no idea, but if he could, he would want her by his side. He had told her such things in his reply letter and that he was to leave the country soon. *One step at a time.* He told himself.

Harry and his fellow pilots from the RAF base, which sat on top of the cliffs, had ventured down to the little village of Portreath to enjoy their last night in England. For some, this would be the last time they looked on the green fields of Britain.

Wing Commander Millward had given them the evening off, for in the morning, they would fly from Portreath to Blida, Algeria, an RAF base that was taken by the British 11th Infantry Brigade not ten days before. The men talked as they walked down Lighthouse Hill about their briefing they had attended earlier that day. They would be part of a North African Campaign called 'Operation Torch.'

Harry could face anything now that he and Margaret were open about their feelings. He sauntered down the hill with his comrades at his side, Guy and Val. Rob was off a-ways chatting with some of the younger gunners. The view was incredible. To their right the cliffs fell away to the churning, frigid ocean far below. A cold wind blew up from the sea and the sight of the sunset was spectacular. In the little valley that wound down to the sea, the village of Portreath was nestled with its white houses among a sea of undulating green hills. Coming down from Lighthouse Hill, the band of pilots passed several cottages and received a few coy smiles from young female passers-by. The lads all went into the Portreath Arms and enjoyed themselves. They took off their aviator jackets to reveal their navy RAF uniforms and ordered food they hadn't touched for months or years. Harry ordered and sat with his friends at a table in the warm, busy pub.

The men laughed, joked, swapped stories, and enjoyed their evening off. Harry couldn't remember a time when he hadn't woken up at 1900 hours only to be sent off on a mission that lasted until 0300 hours the next morn. He was thankful for the respite, knowing they would all need fresh minds and clear heads for the upcoming flight. Besides, he couldn't help but think that it could be the last night he was in England. However, he pushed the thought away. He was to enjoy the evening, not worry about what was to come Over There.

Sitting at the table listening to a senior ace relate his story of landing on a frozen lake in the middle of Norway, Harry reread Margaret's letter. He was ecstatic with her reply, yet he hoped he could survive long enough return to see her. In the meantime, however, her presence in her letters was enough. He savoured every word she wrote. He glanced at the sheet music she had sent in a separate letter. He had learned to read music when Margaret had forced him to, so he was determined to figure out the melody. Oddly enough, there was an upright piano in the corner of the pub. *Now or never.* He knew finding a piano in North Africa would be near impossible. Harry got up and ignored the questions from Val and Guy.

He sat down on the swivel stool that was in front of the piano and tuned out all the laughter and talk. He put the two pieces of sheet music in front of him and took a deep breath. Slowly, he started to touch the keys and play the melody. A, B, C, those were easy enough. F sharp, G. He played the same notes over again and added the low octaves that were written above the melody with his left hand. The talk in the tavern quieted down and before Harry knew it, all the men were listening to the piano. Some of them wore dreamy expressions. Others looked intrigued. The song was titled *'A Butterfly's Flight.'* However, to them, it didn't sound like a butterfly, it sounded like home; like their children playing in the yard. It sounded like their families waving from the front porch. It sounded like their sweethearts' love letters. It reminded them of home and the sweet pleasures they had taken for granted before the war.

Harry finished the song he had played somewhat poorly and shrugged. He had never been much of a musician, but the men didn't care. It gave them a reminder of home when a reminder of it was much needed. Harry folded the sheet music and a few of the men clapped.

"Give this lad a pint for his playing!" A pilot clapped Harry on the back.

"Hip, hip, hoorah!" Val raised his cup for a toast and the other men raised theirs.

# Chapter 22

0500 hours. November 18th. The formation of Bristol Beaufighters followed their new Wing Commander B. W. White. It was around 1,600 km from Portreath to Blida and they had been flying for three hours. Just a little longer and they would be there. Once across the English Channel, they bypassed Brest so as not to fly over occupied France. The Pyrenees Mountains passed beneath them and looked like ripples in a carpet from their height as they passed over the French/Spanish border. The Spanish coast gave way to the Balearic Sea, a body of water Harry never dreamt of seeing, or even knew existed. He was nestled in the cockpit of his Beaufighter, in Wing Commander White's formation positioned to the left of the leader.

The sun began to rise and brilliantly reflected off the Mediterranean Sea.

Algeria was drawing near.

Harry spoke with his gunner, Fredric, or Fred as he was called by everyone. "See anything up there?"

Over Harry's radio, he heard Fred's voice. "Nothing. Clear skies as far as the eye can see." He wasn't far from Harry, but the noise of the duel Hercules engines was so loud, Harry would have had to yell without the radio.

The voice of their leader came in through the static and the great formation all heard his words. "Welcome to Algeria, men." He stated.

There were ten squadrons making their way to the airfield of Blida. In each squadron there were between ten and twelve aircraft. It was a large formation, but some of the senior aces boasted of flying in formations that were twice or three times as big.

Finally, the coast came into view. The blue of the sea and the sky seemed to blend, but there was a tan city with mountains and hills cutting between the ocean and the sky. The formation flew inland for about fifteen kilometres and ducked beneath the few clouds that scattered the clear day. They continued to lower their height and it surprised Harry how green the landscape was. They circled the straight runway of Blida and saw the small town for the first time, a jumble of tan buildings and maze-like streets. To the south was the Chréa National Park where tall mountains rose into the horizon. Some even had snow on them.

The formation slowly landed in pairs and by the time the 600 squadron all landed, Harry and Fred were climbing out of their Beaufighter. Several of the other pilots had taxied their planes next to Harry's. Taking off his mask and goggles, Harry was thankful for the fresh air. It was almost warm enough to feel like they were stepping back into summer. Harry breathed in deep and took in the airport. There were some large hangars on the south side, offices to the north, a street to the west, and nothing but brush and large empty fields to the east.

*Welcome to Algeria, indeed.*

Outside, near one of the office buildings, the pilots of the ten squadrons were given a briefing. Another wing commander who had already been in Algeria for some time addressed the bomber and fighter pilots and informed them of what they would be doing. He stood in the bed of a Jeep and wore the characteristic khaki and brown uniform of the United States Army Air Force.

"The North African ground campaign is currently schlepping through to Benghazi." The man looked like he had seen many missions and had commanded the men who had fought them. "Our aircraft, USAAF, RAF, and AAF are striking at Rommel's supply lines. This includes, but is not limited to sinking ships, shooting down air transports, blocking roads, and strafing motor columns. We're working in tandem with the ground forces. Now that we have complete air supremacy, Rommel's supply lines are being choked. We will further weaken the enemy by attacking the German aerodromes before the ground forces strike and take control. Do I make myself clear?" He paused for a second.

"Yes sir!" They all shouted.

"Good." He climbed down from the Jeep.

That afternoon, in the Mess, Harry sat with Val in a group of total strangers. There was a large group of pilots who had been in Algeria for many weeks. They had taken part in countless operations, one of the men, a B-17 pilot, was going on about the night raid on Tobruk. The raid had happened on September 13th and had been in vain. Naval and air forces had tried to disrupt the city and block the key port of the North African Coast. The pilot explained how his fellow 'Wimpy' or Wellington pilots had dropped flares on the target areas for the U.S. heavy bombers above to see where they needed to drop their loads of TNT. He described it as hell's inferno. The entire city was destroyed and laid to ruin with nothing left but rubble and flames...

Harry listened intently and looked to Val. They both exchanged worried glances. They knew they were about to see war first-hand. The seemingly petty operations they had done in England blanched in the face of what the pilot was describing. He said his best friend went down and his own Wellington was crippled during the bombing of Tobruk. He had barely made it back to their base.

"What would have happened if I'd gone down over the city..." the pilot merely shuddered.

The pilots that had just arrived were then shown to their tents. Harry and Val shared with a few other pilots and slept through the afternoon.

Gunfire could be heard in the distance.

Shortly before midnight, Harry was woken by Val.

"Rise and shine." He joked and shook his shoulder.

Harry sat up and moved his bag he had used as a pillow. He stretched and didn't think the missions would start so soon.

"We're to report in a half hour." Val said into the darkness.

Harry hadn't even changed and was glad he hadn't. His navy uniform was warm against the cool desert night. He was surprised by how cold it was.

They made their way quickly to the office-turned-Ops Room and got their briefing. They were to fly into hostile Libya and destroy an aerodrome near Benghazi. It didn't sound difficult, but the fact that it was over 1,500 kilometres away complicated things. Harry grew nervous as he looked over his Beau, got in, and started her up.

"What's the verse today, Harry?" Val asked from the dorsal gun's position as they taxied down the runway with several other Beaufighters, their fuselages' reflecting the moon's pale glow.

The deadly planes were off in no time.

"It was Joshua 1:9. *'Be strong and courageous. Do not be afraid; do not be discouraged, for the Lord your God will be with you wherever you go.'*"

"Sounds good to me," Val replied as he put on his mask, goggles, and gloves.

Three and a half hours of flight for an operation, Harry had plenty of time to calm his nerves. He wondered how Val was but decided against asking him.

Soon, the formation had left Algeria behind and then Tunisia; finally flying over the Mediterranean. To their right was the westernmost part of the Sahara Desert. Harry looked to his left and saw the formation of nine other planes. The groups of twos and threes made a giant V. Their leader was Wing Commander Dawson, another squadron leader who was leading some of his squadron with Wing Commander White of the No. 600.

The Mediterranean stretched on as far as the eye could see. They were deep in the enemy's territory now. The Eighth Army was fighting for Benghazi under the vast African sky. The Afrika Corps, led by Rommel, had stretched their forces across North Africa, mainly around the Gulf of Sirte in Libya. Now with over 35,000 U.S. Troops landing in Casablanca, Morocco; 39,000 U.S. Troops in Oran, Algeria; and 33,000 U.S. and British Troops landing in Algiers, Algeria; it was time to drive the Desert Fox back to Germany and deplete him of the precious transports his army needed to continue the offensive.

"Benghazi, up ahead," came Dawson's voice as he broke radio silence.

The pilots lowered their planes. Beads of sweat formed on Harry's brow as he flew the Beau a slight eight metres above the sea. Everyone was in formation and if Harry dared to move an inch, the plane would nosedive right into the Mediterranean and he and his gunner, Val, would die. He kept a tight grip on the yoke. The Beaus left propwash behind in their wake and the eerie iridescence of the moon reflected off the sea. Because the formation of nine planes was flying so low, they were almost invisible to the enemy in the Benghazi harbor. No planes could see them from above, nor get beneath them to shoot at them. And the deadly Beaufighter was silent from the front.

The enemy never knew they were coming.

Harry fingered the trigger on his figure-eight style yoke as the formation spread out. The nine planes came straight at the harbor. The arriving transport ships didn't know the enemy was fast approaching. Suddenly, the gunfire started. The pilots strafed the ships. Wood flew into the air; fires broke out on deck. Harry pulled up, nearly hitting a building. Harry climbed into the sky and then spiralled straight down to the harbor where he let loose another round of gunfire. He was unaware of all else and pulled up again. Val was shooting at the anti-aircraft guns in the watch towers, and they exploded as the shells hit the guns. The dark city was now aglow with fire. Somewhere from the east of the harbor, someone was shooting at Harry's Beau. Making a right climbing turn, he radioed to his fellow pilots.

"Ack-ack, 10 o'clock!"

"I've got him!" Guy's electronic voice came in through the radio.

Harry pulled out of the fray to catch his breath for a few seconds. He then whipped the Beau around again and made straight for the cement underground anti-aircraft guns. There were Nazi trucks all around it and the Germans were running for the cement hole. Harry bit his bottom lip and dropped one of his bombs into the fray. Explosions rattled the air and heaved the earth. The cement exploded. Harry swung around and strafed a motor column leaving the port. The bullets penetrated a few of the cars, hit the gas tanks, and they exploded. He pulled up and levelled out, surveying their work. The docks were a web of chaos and fire and black smoke. Almost all the ships were burning or foundering, except for one.

"Any bombs left?" The wing commander asked over the radio.

"This is Cavanaugh. I have one."

"See to it, officer."

The other Beaus were retreating, their work done. Harry levelled out over the ship and released the bomb. It barely caught the ship in the stern and exploded, a ball of fire erupting into the black sky. Hopefully it had caused enough damage to sink it.

Harry strafed the deck as he sped away from the port, leaving the burning pandemonium some distance behind.

"That's it, boys," Dawson's voice came over the R/T and everyone levelled out over the water.

The transport trucks had been totalled, the ships had been blown up, and the Beaufighters had left behind a deadly scene.

Harry's heart finally stopped racing when they came over the Mediterranean. They made their way back home, two planes fewer. One Beaus' engine had caught on fire from being hit by flak and the other had flown too low and had crashed into the dark city, taking out transport vehicles with it as it exploded. The lagging Beau would be lucky to make it. The formation of fighters was stopping in Malta for a refuel before heading back to Blida. The pilot could land there. Harry tried to ignore the

conversations on the radio. Dawson was coaching the lagging pilot along...
trying to help him get to friendly ground, or to Malta, if he could make it.
The frantic pilot on the other end hardly made sense. His gunner was dead.
His plane was hardly staying in the air. Harry heard that one of his engines
had gone out and the other was smoking. He wanted to click his radio off,
but he couldn't. The only thing they could do was listen as the pilot was
forced to bail out, his parachute refused to deploy, and he and his
Beaufighter crashed into the sea.

Harry wanted to forget all that was said that night. He wanted to
forget the fear of the pilot's voice and his panicked last words. But try as he
might, Harry couldn't.

He carried that night with him for the rest of his life.

---

"Gabriella! Oh you'll never guess what I have to tell you!" Betty
ran into the studio where Margaret was playing her cello and Gabriella was
teaching a lesson to Cecil, one of her students.

"Oh, excuse me!" Betty couldn't wipe the smile off of her face, but
she turned to leave so she wouldn't interrupt the lesson.

"Just one moment, Cecil." Gabriella patted the boy on the back.
"Play your arpeggios through again."

"Ok, Miss Sutton!" The young blonde-haired boy was loud but
extremely cute.

He played the scales noisily and with fervour. Margaret smiled to
herself and went back to practicing Vivaldi's Winter arranged for
unaccompanied cello. She watched her mother talk with Betty and could
just make out what they were saying over the musical din.

"I got a job!" Betty exclaimed and Gabriella looked at her as
though she was crazy. "Ted just found me a place in the factory! I'll be in
the assembly line, working for our country! Isn't it exciting?!" She jumped
up and down and squealed.

Gabriella looked pleased for her friend, but confused at the same
time. "Ted? He helped you find a job?"

"Yes! Isn't he just the greatest? Between you and me, I'm going
out on a date with him tonight!" Betty squealed again and then ran back
down the stairs.

Margaret chuckled and found the whole escapade amusing. Silently, she put the information she had just learned in the back of her mind. *If Betty's working at a factory, maybe I could too...*

Margaret and her mother shared amused glances before Gabriella went back to teaching her lesson.

That night, Margaret read a letter from Harry. The words touched her heart and she could almost hear his voice in his descriptions.

*'My dear Margaret,*

*How beautiful the Algerian sunset is. The desert sands that we fly over are golden and there is a halo around the setting sun from the dust that has been kicked up from the wind and the turbines and propellers of the planes. This sunset would be even more beautiful if you were here with me. The endless sand dunes stretch as far as the eye can see.*

*Please tell me how things are with you in New York City. How is Juilliard?*

*I hope you are doing well. I miss you. I had news from home; my mum and dad are all doing just fine. Still no news on Rich's whereabouts, but we would have heard if anything bad had happened. No news is good news, I guess. I'm afraid I can't dig up anything more exciting besides that. It's quiet here this morning. Val's writing a letter as well to his family and siblings. We just got back from a mission. We're all rather tired here, but we can't complain. It's not as bad as others have it. I did see a jackal this morning running across the tarmac some ways off. Being in Africa, I had wishfully hoped to see some animals that were a bit more exotic... maybe a zebra or giraffe, an elephant or a lion. But no such luck. I'll have to settle with scorpions and jackals and birds; nothing I haven't seen before in Australia or England.*

*I miss you.*

*Have a joyful, lovely Christmas.*

*I'll be thinking of you.*

*Ever yours,*

*Harry.'*

Margaret placed the letter on her desk and wrote him a reply, telling him all about Juilliard and how much she had learned. If she was honest with herself, she would admit that she was afraid. *What if something happens to him?* Margaret wished him a Merry Christmas, for the holiday was only a few days away. *What can Christmas be like in the desert?* She thought to herself as she sealed the envelope that was destined to reach Harry a week later in the sand dunes of North Africa.

*"I'm dreaming of a White Christmas,*
*Just like the ones I used to know.*
*May your days be merry and bright,*
*And may all your Christmases be white."*

Margaret listened to the Bing Crosby song and stood in front of the tall window in the kitchen. She watched as people walked here and there on Christmas Eve. It was her favourite holiday. She closed the dimout blinds and went back to the living room where everyone was putting presents under the tree. Samuel wore a festive Christmas sweater that was bright red. Grubbs and Pitcher wore their best clothes, for they were going to go to the Christmas Eve service that night. Rachel and Margaret both had on their pretty dark green sweaters with red bows in their hair. Their black and grey plaid skirts were long and came down to their calves. The Christmas song played on the scratchy record from the gramophone in the foyer. It made the night feel special.

"Shall we go?" Gabriella looked to the others who all eagerly said yes.

She had full charge of the children that evening. Their little mix-matched family was scattered on this Christmas Eve. Mr. Ackerman was visiting his daughter, son-in-law, and Hannah in Chicago. Betty was visiting Ted's parents in Boston and was sad that he had left for the Navy earlier than expected.

The group of six walked out into the dark streets of New York and made their way to St. Vincent Ferrer Church where they sang Christmas hymns and enjoyed the wonderful season and the reason why they celebrated.

Christmas morning was always exciting and this year was no exception. Betty explained to Grubbs and Pitcher that Santa Claus had to cut back with the war on. The children then asked how Santa got past the barrage balloons in London and the B-24s that flew over New York. Gabriella, with the help of Margaret and Rachel, explained Santa's sleigh as best as possible. It was amusing to Margaret, picturing the iconic sleigh flying under and dodging the barrage balloons.

That afternoon, Margaret had her usual call from her father. "Hello!" Margaret picked up the phone, knowing that she would hear her father's voice on the other line.

"Hello, my girl, and Merry Christmas!"

"Merry Christmas, Dad!" Margaret smiled and explained all the things they had done on Christmas; the little presents they had exchanged, the Christmas Eve service, Santa Claus' escapade and imagined escort by the B-24s, and her latest letter from Harry.

"What does Harry say?" The reverend asked.

"Not much. His missions are going well and he's a bit tired. I feel so bad for him... I know he's in so much danger. I wish he didn't have to be. Of course, all the young men have to fight, but... I don't know, I just wish him safe and well." Margaret leaned against the hallway wall.

Christmas carols sung by her family floated down the stairs that were right above her head.

"God will walk with him every step of the way. If it's His will, He will see him through to the end of the war." He paused. "Have you thought any more about... you two?" He inquired.

"It's all that's been on my mind lately." She replied honestly.

"Well, you both have your whole lives ahead of you. I'm happy for you two, but please don't rush anything."

"We won't, I promise, Dad. But I know Harry feels the pressure of the war and that..." She drifted off, not wanting to say the last bit. *His next mission could be his last.* "I just pray for his safety every day." She took a deep breath and changed the subject. "What are you doing for Christmas?"

"The usual. The Cavanaugh's invited me over for dinner and we had a wonderful meal despite the rationing. We are squeezed quite tight here, so sweets are rare and fruit is non-existent. But we had our gardens in the back this summer and no family has gone hungry on this street. If someone doesn't have enough, we share." He explained.

Margaret thought for a moment. "I wish you were here, Dad. I wish Harry was here. I wish this war was over... I just wish I could come home."

"So do I, my girl, so do I."

They talked for several more minutes before they said Merry Christmas and Margaret hung up the phone and took a deep breath. *1943, full steam ahead. It's coming whether we like it or not.*

After the holidays passed and the New Year was welcomed by Auld Lang Syne's traditional lyrics, the late January wind blew through New York. The Statue of Liberty had snow on her brow and there were large ice floes floating lazily around the Hudson. Central Park was knee-deep in snow and the taxis wound through the slushy streets. It was in these conditions that Margaret and Rachel made their way to Juilliard School in Lincoln Center. It was their first time back in a few weeks, but they were ready to plunge back into learning. Rachel, of course, still had school to go to but Gabriella had pulled some strings again that allowed her one morning off a week so she could take her lessons.

"This case is so heavy, I'm sweating!" Margaret exclaimed with a laugh.

Rachel chuckled and held her flute case closer to her so that it would not fall in the dirty snowmelt puddles. Lucky for her, it was much lighter than Margaret's cello case.

The girls emerged out of Central Park and came upon Central Park West Street. They crossed it quickly and went up to West 65th Street. They stopped at an intersection and waited for the pedestrian lights to change green.

"So, what news from Harry?" Rachel was always curious about him.

"They moved east on the 3rd and they're still fighting in the heat. Odd to think they're in the desert when we're here freezing off our toes." Margaret and Rachel raced across the road as the cars came to a stop.

"Very odd. It's like what *Time Magazine* says, '*war is like another world.*' Rachel stated and Margaret painfully agreed.

She was more worried about Harry than she let on.

The office at Juilliard was warm and somewhat noisy from the heating units.

"Miss Meg," Mr. Seymour folded his hands and sat behind his desk. "Happy New Year," he smiled.

"Happy New Year," she sat down in front of his desk with her cello in its case by her side.

"I have a proposition for you." He looked excited. The corners of his eyes turned up as he smiled.

"What can that be?" Margaret asked as she heard Rachel practicing with Dorothy the other office next door.

Mr. Seymour got up and went to the window with the vertical white blinds. "The second semester is starting here..." He said to himself and trailed off. "So, I was wondering if you had any interest in enrolling in Juilliard?" He turned to her and clasped his hands behind his back.

Margaret thought for a moment. "I always dreamt of going to university for music." She said fancifully. "But I never really thought it financially possible."

"Well," Mr. Seymour shrugged. "Juilliard *does* offer auditions and scholarships. Why not try out for them? You have the talent, you have the diligence, and I believe they would offer you some options."

"How would I go about auditioning?" Margaret furrowed her eyebrows, quite intrigued.

"You see, I am on the board. I could put in a good word for you and the judges will surely see your talent. There is a list of songs..." He went to his desk and pulled out a piece of paper. "These are the compositions and movements of symphonies you must play for a cello audition." He handed the list to Margaret. "If you can play those fluently, without any sheet music, and to the calibre Juilliard expects, you could find yourself a student here."

Margaret looked over the list. Almost all of the songs she could already play. "Will you help me?" She looked up to him and he held his hands up.

"I'm afraid I couldn't, seeing as I'm on the board. But Mr. Ackerman would no doubt be willing to help you hear the pieces you do not know and your mother could help you, could she not?"

"Yes," Margaret nodded her head and put the piece of paper in her cello case. "I will practice, and I *will* audition. Thank you, Mr. Seymour, thank you very much! This is something that I've always dreamt about." She couldn't contain her excitement. *An official student of Juilliard!*

"Mum! Mum!" Margaret ran into the foyer and set her case down by the stairs. Gabriella came out of the kitchen with a towel over her shoulder.

"What is it?" She asked, obviously surprised.

"Will you help me? Mr. Seymour told me that I could audition for a scholarship at Juilliard and I have to learn these songs!" She showed the piece of paper to her mother and put it into her hands. Looking over her shoulder, she continued, "I know all of them except these two," She pointed to Haydn String Quartet Op. 76 No. 3 and the first movement of Debussy's Cello Sonata.

"Those two shouldn't be that hard for you to learn." Gabriella mused and looked over the list. "I'm sure you could play them."

"Will you help me?" Margaret looked up to her mother who was still just a little taller.

"Of course I will!" She finished looking over the list and smiled at her daughter. "You a student of Juilliard... who would have thought it? I'm very proud of you, my girl." She exclaimed and turned off the water faucet in the sink that was still running.

Margaret looked to her mother fondly. "Did you know," she sat on the single stool against the kitchen's white wallpaper. "Dad always calls me, 'my girl?'"

Gabriella had a twinge of sadness in her eyes, yet she looked genuinely happy. They exchanged warm smiles.


Later that night, Margaret knocked quietly on Betty's door.

"Betty? Can I come in?"

"Meg! Of course." Betty was reading in bed and patted the side to invite Margaret to sit.

Margaret entered the cosy room that smelled like Betty's hairspray and had several posters of famous classical musicians and current-day singers up on the walls.

"I had a question." Margaret sat down with a bounce.

"What's going on?" Betty put her book down.

"I know how much you like your new job."

Betty nodded.

"Do you think," Margaret paused, "they would hire me?"

"You want to start working?" Betty asked, looking surprised.

"I want to be of help. I play my music and learn from Mr. Seymour and help Pitcher and Grubbs and Rachel with their schoolwork when they need it, but beyond that, I feel purposeless. I know I have my audition coming up and if it goes well, I'll be enrolled in Juilliard and have several classes there to attend. But I get letters from Harry and Dad and they are making such a difference where they are; even Bess in all her volunteer efforts. I want to do something to help the war effort and if that means working with you in the factory, I'll do it." Margaret replied, hoping she didn't sound too pushy. However, she was determined.

Betty thought for a moment. "Well... I assume you've talked to your mother about this?"

"I've spoken to both Mum and Dad about it... not specifically about working in the factory but I'm sure they wouldn't mind."

"Well, you have to check with your mom first, but if she gives it the all clear, I see no problem with you coming to work with me. You'll be busy. We have to be there by four in the afternoon and won't get home until after midnight. And it's tedious. Be prepared to do the same thing a thousand times and then a thousand times again on the assembly line."

Margaret nodded. "I know. I understand and I want to help." She was resolute. "I want to be busy."

# Chapter 23

One week passed. Margaret had applied herself to learning the Debussy and Haydn pieces. She had stopped her lessons with Mr. Seymour for the time being because they didn't want to be accused of cheating as the auditions were fast approaching and he was on the board. Therefore, Margaret spent all day practicing the songs that were on the list. She had them memorized forwards and backwards. Her mother looked on during all of her practicing and Betty and Mr. Ackerman gave their advice here and there. Naturally, Margaret relied on her talent and hoped that it would be enough. Her mother had said that she had some money put away in savings especially for Margaret when or if they had ever met. The money was hers for her education, but Margaret hoped she would get a large enough scholarship so they didn't need it. Hence, her constant practice.

She had also spoken to her mother about working in Betty's factory. While Gabriella didn't look pleased, she gave her permission. However, she advised Margaret to wait until the audition was over to see if she would be accepted in the school. If she was accepted it would take some time to adjust to the new schedule. Once Margaret was settled, Gabriella told her she'd help her apply for the job.

It was February 1st. The audition was that day. As Margaret walked to Juilliard with her mother, she was, for once, nervous about playing. Professors and teachers would be scrutinizing her every move and every note. They entered through the main students' entrance and joined the mass of musicians. Margaret and her mother wove through the many people until they came to the concert hall. Entering the seemingly empty hall, they made their way down to the front. They were both greeted by several of the genius professors and teachers. Margaret was told to walk up on the stage and they would sit in at the long table that had been set up before the front row. The list of songs was before them. Margaret climbed the steps and went to the middle of the stage where a single chair sat.

No music stand.

No list.

Nothing.

Taking out her cello, she put the case behind her. Margaret sat on the chair in her black dress and put the cello between her knees. She quickly tuned it and then paused.

Her heart was racing.

Gabriella sat a few rows behind the professors with her purse on her lap. She made a face that Margaret understood. *Relax.* Taking a deep breath, Margaret heard one of the professors say she could start whenever she wanted to. The verse her father had told her years ago echoed in her mind. *'Be strong and of good courage, do not fear nor be afraid of them; for the LORD your God, He is the One who goes with you. He will not leave you nor forsake you.'* Closing her eyes, Margaret began the first song as the single beam of light fell on her and her instrument from above.

The song was Elgar's Cello Concerto. She had played it so many times effortlessly. This time was no exception. There was not one mistake in it and Margaret knew that she couldn't have played it any better. The next composition was the first movement of Debussy's Cello Sonata. Margaret closed her eyes and felt the emotion of the piece. It moved her and she hoped it moved the onlookers as well. *One mistake... Only one in that song.* She sighed as she prepared to play the next composition. She dared one look at the professors. Their expressions were calculating and judging. But moreover, they were listening. The next three songs went off without a problem or mistake and then it was time for Haydn's String Quartet Op. 76 No. 3. Margaret was a bit nervous about the piece, for she hadn't been playing it very long. Nonetheless, she had to try.

The first half of the cello part for the quartet was flawless. By the end though, Margaret knew the melody, but she had a hard time with the tempo. Nonetheless, she finished it correctly and beautifully. The last song was one of her own choosing. She had debated whether to do Bach's unaccompanied cello, or Schubert's Serenade. Knowing that she could do each one beautifully, she decided on the Serenade. It was her absolute favourite and it made her think of home.

When Margaret felt a song, she could play it better than any professor. The eighteen year old proved it that morning. Pizzicato for the first few bars gave way to the lovely melody. Not only did she think of home and her father, but she also thought of Harry and his loneliness on the North African front. It gave the song another dimension and when it finished, she took a deep breath and heard the professors applauding her audition. The accolades could only mean one thing.

———————————

"Thank you, Commander Groves." Harry saluted his superior and glowed from the praise.

"You have a good head on your shoulders, keep up the good work." Squadron No. 600's wing commander left Harry by his tent that was basking in the hot sun of Setif, Algeria.

Harry smiled and climbed back into his tent for a few more hours' rest. Val looked up from where he was resting on his cot.

"What was that?" He rolled over groggily.

They had been out on a patrol and had found nothing that night. However, Harry had gotten separated from the formation as they were making their way back to the air base in Setif and had spotted an unsubmerged U-Boat that was flying the swastika. He had relayed the information back to HQ and not long after, B-24's had sunk the submarine off the coast of Libya. It was a massive victory, one that Harry was extremely proud of. Not only that, Harry's Beaufighter now boasted four black crosses painted below the canopy. It was a large number for a novice pilot, a large number of enemy planes shot down, and Val teased him about it relentlessly.

"It was nothing," Harry collapsed on his bedroll and plopped his head down on his bag.

Val raised his eyebrows, looking for a further explanation. "He promoted you, didn't he?"

Harry nodded, not wanting to boast.

Val watched him. "Lieutenant Cavanaugh." He thought out loud. "Does this mean I have to start taking orders from you?"

Harry scoffed. "You wouldn't listen anyway," he joked.

"No, I wouldn't." Val chuckled. "All the same, congratulations." He said seriously.

Harry thanked him. He was proud of himself.

The hot African sun started to fall from its high throne in the sky and by the time it slipped below the horizon, the deadly Beaus of the RAF and Boeings of the USAAF would be at it again.

Around 1800 hours, Harry woke up and knew that his day, or

night, would start soon. Val stirred beside him and sat up.

"Bloody rock," Val threw out a rock that had somehow crawled underneath his bedroll.

Harry opened his eyes and saw the red glare of the sun that usually accompanied the sun's setting streaming into their tent.

"At least it wasn't a scorpion. I heard Fred saw one the other day and shot it." Harry sat up as well and put on his aviator's boots. Although he thoroughly checked the toes of his boots to make sure no scorpions or spiders had taken up residence in them first. "What did your letter from home say?" Harry asked Val who had been engrossed in a letter the previous morning.

Val was the oldest of four children. He had two sisters and a younger brother; all three had been evacuated to Cheshire. His parents were still living in Bromley, on the southeast side of London.

"Not much," Val shrugged. "Annie drew me a picture of the old cottage and the family they're staying with. Last time I saw her, I daresay it was two years ago, she was only four. Tom will take good care of her though, he's a good lad." Val slipped on his boots after knocking out some ants that had crawled in them.

"What about Aggie?" Harry picked out his Bible from his bag and leafed through some of the pages, reading the verses that his eyes settled on.

"She's fine, but doesn't say much." Val sounded amused. Agatha was the second eldest and apparently quite the know-it-all.

Harry smiled as a letter from Margaret fell out from between the pages of his Bible. He put it back in and reminded himself to write to her that morning when they got back.

"What's the verse today?"

Harry looked up and relayed the verse he had just saw and read. *"'All have sinned and all have fallen short of the glory of God.'"*

"Hardly encouraging..." Val turned off the small lamp above their heads and went out into the open air.

Harry stepped out of the tent and stretched. The other men were all waking around him, emerging from their tents, ready to start the evening patrols and intruder missions.

"Hardly encouraging, but true, nonetheless. And all the sweeter it makes His grace." Harry's hair stood on end from the chilly wind that blew from the south. The red, round sun was sinking to the west. Harry and Val stood together, looking out over the flat horizon.

"Are we any better than them?" Val asked rhetorically.

"Who?"

"The people we're fighting."

Harry baulked at the question. And yet didn't want to admit to thinking the same thing from time to time. "I don't know if we're any *better*. But the principles we stand for are..." He tried to assure himself and his friend.

Val furrowed his eyebrows and looked to his friend. "I think if I was faced with sitting down with a Nazi one on one, I'd like to talk him into changing his mind rather than just shoot him."

"Unfortunately, we're not afforded that luxury. For some reason, they want to kill us all and take over everything."

"I'm just saying, it's a shame the cost is so high."

Harry couldn't help but agree.

The mess hall clattered with the sound of trays and tired voices. Harry's mood darkened. He had a headache coming on and was starting to feel sick from the greasy beef slather they put on their bread to make it taste better. He sat beside Guy who was chatting and laughing with one of his buddies in the A-Flight group. Harry thought he remembered the man's name was Alfie. Val was quiet too, for they knew they would be called soon and neither of them was very hungry, at least not for what was on their plates. Fred joined them across the table and had an excited look on his boyish face.

"What do you think we'll get to do today?" He asked excitedly as he tore into his hard biscuit.

"You that eager to jump back into the fray?" Harry asked dubiously.

"Aren't you?! I don't care if it's Berlin, Munich, or the damn moon we get to fly to. I'm ready. We can't sit around knocking scorpions out of our boots forever."

"This isn't a game, Fred." Harry scoffed. "When you sit across from a pilot one night and then the next you listen to his final words over the radio," he shook his head, almost unable to finish. "Every time you go up, it's something different... something changes."

Fred shrunk back, raised his eyebrows, and started talking to another one of his mates, ignoring Harry.

Guy had listened to the exchange and went back to eating.

"Don't be short with Fred," Guy spoke quietly and directly to Harry.

Harry eyed him and swallowed the last of his biscuit. "Enjoy your breakfast," Harry snatched his tray and let them be.

He got up from his place, ignored the curious look Val gave him, and went outside. Instead of watching the morning sun rise, Harry watched the northern star peak out from behind the veil of night. He remembered his grandfather just then. His grandfather had told him when he was just a lad sitting on his knee that if the underside of heaven looks so beautiful, we can only imagine what it looks like on top. Harry put his hands deep in his pockets and thought as twilight surrounded him. His nerves were frayed, and he was *tired. So, so* tired. He rubbed his face, his eyes begging to be closed. He held up his hand and saw that it was shaking. He stuffed it back in his pocket and tried to calm his breathing.

*I'm losing it,* he thought to himself and sat down. He closed his eyes and listened to the sounds around him. Behind him, he could hear the din coming from the Mess. Out across the tarmac and beyond the fences of the airport, he could hear the single low-pitched hoot of an owl. The wind was cool against his face as it blew from the south. The earth was warm underneath him and seemed to ground him back to reality. He didn't like to admit it, but he was having nightmares occasionally. The things he had seen... his mind wasn't letting go of those scenes anytime soon. Explosions, bodies thrown into the air by bombs he dropped, and others floating in the water... they circled in his mind when he closed his eyes.

A hand came down on his shoulder.

Harry jumped.

"Easy, Cav." Guy sat down next to him. "You alright?" The senior ace asked with genuine concern.

"I'm fine." He lied.

They sat in silence for several minutes, the night growing darker, the air growing cooler, the stars coming out one by one.

"If you need to talk, the chaplain's a good man."

Harry shrugged. "I'm alright, really."

Guy took a deep breath. "Don't lie to yourself. I did when I first joined up and I wish I had gotten help sooner. It takes more bravery to ask for help than to pretend you don't need it."

Harry thought for a moment. "I guess my nerves are just frayed." He let his guard down slightly. "Sometimes I dream about our missions."

"Those are called nightmares." Guy stiffly chuckled. "I know what you're talking about. It can be terrifying Out There. You feel like you have no control, and it makes you panic."

Harry glanced at him. He had described perfectly what he had been feeling. "I'm glad I'm not the only one who feels that way."

"If we were all honest, each and every one of us would be admitting to the same thing. Except Fred," he shook his head in amusement. "I *do* agree with you; he thinks this is a game."

They were silent for another few moments.

"But you shouldn't be short with him. I've been short with too many a man before watching them go down in the next few hours. You never know which moment will be his last... or yours." Guy pointed at Harry to amplify his point.

"You have a point there." Harry sighed. "What does Claudie say?" HE asked after Guy's wife, deciding to change the subject.

Guy smiled. "She's doing well." He beamed, for they were expecting their first child. "We've been discussing names... She wants Susan if it's a girl. I told her that if it's a boy, he should be named after my dad, John." Guy took a deep breath and smiled again. "I can't wait to see her. It's been a long time."

"Hopefully we'll be on leave soon."

"I doubt that." Guy shrugged. "Tunisia's too close to falling and Rommel can't stay there for long if we keep hacking away at his supplies."

"It'd help if we had more planes. Too many pilots, not enough aircraft... Funny, it was the other way around in England."

"What can we do?" Guy shrugged. "Just keep going one day at a time." He stood up. "Take care of yourself. And I mean that." Guy waved him off and went to one of the hangars to look over their Beaus.

Harry watched him go and thought about what he had said. After a few minutes passed, he saw Fred leave the Mess with a group of younger pilots.

His conscience prickled and then went to war with his pride that reared up. He watched as Fred and the others joked and laughed together. He sighed to himself and got up.

Jogging over to them, Harry stopped Fred. "Fred,"

The younger pilot stopped, eyeing him and looking somewhat annoyed.

"I'm sorry." Harry apologized. "My nerves were getting the better of me."

Fred shrugged and kicked a rock. "It's alright. I understand." He waved to his friends who were going back to their tents to get their kits. "I just find it easier to grin and bear it, you know? What good is worrying? Our time comes when our time comes. No good trying to change it."

"There's wisdom in that," Harry admitted.

Fred nodded curtly and hit him on the arm. "I'll see you in a few."

---

*'March 26th, 1943*

*Dear Harry,*

*Every time I wake up, I wonder what you're doing. No doubt you're returning from a mission, completely exhausted. I truly cannot find the words to explain my concern and sympathy for what you're going through. Please just stay safe and stay strong. My thoughts and my prayers are always with you.*

*Juilliard is everything I expected it to be and more. I learn so much every day and the teachers and professors are all so kind and courteous. I don't know what I was thinking when I was so nervous at my first audition. They want every student to perform to the best of their ability. I am so blessed to be a student there now.*

*Our practices in Carnegie Hall continue and I only wish you were here to see them. It is less spectacular now without the twins and Hannah, but we make do. Our latest news at the house is that we are coming up with a name; a name for the school and a name for us. We have a grand idea that involves War Bonds, but we haven't figured out the details yet.*

*...When will this war end? Just yesterday a formation of planes flew over New York and everyone panicked, thinking it was a raid. But a few level-headed people yelled out, "They're ours!" That calmed everyone's fears. I shouldn't complain. We have nothing of what Europe is going through. In fact, it would seem like the war is a world away if it weren't for the rationing, propaganda posters, dimouts, aircraft factories, and busyness of*

*the Navy Yard.*

*I do have some exciting news! I'm going to start going to work with Betty! She works the second shift at Grumman's factory and together we'll commute down there, work together, and commute back. I'm a little nervous, as I start this week, but I'm glad Betty will be with me. Mum is worried and I've told Dad and he's proud of me. But I'll be fine. I'm just excited to be helping in some way. I feel so useless sometimes. I wish I could be back in London helping there somehow, but God has me here for a reason. It would just be nice to know what that reason is.*

*How are you? Tell me any news you can. I know you're so limited with what you can share, but I'll be happy with any news you can give me, even if it's just what you had for dinner or what the weather's like.*

> *Yours,*
> *Meg'*

Margaret read through her letter to make sure there weren't any spelling mistakes and even if there were, she couldn't do much about them except cross them out. Walking over to the map of Europe and the Mediterranean on her wall, she looked at the blue string she had pinned into it. She was tracing Harry's squadron's movement based on the return address labels he wrote. Margaret had a pin in Blida, Algeria. Then they had moved from Blida to Maison Blanche, an airfield just to the east of Algiers. From Maison Blanche, they had then gone to Setif, about 150 kilometres east southeast of Algiers. She could hardly imagine where they would go next and what dangers he would encounter.

*Please, God, let him be safe. Let him live. Please.*

Down the stairs she trod, thankful that she didn't have to go anywhere that day. It was Saturday and there was nothing to do besides practice and do homework. She greeted her mother with a cheery 'good morning' and set to work on her homework. They lounged in the living room and one by one, the others joined them. Betty came down looking sleepy-eyed and Rachel was on her heels. Margaret ate her toast and said good morning to them too. The three boys then joined them and ate their breakfast.

"So!" Margaret leaned on the arm of the couch. She petted Louis' ears, for he was sitting with her. "What have you all come up with for a name?"

Rachel was the first to speak. "What about the Parkers? We play in the park." She offered her idea.

Margaret made a face and Betty stifled a chuckle.

"Well then, what do you think we should be called?" Rachel retorted to Betty.

"I have no clue..." Betty shrugged and finished her breakfast in one gulp. She vanished into the kitchen to put her plate in the sink.

"Meg?" Gabriella was reading a magazine and put it down to join in on the conversation. "What do you think?"

"I was thinking something official." Margaret replied, formulating an idea in her mind.

"Something like this?" Gabriella wrote something down on a piece of paper.

Margaret got up from the couch, for Grubbs and Pitcher had just claimed it. They plopped onto it and listened to the conversation. Gabriella held up a notepad that had the letters 'NYCCO' on it.

"What does that mean?" Grubbs asked.

"New," Gabriella pointed to each letter. "York, Children's, Chamber, Orchestra."

Margaret nodded, but took the notepad from her mother. She scribbled something on it and handed it back.

Gabriella read it and then turned it around. In large letters was, 'NYYO.'

"The New York *Youth* Orchestra." Margaret declared. "That way Samuel and I don't have to be classified as children." Margaret smiled and Samuel nodded in approval.

"What does that make me?" Rachel objected.

"You're a *child*, like us." Grubbs teased her.

Rachel stuck her tongue out at them.

"*I'm* a lady. I'll be fifteen this year and I think that disqualifies me from being called a child."

"Sorry, Rachel." Margaret shrugged. "You know what I meant."

She stuck her tongue out at Margaret who returned the gesture playfully.

The boys laughed and Gabriella shook her head in motherly exasperation and wonder. Betty came back into the living room.

"What'd we decide on?" She leaned on the entryway.

"I think we have a name." Gabriella stood up. "Everyone in favour of the New York Youth Orchestra, raise their hand!" Everyone's hands went up.

"Well, that's swell! And a fine name it is too!" Betty declared.

Plans commenced soon after the name was decided. Mr. Ackerman came in later that day and helped and contributed all he could. The children had come up with a brilliant plan and it only required Carnegie's cooperation, something they could easily acquire, for the manager was very fond of them. Their plan was to raise money and encourage people to buy War Bonds by holding Sunday concerts at Carnegie's Chamber Music Hall. So many people, Betty and Margaret included, were going to work in the factories and help bring the United States through this war and win it. The children of the house desired the same thing. They would paint banners, signs, and get posters from the War Finance Committee and decorate the hall so it would look like a true Fourth of July celebration. It was sure to be a hit with the children playing patriotic music and encouraging the people to either buy 10 cent stamps that saved up towards a War Bond or buy a whole War Bond.

Mr. Ackerman took care of the official and legal things while the group practiced the songs they would play. They would start the next week and it was exciting for them all.


Margaret and Betty sat quietly together on the hard metal seats that lined the subway car's sides. Margaret looked around her at all the other men and women who were commuting to and from their jobs that Monday afternoon. Some chatted, some read the paper, and some stared off into the distance. Margaret wondered what they were thinking about; she wondered if they had loved ones fighting overseas. They probably looked at her and thought, *what a nice innocent girl, probably on her way to her first day on the job.* Margaret was sure she had such an expression of naivety and nervousness. She fidgeted and twirled the bandana Betty had given her in between her fingers and wondered what her first day would be like.

The factory was loud. Margaret didn't know where to focus. Drills were whirring, machines were beeping, time cards were being punched in, and a general cacophony met her ears. Betty led her to her work station and a man was there that showed Margaret what she would be doing.

"This is the crank that lowers the drill onto the table." He turned a wheel that lowered a spinning drill onto a sheet of metal. "Center the drill over these four marks and drill there and only there. Once you've finished, place the sheets on this pile and another worker will come and pick them up. You got it?"

Margaret nodded.

"Good. Miss Shea, call me if there's any problems."

"I will, Bert. Thanks a million."

The man left amidst the busy factory. Margaret looked to Betty.

"You'll do great." She encouraged her. "Don't forget your gloves." She held up her leather-gloved hands.

Margaret remembered and took the gloves out of her back pocket.

"Don't worry." She let out a soft chuckle. "You look like a deer in headlights."

"I'm sorry," Margaret turned to the machine. "I'm so nervous."

Betty methodically set to work. She was drilling smaller holes around the edge of the sheets she then passed to Margaret who drilled larger ones.

"You'll make mistakes; it's all part of learning." Betty continued. "You didn't play the cello flawlessly when you first started, now did you?"

"No," Margaret responded and took the sheet Betty passed to her on the rolling conveyor.

"Go slow, think things through. It's a piece of cake once you get the hang of it. You'll be doing it with your eyes closed in no time."

"What are we making?" Margaret asked as she centered the drill on one of the marks and lowered the crank.

"We're making a plane." Betty responded.

Margaret's face lit up. "Really?" She had a hard time believing the tabletop-sized sheet of metal was part of a plane.

Betty laughed. "Really." She paused for a moment and motioned to something behind her. "I don't know if you can see it from here... but take a look over there."

Margaret turned around and followed Betty's gaze. Far away, on the other side of the factory floor, there were large pieces of something hanging from the ceiling. They looked like giant torpedoes.

"What are they?"

"They're the middle of the planes. The fuselages. Grumman

produces mostly planes... they make guns as well and communications equipment. Ted pulled some strings for me to get into this factory." She leaned in close to Margaret and whispered, "the pay is a bit better here than the other places."

Thoughtfully, Margaret nodded. She turned back to her work and was somewhat lost in a daze. She was making planes for the war effort. Never in a million years did she believe she'd been in an American factory making American planes next to an American who had become like an aunt to her.

"Thanks, Betty." Margaret said quietly some hours later once she had gotten into a rhythm of the work.

"What for?" Betty asked, sliding a sheet to Margaret.

"Thanks for letting me help."

Betty knew what she meant. "It feels good, doesn't it? I know sometimes the music isn't enough for me. It gives me purpose, I will say that. But whether or not I can play flawlessly pales in comparison to helping and giving my time towards something that will last and make a difference. We're making history, you and I; us and all the women we're working with. I wouldn't want to be anywhere else right now. Well... maybe out on a date with Ted. But we make do while our boyfriends are away, don't we?" She winked at Margaret.

It made her blush. "I guess we do."


That week was the busiest Margaret had ever known. She went to school from 8 o'clock in the morning until 2 in the afternoon and only had a few minutes to stop at home, eat something, and then she was off to the subway with Betty, commuting to the factory on Long Island.

She was starting to get into a rhythm, though; and she liked it. When she and Betty came home late every night, Margaret was so exhausted; sometimes she merely slept on the couch on the first floor. There was no way her legs could carry her up four flights of stairs to the attic. Her hands ached by the end of the week from the repetitive work at the factory and yet she didn't mind it one bit. Every morning she still woke with excitement and readiness to start the day.

When Sunday rolled around, though she was rather spent, she helped turn Carnegie's Chamber Music Hall into a red, white, and blue wonderland. Buntings hung everywhere and *To Have and To Hold – WAR*

*BONDS'* posters were on the doors that led into the hall. *'For Victory!'* banners were also put up along the sides. Not very many people turned up on the first few Sundays. However, as word got out and the weather started to take a nice turn, the hall was graced by more and more citizens willing to give War Bonds.

Men and women alike came in and signed the paperwork and gave their money. Mr. Ackerman collected the papers and then would make a weekly stop at the War Finance Committee building in New York and report in on their earnings. It was a happy time for the children. Not only did they feel productive and helpful, they also had many nice compliments from the people who came to give. They would point and smile at the young musicians, saying how extraordinary they were. The small orchestra would then tell them they would play every Saturday in Central Park once it was warm enough. It was a lovely way to meet fellow New Yorkers and feel the close kinship of countrymen who all were striving for the same thing; winning the war.

It was on a rainy Saturday when the household was surprised by a very unlikely guest. Margaret was in the living room reading her latest letter from Harry. He was describing how he had been feeling rattled lately and was asking for prayers. Margaret read it with concern. She wished she could see him and encourage him... but he was so very far away. She wondered what he looked like now, as it had been almost four years since she had moved. *He probably looks so handsome now...* Margaret thought and then scolded herself for thinking such things. *I wonder if he has a beard. Do they let you grow a beard in the air force?*

The doorbell rang.

Margaret jumped in surprise, quite taken out of her thoughts. The others were all upstairs playing in the studio. Gabriella was in the kitchen and answered the door. Betty was asleep in the chair across from Margaret, her shoes kicked off, her stocking feet propped up on the coffee table. Her mouth was open and she was drooling a little bit. Margaret wondered if she could toss one of the candies she was eating into Betty's wide open mouth. She chuckled at the thought.

"Betty!" Gabriella called from the foyer. "It's Ted!"

Betty stirred and looked confused. She didn't have time to make herself look presentable in front of her boyfriend, for Gabriella led him into the living room. She did manage to wipe the drool from the side of her chin, though.

"Ted!" Betty exclaimed in surprise and leapt up, quite awake now.

"Hi, Betty," his reply was muffled as she threw her arms around him in a tight hug.

Ted was a quiet, gentle man, but not in a weak way. He seemed like he knew what he wanted and would work as hard as he needed to get it. Margaret admired that about him. Betty always talked about his letters and he seemed like a steady, reliable man. Like Rachel had said back at Coney Island during Margaret's birthday, he was a little short; just the same height as Betty, but shorter if she wore her heels. But what was height in the grand scheme of things? Some would probably have said he was boring, but he was sweet and funny and from what Betty said, he was a real gentleman.

Margaret smiled and looked back down to her letter.

"Can I talk with you?" Ted asked Betty as she stepped back.

"Of course. You're all wet." She wiped the raindrops from the jacket of his navy uniform. "What are you doing here?"

"My parents didn't send word?"

She shook her head.

"Ah, well I guess I travelled ahead of their letter and my own."

"We'll give you both some privacy." Gabriella offered and motioned for Margaret to follow.

Margaret didn't want to go, she wanted to hear what news Ted brought, but she got up anyway and gave Betty a wink before leaving. Climbing up the stairs, Margaret followed her mother.

"Why do you think Ted's back so suddenly?" She asked.

"I'm not sure, dear. Perhaps he was injured?"

"He didn't look injured." Margaret thought out loud.

"Well, I guess we'll just have to wait and see." Gabriella responded with not a great deal of patience as they entered the studio and found Grubbs and Pitcher wrestling again; one had a bloody nose and the other wasn't being merciful.

About twenty minutes later, Betty and Ted burst into the studio.

"Guess what!" Betty was holding up her left hand.

"You brought us a pie?!" Pitcher guessed comically.

"What is it?" Gabriella looked up from tending to Grubbs' nosebleed.

Margaret noticed first. "Betty!" She leapt up from where she had been writing a reply to Harry and ran to her friend, giving her a big hug.

"Congratulations!" Margaret squealed.

"What is it?" Rachel stood up from where she had been tinkering on the piano lazily.

Gabriella caught on next and let out an excited, "Oh!" She rushed to Betty and hugged her tightly as well.

"Thanks," Betty laughed, wiping tears from her eyes.

"Hey! What's going on?" Pitcher joined them.

Samuel watched from afar and Grubbs wasn't too happy he wasn't the center of attention anymore.

"Betty and I are getting married." Ted told the young boy.

He made a face. "Oh." He slipped out of the room and down the stairs.

"Betty, I'm so happy for you!" Gabriella told her dearest friend.

"Thank you, Gabriella. I'm so excited. I was so surprised!" She reached out a hand to Ted and he held it sweetly.

It was then Margaret noticed the bandage on his other hand. She didn't want to be rude and point it out. But she had no need, for Grubbs did as he joined them as well.

"What happened to your hand? Did you get shot?"

"It was from an explosion." Ted explained.

"Woah..." his eyes grew wide.

"It was burned pretty badly. Doctors did what they could, but they're not sure it'll heal completely. That's why I was discharged. I'm not of much use to the navy with a hand that doesn't work." Ted explained, offering a shrug.

He held his bandaged hand close to his stomach and his wrist was bent in slightly.

"Congratulations!" Rachel had since come over and given the couple a hug, completely ecstatic for them both.

"Well," Gabriella clapped her hands together. "This calls for a celebration! Stay for dinner, Ted?"

"I'd love to." He thankfully accepted.

"And dessert!" Grubbs added and dashed out of the studio happily.

# Chapter 24

It was a day to celebrate. May 13th 1943, the day the Axis Powers surrendered in Tunisia. Harry had another reason to be happy. He had gotten a letter from his parents who informed him that for the first time in a year, they had heard from Richard. He was working in Prisoner of War camps, making sure the prisoners were well fed, taken care of, and healthy. He had been working in an auxiliary hospital for some time, but would soon be moving. To where, he couldn't tell them. But he was safe, and he was doing his part, making a world of difference to the Allied POWs in different countries.

The men of the 600 Squadron were relieved that the fighting would stop, at least for a while. They celebrated with that in mind, knowing the fighting would be carried farther north and east. Operation Torch was successful, and the Allies gained another victory in North Africa. But now another task lay ahead of them. The soft underbelly of the Axis Powers was now open for the Allied invasion. Soon, the fighting would start anew and the invasion of Sicily would begin. But Harry couldn't help but feel that, yes, they had won in North Africa, but Europe was a whole other story. Europe was Hitler's playground... his home field. They were taking the fighting to him. The Luftwaffe ruled the skies, the Heer had control of the ground, the Kriegsmarine reigned the surrounding seas, and the Wehrmacht oversaw it all. Every road and rail-line from southern Sicily to northern Denmark was watched and owned by the Nazi regime. It reminded Harry of David and Goliath. They were the unarmoured child standing before the two-metre war giant. Their victory would be a miracle... something only God could do.

They were about to take on Europe. They would move north soon, deep into the fray. And Harry had an instinct he felt to his core that the worst was yet to come.

---

Sunday's War Bond rally took place right after church. Margaret hurried to Carnegie Hall and walked quickly down West 57th Street. Samuel was with her and together, they carried large boxes of posters they had just picked up from the War Financial office, and banners they had just made that week.

Margaret repositioned the large box on her hip and they quickly crossed the street. Pedestrians looked at them suspiciously and she knew they probably looked rather silly with their loads. As they hurried down the sidewalk, Margaret's heels clacking on the cement, a voice broke into their trek.

"Hey, look! It's Rachel's friend..."

Margaret eyed a group of three young men who were leaning up against the wall near a cinema's entrance. However, they weren't looking at her. Biting the side of her cheek, she looked over her shoulder at Samuel.

"Come on, Sam." She kept walking.

"That's it, boy," one of the young teenagers started. "You heard the lady. Keep up."

Margaret didn't like their tone. They had almost passed them by when another one of the boys who looked to be around Rachel's age started forward and knocked the large box out of Samuel's hands. They all started laughing. Margaret turned on her heel.

"Watch where you're going!" The boy taunted Samuel.

"Leave him alone!" Margaret was on the verge of being furious.

"What'll you do?" The boy sneered. "Call the police on me? The only thing that's a crime around here is you walking with this..." he trailed off as he looked Samuel over from head to toe.

"Go on, boy. Pick it up."

A moment of tension passed. Margaret was going to put down her box and help him, but Samuel knelt down and began putting the things back that had spilled out.

"Why do you lot have to be so awful?" Margaret huffed. "Because of the color of his skin? Who cares that your skin's white and his is dark? I feel bad for Rachel for having to go to school with such stupid, immature boys."

They were about to continue their taunts when Margaret cut them off.

"It's a shame you children don't have something better to do than discriminate against your own countrymen. It's pathetic. Find something useful to do. There's a war going on, for heaven's sake. I suggest you get busy and help win it."

Samuel had finished cleaning up the supplies. However, suddenly the first boy came forward as though he was going to start a fight. They were quicker however, and started down the sidewalk, walking quickly before they could cause any more trouble.

Margaret huffed angrily. "Stupid boys," She was disgusted.

Looking over to Samuel, she couldn't quite read his expression. She guessed it was embarrassment and perhaps anger.

They walked in silence for a few moments.

"Thank you," he said.

Margaret looked up to him, for he was now a little taller than she was. It was the first time he had really ever spoken to her.

"You're welcome, Sam. I'm sorry about what they said..." She paused. "Do they go to Rachel's school?"

He nodded. "They're usually on the front steps when I see Rachel and the boys off at their school before heading to mine."

Margaret sighed. She had never had to deal with discrimination much before back in England. It was odd to her. She saw colored people exactly how she saw white people. How could people still think they were so different they needed to be separate in almost every aspect of life?

"Well, I'm sorry. It was good of you not to get upset and fight them, though. Things could've gotten out of hand quickly."

He nodded. "I didn't want a fight... at least not with a lady present."

"Thank you. I appreciate that." Margaret smiled thoughtfully. "You should talk more. You're good at it."

He let out a small smile. "Please don't tell anyone this happened."

"On one condition." Margaret responded as they came up to Carnegie Hall.

Samuel waited for her to continue.

"You have to talk to me and the others more often. I understand you're quiet and reserved, I can be too. But you're family, Sam. And family lets each other in on our lives."

He nodded, still with a small smile on his face. "It's a deal,"

Once inside the hall, Margaret deposited her box on one of the back row's seats. Some of the orchestra was already there practicing. Her mother and Mr. Ackerman were down front talking to one another. Samuel put his box down next to Margaret's and joined everyone down front as though nothing had happened.

As Margaret began unpacking some of the things so she could hang them, she wondered if she should tell her mother about the incident. However, she decided against it. Samuel wanted it kept quiet and she wouldn't betray his trust since he was opening up more. As she thought things over, she noticed a lady entering the hall with a young girl in tow.

"Good afternoon!" The lady waved.

"Good afternoon. I'm afraid the concert hasn't started yet. But if you'd like to buy a stamp or a bond, you can speak to Mr. Ackerman."

The lady interrupted her. "No, no, I already bought a bond." She seemed quite scatterbrained and spoke quickly. "I was wondering if your orchestra had any openings?"

"Any openings?" Margaret pondered the request.

She looked down to the girl who was obviously her daughter. They both had reddish brown short hair and brown eyes. They seemed upper middle-class... well-off but not too well-off.

"We are always open to new students." Margaret explained. "My mother teaches piano, Mr. Ackerman teaches everything, and Betty teaches violin and viola. Although she won't be-"

"I wasn't thinking about lessons, my little Elizabeth can play anything!" The lady interrupted her again, replying in her boisterous voice as she cast a glance to the quiet girl behind her. The girl didn't look so little. To Margaret, she looked about twelve. "Can she stay at the school? I heard from someone last week that you all live together?"

Margaret didn't quite know what to say. "You'd have to talk with my mother and Mr. Ackerman." She said simply, motioning to the two adults down by the stage.

Gabriella had noticed Margaret was talking with someone and looked like she might join them in a moment.

"I'll do that, thank you. This is just the sort of thing my Elizabeth needs!"

"My name's Margaret," Margaret forced a smile and reached out her hand, taking a break from unpacking the banners.

"Nice to meet you, I'm Miranda. Miranda Hill." She shook Margaret's hand.

Her daughter looked aloof and somewhat annoyed, as much young people her age usually did.

Leaving her to the boxes and their contents, Mrs. Hill went down the aisle to where Gabriella and Mr. Ackerman were. While they talked and the orchestra tuned their instruments, Margaret set to work putting up the posters and hanging the new banners they had made. She glanced over now and then to see if she could hear what they were saying. Mrs. Hill was handing over papers and the two teachers were looking over them. Margaret finished with the last banner she had wedged underneath a piece of trim. She sighed and looked at her work, stretching her back as she did. She was sore from working all week. Contended with the way it looked, she went over to the stage where her cello would be waiting for her, thanks to Rachel, who had brought it to the hall earlier.

She cast a glance to Samuel and caught his eye.

"We ready to start?" She asked him.

He made good on his promise and replied. "We are. We'll start with *'My Country Tis of Thee.'*"

The others, Cassie, Rachel, Grubbs, Pitcher, Simone, and Grace all looked surprised that he had spoken so much.

"And a wonderful version of it, it shall be." Margaret smiled and they started the tune.

During the song, Margaret noticed that Mrs. Hill had left with Elizabeth following close behind. She couldn't help but wonder what had transpired between them all. *Will this lead to a new addition to our orchestra? Or a new addition to our family?*

---

Walking into the empty Mess, Harry heard a familiar tune.

> *"...sun shines bright on Loch Lomond.*
> *Where me and my true love will ne'er meet again*
> *On the bonnie, bonnie banks of Loch Lomond."*

A man with a low baritone half sung, half hummed the song. Harry looked around, wondering where the man was. He finally spied him in the corner of the dirty Mess carving something out of a piece of wood with a knife.

Their eyes met and Harry dipped his head to him in greeting

before walking over and joining him at his table.

"Are you Anthony?" Harry outstretched his hand. He had asked to meet the chaplain of their squadron that evening before they flew out for a mission.

"Aye," He replied and shook Harry's hand. "And you're Flying Officer Harry Cavanaugh?" He put his carving knife down on the table.

Harry nodded "That's right. I've heard a lot about you from Woodard and Neff."

Anthony went back to carving the wooden stick. "They're good lads, Officer Woodard and Lieutenant Neff."

Harry sat across from him at the table. Wood shavings were at his feet.

"I've known Val for years. It may surprise you, but I was his algebra teacher back in London. That was before I joined the cloth." He continued to carve.

Harry thought for a few minutes and watched the man work. He let his mind drift from the present to the past and thought about his life before the war. He thought about his school, Regent's Park, listening to Margaret play the piano and cello at Lily's End, and he thought of Evan... his thoughts abruptly jolted to a halt. He couldn't ever think about his brother without feeling sick to his stomach. Sometimes he still couldn't believe he was gone. *How things have changed...* He sullenly thought.

"How are you holding up?" Anthony asked without taking his eyes off his work.

"Alright," Harry said slowly as he was pulled back into the present.

He was about to continue when Anthony spoke again. "You sure?" He looked at Harry now. "You asked to see me." He set down the carving, put his elbows on the table, and crossed his arms.

Harry sighed. "I've just felt rattled lately."

Anthony scoffed. "Who wouldn't? Lad, you're being shot at and fired at and you're watching your friends die around you. We have no control Out There." He paused. "Are you a man of faith?" The chaplain asked.

"Yes," Harry replied. "I think it's the only thing that's gotten me through so far."

"Most likely, it is. Keep praying and reading your Bible if you have one. It gets easier, trust me." Anthony took up the carving again. "If you need a Bible, I can get you one."

"I have one."

"Good." He paused and looked Harry in the eye again. "What does it say about your thoughts?"

Harry thought for a moment and shrugged his shoulders.

"You're smarter than an *'I don't know,'* so don't give me that. What does it say about your thoughts in the Bible?"

Harry furrowed his brow and recalled some of the verses he knew. "Whatever is true, whatever is right, whatever is noble, and whatever is pure and lovely and admirable... to dwell on those things."

"Good..." the chaplain nodded. "What else?"

A few awkward moments of silence passed before he answered for Harry who didn't know the answer.

"Take your thoughts captive." Anthony said. "Imagine your thoughts and your fears like flying planes. You're in the Ops Room and only *you* get to decide which thought gets to land. The others you tell to move on."

"That makes sense."

"Good." A wood shaving fell to the table and was blown off by a gust of wind that came in through the open tent flap of the Mess. "And what does it say about control in the Bible?"

Harry thought for a moment. "That God is in control."

"Mmm, hmm... That will help you. It's helped me and it's helped others. At the end of the day, God isn't surprised by who's on the list. He numbered their days and knew when their time would come. Despite the seeming chaos of it, He is still sovereign, even over the airfield."

Harry watched him for several minutes; both of them were lost in thought.

"It's a small world." Harry commented. "You being Val's old math teacher."

"Even smaller when there's a war." Anthony raised and lowered his bushy eyebrows with a smile and handed the carved thing to Harry. "Funny old world..."

Harry looked down to the carved figurine and saw that it was a rugged cross. He smiled to himself and put it in a pocket of his navy pants.

"You have any other questions, lad?" Anthony asked as he stood and stretched.

He was taller than Harry thought and had slicked back red hair and a red moustache.

"I think I'm alright for now. Thank you." Harry stood as well and shook the chaplain's hand, hoping that his advice would help.

---

May 16th, a warm, beautiful spring day. Betty and Ted Wallace had just gotten married down at City Hall. Only Gabriella and Ted's parents had been there, but they were having a celebration at the house where Ted's sisters came and celebrated along with his parents and family. Betty's parents and her younger sister lived in Iowa, so they hadn't been able to make it on such short notice. Nonetheless, it was a wonderful party that lasted from lunch to midnight. Betty had worn a lovely white suit and Gabriella had bought a small veil for her. Ted had worn his Navy uniform, a white suit with white hat and a navy blue double tie. They were the picture of a perfect couple. They smiled all day. The gramophone garbled out happy love songs and dinner was served. It was a beef dinner, something no one had tasted for quite a while. Gabriella and Margaret had cooked it themselves and were very proud of their work.

As the night drew on and the couple danced slowly in the studio, Margaret sat on the stairs watching them through the open door. She smiled to herself and was joined by Rachel.

"Don't you wish Harry was here? You could dance with him." Rachel sighed dramatically. "It would be so romantic."

Margaret chuckled matter-of-factly. "It would be nice..." She patted Rachel on the head. "I never thought I'd be nineteen and have a boyfriend."

"Maybe next it'll be your turn to get married!" Rachel teased and stood up. "Do you want to dance?" The song was now 'The Boogie Woogie Bugle Boy of Company B,' by the Andrews Sisters.

Margaret got up. "Why not,"

She and Rachel shuffled along with the catchy melody. It had been such a lovely day and had ended perfectly.

Late that night, lying in bed, Margaret couldn't help but think of what the next few months and years would bring... She hoped that wherever Harry was, he was alright. Rachel's words echoed in her mind... maybe next it would be her turn to get married. Margaret didn't know what to think about such an idea. She *had* thought about whether or not she would marry Harry. But it felt so far away. And yet here was Ted, home at a moment's notice because of an injury and he and Betty were married. Just like that, Betty's whole life had changed. Margaret wondered. If Harry asked her to marry him right now, what would she say? She smiled to herself and knew what her answer would be. He so very far away though and victory felt so distant despite the news. Margaret had heard that the North African campaign had ended with a huge victory for the Allies. However, there was always another obstacle in the way of victory; what it was, Margaret, nor Harry, could even begin fathom.

# Chapter 25

The earth shook under Harry and he felt like he had just taken a blow to the stomach. The air was sucked from his lungs as the bomb exploded. Dirt and sand rained down on him, nearly burying him in the earth. He spit out sand and silt and crawled to the entrance of his collapsed foxhole. He managed to edge his way out. Emerging into the daylight, he was nearly blinded by the sun. He glanced up. Formations of Junkers and their Messerschmitt escorts dotted the sky and flew in V formation.

Harry reached behind him and helped the other pilot out of the collapsed foxhole. Val coughed, gasping for air.

"You alright?" Harry asked quickly, choking on the sand that had gotten in his mouth.

Val could only nod in between coughs.

"Come on!" They stumbled to their feet and made a mad dash for another underground shelter.

Luqa, Malta.

It was a place that had been bombed, bombed again, and then bombed once more just for good measure.

High in the sky, the Beaufighters and Spitfires chased down the Messerschmitts and Junkers. Every now and then a muffled explosion could be heard, which meant that a plane had crashed, Allied or Axis, Harry didn't know. Out on the tarmac a Junker was covered in flame on the runway it had been dive bombing. The eerie sirens sent chills up Harry's spine. The Bofors, the anti-aircraft batteries, were throwing up Ack-Ack and the black smoke clusters were like lumps of coal thrown up into the sky.

Amidst the chaos, Harry and Val ducked into the shelter of another foxhole where another man was waiting out the onslaught. They dared a glance to the sky and just as they did, a bomb landed on a storage shed about thirty metres away. Harry covered his ears. He felt the familiar kick in his gut and pressure to his chest from the impact of the blast. Sandy soil heaved up out of the ground, orange flames licked the sky, and splinters mowed through the airfield that was, in reality, a combination of three. Luqa, Hal Far, and Safi. The messy airfields soldiered on and no matter how bad the bombing was, there was always a runway that was usable to land or take off on.

A nearby Bofor anti-aircraft gun was unmanned and Harry pointed to it. Val saw what he was planning and reluctantly nodded. The man beside them, a pilot by the name of Peter, joined them in their sprint to the gun. Harry gritted his teeth and looked at the Bofor 40mm. Peter told Harry what to do. But it was no time for lessons. Harry got behind the gun and fired. The massive gun shook. A Junker was making right for them, about to pepper them with bullets. The blast of the gun nearly deafened Harry, but he kept his aim and shouted as the Junker came closer and closer to the sand-bagged area where the three men were.

"HARRY!" Val yelled over the deafening sound of the gun from where he stood, manning the ammunition.

The bullets peppered the wings, but not the fuselage.

They were out of time.

All at once, they flung themselves next to the sandbags to try to get to cover as bullets hit all around them. Harry covered his head with his arms and tasted sand.

In a second, it was over and the plane whizzed by overhead, shaking the dugout. Recovering quickly, Harry looked about and was about to run back to the gun. Then Harry saw Peter.

"Val!" Harry shouted.

Val hadn't heard him. Harry could hardly hear himself over the cacophony.

"Sod it," Harry thought of several other choice words he could've said. "VAL!" Harry threw a handful of sand at him.

He got to his feet shakily, feeling the blasts from more bombs not far away. He went to Peter's side and rolled him over. Thankfully, he was alive. However, he had three, blossoming red patches on his torso. Peter coughed and there was such a look of agony on his face... Harry had never seen a man in such pain before.

Harry instantly put pressure on two of the gunshot wounds. "We need a medic."

Val looked lost. Both thought it, but neither said it... Peter wouldn't live long enough to get to the nearest med tent.

"Come on," Harry removed his now blood-soaked hands and put them under Peter's armpits. "We have to go quick."

A Messerschmitt was circling the airfield with no one in pursuit. Together they half ran, half shuffled to the relative safety of the closest underground hideout.

"He needs a medic!" Harry shouted to the others in the foxhole.

A few men took Peter from them and set him on a stretcher. One of the men started shouting orders.

Harry could hear the Beaufighters and Spitfires returning. Their ammunition was spent and no doubt their fuel was running low.

"Will he make it? We can take him back to..."

One of the men held up a hand and shook his head.

"What?" Harry looked to his fallen comrade. Time was of the essence. They couldn't wait. "We can take him-" He was about to shoulder past the man when he stopped suddenly.

Peter's hand had fallen off the stretcher. Blood dripped thick and warm from the tip of his finger into the sand below.

His chest did not rise or fall.

He couldn't find the words... could hardly find the air to breath. He stepped back and left the foxhole, the barrage of bombs leaving an eerie stillness to the earth. He spat and tried to wipe the sand out of his eyes, but only succeeded in more getting in.

Val joined him, but both stayed silent. There were no words to be said and none that would suffice.

That evening, Harry manned a Bofor with Guy and Val. They were keeping watch, all thankful for the coolness of the night. The stars shone and Harry stared at them, expecting to see a plane pass in front of them, blocking out their light. Everything was quiet. A faint whisper of men talking by another Bofor battery could be heard some ways down the airfield. Harry was glad to be on watch. Even though they weren't officially gunners, they were close to the dark figures of their Beaufighters, should they hear the enemy approaching and need to scramble to their planes. Manning a gun and keeping watch was better than sitting around doing nothing, just waiting for the fighting to start.

"Any news from Claudie?" Harry asked quietly and leaned back against the sandbags. He looked over to Guy's face that was lit up in the moonlight. His face looked just as anxious as Harry felt.

"Just two more months to go... I'm so nervous for her. It's just..."

He shook his head with sadness. "I wanted to be there; for her... for our child." Guy grew quiet.

"Maybe we'll be home soon." Harry replied. No one responded. Harry didn't believe the weak encouragement either.

Guy got up and sat next to Harry, digging something out of his shirt. Harry looked down as Guy handed him a folded up piece of paper.

"Between us," he said, his voice low. "Give this to her... in person... if something should happen to me."

Harry opened his mouth to protest, but Guy continued.

"Write one up for Meg and I'll hold onto it for you." He clapped him on the shoulder, closing the conversation.

Harry reluctantly put the letter in his shirt... realizing that the men all dealt with the reality of their position differently. Some seemingly ignored the fact they could be killed any minute, some prepared for it, and some worried endlessly. Harry rubbed his shoulder that was sore and shoved the heels of his boots farther into the sand to get more comfortable. He wondered what his approach was... probably a mix of preparing and ignoring the fact death was always right around the corner. There wasn't anything he could do if his time was up. However, he tried not to think of the names of the dead that would appear on the list in the morning.

Val held onto a large rifle and looked nervously up to the sky. "News from Meg?" He asked quietly.

Guy propped his legs up on the base of the Bofor and listened for Harry's response.

"She sounds good... cheery. She enjoys her job and her schooling." Harry shook his head. "I just wish this was all over."

They went back to their evening vigil; every man keenly aware that any minute a raid could start. The airfield was deathly calm. There was not a sound; the distant ocean could not be heard, nor was there any breeze to stir the carob trees; not even the crickets chirped. Yet as the hours ticked by in the eerie quiet of the night, Harry thought he heard something. He popped his head out from above the sandbags and listened into the darkness.

"What is it?" Guy whispered.

Harry held up his hand.

Val's gaze raked the sky nervously.

"Stukas." Harry muttered back and cast a glance to Guy out of the corner of his eye.

"Time to get rolling, lads." Guy was the first out of the sandbag enclosure.

Harry and Val leapt out of the circle of sandbags and ran after Guy just as the sirens started. Another team of battery operators came in behind them to man the Bofor they had just left. Harry sprinted as fast as he could as the crews emerged to man the massive machines. His Beaufighter was straight ahead. As he got her started, Fred, who was still his loyal gunner, joined him. He jumped into the Ten-Ton Terror as fast as he could muster.

Harry and Guy's twin Beaufighters took off into the cloudless sky first. Val was close behind them. Harry hoped they'd be able to intercept the enemy in time. No doubt they were just at the coast. It would be a race to get to the right height. Leaving behind the leprous airfields, Harry brought his Beau up and up faster and faster. He sat on his dinghy, was strapped in as tight as he could stand, and his life-jacket was around his neck, digging into his skin. He levelled out and saw the enemy. Radio over his ears, he spoke to Guy.

"Enemy, dead ahead!"

"Roger that," Guy said back.

"Fred, get ready up there! Twelve o'clock!" Harry started to sweat and shiver at the same time against the chill in the night air.

He gritted his teeth harder as the enemy drew closer. The formation started to break and the Messerschmitts started forward to meet Harry and Guy and the few Beaus that were climbing up close behind them.

"How many do you think there are?" He asked Guy.

"About twenty Me's. Ten Stuka. It's a flock. Could be worse." Guy responded.

"Could be better." Harry glanced over to his friend in the massive black figure of the Beaufighter before they broke formation and plunged into the fray.

Harry pulled up sharp after shooting a second's worth of bullets at an enemy plane. The black cross whizzed by his canopy and he climbed up to the right to get on his tail. As the forces were exerted, Harry let out a breath as he levelled off behind the Me 109. He shot at it in two second intervals and within two bursts, the wing was torn to shreds and the engine was on fire. It probably wouldn't make it back to Axis-controlled territory. Harry turned sharply to the right and with the help of Fred they shot mercilessly at a bomber that banked to avoid their fire. However, he wasn't fast enough and bullets raked his fuselage. Harry caught sight of Guy's plane chasing a Messerschmitt through the formation. Then three more Beaus entered the fight. One had a Messerschmitt on its tail and another had just shot down a Stuka. It burst into flames as it collided with the ground.

Suddenly, Harry's second of delay at a wide left turn had given the opportunity for a Messerschmitt to get on his tail. Bursts of gunfire sounded above Harry, and he dove as steep as he dared. He spun around, his wings slicing through the air and still the Messerschmitt stayed on him and shot at him. Harry levelled off, going as fast as he could and then did a dangerous, tight, and tricky climbing left spin. He hoped the Messerschmitt wouldn't follow him, and he was right. He landed right behind the enemy when he levelled off and then burst out his guns. Fred contributed to the melee and before they knew it, the Messerschmitt was hit in the rudder and listing to the side. It wouldn't be long before it crashed. Harry shot one last time at it and damaged its undercarriage. He climbed up and to the right, getting back into the fray, not wasting time on a plane that would go down soon anyway.

A Beaufighter flew underneath him at a dizzying speed. It was Guy.

"Cav!" He yelled over the cacophony of the R/T. "He's on me! I can't shake him!"

Guy's panicked voice came in and Harry turned to get the Messerschmitt that was close on his tail. The fight drew them closer to the coast and before Harry knew it, they were dogfighting over the Mediterranean, north of the island. The Messerschmitt shot at Guy incessantly and was incredibly tight on his tail. Harry dove at the Messerschmitt and shot many times at him. But still, even with the wounds Harry had inflicted, it wouldn't let off. Harry spun his plane to the left to follow the duelling planes, but just as he did, he heard Guy's yell through the R/T and his Beaufighter burst into a ball of flames.

Harry latched onto the Messerschmitt's tail and burst his guns at him. The agile fighter plane banked and avoided the onslaught.

Harry banked his plane to the right and watched as the ball of flames neared the black waves. He watched with horror.

"Come on. Let out a chute." Harry pleaded.

It neared the sea.

"Come on,"

The burning inferno crashed. Steam and smoke exploding into the sky.

"Harry look out!" Fred alerted him to the fighter coming up at 4 o'clock.

Harry swung his plane around and met the attacker head on, ripping apart his fuselage, but unfortunately not downing the aircraft. Harry's hands shook, but he stayed steady as he neared the airfield again. Some of the bombers had gotten through. There was still work to do.

"Val, Guy went down. I didn't see a chute." Harry said as he came up beside Val's Beau.

"What!?" They were fast approaching the airfield that still had bombers diving over it.

"He's gone, Val. There was no chute." Harry didn't have time to say anymore or process what had just happened. He wagged his wings and dove down to a Stuka that was about to release her bombs.

The pilot never got the chance. He was chased off before he could drop a single bomb. Harry flipped his plane around and plummeted down to the airfield upside-down. He shot at another bomber, but they were all scurrying back to their airfields in Sicily. Nonetheless, he damaged a few. He felt numbness take over him.

Once the raid was finished, Harry landed his plane. It rumbled into silence and he took a moment to sit in the silence of the cockpit.

"NO!" He burst out, letting a scream loose. He ripped the helmet from his head and threw it. It didn't go far, but he didn't care. He balled his fists and pounded on the yoke, shaking with rage and shock.

He finally breathed in and out and tried to relax. *No...* He shook his head, his shoulders trembling. He put his head in his hands and couldn't believe it.

The remaining Beaus, fourteen in all, landed and assessed the damage. Harry opened his canopy and stood on the wing. Fred was right behind him, coming out of his dorsal turret. The wind blew the chilly air in Harry's face, and he felt cold inside.

Guy was gone.

Val walked to Harry's plane and looked up at him. He put his helmet underneath his arm and he and Harry exchanged glances as he climbed down from the wing. Fred jumped down beside him and clapped him on the back.

"He died fighting, Cav."

Val's face was grim. Neither he nor Harry responded to Fred.

"He may still have gotten out once he landed..." Harry started. "I tried to help him... I..." Harry set his jaw firmly and closed his eyes as he tried to think.

"It'll keep. There's nothing more any of us could have done. We need to go report in."

Harry couldn't believe that... he couldn't believe there wasn't anything he could have done. There had been and he had failed. He was quiet as they went back to the shelter to give their reports on the damage the raid had caused both to the enemy... and to them.

Harry stayed in the Ops Room for several more hours. He wouldn't leave until the search returned. After the damage was reported, Val and Fred had taken the long, 5-mile jaunt back to the tents and the Mess Hall in the bed of a full transport truck. Harry had assured them he'd join them as soon as he could.

He sat outside the small sand-colored building and watched the darkness, numb and not quite knowing what to think. Eventually, he saw a Jeep approach and several men got out. The man driving met Harry's eyes and shook his head.

Harry felt his world spin around him. He could hardly believe that Guy was gone. It could have been him. It could have been Val. Alone and in the quiet of the early dawn, he walked the five miles back to their tents. It took him over an hour, but he wanted to be alone. He didn't stop until he entered the tent he, Val, Fred, and Guy had shared. Val sat on his bunk looking as numb as Harry felt. Fred was curled up on his cot with his back to them.

"Should we," Val asked quietly and motioned to Guy's cot and personal things.

"Just leave it," Harry shook his head and collapsed on his cot, too tired to think.

# Chapter 26

Bach's prelude from Partita No. 3 played on Margaret's cello almost effortlessly. Nonetheless, she was ill at ease about playing the song in front of her class. Each student in the strings class was being asked to play it and the fast melody echoed in the classroom. She played a little slower than what was written on the sheet music, but then again, she didn't even look at the sheet music.

Margaret had driven her strings teacher crazy. She never looked at the music and every time Mrs. Gloelecki caught her losing her place on the page, she scolded Margaret. But Margaret never lost her place in her head.

"Thank you, Margaret. Jackie? Will you come up now?" Jackie, a girl who played the viola, went up to the front of the class and picked up the spare viola on the teacher's desk.

Margaret left the classroom's cello by the blackboard and sighed. At least her teacher hadn't caught her not paying attention to the sheet music. She had devised a way to play and look at the sheet music blankly. It always distracted her when she tried to read every note and play it. Margaret sat down and looked out the window of the classroom. Birds and butterflies flitted from tree to bush and she smiled to herself. By the time the entire class of seven played, Margaret's ears hurt from all the playing of that one song. At the end of the day, she was glad for the partial quiet of Central Park.

Strolling through the lush park, Margaret listened to the sounds of New York and felt her book-bag thumping against her side. She thought back to the winter's walks on the same street, 65th Street Traverse. Even though she was at Juilliard every school day and took his composition class, she still missed Mr. Seymour's private lessons. He was fond of her and knew that she had a great talent.

Back at the house, Margaret still was not used to Elizabeth living there. She had come to live with them at the beginning of June. It was almost the end of June now and Margaret was still surprised to see the ten year old in the studio. Not only that, Margaret was still getting used to Betty's absence. The kind and funny teacher had moved to Brooklyn with her husband and came in every Wednesday to teach lessons at the house.

However, her list of clients was dwindling, and she only had Simone and Grace now as students. That meant Margaret went to work alone. She had gotten used to the commute and she was now so familiar with her job, she could do it with her eyes closed, just like Betty had said. Granted, her position changed every now and then and her place on the assembly line moved up as she got better at her job. She enjoyed it immensely. It had never felt so good to be so busy.

Margaret entered the kitchen, and Elizabeth was plucking at the strings of a cello in the living room. Her face lit up when Margaret came in. She had taken a liking to Margaret and was like her shadow. The girl's mother popped in every now and then to see how her daughter was doing. But mostly she paid her room and board and didn't come around too much.

"Hello!" Elizabeth greeted Margaret in her pretend English accent.

She thought Margaret and Gabriella's accents were the neatest thing since television and tried to sound just like them.

"It's a lovely day out, isn't it?" She got up from behind the cello. "Will you show me? Teach me? Is it time for our lesson?"

Margaret had generously, or perhaps foolishly, volunteered to show Elizabeth how to play a cello. How she regretted it now.

"Maybe later, Liz." Margaret forced herself to smile as she made a quick sandwich. "I'm off to work."

"Before I forget!" Elizabeth ran to the foyer and returned with a letter in her hand. "Your mom told me to give you this." She handed it to Margaret as her pretend British accent died away.

"Thank you," Margaret finished making her sandwich and went up the stairs and entered her room.

She saw that the letter was from her father. She quickly ripped it open and read it as she changed into her work clothes.

*'Dear Meg,*

*I cannot begin to describe how much I miss you. I have thought about boarding a ship, or flying in a plane just to get to you. I would risk all the dangers; it would be worth it just to see your smiling face again. Still, it is hard to believe that you are nineteen! Where did my little girl go? This war sets up a barrier between countries and we can only hope and pray that it will be over soon. I don't know how much longer I can wait.'*

Margaret put the letter she hadn't finished reading back in the pocket of her overalls and hurried back downstairs.

"Bye, mum!" She called out as she passed her mother in the foyer. "See you after work!" She gave her a hug and a kiss.

"Be safe," Gabriella called as her daughter left the house behind and headed to the nearest subway station.

Once on the rumbling subway, Margaret finished reading her father's letter.

*'News on the home front is the bombing of Northern Nazi Germany. The fighting is being taken to our attacker's home soil. You know I can be somewhat of a pacifist, but everyone seems rather relieved that Germany is getting a taste of what we've gone through here in London. And I rather agree. I just hope this means we are coming into the end of the war years.*

*Now come my questions... What news on your home front? How is America? One reads stories and articles, but I'd much rather hear it from my girl. What news from Harry? And how is Juilliard? You must know how proud I am of you. To be accepted in the prodigious university and to receive so many scholarships; it is a remarkable thing... I am very proud of you. I know that you have a wonderful career ahead of you and God has blessed you with a wonderful gift. How is your mother?*

*I think about her often. And while I am not participating as actively in the ARP, I have more time on my hands. I think about you and I dare to imagine what things will be like after the war. How can we ever go on as before? In my dreams, we are all together. Still, I make no assumptions and only hope that one day our family, all of us, will be together again.*

*Much love,*
*Your father'*

Margaret finished reading the letter and thought about the last paragraph a great deal. *Her family? Together?* Could she even imagine such a thing? Could her *mother* even imagine such a thing? Margaret's thoughts were interrupted by the subway screeching to a halt. They came to her stop and she got up with all the other second shift workers. They trudged out and all the way to their specific factories. Margaret thought about little else that evening. *Could her family truly be together?*

The next evening, Margaret added another pin to her map in her room. She put the blue thread around the pin which was on the tiny island to the south of Sicily. No doubt about it, she was learning her geography, all thanks to Harry. She had gotten another letter from him, and it had broken her heart. He had sadly told her that one of his best friends had been killed when his plane was hit. Margaret looked at her map and wondered where her dear Harry would be led next. Taking a deep breath, she sat down and wrote two replies, one to her father and one to Harry. The hour was late, but she picked up her cello that was leaning against one of the low walls and played a song known to no one but her. Her emotions picked the notes and her feelings determined the melody. The words of the king she had memorized so long ago replayed in her mind as the melody surrounded her.

*'We cannot tell what the future will bring.*
*If it brings peace, how thankful we shall all be.*
*If it brings us continued struggle,*
*we shall remain undaunted.'*

*"And I said to the man who stood at the gate of the year:*
*'Give me a light that I may tread safely into the unknown.'*
*And he replied:*
*'Go out into the darkness and put your hand into the Hand of God.*
*That shall be to you better than light and safer than a known way.'*
*So I went forth, and finding the Hand of God, trod gladly into the night.*
*And He led me towards the hills and the breaking of day…"*
-Minnie Louise Haskins

# Part 2

# Chapter 27

"Gentlemen, listen up. We are commencing a new campaign. Operation Strangle will be simple to state, but damned near difficult to carry out." The colonel stood in front of the line of men who had their backs to an open hangar. "We are to sever the German Army's lifelines south of Rome. Every bullet they fire, every scrap of bread they eat, every tank they move, has to come down our targeted supply routes."

Harry swallowed hard. He had been chosen along with half of the No. 600 Squadron to join the Desert Air Force, or as it was lately called, the First Tactical Air Force. He glanced out of the corner of his eye, not daring to move his head and caught Val's eye from where he stood next to him.

"This will not be a single raid." The tough colonel shook his head. "Sicily is ours and Mussolini has resigned. That's all well and good, but we need a sustained pressure campaign. Sortie after sortie, day after day, we'll hammer bridges, cut tracks, crater roads, and make them spend more time repairing than supplying." The colonel clasped his hands behind his back, his pilot's cap blocked out the hot late-July sun that was burning over Cassibile. "You'll fly low, you'll meet flak and fighters, both, and we will sustain losses. But remember, every locomotive you put down, every ship you founder, is worth more than a dozen tanks destroyed in the line. Let's make them wither on the vine, men. Soon, Italy will be ours."

A moment passed.

"Gentlemen, you've all trained for this. Keep tight formations, mind your altitudes, and hit your marks. You have your orders." The colonel smiled. "Now see to it."

As the sun set, the pilots scrambled to their hangars.

Chocks away.

The Beaufighter Mk 21s took off into the sky, their pilots and gunners manning them with their mission reeling in their minds.

Harry was one of the many. He strapped himself into the cockpit of his Beaufighter and stared out of the canopy. Rolling grey hills rose up on the horizon; the last hues of the sunset were splashed across the sky; they reflected off the glass of his canopy. *Please God, keep me safe.* He gritted his teeth as the plane gained speed on the runway. A moment of weightlessness overtook him as the wheels left the hot tarmac, as the black plane roared into the sky.

Harry had dozed off. He started when his head began to nod and shook his head to rid himself of his weariness.

Val chuckled from where he sat at the table in the Mess.

Harry sighed when he realized his friend was laughing at him and finished his dinner reluctantly.

He didn't feel like eating, for he still felt sick from his last mission, a day raid on a port city that had ended in many RAF casualties. He thanked the Lord that neither he nor Val was one of those counted dead.

"You look awful." Val got up from the table and left Harry alone with his thoughts.

"You look worse." Harry muttered under his breath.

"Heard that." Val retorted.

Harry played with the last bit of food with his fingers and then gulped down the crumbs of the dry bread.

Here they were, making their way up the boot of Italy. Things had changed in the last few months. The Allies were winning and the Allied Air Force almost had complete air supremacy. The Axis air power was a mere shadow of what it had been years ago, thanks to the brave pilots that had first started the offensive in North Africa.

Harry felt under the weather. He had a cold that he couldn't shake, he had a fever most of the time, and whenever he got into his Beaufighter to bomb a bridge or tunnel, he thought of Guy. Since he had lost his good friend, he had seen some terrible things, particularly near the Gustav Line that lay south of Rome. From his high view, he had seen things he didn't want to think about ever again. The terrors of the war were everywhere. He would fly over towns that were nothing more than rubble now; buildings still burning, bodies still scattered amongst the ruins... men, women, and oftentimes even children. The swath of destruction and death the Nazis left in their wake was horrifying. They burned things down and destroyed and killed everything they passed by merely so the invading Allied forces were left with nothing to work with and no one to aid... It was the most animalistic and barbaric thing Harry had ever encountered. To destroy and kill everything just because you could. Nothing seemed more insane to him. They decimated everything they encountered. It made Harry sick.

He closed his eyes, gulped down his water despite the knot in his throat and got up from the table. He left the Mess and gazed out across the tarmac. Marcianise Airfield stretched out before him and the sunset painted the airfield in golden colours. The red tint of the earth of Italy and the golden rays made it feel warmer than it was. It smelled of earth, for it had rained that day. The showers had left behind a clear, glistening evening.

It was finally spring, and the 600 Squadron had been at the airfield since February. Harry and Val, even though they were part of the First Tactical Air Force now, stayed with their squadron and the others that had been chosen to bomb the transport supply lines of the Germans. *Surely the war can't last any longer?* He thought to himself. Many had thought it had dragged on long enough. Harry sluggishly walked back to the barracks.

Gazing up at the Monte Maggiore Mountains in the north, and the Monte Tifata Mountains in the west, Harry admired their radiance. In the evening, they were russet and in the sun during the day they were purple and a deep, distant blue. Harry put his hands into his pockets and felt Margaret's letter. He pulled it out and smiled faintly to himself. No matter the situation, her letters always made him smile. It tied him to the world he left behind when he joined the RAF at the beginning of the war so long ago.

Harry and Val lounged in their barrack room. There were three bunks per room, and long hallways split the two-story buildings. Harry picked his Bible up from the nightstand and sat on his bed.

"Sure beats a cot, eh?" Val said from the bottom bunk.

"It does, that. I'm glad to be out of the tents." Harry agreed and looked through his Bible that had countless letters from Margaret and his parents in between the pages.

"What's the verse?"

Harry was reading part of Luke and read aloud.

"*The voice of one crying in the wilderness: Prepare the way of the* LORD; *Make His paths straight. Every valley shall be filled and every mountain and hill brought low; the crooked places shall be made straight and the rough ways smooth; and all flesh shall see the salvation of God.*" Harry relayed the verse. "Luke 3:4-6." Harry read on silently when suddenly, a loud voice broke into everyone's thoughts.

"Attention to orders." The NCO called out.

There was a great shuffling and commotion as everyone leapt up and stood at attention.

The commanding officer who was with him elaborated. "Enemy transports are soon to be arriving in Rome. Chocks away at 2030 hours."

The Beaufighters soared into the night sky and made their way towards Rome. The dark Italian coast could be seen to their right and as they flew up the peninsula, they spied the Gustav Line. Harry's mouth became dry as they flew over it. Endless networks of barbed wire, trenches, guns, transports, and infantry littered the ground like a deep scar. There had been intense fighting there since February and Harry prayed that the Allies would soon break through and capture Rome, their target. Harry put his attention back to the matter at hand. He had four bombs under his wings that had to be released over the transport ships. Any minute now Rome and the coastal city, Fiumicino, would show on the horizon and the twelve Beaufighters' work would begin.

The cities and towns passed by far below, their lights twinkling in the night, as the formation headed northwest. Sure enough, Fiumicino was right ahead. Harry checked his map he kept in his boot and re-evaluated their position. Their navigator confirmed the location with the other pilots over the R/T and then they started to descend onto the port city. The flat land spread out before them as they came over the river that divided the off-white and terracotta city. Suddenly, anti-aircraft guns started to explode from below and within moments, the bright bursts of flak littered the air in front of the formation.

"Twenty metres!" The leader instructed them, and Harry brought his Beau even lower to the ground.

"Fifteen metres!" The leader commanded them again and they whizzed over the houses of the city.

Harry saw the port just ahead and there were over twenty transport ships coming into the harbor. They had arrived just in time. Harry picked his target and bombs away. One of the bombs exploded on a transport ship. Harry executed a climbing right turn and double-backed over the port, remaining in formation with his group. He dropped another one of his bombs, but it missed its target by a hair. Explosions riddled the air and flak was thrown up into the sky. Harry tried to evade the flak, but it was coming up everywhere. He pulled out of their range, breaking formation, and dove back into the port that was smoking terribly. Harry flew through the pillars of black smoke and above the furious, orange flames. He dropped another bomb on a transport ship that was trying to get out of the mayhem. Thankfully, it exploded into a ball of flame that was much larger than it should have been. Harry looked back at the ship, something he knew he wasn't supposed to do, and realized he must have blown up a ship full of ammunition.

*One more bomb.* Harry wiped the cold sweat off his forehead and maneuvered around the many planes that were diving in and out of the smoking port.

The river Tiber reflected the fires that had sprung up on the water as the wreckage burned. The night was wild with confusion and chaos. Harry eyed another ship that was sailing up the river, trying to escape. He came up behind it and flew lower and lower. He found himself holding his breath as he open fired on the transport ship and let loose his last bomb. However, his bomb missed and landed in the canal. It exploded in the river right behind the ship, thus destroying it. But the anti-aircraft guns let loose on Harry's plane. Suddenly, the controls went lax and Harry fought with the yoke to get his plane back under control. But it was no use. He glanced quickly to his right and saw half of his wing was blown off from an anti-aircraft cannon and an engine was on fire.

Climbing to a suitable height so he wouldn't crash into the houses that were along the canal, Harry managed to bank to the right. His engines sputtered and Harry panicked. *Gone down in enemy territory...* He could see the letter his parents would receive. It was then that fear hit him like a tidal wave.

"Red leader. Engine shot. Losing power." He relayed over the R/T to the leader of their formation.

"Condition confirmed, red three, bale out while you've the height." He responded.

Harry attempted to bring his plane up higher. "Negative, she's seizing."

"Turn southwest if able,"

Harry yelled with exertion, for the Beau was fighting him, wanting to crash and give up. The sweat dripped off his face, he couldn't bail out at such a low altitude.

The plane groaned and grunted and suddenly his port engine burst into flame as well.

"Make it clean, red three." Val's voice shot out over the radio. "We'll mark your position."

Harry pulled the lever that released his hatch. He surrendered the yoke to fate, lifted himself out of his seat and swung himself over to the hatchway.

Nothing was below his feet but open air.

Tree tops whizzed by not far away.

He said a quick prayer and let go.

The cold night air slammed into him, shocking the breath out of his lungs. He pulled on his parachute and thanked God that it billowed out above him without any tears or static. The Beaufighter was flying away from him, the flames dizzyingly bright against the pitch black of night. Time seemed to still as the thundering plane's engine exploded and it crashed into the canopy of trees. A second later and it let out a huge mushroom cloud of flames and black smoke. Harry could feel the shockwave and the heat it released. He took in his surroundings quickly, fighting against his panic. To the north were open fields and vineyards, to the south, east, and west, lay more forest. As he neared the canopy, the real trouble began. He was headed nearer and nearer the burning inferno that had been his plane not moments before. He tried to steer away from it, but the tree canopy was coming up fast. Cursing all manner of vegetation, Harry fell into the branches at a sickening speed. From then on, all else was a blur.

Branches scratched his face, birds flew off in terror, and Harry was hit on all sides by the boughs and branches of the thick woodland. His parachute got tangled in the canopy and he stopped with a stomach-turning jolt in his harness. He felt the heat before he saw it. About forty-five metres away, the fire was raging around the remnants of his plane, its flames licking up to the tallest treetops. Harry wiped something wet and sticky off his face and looked down. He groaned with despair. The ground was at least ten metres away and there was nothing between him and it.

The fire continued to grow.

"Lord, help me." He looked around for any branches he could get a hold of, but there were none. *The last thing I want to do is be burned alive hanging in a tree.*

The only limbs were the ones entangled in his parachute. Harry bounced his weight up and down to try and get the parachute unstuck, but it was no use. He hung there and looked down at the ground and wondered if he could fall that far without hurting himself. He didn't have time to contemplate the situation.

"Now or never," he muttered to himself.

Harry closed his eyes and took a deep breath. He started to undo his harnesses and with every strap he undid, his tension and anxiety rose. The sweat he was dripping in made his hands clumsy. The fire was unbelievably hot. Blood dripped from somewhere on his head. *Last strap...* Harry unfastened it and plummeted to the hard dirt ground. He crumpled, landing on his feet and hearing a sickening snap at the same time... pain like fire shot through him and he howled in agony.

# Chapter 28

Harry's hands shook with pain and fear and cold. He was leaning against a tree and was exhausted. From what he could tell, his ankle had broken when he fell out of the tree. He had retched right then and there and though the last thing he felt like doing was moving, he managed to get a safe distance away from the fire before he took a moment to examine his leg. It was indeed broken, as he couldn't move it without excruciating pain and it stayed at a slightly bent angle. His only choice was to hop on one leg from tree to tree to try to make his way out of the forest and put as much distance between himself and the plane as possible. The tower of smoke that billowed from the wreckage was like a giant beacon telling every enemy in the area 'an Allied plane went down here.' Harry was in so much pain; he was drenched with sweat even though it was a cool night. Sometimes he didn't know whether his face was sweating or still bleeding, but nonetheless, he hobbled on with one good leg. The thought of being captured terrified him... it was the most scared he had ever been in his life and that fear drove him on.

Taking one hop at a time, Harry reached for another tree and stumbled forward. He fell into a patch of brambles with thorns and bit into his fist to stop himself from screaming. Rolling off the thorny patch, he lay on the cool ground that was covered in leaves. *I have to do this...* He panted for air and yearned for a clear path. If he stayed in the forest, he'd be closer to danger and the ruined plane. If he left, he'd be out in the open wearing an RAF uniform, unable to speak the language, with a broken leg. His options weren't good.

*God, please help me.*

He thought about what he should do. Surely, he'd be found if he stayed. Would anyone take pity on him and hide him at the risk of their own lives if he left the woodland? Could he even walk far enough to somehow return to Allied territory? Doubts and questions swirled in his mind, making him dizzy. He opened his eyes and looked up at the tree canopy. *If I don't get out of here, I'll die.* Harry knew it was the truth. It kept repeating itself in his mind. If he stayed where he was, he would die. And so, he rose and continued on, deciding to roll the dice and take a gamble with his life. He had a chance if he soldiered on... granted, it was a slim chance, but it was better than giving up and wasting away in the woods. It sounded grim when Harry thought it, but he'd rather be shot than starve or freeze to death.

Minutes seemed like hours, and hours seemed like days. Harry slid down deep ravines and climbed through thick undergrowth. However, just as he thought he was about to die from pain and exhaustion, he would find new strength and press on for another hour. Before Harry realized it, the dark forest turned grey, and the dawn started to brighten the black night. Harry had never been so afraid to see daylight coming.

Caked with sweat and blood and dirt and grime, Harry hopped to another tree and grasped its bark. He thought he heard something. Opening them slightly, Harry listened. The usual sounds of a forest awakening greeted him; birds chattered all about him. The leaves rustled in the morning breeze. However, he heard the rumble of an engine straight ahead. It passed within a few seconds, and silence ensued. *I must be close to a road.* He thought as he heard the same kind of quiet car engine grow and fade. *Just to that stand of trees...* Harry pushed himself onwards as the grey of the morning surrounded him.

Just ahead of a clearing in the forest, was a series of trees with thick undergrowth at their base. Harry crawled across the clearing and felt pain shoot up his leg, but he was almost numb to it now, having felt it the entire night.

Harry reached the undergrowth and peered through. The forest came to a half before a smooth stretch of pavement that went as far as the eye could see in either direction. The road was not busy, but the last thing Harry wanted to do was be picked up by a truck full of Germans. He couldn't even imagine what they did to their prisoners of war. He had heard stories... words like camps, prisons, and torture murmured around the Mess halls. He gritted his teeth.

Squeezing underneath the bushes and brambles, Harry was right in front of the road. He got up on his good leg and started to hop across the street. He could scarcely pick up his left leg, so he merely dragged it along at an awkward angle. Thankfully, there were no cars and Harry thanked God for it. Just as he was nearing the other side and coming off the pavement, he slipped. His good leg went out from underneath him and he fell back onto his injured ankle. He howled in pain as all his weight came down on his injured leg. He toppled into the ditch as everything surmounted, the weight of everything crashing down on him at once.

His vision flickered. His eyes fluttered. And he blacked out, completely exhausted... at his wit's end with nowhere to go and nowhere to hide.

---

For the last time, Margaret showed Elizabeth how to hold the bow.

"You have to grip it but let it hang loose." She was growing impatient with the young girl.

It was useless, Elizabeth, no matter how hard she tried, could not hold the bow correctly. She sagged her shoulders and sighed with despair.

"I can't do it!" She put down the bow and got up from behind her small cello.

She stomped out of the room, her reddish brown hair bouncing with every step. Margaret didn't even try to stop her. She sighed and shook her head, for she had gotten frustrated too.

They had been at it for over a half an hour and this had gone on for the entire weekend. Margaret put the cello back in the hidden room in the studio and gazed at the other single cello that was against the long wall. When she had first come to the house, the celli had been covered with dust. But now they were well loved and used often. Margaret fingered the scroll of her cello and left the secret room behind. She rolled the shelf back in front of the doorway and left the studio, turning off the lights as she closed the door behind her.

The air was chilly and Margaret shivered as she entered her room. She had left her window open to let in the warm afternoon sun and now the cool March evening breeze wafted in. She closed her window and gazed out into the street.

*Five years... Five long years...* It had been so long since she had seen her father, Harry, and Bess, that she was starting to wonder if things would even be the same when they reunited. She was a different person now... and she wondered if Harry, Bess, and her father would be different as well.

Picking up her Bible from her shelf, she read a few verses of Galatians and found comfort in the words and promises. Margaret paused in her reading and thought back to her fifteenth birthday that seemed so long ago. She would be twenty this year and she could hardly believe it. No longer was she the girl lost in the hustle and bustle of New York City, or pining for her home so very far away. She was a young woman now with a good job and a bright, promising career ahead of her. Juilliard was everything Margaret had ever hoped for and more. This winter, she would have been going to Juilliard for two years. She only had two more years to go and then she would graduate. After that, it was all up to Margaret's imagination. She could give lessons, be a teacher, become a professional musician, or join an orchestra or symphony... Her possibilities were endless. However, Margaret forced herself to remain sensible and not let her imagination run too wild. Her father's letters always helped with that.

Margaret sat at her desk and glanced over the latest letter from her father. He had given her the usual news. Bess was nearby doing work here and there and volunteering wherever she was needed. The sermons were going well and he had said they were always more than full. People had started to fill the church more than ever before. There was now standing room only. He also said how Mr. Burdelik, Margaret's music teacher from years ago, had returned from the British Expeditionary Force with a slight wound, so he was now playing the piano and the organ for the sermons. She had recently had a brief letter from Harry. Their squadron had moved again and they were busier than ever. Margaret wished he could tell her everything they were doing, but it was all hush-hush. *Someday we'll be able to sit and talk all day about everything that happened.* She hoped it would truly happen someday and it wasn't just wishful thinking on her part... a blind hope.

A voice broke into Margaret's thoughts. "Meg! Time for dinner!"

It was Rachel.

"Coming!" Margaret called back and dashed out of her room to join the others around the dinner table.


"Amen," Gabriella finished the prayer and the family of six started to eat the dinner of chicken soup with homemade bread.

Margaret had made the bread from the recipe Bess had sent her some weeks ago. She was proud of her work, for it used as little ingredients as possible, but it tasted very good.

"How was your cello lesson, Liz?" Gabriella asked from her place at the head of the table.

Elizabeth furrowed her eyebrows and pouted. She looked intently at her soup and didn't say a word.

"I'm afraid we're still having trouble with the bow." Margaret replied meekly and smiled kindly to Elizabeth who was still pouting.

"Well, perhaps we could ask Betty to come over and give you a few lessons. She is very good at teaching and I'm sure she could help you." Gabriella offered.

Elizabeth seemed to brighten at the news.

"When will Miss Betty come to see us?" Pitcher asked as he took a bite of bread.

It had been a few weeks since she had come to the house to give a lesson. Margaret missed her and she was sure the others did as well. Obviously, she was very busy with being a wife and working her new job over in Brooklyn at a music store.

"I don't know," Gabriella answered. "But maybe we could pop in and see her. Wouldn't that be lovely?" She smiled and Pitcher and Grubbs exchanged excited glances.

"Hannah said in her letter that she still couldn't believe Betty was married." Rachel put in. "I hope that when the war's over Hannah can come back and live with us." She said hopefully.

No one said anything for a while, for they all new that this war had changed things for them and that their lives would never be the same after it. Who knew what the future held? The Moser twins had not been seen for at least a year, Betty would never return to live at the house, and Hannah still lived in Chicago with her parents. Everyone at the table knew, deep down, that their lives would never be the way they were years ago, yet no one wanted to admit it.

---

The sun was rising in the sky when Harry woke with a start. Someone had screamed. He opened his eyes and saw a woman running away from him. His breath faltering, Harry propped himself up and watched as the woman ran down the road and disappeared into a driveway. His heart rate quickening, Harry tried to get up, but it was no use. Even if he could get up, he wouldn't have been able to get out of the ditch. He was stuck. And now he was imagining what would happen next. Someone had found him... they would call the authorities... he'd be imprisoned.

Harry tried to get his wits about him. It took him several seconds to sit up and then get to his feet. There was a fence along the road, in the same ditch he had fallen into. He grasped the split rails and using it to support himself, he started to hurry away as quick as he could.

However, he did not get far before a man came out of the same driveway the woman had gone into.

He marched furiously after Harry.

Harry quickened his pace.

He yelled out in Italian and the woman spoke something too. They started to argue and looked furious at each other.

A splinter dug into Harry's palm, but he kept hobbling away from them, oddly aware of his raspy breathing and how thirsty he was. His head was throbbing.

The arguing behind him ceased and the man ran after him. He caught up in a laughable amount of time and grabbed Harry's shoulder.

Harry stiffened and swung around to meet him, withdrawing his aircrew knife at the same time.

They stood at an impasse. The Italian held up his hands and his wife caught up to them. They exchanged apprehensive looks, and Harry knew he had to make a choice and take a chance.

*Please, God, let this be the right decision.*

Slowly, Harry lowered his knife.


When Harry awoke, he thought he was in a dream. He was on a bed in a small clay-stucco room with yellow gingham curtains and birdsong filtering in through the open window. Harry tried to stir, but as soon as he moved, pain shot up his leg.

Everything from that day came to mind... the man and woman instructing him as best they could to lay back down in the ditch, covering him with debris... Their return in a cart pulled by a donkey... smuggling him into their farm and very home. Hushed, panicked voices... He realized just how fortunate he was... just how blatantly God had delivered him.

Suddenly, the small door opened, and the man came in. He slammed the door hard behind him and his intense dark eyes looked straight down at Harry. The man grumbled under his breath in Italian with his deep, intimidating voice. He spoke a string of words Harry did not understand, but he listened.

Watching in confusion, Harry's head throbbed. "Thank you for saving my life."

The short woman peaked into the room and asked a question in Italian.

"Get out of here, woman!" The man yelled then stopped pacing.

"I think we understand each other?" Harry managed to sit up. "English," he put his hand on his chest, then outstretched it to the Italian man.

The man glared at Harry. His eyes looked like they were burning with anger. "Thank my wife and her faith. I would have left you." The man responded curtly.

Harry swallowed, his dry throat scratching. "You don't have to keep me here. I know the danger it puts you in. I can leave." He offered even though he knew he couldn't walk and wouldn't know where he was going.

"Do not tempt me." The man paused, eyeing Harry. "We have to get rid of that." He pointed to Harry. "The uniform."

Harry agreed. He started taking off his jacket and the man helped him with the rest. His pins and insignia, the man took off and pocketed, obviously to dispose of, perhaps in some river or buried so no one could find them. He helped Harry into a change of his own clean clothes and eyed his dog tags.

"Those too," he held out his hand.

Harry looked up at him, exhausted just from the simple act of changing clothes.

"I can't," Harry couldn't part with them... they were his last link to the RAF.

The man still held his hand out, his dark brown eyes firmly locked on Harry's.

A few moments of silence passed. Harry realized he was in no place to negotiate with these people; besides they had just saved his life. He took off his identification and handed them to the man who swiftly left to burn his clothes and bury his belongings.

Harry sat up in bed and rubbed his face, it was still caked in dirt and blood and grime. The door quietly opened a few seconds later and the woman entered. She walked over to Harry with a bowl of water and a towel. She put them on the bedside table to Harry's left. Leaving for a few moments, she returned with a plate of bread and cheese, and a glass of water.

"Giovanna." She dipped her head to Harry.

"Harry Cavanaugh," Harry dipped his head to her as well in greeting. "Thank you... thank you so much."

She wrung out the towel in the basin of water and handed it to Harry who thankfully wiped his face with it. She repeated that until all the blood and grime was gone.

"Bruno Russo," she inclined her head to the door.

Harry took that to mean it was her husband's name. "Thank you." He told her and offered a slight smile.

The poor woman looked terrified behind her calm appearance. Harry had gotten used to seeing fear in someone's eyes even when they didn't want to show it. She spoke something in Italian, crossed herself, and motioned to the food and water, handing the glass to Harry when he couldn't reach it.

"*El doctore...*" Giovanna pointed to his ankle.

Harry drank and felt incredibly guilty.

The Italian woman left the room and closed the door behind her. Once Harry ate the food she had brought and drank the entire glass of water, he put his head in his hands. He heard children running through the house. *What have I done?* He couldn't imagine what would happen if they were found out. On the other hand, he physically couldn't leave. Part of him wished Bruno had killed him back in the ditch. It would have been easier than this. How could Harry endanger these innocent civilians? How could he allow them to risk their lives and their children's lives for his sake? There was no winning in this war. Someone always had to pay the price. As darkness crept into his room, he fell asleep with a painful throbbing in his left ankle, so painful he almost couldn't stand it.

# Chapter 29

Right before she headed off for school, Margaret gazed at the map that was on her wall, framed by the rows and rows of shelves. *Another day and no news...* She looked at the blue ribbon that skipped from the tiny island of Malta up to the western side of Italy. *Where will he go next?* Margaret longed for news and an update on where her dear Harry was. Grabbing her book bag, Margaret left her room and closed the door with a slam.

Central Park was busy as commuters walked to their jobs. Rachel and Margaret went along together, each with their book bags slung around their shoulders. They had made the commute hundreds of times and knew it by heart. Every pothole, every rise in the sidewalk, they knew. They crossed Lincoln Center and entered the famous Juilliard School. The two girls parted in the hallways that were lacking in attendance. All colleges were low on young men and women earning their degrees. The young men were off fighting overseas and the young women had taken the men's places in the factories to help with the war. It was another average day in New York City's Juilliard School. It was another day that the war was not over and it weighed heavily on everyone's minds.

That afternoon, as Margaret and Rachel got back from school, the other children were returning as well. Grubbs was showing off a new harmonica he had found on the sidewalk and Gabriella was scolding him to wash it before he played it. Samuel, the young composer that had recently turned eighteen, was scribbling quietly at the table, and Pitcher was practicing his curveballs out the back door as Louis bounded after them to chase them. It was a busy house and the chatter was constant. Rachel was talking loudly on the phone and Margaret peeked into the back hallway and told Pitcher to go outside before he broke a window or went right through the wall. The corgi bounded after him. Walking back to the foyer, Margaret scanned the table with the gramophone for any letters. There were none. She sagged her shoulders and entered the kitchen to see Grubbs rinsing off his harmonic. Gabriella was red in the face as Elizabeth ran into the kitchen with her pretend British accent.

"Can I pop down to Macy's? I saw *the* cutest dress when we walked by..." Her request was silenced as two people entered the loud house.

"Gabriella! Meg! Rachel!" Betty and Ted Wallace came into the house and joined the busyness.

"Betty!" All their faces lit up and the noise picked up again.

They were all excited to see the former teacher and her husband. Ted was a fun-loving guy and despite his injury that would never quite heal completely, he was as lively as Pitcher. The boys all went outside to play catch. Inside, Margaret and Gabriella and Rachel all hugged Betty and they exchanged news. It was lovely to have Betty back and all of Margaret's previous worries and doubts melted away. However, she kept an eye on the clock. She and Rachel had gotten home early from Julliard, but she would have to leave soon for work.

"Ted's found a job at the library! Can you believe it?" Betty plopped down on the couch in the living room and the other girls sat around her. "Ted! In a library!" She exclaimed. "I never would have guessed he'd want to work there. I come home from Kochanek's, it's always 'Betty this' and 'Betty that.'" She beamed and Margaret smiled with amusement and happiness. "But I wouldn't change it for the world." Betty tossed her light brown curls off her shoulder. "What about you all? How's the school running?"

"We're steadying the buffs. Mr. Ackerman comes by two or three times a week and gives a few lessons. But things have quieted down and usually it's just us here." Gabriella replied.

As she spoke, Margaret watched her mother and noticed a hint of worry in her eyes. She reminded herself to ask her mother about it that night.

"Well, I'm glad. I *do* miss teaching, but I *love* living in Brooklyn. It's not as pretty as it is here, but it's just the right size for us." Betty explained.

"Meg's been trying to teach me how to hold a bow." Elizabeth said in her regular voice.

"Has she?" Betty smiled and looked to Margaret. "How has it been going?" She asked when she saw the look on Margaret's face.

"Not good, I'm afraid. Perhaps you could help her, Betty. I'm sure you could teach her better than I could." Margaret sat on the arm of the couch next to and above Betty.

"Don't worry, Liz, we'll give it a go before we have to leave." Betty nodded and smiled to Elizabeth whose face had brightened up.

It was a quick visit, for the Wallace's were on their way to Coney Island for an evening on the boardwalk. Margaret took off for work a little before they left.

"Are you still waiting to hear back from Harry?" Margaret's friend inquired.

Sighing, she nodded. "Yes, I still haven't heard anything yet." She told Emily, the young lady who had taken Betty's spot on the assembly line to Margaret's left.

Margaret was thankful Emily had been put on the same line as her. They were close in age and got along terrifically. They had even gotten together a few times to see some of the popular movies that had come out recently.

"Well, I'm sure you'll hear back soon." Emily encouraged her. She fixed her red headband she wore tied up over her short black hair.

"I hope so." Margaret replied. "It's driving me crazy not knowing whether he's alright or not. I think I would've heard if anything bad had happened."

"I'm sure you would have. Although there's probably quite a gap between things happening on the front lines and the time it takes for word to get back to us." Emily offered her encouragement.

Margaret thought about what she had said. "Hopefully I'll hear soon."

She smiled to her dear friend and they went back to work. However, she doubted her own words. Something deep down made Margaret feel like something was wrong. She didn't know how to describe it, so she didn't attempt to tell Emily about it. Perhaps she was right, perhaps she was wrong... she just prayed that Harry was alive and well and their letters had just been mixed up. *Please, God, let him be alright.* She prayed that short prayer more than she ever had before.

Upon returning home from work around midnight, Margaret found herself in the living room alone with her mother who was reading. The others had all gone to bed.

"Mum?" Margaret asked in surprise. Usually her mother didn't wait up for her. "S'everything alright?"

Her mother's brown eyes looked up from the cover of Times magazine. "Oh yes, just couldn't sleep."

Margaret nodded, completely understanding.

"How was work? How's Emily?" Gabriella asked.

"Work went quickly, and Emily's great. She's taking next week off to visit home. Her brothers will be on leave and she hasn't seen them for over a year." Margaret sat down on the couch, quite exhausted. "Can I ask you something?"

"Of course," Gabriella put down her magazine and grabbed a blanket from the back of the couch.

"I don't know how to say this..." Margaret trailed off. "But... Is everything alright? Only I heard what you said to Betty about things slowing down and us steadying the buffs. But I noticed... I don't know, you just seemed worried." Margaret watched her mother's face as she listened to her.

"We *are* steadying the buffs... But it's a bit harder than I thought it would be. No one is interested in music these days. Who can blame them?" She lowered her voice and sighed. "We're struggling a bit financially. Betty's gone and so is what she used to contribute to rent. Not enough lessons, too many bills. The time may come, Meg, when we might..." She shook her head, deep in thought.

"We might have to close the school?" Margaret already knew what was coming.

"Yes. Or move to a different place. But that's a long way away. And we would make a great number of changes before that happened. For instance, if any of the children *can* go home to their parents, like Liz and Andrew, whose parents are alive and well... well, they would have to go."

"I can help. My pay from Grumman, I can contribute more."

Gabriella smiled. "I know, and we may need it. But for right now, we're steadying the buffs. Something'll work out, and if it doesn't... this is a big house. We don't need all this space."

Margaret nodded thoughtfully. It made sense. Part of her was scared at the prospect of having to leave the house that had become a home. But she was also growing and maturing and she wasn't a child anymore... she knew things changed and all you could do was walk through those changes as courageously as you could.

*What did the king say?* Margaret thought to herself. *We must remain undaunted.*

Now was the time to live that out more than ever.

---

Harry woke up with a start from his nightmare. His head throbbed and his wrapped ankle stuck out awkwardly.

He was now faced with a terrible decision that he had to figure out by dawn. The doctor had come at midnight that night, waking Harry out of a deep sleep. He had told Harry in very broken English that his leg needed to be operated on. He could either get the operation done in the back room in the little Italian casa and risk infection or let it heal on its own and pray that the bones healed correctly. Harry was undecided, but he was leaning towards one option more than the other. He was just thankful the doctor was willing to treat him.

Morning came, the early birds chirped away. Harry sat up in bed and waited for the family to wake up as well. About twenty minutes passed before a little head peeked into his room. Harry raised his eyebrows. The little boy raised his eyebrows as well. Harry waved weakly. The little boy waved back. He chuckled underneath his breath and was pulled out of the doorway. An older boy peeked into the room. They were whispering to each other. Suddenly, a voice called them, the voice of their father, and they disappeared.

Giovanna entered a few moments later. She brought Harry a meager breakfast and he thanked her heartily. He wished he could speak with her, but it seemed the only person in the house who could speak some English was Mr. Russo and he didn't seem too happy to have Harry there. Harry didn't blame him. If he had been in that position, he would've had a hard time putting his family in danger for the sake of a stranger. It reminded him of the good Samaritan...

The Italian woman left as Harry ate. Once he finished and put the plate on the nightstand, he looked up in surprise. The older-looking boy who had peeked through the door was climbing in through the window.

He swore at the brambles he was climbing through.

"You can speak English?" Harry asked as the boy who looked to be about eight climbed down from the window and onto a chair.

"My name's Antonio. My brothers are Pietro and Andrea. Papà's very angry at you and Mamma. But Mamma is Catholic and says it's the Christian thing to do... otherwise she'd have to pray her rosary for a very long time."

Harry half-smiled in grim amusement. "Tell her thank you for me, alright?"

"Thank you is *grazie*." Antonio stood at the foot of Harry's bed. "Now you can thank her." He was silent for a moment and looked down at Harry's leg. "Are you going to die?"

"Not right now, thanks to your parents." Harry replied.

Antonio looked deep in thought. "Papà hates you because you killed his brother... and my aunt and my cousins."

Harry furrowed his eyebrows. "How does he figure that?"

"Uncle Mario lived near the big monastery at Monte Cassino." Antonio motioned with his hands at how big the monastery was. "But it was attacked in *gennaio*."

Harry stared at the face of the young boy. He had often thought of the civilians the First Tactical Air Force was putting in danger... and how many civilians were killed because of the bombing missions they carried out.

"I'm sorry, Antonio." He truly meant it.

The boy didn't know what to say and merely climbed on the wooden bedframe and shrugged. Suddenly, the doorknob rattled. Antonio dashed to the window and was gone from sight before Harry could say another word. Giovanna entered with the doctor following. Harry took a deep, shaky breath. It was time for him to make his decision.

———————

Several days passed before Margaret received a letter that contained news. However, as she walked into the foyer from a long day at school, her heart stopped, not from excitement, but from dread.

The letter was from Mr. and Mrs. Cavanaugh. She had never had a letter from them. *Something must be wrong!* She panicked and ignored the innocent questions from Elizabeth who was sitting on the stairs with Louis beside her. Margaret was crying, her breath taken away in fear and panic.

*'Dear Meg,*

*How sad we are to write to you with this news. I wish we did not have to tell you this. Our dear Harry's plane has been shot down over Italy. The telegram we received explained how they were sure he had gotten out before it went down. But beyond that, we have no other news.*

*Oh, dear Meg, please be praying for him. He is in God's hands, as he always has been. But pray that he is safe. Perhaps the coming month will bring the liberation of Rome, and he will be reunited with his countrymen... But how can we be sure?*

*Please pray for our Harry's safety.*

*Your affectionate neighbors,*

*Mr. and Mrs. Cavanaugh.'*


Margaret gasped and dashed past Elizabeth and Louis. She ran all the way into her room and closed and locked the door behind her. She cast herself onto her bed and imagined the worst of things. Her fears were what made her sob, not simply the news. A few minutes later, a knock sounded on her door.

"Come in," Margaret sniffed and wiped off her wet cheeks.

"The door's locked, Meg." Rachel's voice replied.

Getting up quickly, Margaret unlocked the door and went back to her bed and she shuddered with every sob.

"Lizzy told me..." Rachel sat next to Margaret. "Is he..." She couldn't say the one word they never spoke of.

"No," Margaret sniffed and cried. "But his plane was shot down over Italy. They have no other news. What if..." Margaret was plagued by the thoughts.

"Don't do that to yourself," Rachel took her friend's shoulders and stared at her. "Don't assume the worst when you don't know. He could be fine!" Rachel shook sense into her best friend.

Margaret looked to Rachel and hugged her. "You're right. I wish mum was home from the store." She took a shaky breath. "Oh!" She let out her breath. "I always prayed that he would be spared... God help him. Please, God help him."

Margaret and Rachel embraced each other as Margaret's sobs quieted overtime. It was not the worst news; Harry was not dead. But the thought of him in Nazi-occupied Italy was enough to send Margaret over the edge with worry. And yet she prayed. She prayed fervently to God that Harry would be spared. She could not imagine what would happen if he was taken...

The last pin was on Marcianise, Italy north of Naples and the blue ribbon hung limply from it. Once Gabriella had returned, she and Margaret had talked extensively about Harry and now she was feeling calmer. God was with him wherever he went, whether he was with his squadron or on his own in Italy. She looked down to the shelf that was right below the map and it had Harry's latest letters folded neatly on the top. She read through a few and missed him more than ever. That night she went to work and was comforted by Emily and Heather, another one of the girls she had gotten to know on her line. She was so thankful for them. Together, the three young women took a moment during their break and formed a small huddle, holding each other's hands. Together, they all prayed that Harry would be alright, that he would be safe, and he would find his way back to friendly territory, and maybe, just maybe, the war would be over soon.

---

*Two weeks down... six to go.* Harry hobbled over to the small window in his small room and was glad to finally be standing and moving about the house for the first time in weeks. Granted, he had crutches that the doctor had given him, but at least he could move about. He had decided to let his ankle heal on its own after the doctor had set it. The surgery was too risky and he thought if it healed enough for him to walk and get to friendly territory, he would be more than satisfied with that.

The Russo's had been so very good to him. He never saw Bruno Russo or the younger boys, but Giovanna came in frequently to bring meals, and Antonio came in through the window and brought Harry books and things he had found outside; rocks, sticks, bird nests, and he even brought Harry their barn cat once to keep him company. He talked endlessly about all the things he did every day. He talked about going out to their vineyard in the morning with his father and wandering around the hay field and caring for their animals. He spoke very good English and Harry asked him if they taught it to him in school. Antonio had shaken his head and said that his father had taught him... just in case they ever had to go to America.

It was apparent that the Russo's were not Nazi-sympathizers, as Harry was still alive, but it was a dangerous time. Harry was sure Mr. Russo kept his children away from him so that word wouldn't slip. Antonio was old enough, but the younger children might talk. And loose lips could be deadly to any and all who knew you. Harry never left the room either. If someone stopped by or saw him accidentally, it would spell disaster for all of them. His blond hair and blue eyes were enough to make him stick out like a sore thumb. Thankfully, Harry didn't mind the small room. It gave him time to think and heal and breathe. He didn't have to wake up at dusk to go out on a mission. It was his first real break from the war since it had started. True, he had been on leave occasionally when his squadron had still been based out of England. But the moment they had gone overseas, no leave was given them. They were too valuable... too needed.

Often, Harry lay awake, staring at the ceiling, deep in thought. He thought of Val and what he was doing. He wondered if Val was still alive. It was a possibility that was always at the forefront of the pilots' minds. He also found himself thinking about home, Lily's End, his old school... and most importantly, Margaret. He wondered what she was doing, what she was thinking, and if she was alright with the news of his predicament. He wondered if he would live to see the end of the war and a time of peace... At that moment, it seemed distant. England seemed like a world away and London felt like a faraway dream.

The doctor visited every other week to check Harry's progress. Harry didn't understand much of what the Italian doctor said when Bruno wasn't there to translate, so he was unsure of his progress, but he hoped for the best.

*Will I be able to walk? Will I be able to fly?* Harry tried not to dwell on those two questions for too long. It was something he didn't even want to consider. *Thank you, God.* He still couldn't believe he was alive. How fortunate he had been when so many were dealt the worst possible scenarios. *I'll never take another day for granted.*

The day finally came when Harry's cast could come off.

It was about midnight when the elderly doctor came in by way of the vineyard. He went to Harry's room and Harry sat up in bed. He looked up expectantly and watched Bruno take a seat in the corner where he would observe the diagnosis, his arms crossed, and a grave look on his face.

"*Buonasera, signore* Cavanaugh." The doctor shook Harry's hand.

"Good evening, *doctore*." Harry greeted him.

The doctor then set to work. Harry watched with apprehension. He had a sharp pair of tools that looked like scissors that went through his hard cast and the gauze it was wrapped in. Harry prayed the whole time, hoping that his injury had healed. The cast came off in full and Harry moved his toes. It felt extremely peculiar to be moving his leg after almost two months of restricted motion. His leg also felt incredibly light and fragile. The doctor examined his ankle and flexed it. Harry's ankle joint was stiff and he was reluctant to move it, but it moved. Right as rain, it moved and there was little to no pain. Harry smiled widely and the doctor held up his hands with satisfaction.

He spoke swift Italian and motioned for Harry to get up. Bruno didn't offer to translate. The doctor backed up and Harry carefully swung his legs over the side of his bed.

Slowly, ever so slowly, Harry put some weight on his left leg. He felt weak and his ankle felt sore, but his weight held. Harry smiled again and the doctor nodded.

"Thank you, sir." Harry held out his hand. "I can't thank you enough."

The doctor shook his hand and said something. He gave Bruno a pointed stare. This time, Bruno translated.

"No running for at least two weeks. Limit your walking time to twenty minutes for the first week and then gradually increase it." Bruno relayed the message.

The doctor put his instruments back in his medical bag.

Bruno stood up. "He says you are one fortunate pilot!"

———————————

*It's May!* Margaret thought in despair as she sat in Central Park with her cello on her knee. Still no word on Harry's condition and she was beginning to doubt whether she would hear from him again while the war raged on. In her heart, she could not help but think that he could be a prisoner of war, locked in a German jail somewhere in deplorable conditions... *No!* She shook her head to rid herself of her thoughts.

Picking her bow up off of the bench, she set to work playing Bach's Cello Suite No. 3. It was a composition she had just learned and in its entirety, was twenty-four minutes long. Needless to say, she hadn't memorized it yet.

Playing always calmed her aching heart. Margaret closed her eyes and lost all sense of time as she disappeared into the realm of the musical world. She played all her thoughts and worries out and was unaware of the small crowd that had gathered around her. Margaret played the cello suite and sought the comforting musical notes that radiated from her instrument.

She played quickly and precisely, the notes and patterns she had learned instinctively came back to her and the sheet music wound through her head like a thousand pieces of paper swirling in a windstorm. Unaware of all else, Margaret finished the four minute prelude and took a deep breath as the final notes radiated through her little corner of the park. She had chosen a bench near a bridge and was surprised to see a group of about ten people clapping in front of her. Men in suits and women in summer dresses applauded the accomplished musician.

"Thank you," Margaret smiled and got up.

She hadn't intended to draw a crowd. It had simply been such a lovely day; she wanted to play outside instead of in the studio as she always did. As the crowd began to disperse and disappear, she put her cello back in its case ever so gently.

"Good day, Margaret!" A familiar voice sounded behind her.

Margaret looked over her shoulder to see Mr. Seymour, her previous cello teacher, with a friendly smile on his face.

"Good afternoon, Mr. Seymour!" Margaret hopped up and shook his hand. "I haven't seen you for a few months!"

"It has been a while, hasn't it?" He nodded. "I heard your playing clear across the park and thought to myself, *that must be one of the students from Juilliard!* Turns out I was right." Mr. Seymour adjusted his fedora hat that was placed on top of his brown, slightly grey hair.

"Yes, it was a lovely day and I needed an excuse for a walk." Margaret picked up her cello case.

"A lovely day indeed. And how has Juilliard been treating you?" He inquired.

"I've learned so much." Margaret started across the bridge. "I still can't believe I get to attend. I miss your classes." She had finished his composition class and had taken another in its place the previous semester.

"Well, we are lucky to have you. And if you're ever in search of a job or a place to teach..." Mr. Seymour took off his hat in an amicable gesture. "All you need to do is ask. Have a wonderful day, Miss Sutton." He put his hat back on and tipped it to her.

"Thank you, Mr. Seymour. Enjoy the lovely day," Margaret smiled and watched him go.

She sighed and leaned against the bridge's railing, admiring the pink and white cherry blossoms and the budding green leaves on the bare branches of the trees. The water trickled and gurgled underneath the bridge and the birds chirped high in the trees. Margaret couldn't help but feel at peace as she left the tranquil scene behind and made her way from the budding park to the busy streets of New York City, all the while with her cello at her side and Bach's playful, elegant compositions playing through her mind.

———————

The sun had set over the Tyrrhenian Sea.

Midnight, the 15th of May. Harry, with help from Giovanna, had packed a satchel of food and provisions.

Giovanna brought him some extra supplies like a blanket and a change of clothes she had taken from her husband's things. However, Harry refused them politely. The less he had to carry, the better.

Antonio lingered in the room, sad that Harry was leaving. Giovanna wished him well, translated by her son, and as he was saying goodbye, the door opened. Bruno Russo stood in the doorway. The few times Harry had seen him over the past two months, he seemed to be a very proud man. Harry was humbled that he had consented to helping him.

"Thank you, Mr. Russo." Harry dipped his head to him. He had so many things he wanted to thank him for but couldn't find the words.

Bruno stepped forward and shook Harry's hand. "I am relieved no harm has come from this. I was doubtful at first. Giovanna was right, I must admit." His wife beamed. Bruno held out a revolver, the handle towards Harry.

Harry was confused.

"I want you to have this. You have a greater need of it than I do."

Harry took it with many thanks.

"Thank you... for getting them out of our country."

Harry dipped his head, many unspoken things passing between them.

They shook hands and parted as friends.

So, as Harry set off, Margaret was in the studio of the house at 6 o'clock practicing her cello. She was playing the touching, sad-sounding composition of Albinoni's Adagio and prayed earnestly that her Harry would be safe wherever he was.

Harry kept the gun in his belt, underneath a coat that Bruno had given him. In his pocket was a map that would lead him to Anzio, the only place north of the Gustav Line that held Allied forces. Antonio had given him a walking stick he had found in the vineyard and Harry used it with every shaky step he took. Harry couldn't thank them enough and he promised that after the war, if he could, he would properly repay them for the kindness and mercy they had shown him.

Walking slowly south, Harry stayed to the west of the road that ran through the forest where he had crashed two months ago. The only towns he had to pass were Ardea and Colle Remito. That would be the easy part. Then, he would have to somehow sneak into Anzio. That would be the hard part. Bruno had helped him acquire some false documentation should he be caught, but Harry would need a lot of help from the Lord. He prayed as he limped through the dark woods and hoped that he was doing the right thing.

It would take Harry eight hours to reach Anzio and that was without any problems. He walked for a great deal of time before he stopped to rest his left ankle. It was swollen, but he could put his weight on it. However, Harry had a feeling that something wasn't quite right with it. He didn't know why, but it still felt odd to him and clicked when it moved a certain way. He pressed forward and snacked on the pieces of bread Giovanna had packed for him.

Two hours passed and Harry skirted Ardea easily. The city was asleep and did not stir. *Just get me in a plane!* Harry thought to himself as three hours elapsed and then four.

He was halfway there.

Harry trudged through fields, vineyards, and passed as a shadow through dark city alleyways. Every now and then he would see a Nazi car go by with personnel inside. From where he was hiding, he wondered where they were going and if perhaps the Allies had attacked the Gustav Line and were advancing on the Germans. If that were the case, it was just a matter of time before Anzio was freed. He wished he knew what was going on with the war. For two months he hadn't a word. He didn't know whether the Allies had made any progress at all. It would've helped immensely, knowing what had happened since his plane had gone down. But he couldn't just walk up to the Germans and ask for news and Giovanna and Bruno had not had much news to share with him, secluded as they were on their farm.

As Harry passed the tiny town of Lavinio and neared Anzio, he grew nervous with every step. Darkness was starting to wane and the last thing he wanted was to be caught so close to his freedom. His ankle was now throbbing, but he could care less. If he could take one step, he pressed on. His life depended on it. The streets were quiet, and the tiny houses lined the narrow, paved streets. Harry walked down a side road with his walking stick in one hand. He tried not to look suspicious and blend in, but how was an Italian supposed to look walking through the city alone? He didn't know, but he hoped no one would emerge from the silent darkness to question him.

Suddenly, a car backfired. Harry instantly thought it was a gun. However, he saw an open car come rumbling down the street and he ducked into an alleyway. He hoped the driver had not seen him. Harry pressed himself against the cool building and watched as the car rumbled by. There were about seven people in it.

Wehrmacht soldiers.

Germans.

The sound of the car braking made Harry's blood run cold. He started walking swiftly down the alleyway, trying to get away without looking out of place. There was nowhere to hide. The alleyway was long and there was not any cover to be seen, only shuttered windows and locked doors on either side. Harry knew because he tried them quickly to see if they would open. He knew that if he ran the rest of the way out of the alley, the soldiers would be on him in an instant and there would be no explaining his way out of it. Besides, he couldn't outrun them. Therefore, he hunched his shoulders, walked with a limp, and tried to stay calm.

His heart beat rapidly in his chest.

A flashlight shone down the length of the alleyway.

A shout echoed down the walls that fenced Harry in on both sides.

Harry stopped.

*God help me.*

He weighed his odds. Could he run? If he tried now he might be shot in the back. If he stayed, what would happen? There was only one way to find out.

# Chapter 30

The soldiers came down the alleyway, shining their flashlights right in Harry's face without mercy.

They spoke in German to each other. One of the men who had a grey helmet on held out his hand.

"*Papieren.* Papers. Now." The man ordered.

Harry reached into his coat, his other hand held up in surrender and withdrew the papers Bruno had given him. Harry knew they were terribly done. He had seen false identification cards during his RAF training, but these weak forgeries were his only chance. He hoped the lack of decent light made it hard for the Germans to tell a difference.

The man turned and showed the other soldiers the papers. They spoke rapidly. Harry kept his eyes low.

The soldier said something in German and shook his head, tut-tutting.

Harry took it as sarcasm. Not a good sign. He spoke up, saying he was going to work in Italian. Giovanna had taught him what to say. Antonio had drilled him on it.

The men with the swastikas on their sleeves didn't seem to understand him. The man who must have been their leader with his grey uniform and grey helmet looked at Harry with a stone-cold face.

Harry stared right back at him. He felt like he was in a nightmare. He had never looked the enemy in the eye before; always his fighting had been from a distance. But as he stood in front of his enemy, Harry could have sworn the man was issuing him a challenge. Suddenly, he ripped the paper in half.

"*schmutziger Saukerl.*" He sneered.

The other men rushed at Harry.

He didn't even see them coming.

They grabbed him by the arms and shoulders, their combined strength was more than Harry could fight off. They pinned him up against the wall. They took the revolver from his belt. Harry couldn't beg for mercy; his language would give him away instantly. The leader pulled out a heavy-looking handgun and raised it at Harry, cocking it at the same time. He seemed amused Harry wasn't yelling or screaming or bargaining for his life.

Harry raised his chin defiantly, still struggling against the men who held him. The only thing Harry could think of was that he couldn't believe how bloodthirsty the Nazis were. They would do anything to shed blood...

The leader grinned. "Tell me," he said in English, so seemingly pleased with himself.

Time seemed to slow.

*Is this really how I die?*

The man lowered the barrel of the gun. "How does a blond-haired and blue-eyed *Saukerl* such as yourself end up here? *Ja...* English?"

Harry had never felt more alone.

The soldier aimed.

Harry couldn't tear his eyes away from gun that was aimed at his head. He was half-ashamed he didn't have any final words or any other final thoughts except for the panic that washed over him and blinded him to any other feeling.

"HALT!" A voice commanded all their attention.

At the end of the alleyway, the same direction the soldiers had come from, stood an imposing figure. The leader who still had the gun pointed at Harry shone his light on the newcomer and shouted something in German. The other man responded with a low, authoritative voice. He joined them all and looked at Harry. Shaking his head, he looked back to the soldiers who looked puny compared to this man. He wore a lieutenant's grey service hat and a spotless grey Wehrmacht uniform. A trench coat was over his shoulders, and his grey trousers were tucked into high, shining boots. The swastika and German eagle pins were shining on his lapel, reflecting off the beams of the flashlights. Harry caught sight of his face that was stoic and hard and rough as a flashlight passed over it. He continued speaking to his fellow soldiers. Harry was still held against the wall, waiting for his fate to be dealt out. He tried to survey the area to see how he could get out of this, but there was no way... not now anyway. He struggled and yet the soldiers' grip was like iron. He hoped whatever it would be, would be quick. There were worse deaths than the barrel of the gun pointed at his face.

The supposed leader's voice was rising. The newcomer seemed angry and annoyed. They started to argue more vehemently. Both were gesturing at Harry. The shorter soldier picked up Harry's torn papers and the taller man took them from him, yelling loudly. Perhaps they were deciding his fate; arguing about how they'd kill him. Suddenly, the quarrelling stopped. The taller man seemed pleased, the helmeted man who must have been less in rank, looked annoyed. The other two soldiers behind them shone their flashlights right at Harry's face.

The taller man took off his trench coat from around his shoulders and passed it to one of the soldiers with the flashlights. He strode up to Harry and stopped about a foot from his face.

"Do you want to know what we were debating?" He asked in English, albeit with a heavy German accent.

Harry wanted to spit in his face. Yet, he kept his composure. This soldier was playing a game with him.

Without warning, he punched Harry hard in the stomach. The breath was knocked out of him. He went to double over from the pain, but the other men held him up. He coughed and grimaced.

"*Sprechen, Engländer,*" the soldier hit him again, this time across his face. "Don't be shy." He hit him again. "Show them who you are." He punched Harry under the nose.

Harry spat out blood. He could hear the other soldiers laughing at him. He was trapped. What could he do? His head was starting to get dizzy; his vision blurry. There was a roaring in his ears. Pain flared like explosions every time he was hit. The soldiers held him back with difficulty.

*Make it stop...* Harry was growing desperate. He didn't know how much more he could take. He took hit after hit after hit. The men holding him up grabbed him by his hair, exposing his face and chin and neck and stomach to blow after blow.

"We have a place for you, *Engländer.* You'll break eventually and when you do, your information will be valuable to us." The man crooned. "Or perhaps we'll just throw you on a train with the rest of the trash."

Harry yelled in rage and pain. He ripped his arms away from the soldiers, clamping them around his attacker's throat. He ran him straight into the opposite wall, knocking the breath from his enemy's body and his cap from his head.

He wasn't proud of the many expletives that shot out of his mouth like bullets, but he was enraged.

Harry only had time to deal him a few blows before the other soldiers drug him off and pinned him to the ground, knees into his back and shoulders, hands behind his back, handcuffs strapped on, a gun to the head.

The tall soldier seemed amused. He dabbed at the blood on his lip, for Harry had busted it open. He spoke to his comrades, obviously boasting.

"You'll talk eventually, *Engländer.*" He told Harry, his chin held high, as they hauled him to his feet.

They led him to the car parked down at the end of the road. Harry tried to struggle, but he hurt all over. He teetered on the edge of consciousness. He dug in his heels, but they shoved him, and he nearly fell again and again. They loaded him up in the back, handcuffing him to the side. The tall man had a few words with the others before two of the first three soldiers Harry had encountered got into the car, leaving the other two behind.

Harry felt cold... down to his very core. He stared at his hands right in front of him and couldn't process what was happening. He sat in the bed of the small transport truck and wondered if he could squeeze his hands out of the handcuffs. He tried, but they were too tight. Where they were going, he didn't know. The car rumbled down the main road and then turned off onto a side road that was smaller. With every passing second, Harry tried to think. They turned a few more times and the car hit a pothole and jostled Harry, knocking him into the side of the truck. He grimaced. With each breath, Harry grew more terrified. He licked his lip that was still bleeding and noticed with a grimace that his front tooth was loose. He twisted his wrists around in his handcuffs.

Suddenly, a bullet rang out.

The truck lurched. Harry ducked.

Another bullet.

The truck stopped accelerating and veered off the road, coming to a halt as it crashed into the ditch. Harry looked up now, taking in his surroundings. Mature trees lined the road, but houses, all but rubble now, were to the right of the road.

Then, someone jumped from one of the blown-out windows and ran towards him, rifle in hand.

Harry looked to the cab of the truck. Both men were dead. He watched in shock as the man rifled through their shirts and came to the back of the truck. He hopped in the bed. He was tall and had a rugged face, as though he had spent every day since birth outside. He unlocked the handcuffs, stowing them in the pockets of his civilian garb.

"Come on," he grasped Harry's upper arm and half-drug him out of the bed. "We gotta get outta here."

Harry recognized the American accent and wordlessly followed as the man who was obviously an American soldier went to the cab and pulled out the bodies.

"What are you doing?" He asked, shaking himself from his shock.

"Their clothes." The man didn't bother explaining. He ripped the shirt and pants and boots from one of the men and proceeded to change as quick as he could. Harry followed suit and also took one of the rifles from the cab of the truck.

Once they had changed, they drug the bodies towards the houses and tossed a piece of blown-apart roof over them. Harry hadn't realized how heavy a body was. He shivered at the blank stares on their faces and the bullet holes in their heads. *He killed them.* He couldn't help but think. But it had been either him or them. And despite the shock of what he had just done, he was glad.

"Come on," the man instructed in a hurried whisper.

And they were gone.

"Who are you?" Harry asked, panting, still feeling the pain from every blow the soldier had dealt.

"Dirk Gates. Squadron leader." He continued, "my plane went down a few days ago. I take it you're Royal Air Force?"

Harry dipped his head.

"Where'd your plane go down?"

"Fiumicino. About eight weeks ago."

Dirk looked impressed. "How'd you stay alive that long?"

"I stayed with a family." Harry said as he followed Dirk into the fields and they hurried for the distant cover of a copse of trees. "Where'd you go down?"

"There'll be time to explain later." Dirk said, out of breath too. "I was on my way to Anzio."

"Well, thank you." Harry felt slightly ashamed he had been saved yet again... "You didn't have to put yourself in obvious danger for me."

"I watched the whole thing." Dirk explained as they crossed a creek. "Trust me, I don't like them any more than you do. What's your name, kid?"

Harry walked with the gun at the ready, though there wasn't much about except for a few farms that had been decimated.

"Harry Cavanaugh. Flight Lieutenant." He replied curtly, taking in the scene of destruction as they neared what used to be a farm.

The barn had been burned down and the house along with it. The stone walls still stood, but the roof was gone. Harry wondered who had lived there... if they had gotten out in time...

Harry cleared his throat, gripped the gun tighter, and continued forward. Dirk strode quietly by Harry as they left the farm behind and walked down the side of the road.

As daylight grew, the trek became more perilous. The fighting wasn't far off. The farms and homes along the way were nothing more than smoking piles of black, charred rubble. Harry could even hear gunfire ahead.

Therefore, they decided to camp out in the undergrowth under a pair of massive bushes that weren't far down a side road. They could just see the main road at the end of the lane, but they couldn't be spotted if a car were to pass by because of the stone fences on either side. They waited out the day in relative silence. Harry lay on his stomach as they kept watch.

"So," Harry whispered, they dared not to raise their voices. "Where'd you go down?" Harry split the last of his food with Dirk who looked as hungry as Harry felt.

"Monte Cassino." Dirk said, not meeting Harry's eyes.

"What were you flying?"

"B-17." Dirk sighed. "Crew didn't make it."

Harry dropped his gaze. The B-17 bomber's had, on average, ten crew members. To lose nine during a mission was a rough thing to live with when you were the only survivor. Those men you flew with, they became your family. Harry knew how devastated he was after losing one friend. He couldn't imagine losing nine... especially all at once.

"You? What were you flying? You strike me as a Havilland kind of guy." Dirk asked.

Harry cracked a grin. "Beaufighter."

Dirk nodded thoughtfully. "Nice. Did you have a gunner with you?"

"No," Harry replied.

He was thankful it had just been him, and he hadn't had anyone else in the plane when he went down. He didn't need another man's death on his shoulders.

"We were bombing the transport ships coming into the harbor." He added.

Dirk was looking at something far in the distance. "Funny how dealing out death becomes just another day... just another day at work."

Harry knew what he meant. Dirk laid down to doze off and Harry took the next watch. It must have been late afternoon. During the whole day, Harry heard gunfire... it wasn't far away, and he wondered how close the fighting truly was. They were near the outskirts of Anzio. Since they were going to stay put for a little longer, he took his boot off. Looking at his ankle, he grimaced. It was still bruised and yet it was more swollen now than it had been the previous morning. He knew he hadn't reinjured it, but it just didn't feel right. He supposed walking and running on it all night hadn't helped. He felt his loose tooth with his tongue absent-mindedly. It was still moving more than it ought.

"What'd you do?" Dirk asked about his leg, clearly not sleeping.

"Fractured it." Harry replied as he put his boot back on and tied up the laces tightly.

"How'd you recover?" He seemed impressed... maybe more amused. "With the family?"

Harry nodded. "I should be dead."

Dirk closed his eyes and went back to trying to sleep. "We all should be dead. None of this makes any sense, but here we are living in it."

Harry didn't know if he agreed, but he shrugged in reply and put his boot back on and went back to keeping watch.

By the time the stars came out, they were both stiff from crouching under the undergrowth all day and sleeping on the hard-packed dirt. But Harry felt like his wits were restored... temper settled.

"Are you ready?" Harry asked.

"Anzio's so close; I can almost see her church steeples." Dirk took a drink from his canteen he had hidden in his shirt and offered Harry a drink as well. "Now," he paused. "The fighting's going to get thick up ahead.

There'll be snipers and every road is going to be a battleground... friendlies on one side, the enemy on the other. Once we cross the line, we're home free. Until then..." Dirk half-shrugged. "It's a good thing we're in uniform. We'll try to blend in and get as far as we can. If we're compromised, we run... as fast as we can and see how far we can get."

Harry raised his eyebrows. "Doesn't sound like much of a plan."

"Oh really?" Dirk laughed under his breath. "You got a better idea? A better place to go? A hotel room maybe with full room service, a nice hot shower, and a comfortable bed?" He looked irritated as he finished his sarcastic remarks.

"If we're caught, we might as well go back and find those soldiers who were going to shoot me point blank. Rather that than be held prisoner by the SS." Harry glared at him as they climbed out from under the bushes and emerged onto the dark road.

Dirk held up his hands. "What do you want from me, kid?"

Harry stifled his rising frustration and turned down the main road. "Come on," Harry started down the road that was cloaked in shadows, illuminated only by the half-full moon.

"Fine," Dirk caught up to him. "Don't get jumpy now."

Harry rolled his eyes.

Sure enough, the gunfire grew closer. Harry's anticipation grew and yet he felt calmer than he had in a long time. He thought of Margaret and looked up at the moon and stars that were shining down on them. *It's going to be a long night... God, please let us live. Let me live to see her again.*

The two men passed in and out of the shadows as they came upon the ruins and destruction and rubble of Anzio. There were Wehrmacht soldiers everywhere, but Harry led the way to the first of the half-charred buildings and found a still-standing two story home. He went up to the second floor and they looked out of the blown-out window. They had a fair view of the next few blocks and the streets that started into the city to their left. To their right were drainage ditches and a grove of olive trees.

Trucks rumbled in and out of the streets and gunfire could be heard dead ahead.

"Let's hold up here for an hour or two..." Harry recommended. "We can watch for any patrols and see which roads aren't busy." As he spoke, he took off his grey coat and ditched the look of a uniform. "We'll blend in better." He shrugged. "I don't feel like getting shot at by our allies."

Dirk shrugged too and followed suit. Harry couldn't help but shiver at the missing warmth of the coat. He wished he hadn't left his civilian clothes behind, but what could he do about such things now.

For several hours they watched the flow of the city... the streets were indeed used to their left, but to their west it was fairly quiet... save for the gunfire near the beachhead where the Allies were. There was one patrol that went by on the road below them, but it had been over an hour and they had not reappeared.

"I think we need to move," Dirk whispered after some more time had elapsed. He cast a furtive look up to the sky. "Clouds are coming in."

Harry followed his gaze and noticed that the moon was dimming as clouds rolled in from the sea. He nodded in agreement. "Let's make for the ditches and stay low."

They left their post behind.

Together, they slipped into the gloom of the ditch that was almost as deep as they were tall. Their black leather boots squelched in the mud. Harry took his shirt off and ran it through the mud, trying to blot out all the color he could. He smeared it on his arms, neck and face. His grey pants blended in well enough, but he wanted to be as invisible as possible to any snipers if possible.

"Come on," Dirk motioned down the ditch after he was thoroughly covered in mud as well.

They went as far as they could before the culvert split in two and shallowed out. They climbed up the bank ahead of them and peered out. They were looking out onto an intersection of five roads. In the middle was an old fountain that had all but been destroyed. Down one of the roads, Harry saw a group of men standing together and talking. Tents were behind them and a tank. He most certainly wanted no part in that. He suddenly felt entirely out of his element... he wasn't an infantryman. He had hardly been prepared for such an event in the few weeks of training he had gotten during basic and the scattered briefings they had since then. His place was in a plane, not on the ground with a gun and a knife. His respect for the ground forces soared... he didn't know how they did it day in and day out.

Dirk touched his shoulder to get his attention and pointed down one of the quiet roads. Harry nodded, seeing it as their best option.

Harry ducked behind a half-collapsed wall. He peered out and saw there was a narrow street running to his right and left.

They turned right down another street and then cut through a pile of rubble that had been a home before it had been bombed. Whether it had been Allies or Axis who were responsible, no one knew. Everything was muddled now. The lines were blurred. However, there was a very distinct line ahead that was not... Gunfire sounded. A flare went up into the night sky, illuminating everything for several moments.

Harry ducked behind a wall and Dirk did the same.

"Let me go first, kid." The USAAF pilot stepped up and peered out into the street. "A few soldiers to the left. But no other way to cross the street." He whispered. "Let's go."

It was only ten metres to the other side of the road where the next set of houses and ruins were that would provide cover. The soldiers were busy to their left. Dirk ran and got to safety in no time. Harry steeled himself, swallowed, and ran too.

*Just keep going.* He told himself as he collided into the wall and they ducked into an abandoned house, one of the few that were still standing.

Inside, it was silent and nearly pitch black. Dirk navigated through the house and to the back, climbing out through the kitchen window. Harry followed, holding his rifle tightly. Outside, the backyard garden was overgrown and they wove through the tall weeds that were over their heads. At one point it must have been a beautiful garden... its tenants now either dead or gone. Harry held his breath, listening for any noises or sounds of the enemy. The gunfire up ahead was getting closer. Sudden bursts of machine fire split the cool and peaceful night air.

All of a sudden, the gun fire was behind them.

Bullets sliced through the tall grass around Harry and Dirk.

Harry leapt into action.

Dirk grabbed him and hauled him to the right. Harry stumbled for footing and saw that Dirk was aiming for the shed to their right. He could feel the bullets hot on his heels. There must have been a sniper in the second floor of the house they had just come out of. They reached cover. Dirk raised his gun and stole a look around the side of the shed. Bullets peppered the wood. Splinters flew up and around them. Harry had had enough. He climbed the fence the shed backed up to.

"What are you doing?" Dirk hissed.

"Follow me." Harry jumped down to the other side, not waiting for Dirk who followed him a second later.

The voice in his head echoed between his ears, *just keep going.*

Along the alleyway, Harry stole through the shadows. He knew the gunman would be on their heels or relay it to someone who would be chasing them in moments. The sooner they got to friendly territory, the better.

They wove through several more streets and blocks of rubble until they got to a place where they could go no further. All before them were scores and scores of Wehrmacht infantry and equipment. There were tanks and heavy heavy artillery. Tents were set up here and there. They were in the thick of it. He and Dirk were hiding behind a half-demolished wall and were figuring out their next move. They laid on the ground with their backs pressed up the wall as close as they could get so they wouldn't be spotted. They had to be close. It felt like they had spent hours dodging the enemy and steeling through the darkness.

"We make it through that street," Dirk pointed to their right. "We're in the clear."

*Just keep going.*

Harry's heart beat wildly. They should wait for a skirmish... something where they could slip through... but there was no time. The enemy was everywhere. Gunfire exploded on the next street over. They could even see the burst of orange-white fire from the guns and occasional explosion of grenades. To their left was the concentration of the enemy. However, Harry knew there was a sniper in every window of the building in front of them. They were about to enter the fray... bullets coming and going from every which way.

"We *have* to go around them." Harry thought out loud.

Dirk bit his lip, thinking about their situation. "Best route out is that way, but it'll take us farther from the line." He pointed away from where the soldiers were.

Harry followed his gaze and nodded. "We have no other choice. Maybe we can slip through along a ditch."

"Worth a try." Dirk said as quietly as he could. "I don't feel much like getting shot in the back."

Harry crawled along the floor to the open doorway in the stone wall. "Or the front," he murmured under his breath.

Together, they slithered along, staying low and out of sight. They were grateful for the cloud cover and the seeming safety it had granted them as they slipped through to a side street that looked strangely quiet.

Harry walked along the buildings' walls, rifle at the ready. A stone fell from above and he halted, aiming his gun.

But there was no one there. He swallowed his panic and continued, footstep after agonizing footstep. Soon, the sun would start to rise... they had to reach the line before then.

They came to the end of the street and Harry held up his hand. A truck rumbled by, passing them as they hid in the shadows. However, it stopped some distance away and the soldiers started to get out. One of the men shouted in German as the other dispersed into buildings all along the street.

Something was about to happen. Harry and Dirk exchanged glances.

"There's no going around them." Harry whispered. "The sea's at the end of that street."

"What'd I say earlier, kid? We run." Dirk slapped him on the back.

Harry resolved himself.

"On three," Dirk got his feet underneath him, ready to run.

"One," he started.

*Just keep going.* Harry crouched.

"Two."

*Just keep going.* The thought drove him.

"Three,"

Together, they left the shadows behind, feet skidding on gravel.

And they ran.

The cobblestones underfoot were littered with debris. Harry leapt over a boulder and Dirk swerved. He had never run so fast in his entire life, nor had his heart ever pounded so.

Ten metres...

Five metres...

They just kept running, hoping not to be seen. They were so close.

Dirk got to the building first and slammed into it.

Suddenly, Harry tripped on a piece of rubble. He smacked against the cobblestones and just as he did, a flashlight shone their way.

"Come on!" Dirk called.

Harry leapt to his feet and they crashed through the doorway of a building, bolting the doors behind them.

Once inside, they were in a whole other world of danger. Shouts came from the street they had just crossed. They were being pursued.

Footsteps sounded on the floor above.

Dirk's eyes flitted upwards.

A gunshot rang out, missing Harry's head by an inch. He ducked and Dirk fired, shooting their attacker several times in the chest.

Harry and Dirk ducked into a side room, hearing their enemy above coming for them. More gunfire filled the air along the street now.

Dirk reloaded his weapon and grinned. "Time to play."

# Chapter 31

Jackboots were hammering the stairs. The ends of rifles were pounding on the door Dirk had bolted, gunfire ripped into the locks. Harry plastered himself into a corner in the back hallway. Men were coming from above and he watched the stairs from where he stood, his rifle aimed at the steps. A soldier came into view. He pulled the trigger and the man shouted and crumpled to the floor, having been shot in the chest. The other soldiers stopped.

Bullets tore through the corner Harry was hiding behind. He grimaced and could hear Dirk in the other room fighting hand-to-hand with someone. Harry dashed across the hall while the stairs were clear and into the room the noises were coming from. The soldier was coming at Dirk with a knife, both guns having been kicked out of reach. He didn't see Harry coming. Harry shot him in the back and he fell. Dirk grabbed his gun, nodded his thanks, and the house grew quiet again. They peered out into the hall. Bullets rang out. The enemy had come downstairs, and they were in the first-floor hallway Harry had just left.

Harry went back to the body of the German and searched him. Sure enough, there was a grenade in his belt. Grabbing it, Harry pulled the pin and threw it down the hallway.

"Run!" Harry yelled and they ran down the hallway, out the door, and into the open air as everything turned to confusion and chaos behind them.

Landing hard on the rubble-strewn street, Harry covered his head with his hands. More than half the building exploded, and flames erupted high into the sky. A cheer went out from the Allied side... which was right in front of them. Harry, his ears ringing, got to his feet, his boots crunching the rubble and gravel underfoot, shots ringing out all around him.

*Just keep going.*

Time seemed to slow. Dirk was right beside him as they sprinted across the narrow street, panic propelling them. Bullets cut through the air. They sprayed the ground, kicking up dust and gravel at their feet. Harry felt like he couldn't run fast enough, his legs not keeping up with his racing pulse. The smoke from the grenade floated through the air making it hard to breathe. Harry made for an opening in a ruined structure. He leapt over a half-wall and landed, rolling to break his fall. He rolled and rolled and ended up on his stomach. He coughed dust out of his lungs, hearing Dirk do the same next to him. As the world stilled and it sunk in that Allied-controlled territory was what he lay on, he realized...

He was safe.

For now...

Men approached them... They shouted and had their rifles pointed at them.

"English! English!" Harry held up his hands. He felt more panicked now than he had in that house of Germans.

Dirk was doing the same thing next to him. They held up their hands,

"English, English, English! Don't shoot! Don't shoot!" Harry cried as Dirk said his name and rank and unit over and over again.

The men stopped and quieted as a superior pushed through.

Harry breathed a sigh of relief, still laying prone with his hands in the air. He coughed out dust again and heard the superior officer give the others orders... blessedly, in English.

He dropped his head in the dirt, relief washing over him so strongly he thought he might cry.

*Thank you, God.*

Dirk and Harry were hustled back to safety, away from the front lines. Dirk had protested, wanting to fight. But they needed to be checked in and have reports taken.

As they walked through the Ally's side of Anzio, Harry was absorbed by the Red Cross tents and American and British and Canadian uniformed army personnel. He had never been so glad to see his comrades in arms before in his whole life. And it wasn't until he was lying in a cot some hours later in a tent full of fellow British soldiers, did the full weight of the last few days, weeks, and months hit him. He curled into a ball and silently wept, exhausted and properly spent.

---

In St. Patrick's Cathedral, Margaret listened to the heavenly voices of the choir as tears fell down her cheeks. Over two months and there was no news on Harry's whereabouts. Margaret cried quietly and her mother put her arm around her during the Sunday service. They were singing a hymn in Latin and even though it was supposed to be glorifying, all it reminded Margaret of was a funeral hymn.

"Chin up, my girl." Gabriella smiled to her daughter and Margaret wiped the tears from her eyes.

"You sound just like Dad," She forced a smile and closed her eyes to take a deep breath.

Rachel patted Margaret's hand from her place beside her in the pew. "Maybe you'll hear from his parents soon." She offered her encouragement and then they all fell back into silence as the choir finished their hymn.

The next day, Margaret and Rachel walked arm-in-arm for encouragement as they took a short stroll through Central Park. They had parted ways with the boys back near the ball fields over an hour ago and were now turning towards home. Margaret hoped with all her heart there would be a letter on the foyer table right beside the oh-so familiar gramophone. They walked through the warm summer day. It was overcast and looked like it would rain.

"We should hurry," Margaret remarked, considering the dark clouds that were gathering

Rachel followed her gaze towards the sky. "I hope the boys pack up soon. Samuel hates getting caught in the rain."

Sure enough, as they left the park and neared home, the skies opened and they ran as fast as they could all the way home, Rachel squealing and Margaret just hoping there would be good news when they returned.

*Please God, I'll never ask for anything again, just please let there be a letter... Please!*

Margaret opened the door, as she was first up the front steps and rushed into the foyer out of the pouring rain. Her gaze scanned the table. Her heart skipped a beat. There it was! A letter! She rushed to it and saw it was from Harry. The address said Rome. She ripped it open and read it, standing as still as a statue. Rachel anxiously read over her shoulder in rapt attention.

*'June 8th, 1944*

*Dear Margaret,*

*I am safe.*

*I went down during a mission and broke my ankle quite badly. Since I was in occupied territory, I couldn't write. I recuperated with a good family. How could I have been so fortunate? I thank God every day that He spared me.*

*Oh, Margaret, I cannot give you all the details... I wish I could. America is so far away, and this letter will not reach you for at least a week. I miss you dearly. How I wish I could see you... talk to you... and tell you everything. When we are reunited, I will tell you everything...*

*But I am safe. I made it to Anzio after my ankle recovered. It was freed by the Allies three days ago. Now I'm in Formia and will be leaving today to reunite with my squadron back in Marcianise. I'm taking a physical exam this week to make sure my ankle is alright and when I pass, I'll be back to flying. I know I don't have to ask you, but please pray. I pray every day that the war will be over soon. It has to be. We are making our way north. It can't be long now.*

*I should go; everyone's jogging to the Mess.*

*Goodnight, my darling.*

*I love you more than words can say.*

*Your Harry.*


*P.S. Would you be able to have your picture taken for me and send it in your next letter? As I was recovering, I would have given anything to have a picture of you.'*


Margaret clutched the letter and let the words penetrate her heart. *He's alive! He's well!* Margaret couldn't wipe the smile off her face as Rachel gave her a hug.

"What's all the commotion about?" Gabriella asked, coming down the stairs.

"It's Harry!" Margaret held up the letter and threw her arms around her mother in joy. "He's alright!"

Gabriella was ecstatic to hear the news.

The boys entered at that moment with smiles on their faces even though they were dripping wet and quite out of breath.

"Why's everyone hugging and crying and happy?" Grubbs asked, kicking off his shoes and looking confused.

"Oh come here!" Margaret hugged him.

"Get off me!" He slipped out her grip and he and Pitcher ran upstairs.

"You two change your clothes before you track water all over the house!" Gabriella called after them.

"That's great news, Meg." Samuel smiled and gave her a hug in support.

"Thank you. I'm so relieved." And how true that was.

Margaret was beaming and she thanked the Lord constantly as she made her way to work. Once at the factory, she punched in and ran to her line.

"Emily! Heather!" She saw her two friends standing together talking before they started work. "Harry's alright! He's back safe and sound!"

"Hooray!" Emily held up her arms triumphantly.

Margaret embraced them both in a group hug.

"We knew he would be." Heather said as she hugged Margaret. "That's such good news."

Breathing a sigh of relief for the first time in a long time, Margaret agreed wholeheartedly. They set to work, chatting happily during the whole shift.

Once Margaret returned home late that night, she closed the front door quietly behind her and locked it. She clicked off the lamp in the foyer and headed up to her room. The whole house was quiet and asleep. Avoiding the stairs that squeaked and creaked, she ascended the several flights before collapsing on her bed to reread Harry's letter. She smiled to herself and went to her desk, spending hours on a return letter that ended up being three pages long. She added more pins to her board in the town of Fiumicino, Anzio, Formia and back to Marcianise, where his Squadron would be. Nothing could describe the peace and happiness that had settled over her.

*Thank you, God.* She held his letter close, wondering what the whole story was. She wondered how he had gotten out of Nazi-occupied territory and back to his base. He'd have quite the tale to tell when they finally reunited... Margaret smiled. *What a day that will be.* She couldn't wait to hear everything... and she wanted to know every detail from the beginning. Ever since Harry and his family had moved next door, they hadn't spent more than a week apart. They were going on five years now. *Soon... it has to be sometime soon.* Not that she wished ill for Harry, but if he wasn't cleared on his physical exam, perhaps he would be honorably discharged... That meant he'd be sent home and out of the fray. And maybe, just maybe, that meant she could see him.

*I have to get a picture for him.* Margaret reminded herself as she climbed into bed. She fell asleep and dreamt of planes and oceans and her dear Harry.

As the week marched on, the whole world seemed lighter to Margaret. She was content knowing that her letter was on its way to Harry in Italy and she wrote several letters back and forth to her father. She could tell her father was growing tired of the war. It seemed like it had taken up an entire lifetime. Margaret wrote encouraging words to him and included several verses that would help him endure the dark days of life on the home front.

So the house slipped into the warm days of summer as everyone relaxed and played and felt no guilt in not doing any schoolwork. Nonetheless, they were all busy as bees with their garden they had expanded and the War Bond concerts they still held. Their garden took up the entire backyard and cucumber vines were starting to climb up and over the fence that separated their lot from the next. They tried new recipes as their gramophone played Bing Crosby's latest hits like, 'Swinging on a Star' and 'I'll Be Seeing You.' They were toe-tapping tunes that made Margaret think of the Moser twins and how much everyone missed them. She wondered what they looked like now, for they would be twelve already this year.

As the sun beat down on Margaret and Rachel and Gabriella in the garden, Margaret wiped her glistening forehead with the back of her gardening glove.

"I wonder why we haven't heard from Hannah in so long." She thought about her dear friend she had grown to love as a sister in her first few years in New York. "How old is she now? Eighteen? I bet she's a regular Bette Davis."

"We heard from her in January," Rachel remarked as she paused in her weeding.

Gabriella got up and dusted off her sun dress, her knees dirty from kneeling in the dirt. "Perhaps she's busy like the rest of us." Gabriella commented and picked up the bucket of weeds she had filled.

Margaret sat in the dirt, not caring if her dress got dirty. "I wonder if she's going to pursue a career with the Chicago Philharmonic Orchestra..."

"I don't think anyone is pursuing careers these days, dearie." Gabriella dumped the weeds into the compost bin at the back of the yard as the song *'Don't Fence Me In,'* by Bing Crosby and The Andrews Sisters garbled out of the gramophone that was set on the back steps.

*"Oh, give me land, lots of land under starry skies*
*Don't fence me in.*
*Let me ride through the wide open country that I love*
*Don't fence me in."*

Margaret hummed to herself as she went back to weeding the tomatoes. The sun warmed her back. The tall plants smelled funny as she pulled up some grass underneath them and she wrinkled her nose. She hated tomatoes.

She contemplated the relative quiet. Selfishly, she was glad that Elizabeth had moved back with her family for the summer. It was nice not to have someone constantly mimicking her and following her around, even though she was a dear girl and meant well.

Suddenly, a ball came flying out the back studio windows from above. Luckily, the window had been open. The ball landed with a thump in the green beans.

"Potter Watson!" Gabriella yelled up to him.

Rachel giggled when she heard her use his full name.

His head poked out of the window and he looked down to them. "I'm sorry, Miss Gabriella! Did I hit you?" Pitcher asked.

"No! But what did I tell you about throwing balls in the house?!" She scolded him.

"Not to?" Pitcher's innocent voice made Margaret chuckle. She and Rachel exchanged amused glances.

"That's right! Now why don't you and Grubbs go down to the park with Margaret and Samuel? You can throw your baseball all you want out there." Gabriella volunteered her daughter and the other eldest member of the house to go with them.

"Mum..." Margaret sighed low enough so Pitcher couldn't hear her as he disappeared. "They're old enough now; they don't need us along."

Indeed, Pitcher was thirteen and Grubbs was fourteen now. They had graduated middle school the previous May and were turning into fine young men.

"Just go, it'll be fun." Gabriella offered her meager encouragement and then went back to weeding on her hands and knees. "Take Samuel with you too, he needs to get out a bit."

Resolving herself to babysitting, Margaret got up, dusted off her dress, sneezed, and hopped over the gramophone that was on the floor in the threshold playing 'Shoo, Shoo Baby' by The Andrews Sisters. At least she wouldn't have to weed the smelly tomatoes anymore. She changed into a clean dress in her room and put on a pretty hat. She peaked into Samuel's room and told him he had to go with her and the boys. He looked up from writing something and sighed. Margaret shared his sentiment as she descended rapidly down the stairs. Her brown curls bounced on her shoulders as she jumped from the last step. Grubbs had a baseball mitt on his left hand, as did Pitcher.

"Come on, boys," She opened the door for them and they all filed out into the warm New York City streets, Samuel close behind.

As the boys played with the other ballplayers, young and old, in the wide-open baseball fields, Margaret and Samuel took a stroll around the sidewalks that encircled the lush, green grounds.

"We haven't had a chance to play in the park yet this year." Margaret remarked.

"It's been a busy start to the year." Samuel responded, his hands clasped behind his back.

Margaret nodded in agreement.

They walked past a bridge and heard a melody coming from beneath it in the cool shade. Margaret stopped and looked to where the sound was coming from. A lone trumpet player tolled out a jazzy, slow tune. Margaret recognized it as, 'Do Nothing until You Hear from Me' by the famous Duke Ellington. They sat on a bench to the outside of the bridge and watched the African-American man play his trumpet in a ritzy suit. Margaret tapped her toe and saw that only a few other people were watching. The solo trumpeter took a deep breath when he had finished. Margaret smiled to herself and got to her feet and clapped. The man whisked off his hat in thanks to his small crowd.

"Afternoon, Samuel Miller." He inclined his head Samuel's way with a smile.

"Afternoon, Uncle Charlie." Samuel responded with a faint grin.

Margaret watched curiously with surprise. "He's your uncle?" She asked quietly.

"Oh, miss, this here's my favorite nephew." Uncle Charlie chuckled, hearing what she had said.

Margaret could tell Samuel was embarrassed. "Well, it's a pleasure to meet you." She shook his hand. "Your playing was wonderful."

"Thank you, miss; music is the breath of my life. Praise sweet Jesus!" He gave her a huge smile.

"Say hello to Aunt June for me." Samuel said as he cut their conversation short.

"Oh, you can bet I sure will, Samuel. Wish your mamma the best for me." He watched them go as they left the bridge behind, strolling back over to the baseball fields.

They were quiet for several moments.

"He seems really nice." Margaret remarked.

"Hmm..." Samuel sighed.

They sat in the grass and leaned against a massive tree as they watched the kids play in a baseball game against the adults.

"If you don't want to talk about it, we don't have to. I was just observing that he was nice." Margaret smoothed her skirts.

Samuel lapsed into silence. Margaret turned her attention to watching the boys play; only slightly wondering why Samuel wasn't keen on his family.

"So, are you excited about working at the navy yard?" She changed subjects.

"I am," he nodded. "I'm ready to help. Maybe even next year I'll enlist."

Margaret thought about what he said. His enlistment would be very different from that of the other young men his age. While he could be part of the army, navy, or air force, he would start at the very bottom while others started much higher simply because of the color of their skin. Margaret bit her lip and thought about it. She was proud of Samuel's humility in wanting to help a country that wasn't always the most gracious to men of his ethnicity.

"Well, I'm sure you'll do wonderful." Margaret smiled encouragingly.

"I wish I could do more." Samuel crossed his arms and watched as Pitcher hit a home run and came sliding into home base, making all the adults throw their mitts at him in mock frustration.

Margaret knew how he felt. She knew how much she had wanted to do her part, and she was just a girl. She couldn't imagine how a young man must have an even greater sense of duty to his country.

"All in good time, Sam. You've graduated high school and soon you'll start your work with the yard. Before you know it, you'll be overseas fighting for our country."

Samuel didn't look convinced. Margaret didn't blame him. It would be a hard road for him and a long time before he could join in the war effort the way he wanted. She turned her attention back to the fields where they were starting a new baseball game. Despite all the unresolved situations around her, Margaret relaxed and put her worries at ease, breathing in the warm, heady breeze that smelled of sunny grass, dust from the ball fields, and a city baking in the sun. A delicious, comforting feeling surrounded her that could only be found in Central Park in summertime.

---

June 20th, 1944. Harry lay on the lush grass and watched the fluffy white clouds roll by. Not a single mission for two weeks. He was starting to like Voltone, the tiny city to the northwest of Rome.

The City of the Seven Hills was in the hands of the Allies.

Anzio was free.

Rome was free.

The Gustav Line had been smashed by the combined forces of the Eighth and Fifth Armies and now the Allied advance was quickly working its way up the rest of Italy. The Alps did not seem so far off. However, their gain was not without consequences. The Canadian Forces had sustained terrible losses, for Rome was ordered as their goal no matter what... no matter the cost. The German opposition was heavy but on June 4th, Rome was theirs and the German Tenth Army had been allowed to escape, not without a great deal of conflict and disagreement between the commanders of the offensive army.

D-Day was a morale booster to say the least. Now that Allied troops had a foothold in France, victory was imminent. Seven divisions of French and American troops had been pulled out of the Italian Campaign to take part in a southern invasion of France. That left the remaining Allies in Italy to focus on their next target, Florence. It wouldn't be long now. They already had control of half the country.

Harry thought over his last letter he had sent to Margaret. It always made him smile when he received news from her and this time was no exception. She had sent him her picture. Harry pulled it out of his shirt pocket and looked at the beautiful portrait. Her curly brown hair was the same, yet her face looked older and more mature now. She was twenty after all. *And I'm soon to be twenty two... When did that happen?* Harry sighed and looked back up to the sky that was pure blue with white clouds floating across it. *I've got to get back in a plane.* He was starting to grow lazy.

Jumping up, Harry jogged back to the tents at the far side of the field. It was in this field that their base was. The planes were also at the far side and their tents were kitty-corner to the massive ten-ton terrors.

"Morning, Val!" Harry ducked into their tent and sat down on his bedroll.

Val was lounging on his bedroll and reading a magazine. A radio he had bartered off a fellow pilot was playing. A song was trying to come through but Harry couldn't quite make it out, the static was too loud to hear any clear notes.

"What's the verse today?" Val yawned, slapped the magazine closed, and got out of the tent to stretch.

"Ephesians 6:13. *'Therefore take up the whole armour of God, that you may be able to withstand in the evil day, and having done all, to stand.'*" Harry read the verse out loud.

"Amen!" Val exclaimed. "I'm going to get something to eat; I'll meet you in the Mess."

"Yes, *lieutenant*." Harry mock saluted him.

Val rolled his eyes and left.

Harry chuckled. Val had been promoted not long after Harry had been shot down.

Picking up his Bible, Harry said a quick prayer for all the men who were fighting that day while he and his fellow pilots waited for orders. He also thanked God he was still able to fly. He had come close to not being able to.

Upon arrival at the RAF base in Marcianise, Harry and Dirk had to take physical exams to make sure they were well enough to still fly. Harry had barely passed. The nurse had examined him and wasn't too pleased that his ankle was slightly swollen. But he assured her it was healed. Thankfully, she passed him.

Harry felt like he still had work to do and the last thing he wanted was to go to southern Italy away from the fighting and convalesce or get the operation he had opted out of.

Dirk, having already been replaced in his squadron, was now temporarily staying with the No. 600 until another USAAF squadron came their way. He was a good pilot. Harry had flown a mission with him when they had provided night cover for Allied transports coming up from the south. He was a *very* good pilot and whenever they ate together, Harry felt inclined to pick his brain. Dirk was an only child and had grown up in Texas. His father was a crop duster, and his mother was a teacher. He told stories about flying with his father when he was three and saying that it was in his blood to fly. Some of the Brits laughed and said, 'what stuff!' However, Harry believed him.

That evening, Harry walked into the large, green tent that was their Mess for the time being. Ducking under the awning, Harry filled up his plate with the meal of lamb, brioche, and noodles with some kind of creamy sauce. A local farmer had donated the meal, and his wife had made the noodles and bread. It was eagerly eaten by the pilots who were growing tired of their usual meals that always tasted bland. Harry sat across from Val who was sitting next to a senior ace who had just joined their squadron, William Lincoln. Will was telling quite the story and Harry listened in.

"Back in '42 we were part of a thousand-bomber raid called

Operation Millennium."

"Thousand bomber?" Val's eyes grew wide.

"That must have been a cloud!" Another pilot, whose name Harry thought he remembered was John, whistled low with fascination.

"It was," Will was probably in his forties but had the wrinkles and grey hairs of a sixty-year-old man. "I remember it like it was yesterday. May 30th, early in the morning the Commander in Chief sauntered into the Operations Room with a characteristic hunch to his shoulders. He sat down and the weather forecast was placed in front of him." Will leaned back in his chair. "He sat like so and I knew it wasn't a good forecast. That night was our last chance to try launching this titanic experiment, or else we would have had to wait another month. We all held our breath, waiting for the Commander to say something. He finally moved, lit a cigarette, and traced his finger across the map of Europe. Then..." Will leaned forward and brought the men who were listening into suspense. "He said, 'the 1,000 Plan tonight.' And his finger was on the city of Cologne."

"Did you fly then?" Harry asked as he started to eat.

"We certainly did." Will responded. "It was one of the most important cities in all of Germany *and* the most heavily defended."

"I heard that it had more than five hundred light and heavy anti-aircraft guns." Val stuck his spoon into his pasta and tried to get it to his mouth.

There were no forks to be had, so most of the men were opting to eat the pasta with their hands.

"Mmm," Will nodded. "And a hundred and fifty searchlights that worked in coordination with the gunmen."

John whistled.

"What did you do? I mean... how did you *do* it?" Harry asked, grabbing a handful of noodles and eating them, enthralled in the story.

"Mid-air collisions were the greatest threat if you didn't count the flak and fighter planes. Just imagine friendly aircraft diving and climbing and trying to get back on a narrow course with one thousand aircraft surrounding you. The boffins figured out the statistics on how many planes would go down in mid-air collisions."

"How many were suspected?" Val asked.

Harry stopped eating to listen, thinking the number would be over 200. The odds were insane and yet he would have done anything to see a thousand of their planes flying over Germany.

"One collision. Two planes." Will replied and grinned from ear to ear.

Harry laughed and Val scoffed.

"Those were our thoughts exactly." Will chuckled. "You should have heard the laughter in the room. One wag from the 50th Squadron at Skellingthorpe asked whether the boffins had also worked out which two aircraft it would be. The briefing officer, having caught onto our sarcasm, replied that he had it on the highest authority that it would be a Tiger Moth and an Anson." Will chuckled. "The pilot who had made the wise-crack shut himself up pretty quick, for he flew the Tiger Moth. And if one plane comes out of a collision between an Anson and a Tiger, it would no doubt be the Anson. She's a big ole plane, that's for sure."

Harry and Val exchanged amused glances and Val clapped Will on the back.

"Them boffins think they know everything." John remarked from where he sat across from Will.

"Thanks for the good laugh." Val got up.

"At least we get some good stories out of this mess, don't we?" Will dipped his head in leave as the pilots started to disperse from the Mess.

# Chapter 32

Harry sat in the Mess until it was nearly cleared out. He studied the grain of the rough wood of the table. It sat on hastily made sawhorses that had been brought with their constantly moving squadron. He thought of home and wondered what his family and Margaret were doing at that moment. He had no idea where Richard was and could be anywhere between Russia and France.

Suddenly, raised voices coming from outside caught his attention. He got up and exited the large tent. What he saw surprised him.

Dirk took a hefty punch to the eye. The attacker was one of Harry's squadron pilots, the one who had been sitting with he and Val and Will earlier.

"Hey!" Harry rushed down the small incline, about to intervene.

Curses and expletives shouted by Dirk met his ears. Dirk brawled with the pilot, punching him in the face and stomach.

The commotion was drawing more attention. Harry entered the fray as the RAF pilot, John, came at Dirk again, fists swinging.

"John! Dirk! Stop! Are you both out of your bloody mind?" Harry grabbed Dirk by the shoulders and hauled him away from the fight.

"You shameful coward! You have *NO IDEA!*" Dirk shouted and struggled to get free, but Harry held on tight.

A few other pilots grabbed John before he could get another hit at Dirk.

"Your lot are all so thirsty for blood, you don't care who gets in the way!" John shouted at Dirk before he was absorbed into the crowd that had gathered.

Harry held Dirk firmly and was aware that their wing commander had just shown up.

"You better have a good explanation," Harry hissed at his friend.

Dirk growled and wretched free, wiping at his nose that had blood streaming out of it.

"Would someone care to inform me as to what's going on here?" The wing commander asked with his steely voice. He eyed Dirk.

"It was me, sir. I started the fight." Dirk's voice rasped as he panted for breath.

The commander simply looked Dirk over from head to toe. *Pathetic.* His gaze seemed to say.

"Perhaps it's time you re-joined your American forces again, Squadron Leader Gates." He didn't need to say more as he eyed the blood dripping from Dirk's nose and onto his shirt. His gaze flicked back up to his eyes and he turned away without another word.

Dirk cursed his own foolishness under his breath.

"Come on," Harry grabbed his shoulder to lead him away.

Dirk merely shrugged him off and walked away from the base, disappearing into the night.


"What was that all about?" Some hours later, Harry peered inside Dirk's tent to see him sitting at a small table that separated two bedrolls. "Dirk?" Harry said it louder, for the rough American pilot was still staring off into space.

"Hey, kid." Dirk kept his elbows on the table and his hands clasped under his chin, still not looking up. He had washed the blood off his face, but not his shirt.

"Well?" Harry glanced at the small lamp that was hanging from the tent's main pole that ran horizontally. A bug was flying around it and bumped into the glass every other second.

"Have a seat." Dirk nodded his head towards the tiny stool that was opposite him. Dirk looked to Harry. "I have one problem with this war."

"What's that?" He asked as he sat.

Dirk shook his head. "These boys don't know who they're fighting." He looked down. "There were ten of us…"

The words hung between them for several seconds.

"I'm sorry, Dirk." Harry meant it.

"We bombed Monte Cassino all right, but three of my men were gone by the time we got there. My co-pilot was one of them. Flak took two more of my men after we dropped our bombs. We had five men still alive, myself included. But there were only four usable chutes." His face grew distant, and a shadow passed over it. "I tried to give it to him. I tried to send him out with mine, but…" Dirk didn't finish. He shook his head.

Harry knew he wasn't telling him half of what had happened.

"We had to leave him behind. We knew he couldn't survive, but still… I should have stayed. We should have tried something, anything, to save his life. It all happened so fast..." He continued. "Ben died an hour after we chuted out. He landed badly. It was just me, Dom, and Hersch." He paused. "We tried to hide in the city, tried to get out before dawn. It was no use. We didn't last three hours before they found us. We didn't even make it till dawn."

Harry listened and took a steady breath. "What happened?"

"The enemy found us and took us into custody. They tortured us."

He didn't speak for so long, Harry thought he wouldn't continue.

Dirk cleared his throat. "We fought back when they came to transfer us. When we resisted, Dom was shot in the head. In the confusion, Hersch and I were able to run. We were separated. The next thing I knew, I was hiding under a transport vehicle watching as twenty or more surrounded Hersch and took him. I should've helped. And my God, forgive me," Dirk's forehead crumpled in sudden despair. "He was Jewish."

Harry's blood ran cold.

"I should've run from where I was hiding and killed as many Germans as I could before I died. It would've been more merciful even to shoot Hersch before they could take him. But I couldn't... I was frozen. I don't know what was wrong with me. I felt like a child again." He let out a long breath and rubbed his face as though he was rubbing the memories away. "I should be dead... or at least a prisoner. It's not right I got away unscathed when everyone else died and Hersch was taken. Who knows where he is now? Being a Jew... Oh, God, he was *Jewish*. There's no worse fate than the one he was dealt. I'm a terrible coward." He added more expletives to his self-derision.

Harry got the sense Dirk was finished and shook his head in disbelief. "I'm so sorry," he didn't know what else to say as his own guilt washed over him that he had lived and Guy hadn't.

It was true that Dirk had perhaps abandoned one of his men... as a squadron leader it was the last thing he should have done... but Harry knew that things happened in the moment, and you have to make a decision. The difficult part was living with those decisions once they happened.

"That flying officer, John Hutchins?" Dirk's voice changed, his tone bitter. "He was questioning this whole war... He was wondering if we were any better than our enemy. He was mumbling about wishing for a truce." Dirk said quietly. "He was saying, 'how could the Germans be that bad?' I'll tell you, Harry, what I saw them do to my friends convinces me that those who wear that red and black and white swastika on their arms and raise their hands to heil their Hitler... they have no conscience, they have no morals, they have no heart." His next words were so full of horror, the hair on Harry's arms stood on end. "They... are *monsters*."

Harry waited a moment before he responded. "Hence the fight."

"Hence the fight." Dirk nodded. "I called him an arrogant... Well, I won't repeat what I said. But this war is worth fighting for, Harry, I know that without a doubt. Imagine if we had given up after Pearl..." He looked out of his tent's entrance. "Where would we all be?"

Harry often wondered the same thing. If it wasn't for the combined Allied efforts of the Navy, Army, and Air Force during those first few crucial years of the war, what would be left? He shuddered at the thought.

"Imagine the swastika flying in front of Buckingham Palace like it is in Paris..." Dirk wondered aloud. "Imagine the Japanese landing on the shores of San Francisco, or a U-boat sailing up the Hudson."

Harry's attention shot up at that. What would that have meant for Margaret if their enemies had advanced more than they had at the beginning of the war? What if the fighting had been brought to America's mainland shores? He couldn't imagine. He swallowed.

Dirk continued, nearly answering his what-ifs. "We'd all be living in fear. Millions would be slaughtered only because they were different."

"It doesn't help anything to speculate, Dirk." Harry didn't know if he could continue down the path this conversation was going. "It didn't happen. For that, I thank God every day. I know you have strongly held beliefs and you've been through things and seen things I can't imagine. But for my wing commander's sake, just..." he stood up. "Try not to start any other fights." He offered a weak grin.

Dirk nodded, still grave.

Harry was about to go when he turned back around. "I don't know, or I can't remember if I ever thanked you. You didn't have to intervene back there near Lavinio."

Dirk looked up now. He shrugged. "I was done leaving people behind."

Carnegie Hall was quiet as the group of six entered the hallways and antechambers. A few violins could be heard as they prepared to play and the piano was being played quietly. Upon arriving in the room, Margaret said good evening to everyone and hopped up onto the stage that she had come to know so well. She placed her cello case beside her chair and opened it up to reveal the shining polished wood.

"How are you, Simone? Grace?" She smiled up at the sisters.

"We're doing wonderfully!" Grace stopped tuning her violin.

"And how are you, Meg?" Simone asked. She was only two years younger than Margaret and had grown up so fast. *We all have grown up so fast...* Margaret thought.

"I'm fine, thank you." Margaret said as she unscrewed her endpin and got behind her cello. She took a deep breath and watched as Samuel got out the sheet music.

It was Sunday night and they were playing a small concert to promote War Bonds. There was already quite a crowd that had gathered. Margaret felt slightly abashed that she was late.

"We're going to play Vivaldi's Winter." Samuel said as he passed out the sheet music.

As everyone looked over the sheets, Rachel commented, "Oh, we're changing things up a bit!" She set her flute on her lap. "Winter in summer." She said amusedly.

The music was effortless and flowed from the musicians with emotion and passion. Samuel conducted them with grace and poise and together they all delivered a beautiful performance. They went through two of the other Four Seasons and Simone and Grace did a wonderful job with Vivaldi's Summer. They did not perform it as Hannah had years ago, but it was beautiful and they were extremely talented sisters.

The evening concert ended with a large round of applause. All the older folks who came to watch them play were thrilled to see such a wonderful generation of music-lovers rising up; destined to take their places in hallowed halls of esteemed symphonies. All the musicians started putting their instruments away for the evening, pleased with their performances. The adults lingered in the hall purchasing war bonds, talking, and chatting. Grace joined Cassie at the piano. She was always eager to learn the ins and outs of different instruments. Cassie gave her a few pointers as Simone packed up their violins. Margaret got up and set her cello in its case and set the lid on top. She got up to join Cassie and Grace at the piano. She listened in as Grubbs and Pitcher argued over who would take down the music stands.

"C, D, E, F, G, and then A, B." Cassie played the notes and Grace observed with patience.

"What are the notes for the song by Schubert? The... Oh what is it called? The Serenade I think it was." Grace asked.

"I don't think know that one..." Cassie scratched her head, her blonde curls were done up perfectly.

"I think I remember how it goes." Margaret said carefully, she didn't want to sound like a know-it-all in front of everyone, nor step on Cassie's toes.

"Show me!" Grace scooted over on the bench and Cassie was pushed to the edge. Margaret showed her the first few notes and the cascading scales that came down with her right hand.

"Meg!" Rachel called to Margaret.

"Yes?" Margaret looked out from behind the tall grand piano.

"Are you done with your cello? Can I take it for you?" Rachel offered, as they often did for each other.

"Yes, thank you, I'll be right there." Margaret showed her the last few notes and just as she did, she heard a terrible crash, a loud gasp, and yell.

Margaret held her breath. She had forgotten to lock the lid of her cello.

Bolting from the piano, Margaret jogged to the edge of the stage. Below her was a group of shocked faces who looked down at the base of the stage by the front stairs. Margaret gasped when she saw it. Her beloved cello hadn't made it. It was a four foot drop.

"Oh, Meg!" Rachel was starting to cry. "I'm so sorry! The lid wasn't locked! It just opened right up and it fell!" She cried out and put her hands to her mouth in shock.

"It was me, I left the lid open." Margaret jumped down the four foot drop and went to her cello that was in pieces. She let out a stunned breath and felt like crying as she knelt in front of it, the strings and neck broken, the body in pieces.

"Perhaps we can save it," Gabriella approached as all the adults left to give them some privacy and the children looked down from the stage with wide eyes.

The cello lay in pieces that were scattered all around the floor. Its neck lay limp and a few of the strings had broken from the impact. One of the pegs was out of its sockets and the body's wood had cracked terribly. Margaret tried her best not to cry, for she didn't want Rachel to feel any worse than she already did. She barely kept the tears back as she picked up the neck of her cello.

"It's useless. It's broken." Margaret stated the truth, and Gabriella put her hand on her daughter's shoulder.

"I'm so sorry, Meg!" Rachel knelt down next to her. "If I had known..."

"Don't blame yourself." Margaret got up and hugged her friend who had also gotten to her feet. "It was completely an accident." Margaret sighed and wiped away a stray tear from her eye. "It was all my fault. I forgot to lock the lid. What should we do with it?" She looked down with indecision to the body of her cello.

"If I can help," Mr. Seymour stepped through the crowd. "Maybe we can keep the pieces for spares. I'm afraid the body is damaged beyond repair," He picked up the neck. "But perhaps we can salvage a *few* of the pieces."

Margaret nodded, still in shock. *Now what will I do? Liz's cello would be too small and we have no other... Oh, my poor cello!*

Late that night, Margaret had gotten a letter from Harry and it had cheered her up. But as she lay in bed that night, she cried quietly and looked at her empty cello stand in the corner of the large room with the pretty white walls. Margaret sniffled in the dark and heard a floorboard squeak. She looked up and saw Rachel in the doorway.

"Are you alright?" Rachel went to her bedside and knelt in front of her.

Margaret took her friend's hand for comfort and stifled a sob.

"Is it Harry? I saw you disappear up here after dinner." Rachel's voice was low.

Margaret chuckled through her tears. "My cello," she buried her face in her pillow and cried and laughed all at the same time at the pettiness of the situation she was crying over.

Rachel burst into a muffled laugh. "Oh, how can I ever make it up to you?" She sighed.

Composing herself, Margaret sat up. "It's alright, Rachel, really. I just hope that I can buy another. Mr. Seymour seemed confident that he could find a reasonably priced, good quality cello." Margaret nodded and took a deep breath. "We'll figure things out." She forced a smile through her tears and laughed a little.

Rachel chuckled and hugged her friend. "Your poor cello!"

"Yes indeed, my poor cello." Margaret replied.

The two girls cried and laughed together and Margaret was thankful for Rachel's never-ending friendship.

---

"Blimey, Americans!" Someone called from outside.

Harry ducked out of his dark green tent. What he saw was rather different from what he had grown accustomed to seeing at the RAF bases.

A group of about eighteen men were in three Jeeps rumbling towards the camp. The late afternoon sun shone down on the grass airfield and the windshields of the Jeeps reflected off the sun, making a terrible glare. Harry furrowed his eyebrows when he realized they were all singing jovially.

> *"Oh! How I hate to get up in the morning!*
> *Oh! How I'd love to remain in bed!*
> *For the hardest blow of all, is to hear the bugler call;*
> *you've got to get up, you've got to get up,*
> *you've got to get up this morning!*
> *Someday I'm going to murder the bugler;*
> *someday they're going to find him dead!*
> *I'll amputate his reveille, and step upon it heavily,*
> *and spend the rest of my life in bed!"*

They sang out jokingly and loudly as the Jeeps rolled to a stop in front of the tents and the large Beaufighters that were behind them.

A tall man jumped out of the lead Jeep and Harry noticed his three-wing insignia on his shoulder. *A Senior Airman...* Harry noticed, intrigued. The 600 Squadron's Wing Commander Stephens introduced himself and found out what was going on.

From what Harry could hear, he gathered that the American USAAF pilots were there for the same reason they were, to damage Italian railroads, bridges, and other things that the Second Tactical Air Force was responsible for. The Senior Airman also brought orders with him. There was news about a lead from headquarters that a large group of transport conveys were making their way from southern France to Northern Italy.

Val squeezed in next to Harry.

"What's all the hullabaloo about?" He asked quietly.

"New pilots to help us out on a transport raid. Looks like a whole squadron." Harry replied, quite interested.

"Sounds like we're going to need all the help we can get..." Val remarked.


That evening, the new pilots proved a welcome relief from the exhaustion and haze the pilots of the No. 600 Squadron had fallen into. They were funny. At times they were hilarious. They were young, most of them under the age of twenty-five, and they were completely dedicated to their job even though they knew how to have a good time. Needless to say, Dirk was more than happy to see fellow Americans again.

Every Brit sat around the tented Mess and listened to the American's tales and jokes. Harry sat with Dirk by a group of boys whose names were Junior, James, and Hooper.

Hooper quieted down after a good laugh and then took a deep breath. "I have a story for you all..." He put down his cup.

"Go on then," Harry encouraged him from where he sat on the top of the table behind Hooper.

"Alright," Hooper leaned forward. "So I'm in Catanzaro," he started, puffing on his cigarette like he owned the place. "First week there, I'm strolling through this little neighborhood, right? When I spot this Italian girl... She's beautiful. Made me forget the war, the noise, everything. Hell, even the food." He chuckled and the pilots listened. "So, I walk up to her, give her my best grin and say 'sweetheart, I'm a pilot. I fly faster than any man you've met.'"

The table chuckled. Hooper took a drag of his cigarette.

"She looks me dead in the eye and says, 'hmm... but can you land?'"

The group erupted, half the men choked on their drinks, the others laughed til they were red in the face.

Hooper shrugged, grinning. "What can I say, boys? Italian women are picky—if you can't land smooth, you don't get to taxi." Everyone laughed. Hooper took another drag. "She turned on her heel and left me standing there like a chump. Last time I talk to an Italian woman, mark my words."

"American gals back home?" James mused, "you buy 'em a Coke, they'll give you a smile. Italian gals? You buy 'em flowers, wine, a whole dinner... and they'll still look at you like you've tracked mud into their church."

Harry chuckled; glad he had no interest in getting to know any of the local young women.

"I've got a story," Junior started, "so, the Jerries, man, they're a few sandwiches short of a picnic, right? Picture this... plane full of German paratroopers flying over Greece. The instructor's yelling at 'em like they're late for the Fuhrer's speech. 'Schnell! Schnell! Out the bloody door!'" Junior did a terrible German accent, drawing a few chuckles.

"'Schnell! Schnell, you cowards!' He's pushing 'em out one by one like a butcher shoving sausages into a bag. But there's one poor guy, right? He's got his hands glued to the doorframe, kicking, shouting, screaming. The instructor's red in the face. 'Out, out! No room for cowards here!' So, he gives him the boot, and this guy's flying out the door like a drunken pigeon on a windy day. The rest of the paratroopers start laughing their asses off. The instructor looks around like he's lost his mind. 'What's so funny?' One of the lads pipes up, 'Funny, sir? That was the pilot!'"

Junior burst out laughing, and even the crusty old sergeant's lips twitched. The rest of the crew slapped him on the back, laughing away.

Harry couldn't remember a time when he had felt so carefree oversees. Never had he laughed this much since the war had started.

"Poor Junior, always such childish stories. Can't think of any new ones except the same old lame jokes." James chuckled and another older ace continued.

"Ah, don't listen to him; he doesn't even have a beard!" The senior ace twirled his moustache gloatingly and Junior glared at him.

"Probably because he's not old enough to grow one." Dirk laughed, playing with the toothpick he was chewing on while Junior turned red.

"Alright, alright!" Junior rolled his eyes and laughed at the joke that was at his expense.

The next morning, Harry was still chuckling over the previous night. The Senior Airman, Vince Goddard, had told some gripping tales about flying USAAF heavy bombers over France. Now here he was in Italy, leading a group of boys who were nearly twenty years his junior and had little experience. Their squadron had seen some sorties, no doubt of that, but most of the pilots had never returned. Goddard was the only one left who had been in the squadron when it had been put together in '41. These boys were ready for action though and a transport raid was a good way for them to get experience. The anti-aircraft guns were not always that aggressive and the ships were easier to founder. Without fighter escorts, the ships were like fish in a barrel. The pilots of the 600 had also made the discovery that if they dropped their spare fuel tanks on the ships and then strafed them, they exploded and then sank the ships without having to use any bombs or torpedoes.

The Italian sunrise was pink and gold and orange. Harry secured on his lifejacket, ate a bland K-ration one of the Americans had given him, and slung his dinghy over his back. He thought over the verse he had read that morning. It was Psalm 18:32-34. *'It is God who arms me with strength, and makes my way perfect. He makes my feet like the feet of deer, and sets me on my high places. He teaches my hands to make war, so that my arms can bend a bow of bronze.'*

"What's the verse today, Harry?" Val came up behind him and asked right on cue.

Harry relayed the verse and Val clapped him on the back.

"Good verse for a good day." He smiled as they made their way to their Beaufighters.

It was their first flight in weeks, and Harry felt eager to get back in his plane. As Harry neared it, he saw that Junior was leaning up against the fuselage.

"Hope you don't mind me as your gunner?" He grinned.

"Not at all," Harry replied. "Promise I'll get you back in one piece."

"Don't make promises you can't keep." Junior joked, chewing his gum. He shook Harry's hand and entered the hatch that led to the plane's dorsal turret.

Harry climbed up through the cockpit's hatch. Once in the small space that smelled like old rubber and metal, Harry took a deep breath.

*I could do this with my eyes closed.* He thought to himself, for he had lost count of the number of raids they had gone on.

Harry put the picture of Margaret on the display of his controls before he secured his harnesses and put his map in his left boot where he could reach it. The entire line of fifteen Beaus went through their flight checklist and Harry knew the Americans were nearby doing the same in their P-51 Mustangs.

He went through the list he had gone through countless times before. His headphones were cupped over his ears and his oxygen mask hung limply to the side. His aviator goggles were on top of his head and he was fastened securely to his seat. Sitting on his dinghy, Harry got the 'ok' that his chocks had been taken away. They would go from Voltone, Italy to the Ligurian Sea. Their path was marked in red on the map and the transport ships were tiny x's straight south of Genoa, Italy.

*Wish me luck, Meg.* Harry thought to himself as he pushed his throttles forward and pulled up on the yoke.

The Beaufighter soared into the sky and Harry glanced down to the green field that was quickly shrinking. He settled in behind Wing Commander Stephens and Will's Beaufighter. The many formations of three, USAAF and RAF combined, started northwest and left behind the shimmering coast of Italy as the golden sun rose behind them in the early morning light.

It was about 300 kilometres until intercept. Harry settled into his seat and took a deep breath and licked his lips. The radio was quiet as they started their journey and Harry was lost to thought. Harry remembered Margaret skipping down the sidewalk by Regent's Park… coming in late to church because she was busy feeding the ducks in the pond. That all felt so long ago. He smiled to himself and then remembered they were an ocean apart.

*Someday we'll be together. Someday I'll be home.*

The sun sparkled on the wave tops and the quiet waters. It was almost serene. Harry spotted flocks of white birds flying low beneath them. Sparse islands broke through the surface of the sea and trees shaded the small patches of land. The wind was calm and the drone of the Hercules engines lulled Harry into a trance that was only broken by a rattle of metal.

The hour quickly wound out and the planes dropped in height. Each with four bombs under their wings, the formations levelled out over the waking waves of the Ligurian Sea at roughly 900 metres. Radio silence was broken.

"Transport ships ahead." The wing commander stated. "You know the drill."

They did. Red leaders would go for the lead ship. Blue wing would get the back. Yellow and white would go for the sides, and black was responsible for escorting red and cleaning up the mess the others left.

Harry was in the red wing, so he would be going for the front with Will and Stephens. The formation pulled to the north as the blue formation turned to the west to catch them from the rear.

It would be easy.

Red wing was the first to see the ships on the horizon. Harry whipped off his sunglasses with shock. His mouth gaped open when he saw what was leading the ships.

"Wing commander, that is no transport ship!" He spoke into the R/T with alarm.

"That's a bloody Nazi destroyer." Will cursed.

Sure enough, leading a score of transport ships was a massive Nazi warship. Huge anti-aircraft guns were pointed at the sky... the bane of aerial bombers.

The wing commander swore. "What on earth's a destroyer doing all the way out here?" He said quickly and then regrouped.

The wing commander had permission to abort the mission, but Harry knew by the tone in his voice, they weren't going to. In the hour it took for another squadron to join them, the ship could be nearing the Italian coast and Axis aerial, naval, and ground cover.

"Black, and white leader, join us in the front. We concentrate our bombs on the prow. We take down the destroyer first." He commanded.

"White, focus on those conveys." Wing Commander Stephens said loudly through the R/T.

All sense of serenity was lost as the destroyer burst into action to protect the transports that were obviously carrying something valuable... Something like artillery and ammunition.

Red leader was the first to dive on the destroyer whose flag poles proudly waved the swastika. Harry and Will were close behind Stephens.

"Say a prayer, Junior!" Harry called back to his friend who was in the top turret.

"Say a prayer and just keep shooting!" He replied, full of young energy and blind bravery.

The flak was terrible from the warship. It shook Harry's Beau violently and many small holes formed in his wings when he swerved to avoid the explosions. The transport ships were being bombed by the other USAAF and RAF planes and the spare, empty fuel tanks were falling from the sky with precision onto the decks. Another plane would then come behind and strafe the deck, exploding the ships. The combined forces of the RAF and USAAF attack fighters gave the convoys everything they had. But Harry had no time to watch the melee. He levelled his Beau out and kept his grip firmly on the yoke. His heart was beating fast as he got up close and personal with the destroyer and the hundreds of men that were scrambling to their guns to counter-attack.

"Bombs away!" Harry called out as Junior set his machine gun loose, hitting anything that moved.

"Bombs away!" Came the other voices, including the Senior Airman who was the black leader.

Harry released two of his bombs and winced as a massive explosion sounded behind him and rocked his plane brutally.

Some of the bombs had missed, but Harry still had two more and the explosion was large on the destroyer. Suddenly, the two massive twin guns on the foredeck swung into action and let loose a deafening fire.

"They're just showing off!" Junior laughed.

Harry wasn't so amused. He had seen what anti-aircraft cannons of that size could do.

Every bullet was let loose as the formations broke and went for anything they could. Harry stayed behind Will and Val stayed behind Harry. Red leader had double-backed and had let loose another set of bombs on the prow of the destroyer, but they had only done minor damage. The bombs intended for transport ships were not powerful enough to break all the way through the hull of the destroyer and make her founder. Harry risked a second to look behind the destroyer where orange mushroom clouds were billowing out from the transport ships. They were larger than they should have been, assuring the fact that they were indeed full of ammo. Harry dove down beside Will, the senior ace, and followed him with his bombs. He let one loose over the destroyer as Val followed directly on his tail. A second of silence passed before part of the deck burst into another huge cloud of flames.

*This isn't working!* Harry's propellers beat at the air furiously as he swung around behind the ship and strafed the deck.

Planes were flying everywhere, bombing, strafing, and machine gun fire was coming from below and from above. Black clouds of flak were everywhere. Harry had never seen anything like it. He pulled up over the destroyer just in time to see something that stopped his heart and almost made him stall his plane. Val's decorated Beau crashed into the sea among the smoking transport ships. Time seemed to stand still for a second and then Harry circled his plane and levelled out over a transport ship. There was so much going on, he didn't have time to process what he had just seen. He dropped a fuel tank and then heard Will's plane strafe it behind him. The transport ship blew up into a million pieces and was no more.

"White leader is down." Someone said on the radio.

Harry hoped Val had chuted out in time. He circled around.

Red leader was still trying to damage the prow, but he was out of bombs and resorted to strafing the deck into splinters. Harry gritted his teeth and yelled over the radio,

"I have one left. Where do you want it, Red Leader?"

The answer didn't come soon enough. One of the young USAAF pilots from blue group replied first.

"Get him in the stern, red three!" He yelled out in reply. "They're crippled if they're-" Suddenly, his plane burst into flames, for he had been flying too close to the destroyer; one of the cannons had gotten him.

His sentence was cut off.

"He's right! He's right!" Junior woke Harry up from his shock, however his voice cut in and out. "His brother... Fletcher Class... they crippled the enemy! Listen to him!" Junior yelled from the top turret.

"No!" Red leader's voice came in. "Drop your bomb on the prow, red three, that's an order!"

Harry had to choose. Their planes were dropping left and right. His heart was racing; his mind was reeling and the image of Val's plane going down and the kid whose plane had just burst into flames flashed through his mind in less than an instant. He pulled his plane up and looked far down to the twin stern guns that were pointing straight at him.

He knew what had to be done. He dove quickly.

"Sorry Junior, I said I'd get you back in one piece, but I don't know if that's going to happen." Harry gripped the yoke of his Beau even tighter.

"We've got to get him, Harry. Do you what you have to."

Harry dove.

He was headed straight for the damaged stern deck of the giant ship.

The twin guns seemed to be beckoning to Harry, urging him to come closer so he'd be in range. Harry pushed his throttles full forward and thought of Meg. He didn't know if he'd be able to pull up in time, but he had to drop his last bomb and do it at the right moment and in the right place... he had to be exact.

"Red three! To the prow! That's an order!"

He gained speed.

The gunfire started. It peppered the air around him and sparked against his wings and canopy as the bullets hit. His arms shook from holding onto the yoke of his plane so tightly. Any second his plane could be hit and turned into an inferno.

Harry looked down to Margaret's picture on his cockpit's controls and felt wretched at what his death would do to her. He wasn't afraid to die, but he was sorry it would hurt her so.

The machine guns on board the destroyer shook the plane. Their Beaufighter machine guns fought back. Harry and Junior spat out bullets in two second intervals and then stopped. He needed to focus.

*Three...*

The destroyer came closer. Hary angled upwards.

*Two...*

Harry was vaguely aware of his commander yelling at him to abort.

*One...*

The ship was so close, Harry could see the faces of the men firing the guns.

*ZERO!* Harry let his last bomb loose and it flew right into the damaged stern deck.

As soon as he dropped it, Harry pulled up with everything that was in him. He cried out from the effort. A split second ticked by before the bomb found its mark. The entire stern of the ship blew up into a large ball of flame.

All at once as Harry's Beaufighter climbed steeply and he banked to the right, they were hit. The fuselage of the plane was ripped nearly in half. The engines burst into flame. . Harry grabbed the picture of Margaret... if he died, he would die with her picture in his hand.

The controls went lax.

Fire surrounded them.

The Beau fell nose-first.

And then they hit the water.

The impact and sickening speed threw the plane like a toy.

Everything went black.

# Chapter 33

Margaret was jolted out of her sleep. Her eyes flew open. She had been dreaming she was falling off a building in the city, only to wake up as she hit the ground. Taking a deep breath, Margaret groaned and rolled over. She turned on her flashlight and felt her heart racing. Her clock said it was one in the morning.

Margaret couldn't fall back asleep for the life of her. She got up from her bed and went to the window, looking out into the empty street. She wrapped her robe around her matching floral pajamas and stood there for a few moments. Margaret bit her lip and couldn't help but feel sad. Her palms were sweating, and she didn't know why. But she couldn't shake off the feeling of sadness that was welling up inside her.

*I want to go home.* She thought as a wave of homesickness washed over her. New York City had become dear to her; there was no doubt about that. But she wanted to go *home.* She wondered if there were liners still going from New York to Southampton. Perhaps she'd look into it. She missed her father. She missed Bess. She missed Lily's End and the streets of London that were so familiar to her, like a dear friend. More than anything, she missed Harry, and she wanted to be with him more than words could say.

Margaret walked to her map that charted Harry's progress across the Mediterranean. Her last pin was on a little town to the northwest of Rome. She hoped she would hear from him soon. The little blue ribbon was reaching the end, and she wistfully hoped that it would mean the war would be over soon. *It has to be. He has to come home soon and I must see my father soon... We've never been apart for so long!*

---

Meanwhile, Harry came to.

He opened his eyes and realized he was still in his plane. He panicked. Water was rushing in on him. It was nearly up to his neck. He unbuckled himself with some difficulty and found the lever that released the plane's belly hatch.

It didn't budge.

*Please, God.* He begged and pulled again, kicking the hatch as well with his right leg. Something was wrong with his left...

The water was up to his neck. He kicked the hatch again. Finally, it gave.

Water came rushing in from below. Harry took a deep breath and swung his legs over and pushed off the canopy to gain some momentum.

He descended out of the belly of the plane.

*Where's Junior?* Harry thought as his lifejacket buoyed him, half-conscious to the surface.

As he breached the water gasped in air, the last thing Harry remembered seeing was a wall of flame in front of him. The destroyer was burning and sinking, men leaping off the ship in frenzied panic. Harry's head lolled backwards, the world spinning around him, and his consciousness gave way.

Harry was pulled out of the water and into a dinghy. He gasped in shock, coming around. He had been floating in the water completely lifeless for some time.

"He's breathing!" Wing Commander Stephens exclaimed as he and a few others hauled Harry into a boat.

"Junior," Harry said through gritted teeth.

He hurt all over as he was drug farther into the dinghy. He leaned up against the side with his eyes closed, he was hardly aware of what went on around him.

The fellow men in his boat paddled amongst the wreckage that had floated away from the flotsam.

Men were yelling... shouting in a language Harry didn't understand.

Gunfire rang out.

Water was splashing.

They were rowing farther out to sea.

When Harry's head cleared enough to open his eyes, the stars were out and Stephens was leaning over him, dabbing at his face with part of his shirt he had ripped off.

"My head," Harry groaned.

It ached terribly. He tried to touch it, but the wing commander stopped his hand.

"I wouldn't do that if I were you. We might lose you again." The wing commander was beat up and his voice was raspy and gruff.

"What happened?" Harry's eyes flickered closed.

"Your plane went under. It's some miracle you're still alive." He replied.

"Where's Junior?" Harry asked quietly, his lips hardly even moving.

The wing commander looked away and then back at Harry. "Junior didn't make it."

The news rocked Harry's mind again. He grew dizzy. The sky above him was spinning.

"The Germans who abandoned ship tried to take our dinghies. We had to scare them off and put some distance between ourselves."

Harry's world had already faded to blackness, and he didn't hear any more.


Stars shimmered down on Harry as he opened his eyes again. It was dark out. He was cold. There was not a sound, save for the lapping of waves and the breathing of the men in the dinghy. Harry looked up to see Val sitting silently, staring down at his hands. Half of his face was covered with cloth.

"Am I dead?" Harry asked.

Val looked to Harry. "If you are, that means I am. I don't feel very dead though." Val replied gravely. "You alright?"

Harry groaned and touched his forehead where a strip of cloth was.

He had obviously cut his head. Then he looked down and as he did, a new wave of pain washed over him. His left leg, right in the middle of his calf, was sticking out awkwardly at an angle. Harry's breath shuddered as the pain hit him. He thought he was going to be sick.

"You're a bit banged up," Val said in a whisper.

Harry pushed himself up slightly so he could see what was about him. What he saw baffled him. In the dinghy were seven men and another floating lifeboat was tied to theirs. It carried eight men.

"Fifteen," Harry said. "Is that it?" He asked Val.

Val nodded, not wanting to wake the others. Harry studied the faces. He saw Wing Commander Stephens, Hooper, and a few others he recognized. But Will and his gunner Fred, Senior Airman Goddard, and James were all missing...

"What happened after I went down?" Val asked Harry.

Harry winced and tried to ignore the pain of his broken limb and the sickness he felt in his stomach.

"Stephens kept at the front of the ship, strafing it. Then... what was his name... Charlie... suggested bombing the stern right before his plane was hit. I went after it. Bombed the deck. We were hit and I couldn't pull up fast enough. We dove right into the water. I don't remember much else."

"Well," Val scooted next to Harry and lowered his voice. "Stephens said his plane was shot down right after you went under. Only about four transports got away. I guess a few planes made it through the ordeal and went after them, but then they turned back to Italy when their fuel was running low." Val explained.

"How many planes got away?"

"Stephens said four of ours, five for the American's."

Harry shook his head. Their entire squadron had almost been wiped out. "Injuries?"

"Scratches... Bullets... I think you're the only one with a broken bone, but Peter thinks he has a broken rib. Stephens has a bullet between the shoulder blades; Hooper has bullets in his arms and legs... I guess his gunner, Stuart, got hit right in the small of his back." Val lowered his voice. "Dirk has shrapnel in his legs and a bullet in the chest. We're surprised he's lasted this long." He added quietly.

"Dirk?" Harry asked, looking over to the other lifeboat where he saw two men laying down amongst the others... sure enough one was Dirk.

They both didn't look good. They were pale and blood covered their khaki uniforms.

It made Harry sick. He balled his fists and leaned back against the side of the dinghy. It was then that he felt something in his grip. He opened his hand and saw Margaret's picture. He leaned his head back and looked up at the sky. The pain he felt in his leg was almost too excruciating to feel. The constant motion of the lifeboat didn't help.

"What about you?" Harry asked Val in a strained voice.

"I'm ok, a bullet in the arm and a bad burn to the face." Val motioned to the handkerchief that was tied around his head and his right eye. Another was tied tightly to his upper forearm. "Nothing life-threatening... At least for now." Val huddled down in the cramped two-man dinghy that was keeping seven men afloat.

Harry tried his best to sleep that night, but it was no use. Whenever someone moved, the man next to him would growl and mutter to himself. No one dared to stir, lest they disturb or hurt the man next to him. During the night, probably around 2, Harry saw a light. He lifted his head that still ached and saw that a man was holding a flashlight. He thought his name was Daniel, for he was part of his squadron, but he couldn't be sure. He was holding his flashlight on a piece of paper.

"What do you have there?" Harry asked quietly.

"Map," Daniel replied. "We're floating northwest." He clicked the light off to save its battery. "If we keep heading more north than west, we'll end up on the shores of Sanremo. Nazi territory, that is. However, if we angle west, we could get as far as Cannes. No one is in any shape to paddle, though." Daniel folded up the map with his good arm; his other wrist was broken.

Harry just hoped someone would find them soon.

At least it wasn't freezing out, or else their night afloat would have been even worse. It was cool, especially because they were all soaked to the skin, but it was bearable. Nonetheless, Harry's teeth chattered.

"I can row." Harry replied as he sat up.

His head swam, but he liked the idea of washing ashore on French territory where there were French resistance fighters, more than finding himself on Nazi-controlled Italian soil again.

"You sure?" Daniel looked up with a hopeful expression.

"Give me an oar." Harry outstretched his hand. Daniel handed him an oar he had been sitting on, and he took one himself.

Daniel used his good arm, and Harry used his upper-body strength to pull both of the dinghies through the midnight waters. He just thanked God he didn't have any bullets in him... the slow infection wasn't something he wanted to experience, yet he feared it for his friends.

"This is hell," Daniel muttered to Harry.

"No," Harry shook his head. "Hell would be warmer."

Margaret cancelled their plans to go cello shopping the next day. She didn't feel up to it and was tired from not getting much sleep the night before. Her mother was worried about her but didn't press the matter. Everyone noticed that Margaret seemed subdued that day. She spent most of the afternoon in her room writing to her father and looking out her window. She missed home so much she could hardly stand it. Earlier, Margaret had asked her mother if liners still travelled to and from England and America. Unfortunately, they didn't, and the ones that did cross the Atlantic only carried passengers on military or government assignment.

Hopes dashed, Margaret resolved herself to her fate. She went to bed that night praying earnestly for her father, Harry, and her country. *Please, God, let the war end soon.*

The next morning, at the crack of dawn, the phone rang. Already up, Margaret went downstairs and picked it up before it woke up those who were still sleeping.

"Hello?" She spoke into it, wondering who it could be.

"Meg? Is that you?" A woman's English-accented voice spoke over the garbled telephone line.

"Mrs. Cavanaugh." Margaret grew worried.

"Yes, it's me, dear. I'm glad you were the one to pick up." She paused and took a deep breath.

*This can't be good!* Margaret started to panic. "Oh please tell me it's not about Harry..." She tried to hold back the tears.

"We received a telegram this morning. I'm afraid it *was* about Harry." She spoke slowly. "I thought... well I thought that I should call and tell you right away what's happened." She was hardly stifling a sob.

"What's wrong?" Margaret held her breath.

"I'm afraid, dear, that Harry went down yesterday over the Ligurian Sea." Mrs. Cavanaugh said. "Harry's plane was shot down and they tell me... Oh, my dear Margaret, they say it's very likely he didn't make it." Mrs. Cavanaugh's words made Margaret freeze. She was crying on the other line.

Margaret didn't breathe. She didn't move. She just stood there staring blindly at the wall in front of her. Gabriella was coming down the stairs and Margaret could hear her footsteps. She was lost for words.

"There may be a small chance he lived..." Mrs. Cavanaugh said through her sobs. "He went down with several other pilots. But they say it is very unlikely..."

Margaret closed her eyes and tried to take it all in. "Thank you for calling... to tell me." She started to cry, and she put her hand over her eyes in despair.

"I'm so sorry, Meg." Mrs. Cavanaugh offered some small encouragement and all Margaret wanted to do was jump through the phone and give her a hug. She had acted as a mother to Margaret on more than one occasion.

*Dare I speak the words?* Margaret thought. "If he is alive, I know that God will see him to safety."

"Pray for him... pray he is alive." Mrs. Cavanaugh paused. "My dear boy. My dear, dear boy..."

Margaret nodded her head and took a shaky breath. "I love him, you know." She admitted. Not able to hold it back any longer, she started to sob.

"Oh, my dear. He loves you too, so very much." The line was quiet for a moment as they both cried. "Take care, darling. We'll be in touch."

The line went silent. Margaret put down the phone and sobbed and trembled. She sank down to the floor in the hallway and sat there with her back against the wall crying her heart out. She had never cried so hard in all her life. As soon as Gabriella heard she had put down the phone, she came into the little hallway and sat beside her daughter and held her tight. Margaret sobbed into her mother's shoulder, and she patted her back, crying as well.

Gabriella had no words to try and cheer her daughter. There was nothing that could be done or said to take away the pain.

---

None of the men had been so thankful to see the dawn in their entire lives. A few of the men had joined Harry and Daniel in their rowing in a desperate attempt to alter their course. Daniel, their designated navigator, tracked their progress and reported that they were now sailing straight for the Italian/French border. But their progress was slow. No one could row now. No one could even sit up. They laid there in their dinghies and watched the sun climb and fall in the sky. All the men had their eyes to the sky and never looked away from the clouds that passed by overhead. Perhaps someone would come looking for them. Maybe there was a slim chance that Allies would fly overhead, although it was a far-fetched chance. Even if the planes that got away were able to get back safely, it was not a good chance they could even be found in the vastness of the sea.

One of the pilots produced a pack of something.

"Who wants a Horlicks?" He asked and took one for himself then passed the bag of tablets around.

So it began.

The day passed and the sea was as calm as anything. The only thing that broke its stillness was a pod of dolphins that swam around the dinghies. Day passed into night and night turned into early morning. The grey stillness was silent and all that could be heard were the mutterings of the men and the groans of the injured. Three of the men died that night from their wounds. They were taken of their belongings and forever entombed in the sea. Stephens had said a prayer. It was the darkest night Harry had ever known.

Harry's leg throbbed and he refused to lift his pant leg to look at it. He grew sick whenever he saw the wretched position it was in, so he merely put his aviator's jacket over it and refused to think of it. His head was feeling better, but whenever he touched it, it stung like a thousand needles.

The Horlicks energy tablets were their only food, and Harry learnt the true meaning of the word hunger. Around 0700 hours, something broke the stillness.

An engine.

All the men sat up as best they could; from across the dinghy, Stephens squinted in pain as they all looked up to the sky.

Not just one engine. Eight engines. Two B-24s were flying directly above them. The men began to signal and wave frantically. Harry joined in. It was their first glimpse of a friend in days. Sadly, the engines grew faint as they flew away. They hadn't been spotted.... at least not yet.

"They're looking for us." Daniel stated hopefully.

"No, they're probably looking for the destroyer we blew up two days ago." Hooper replied.

"Oh, shut up, Hooper! What do you know?" Roger, a high-strung American who was a lot like Hooper, retorted harshly.

"Leave him alone." Harry muttered.

"Oh, you would stand up for him, you pig-nosed, Brit!" Roger stirred up more trouble.

"Be quiet, Roger!" Stephens barked and the dinghies grew silent again.

Arguments broke out all morning and just when Harry didn't think it could get any worse, it got worse. A storm ensued and the dinghies that were tied together flew up and down the crests of waves. Valleys and mountains formed in the sea that had been so calm, so clear, and so blue just that morning. The grey clouds rumbled, and lightning struck the surface of the sea. Harry's lifeboat capsized because there were more men in it and they had the hardest time righting it in the flotsam and chaos of the storm. The salt water stung all of their wounds. They all tried to get back into the boat, but some were weaker than others and there was so much confusion. They lost a man who had been taken too far away by the waves. He hadn't been strong enough to stay near the lifeboat. They couldn't reach him, and he was lost to the giant hills and valleys of the waves.

The churning sea seemed to amplify all of their problems. Dirk was doing bad; extemely bad. The storm finally settled and they were all asleep with exhaustion. Most of the men in the other dinghy were all motionless with fatigue. Harry found himself slipping into a deep sleep too and not even a distant lightning bolt could jolt him awake.

That night was longer than any of the others. The Horlicks tablets that were keeping them alive were running low, but Hooper found a bag of peanuts in his back pocket they all shared.

Harry reached into his coat and pulled out his picture of Margaret. She looked beautiful. She looked peaceful. Harry stared at the picture until it was too dark to see. He held onto it tightly and it got him through the never-ending painful silence of that night.

The breaking of the dawn was beautiful, but the men were too sick and tired and in pain to see it. They did not even stir or lift their heads. Thankfully, they had filled up on rainwater, but they were hungry beyond belief and sore and every inch of them hurt. Some of the wounds were festering... Harry sat up against the wall of the dinghy and touched

Val on the shoulder from where he lay next to him, careful not to touch any of his wounds. Val didn't move.

"Val?" Harry shook him harder in a panic.

"Mmm?" Val stirred.

Harry let out his breath in relief and sighed. "The sun's up. You hungry?"

"I could eat an elephant." Val turned over to lie on his back. He gazed up at Harry with his good eye as Harry handed him a tablet. "What's the verse today?" He looked exhausted and pale and thin. Harry feared for him. "It better be a good one."

"*'Blessed is the man who trusts in the Lord, and whose hope is in the Lord.'*" Harry clasped his shoulder.

Val sighed. "I have one for you." He thought for a moment and then spoke; his voice raspy. "*'The Lord is my Shepherd, I shall not want.'*" Val hesitated... he looked like he was thinking hard. "What's the next line?"

It was Hooper who interjected from his position at the far end of the dinghy. He didn't look up, he didn't move, but he spoke in a clear voice, "*'He makes me to lie down in green pastures.'*"

"That's it." Val confirmed and continued the Psalm. "*'He leads me beside the still waters. He restores my soul;'*" a wave rocked the boat. Val grimaced. "*'He leads me in the paths of righteousness for His name's sake.'*" Val paused again.

Stephens interjected, "*'Yea, though I walk through the valley of the shadow of death, I will fear no evil; for You are with me; Your rod and staff, they comfort me.*"

Val looked to the sky and took a deep breath. "*'You prepare a table before me in the presence of my enemies; You anoint my head with oil; my cup runs over.'*"

Harry finished the verse... "*'Surely goodness and mercy shall follow me all the days of my life; And I will dwell in the house of the Lord forever.'*"

All of the men listened, even if they were too weak to lift their heads. The passage comforted them and in that moment, they many made promises, pleas, confessions, and hopes to the Lord, even if they had never touched a Bible once in their entire lives.

As the men settled in for another uncomfortable day, Harry

silently prayed that today they would be freed from their tiny floating island. They couldn't be left at sea for much longer or else... Harry didn't want to think of what would happen. They had been saved from the fight for what? To die of starvation at sea? They *had* to be found. Surely there was *someone* out there looking for them.

Sadly, the day passed without a single plane or boat to come and rescue them. The men settled in for the night and grew despondent that they only had a few Horlicks tablets left.

As Harry slept fitfully, he heard coughing. Looking up, Harry saw that all the men in his dinghy were fast asleep. He looked over to the other lifeboat and saw Dirk coughing. Harry reached over and propped himself up to better see his friend.

"Are you alright?" Harry asked in his exhausted voice.

Finally, Dirk was awake and responsive for the first time since they went down.

"I've been better." Dirk's eyes hardly remained open.

"Hold on a little longer." Harry pleaded. "We're sure to be rescued in the morning. The Boeings will come back."

Dirk chuckled dryly. "Dying wasn't exactly on my to-do list today, kid. But sometimes things happen when you don't want them to." Dirk started coughing again.

Harry gritted his teeth. "Come on. You can pull through this." Harry moved slightly and gasped in pain from his leg.

Dirk closed his eyes as he lay on his back; his breath was extremely laboured. His khaki shirt was caked with dried blood.

"You saved my life." Harry said so quietly he wasn't sure Dirk could hear him.

"Well," he sighed. "You would've done the same for me." He tried to grin. "Just don't waste it." Dirk said from his dinghy and then attempted a deep breath which turned into another cough. "I'm ready." He said, a tear falling from his eye. He looked over to Harry. "I was ready to die back in Italy with my crew..."

Harry took a shaky breath. "Thank you... Dirk."

"Do me a favour?" Dirk coughed and when he removed his hand from his mouth, blood was there.

"Anything," Harry nodded.

"Find Hersch. Even if he's gone, just say a prayer over him. If he's alive, tell him I'm sorry. He was a good friend... and I left him." Dirk put out his hand for him to shake.

"I will," Harry promised, tears in his own eyes. He shook Dirk's hand and kept holding it when Dirk didn't let go.

"Michael Herschel." Dirk said, his voice so quiet, Harry could hardly hear him.

Silence settled over their rasping whispers and yet Harry still held Dirk's hand as though holding him back from death. Several minutes passed before Harry spoke what had started rushing through his mind.

"Dirk?"

The American pilot opened his eyes ever so slightly.

"I'm not... I mean, I don't know how to say this... But do you know where you're going?" He had never had the bravery to speak outright about salvation with his friends, but it may be the only chance Dirk had.

Dirk actually grinned. "Been saved since I was eight, kid. I know I'm going Home."

Harry breathed a sigh of relief. "I'll see you again, then,"

But his words were never heard. Dirk was staring unblinking at the sky, his chest not rising nor falling. His hand was limp.

Harry didn't know what to do as he looked at the empty shell of his friend for countless minutes. After some time passed, he watched numbly as a pilot in the same dinghy Dirk was in silently and respectfully patted his pockets to make sure there wasn't anything there they could use for survival or give back to his family. The pilot took Dirk's dog tags and handed one to Harry. He took the other and tied it to one of Dirk's boots. Someone said a prayer. The sun was hot on their backs. Dirk's hand started to grow cold. And only when they finished praying did Harry let go of Dirk's hand. Together, the men reverently gave him over to the dark, deep tomb of the sea.

# Chapter 34

The ARP pin was at the bottom of Margaret's wooden box. She was going through all her letters from home and from Harry. She smiled to herself and fingered the golden crown and the letters 'ARP.' She rummaged through more of the memories and found birthday cards on VIM wrappers and grocery bags. Home seemed so close, yet so far away.

It was the first of July and still there was no update on Harry's condition. She knew not whether he was dead or whether he was alive. He had gone down on the 21st of June, but Margaret had to believe he was still alive. She couldn't think of him as dead and she couldn't imagine it.

She turned on her small stool that was always before her desk and saw her new cello on its stand. Ever since the day she had felt homesick, her desire to play had vanished. She had bought the cello more for her mother's sake, for she didn't want to play it.

In the darkness of the night she cried herself to sleep.

Doubt gnawed at her.

*What if Harry is dead?*

Margaret had spoken with her father and Mrs. Cavanaugh again since hearing the news. They both believed the worst. Margaret resisted it with everything in her, but she knew she was being foolish. She stopped playing her music. She went to work every evening. She thanked God school wasn't in or else she would have given up on that too. At the moment, she wouldn't even enrol in the fall. Her heart simply wasn't in it. How could she live in a world where there was no Harry Cavanaugh?

Sitting on one of the benches in the park, Margaret watched the boys play baseball on a warm Sunday afternoon. Samuel had joined Pitcher and Grubbs. She marvelled at how much they had grown. Grubbs had grown so much taller and had leaned out. He'd be a good-looking young man in the future. Pitcher seemed the same, just taller and more mature. Samuel was starting to grow sideburns, and he had grown in stature and strength since starting work at the Brooklyn Navy Yard. Margaret hugged her knees to her chest and let a few tears fall.

"Oh, God, I miss him." She prayed out loud and sniffled and thought of Harry, saying prayers for the Cavanaugh family.

*He's gone... he was never meant to be mine and I was never meant to be his. Time to let it all go... all those hopes and dreams... He's not the one I'm meant to marry... just a friend... just someone I knew.*

She put her head in her hands and cried. Not wanting to draw attention to herself, she put her purse over her shoulder and started back to the house, wiping away the tears that streamed down her face.

*How can love hurt so much?*

---

July 1st.

The clock on the wall ticked.

IV's dripped.

The room was quiet.

The men were all sleeping.

It was a miracle, yet there they were, safe and sound.

Harry lay on his starch-white hospital bed as the anaesthesia wore off. He looked down at his leg that had just been operated on and it was straight. He thanked the Lord and took a deep breath as he thought back to the deplorable state they had been in when they had been picked up.

The day that their tablets ran out was the day they were found by a fishing boat. They had spent eight entire days in their dinghies and had not been five kilometres from the coast of Corsica. Obviously, Daniel's predictions on where they were had been entirely wrong. Their saviours were free French fishermen who had taken them to a hospital right away. Out of the fifteen pilots who had lived through the first day, only seven were still alive. That included Harry, Val, Wing Commander Stephens, and Daniel of the 600 squadron; and Roger, Hooper, and a pilot whose name was Edward, of the USAAF forces. However, that did not include the possible eight pilots who most likely got away after the battle. It was a large loss, but the German's loss was greater. They had lost a Nazi destroyer and countless transport vessels carrying important ammunitions and firearms.

Harry was only thankful to be alive.

"How are you feeling, Val?" Harry looked to his right and saw Val lying on his left side facing him.

"Better." Val sighed.

His face was still bandaged, but his bullet wound had been seen to and soon there would just be scars, ghosts of what they had once been.

Harry smiled. "Good." He was still groggy from his operation.

Harry felt optimistic. He had had his surgery; he could only get better. However, the weight of the last week was crushing. He had never seen anything like it. Going down in enemy-occupied Italy had been easy compared to the past week afloat at sea. He closed his eyes; but all he saw were faces...

Later, one of the doctors came out of the back room and spoke quietly to a nurse. Harry watched them and wondered what they were talking about. They spoke swiftly in French. The doctor looked Harry's way and then nodded to the nurse who then closed the door behind him.

She walked over to Harry, "The doctor hopes you are feeling well and are doing better?" She asked in strained English.

"I am," Harry nodded. "Thank you." She started to walk away. "Excuse me?" She turned back around to listen to him. "Is there any chance I can send a letter to England?"

She shook her head. "Not yet, *monsieur*. We will tell you when."

Harry relaxed, but he couldn't get the thought out of his mind that his parents and Margaret most likely thought he was dead.

"And my belongings?" He spoke up, worried that everything that had been on his person when he had gone down would be lost.

"At the foot of your bed, *monsieur*. Would you like your things?" She approached him again.

Harry nodded, feeling nauseous and slightly panicked for some reason. The young lady put the bundle next to Harry so he could look through everything. His uniform was neatly folded and had been washed, but the bloodstains remained around the collar of his shirt. He didn't know where the other bloodstains had come from on his pant legs, most likely from another injured pilot. In the pocket of his shirt was Dirk's dog tag and Margaret's picture. He fished both out and put them on the small nightstand to his left. Margaret's picture was wrinkled and stained from getting wet, but it was still her kind, smiling face.

Harry was content. The nurse left him after putting his clothes back at the foot of his bed.

"You can get rid of those." Harry said, his eyes closing, heavy with fatigue.

The nurse nodded and left, but Harry didn't notice. He fell asleep looking at Margaret's picture with the sound of a French radio in the distance.

The next morning was bright, and the sun shone into the windows that were behind the long line of beds in the hospital. Harry woke up peacefully, yet stiffly. His left leg was in a cast that went all the way up past his knee. He couldn't move it, but at least it had been taken care of. Harry smelled the fresh, warm air that came in through an open window at the far end of the long hospital room. However, Harry couldn't quite remember where they had ended up. *What city am I in?* He knew they were in Corsica, but beyond that, he was clueless.

A nurse in a white uniform entered the long room and put some things down on a tray.

"Excuse me, miss?" Harry called her over quietly so that he wouldn't wake his comrades.

"*Monsieur?*" She walked over to him.

"What city are we in?"

"Calvi, on the northern coast of Corsica." She smiled. "And this will be your second day you've been here." She explained patiently.

"Thank you," Harry said.

The nurse nodded her head and then went back to what she was doing. Harry touched his bandaged head and sighed.

He felt spent... his strength was gone, his fight had vanished. In his mind and in his heart, he felt ready for this all to be over... He wondered if he would be discharged or if he would be put back with his squadron once his leg healed. The softness of the pillow under his head and the mattress under his body felt entirely too soft, but he forced himself to relax. He wouldn't be going anywhere any time soon. The rest would sort itself out...

After all the men woke up, they had their meagre breakfast. They had to carefully transition into eating a full meal, or else they would have gotten sick, or worse... they could die. Harry finished his small bowl of soup and drank two entire glasses of water. He had never been so thankful for either before.

The doctors made their rounds next. Harry was second to last in the row of beds. On one side was Hooper and on the other was Val. Hooper's bullet wounds were bad and had become infected, but from what the doctors said, they were confident he'd make a full recovery. It would just take time.

"Good morning, Lieutenant Cavanaugh," the French doctor shook Harry's hand. "I am Dr. Dubois. And I am honoured to shake your hand. Your leg was in rough shape when you got to us."

"Thank you for fixing it, doctor." Harry smiled.

"Well, would you like to hear the good news first, or the bad news?" He sat on a stool by Harry's bedside. He had several instruments and tools in the pockets of his white doctor's coat.

"I'll take the good." Harry replied.

"Your head is going to heal completely. There is a gash going from the middle of your forehead," The doctor pointed to his forehead. "And it goes around to behind and above your right ear." He traced the gash with his finger on his own head. "Any deeper and it would have gone to the bone, but thankfully it didn't. You may still have symptoms from your concussion... dizziness and nausea are to be expected for some time. But tell us if it gets worse."

"What about the bad news?" Harry inquired and prepared for the worst.

The doctor hadn't said anything about his leg yet.

Looking down and folding his hands, the doctor started. "Your leg is in very bad shape. I will be honest with you, lieutenant, for I have learned that soldiers like to be told straight out..." He cast a glance over his shoulder to the line of pilots whom he had just looked over. "The truth is your leg has broken and fractured in many different places. Your ankle, as well, has several fractures that look like they weren't properly set, or healed. I gather you took an injury there some months ago?"

"Yes," Harry nodded. "I broke my ankle in Italy."

The doctor nodded. "Apart from those fractures that did, unfortunately break again, the bones in your leg and ankle have... well they have nearly shattered. Because your leg was misplaced for over a week, even if it *does* heal, it will be very, very weak." Then he paused and looked Harry in the eye. "I'm sorry, but you may never be able to walk on it again."

Harry listened and gritted his teeth. He didn't know what to think.

*Shattered.*

"You're confident that I won't ever be able to walk?" He looked to the doctor with determination. He wanted a definite answer.

"At the end of the day, it will be up to you. If you remain here we will do all we can to make sure your bones heal in the way they are supposed to. However, if you want to take the chance, I know doctors in Rome who could look at your leg. There is a surgery that I am inexperienced at doing involving pins and screws." He smoothed his white moustache. "Either way, you will go home, lieutenant. We will send you all home to convalesce as soon as possible; within the week if we can arrange the transportation. Diverting to Rome for this surgery would put you behind... you likely wouldn't return to England for weeks. The hospitals in Rome are overrun with men from the front lines. Canadian, British, American, French, Italian, Polish... There are just as many translators as surgeons. It may take time. It will be a great risk crossing the sea again. Rome is still only recently liberated. But the choice is yours. And before you ask, it must be Rome. It is the nearest place you could have the surgery. The sooner the better if you wish to have a chance at walking again. I will let you think on it tonight. Give me your answer in the morning." Doctor Dubois shook Harry's hand and went lastly to Hooper.

Harry had a lot to think about. He glanced to his left and his right and saw the men he had come to think of as brothers. They had been through much together in the past few weeks and this new venture would mean leaving them all behind, even Val, whose side he hadn't left since training. *Those days seem so far away...* Harry beckoned a nurse over and asked if he could write a letter home. She finally said yes and Harry began relaying what had happened to him after the nurse supplied him with a pen and paper. He returned the note to her, and she assured him that it would be sent off and his parents would receive it in about a week. He didn't write to Margaret, for it would take too long to arrive. He had asked his parents to call her as soon as they could, that way word would reach her sooner. Harry was glad to finally let them know he was alive and well.

Praying for some time before he went to bed, Harry wished he had his Bible and his letters with him. However, he was almost certain he would never see those keepsakes again.

By the time the sun rose the next morning, Harry had made up his mind and yet the decision sat uneasily with him. *Am I doing the right thing?*

---

The sun was shining brightly, and the warm summer breeze lifted the brown curls off of Margaret's shoulders. She watched as Rachel kicked a wave on the shores of Coney Island. The two young ladies were taking a day to sightsee around the city. It was the 6ᵗʰ of June, and the warm sun was shining down on them as they meandered on the beaches of Coney Island. This was their first stop. Next, they would go to Breezy Point and explore the sand dunes and have a picnic. It was a beautiful, sunny day and both girls were thankful to get away from the hustle and bustle; Margaret especially. Rachel believed Margaret needed time away from the house. If she wasn't at work or wandering around the park, she was up in her room pouring over the last three years' worth of letters from Harry. Her heart was broken. That week had been the longest in her life and she wondered if she would ever recover.

The girls waded into the chilly waters and splashed about to try and forget their troubles. The Island wasn't too busy, for it wasn't a very hot day. But there were people up by the amusement rides and attractions, meandering on the boardwalk and enjoying the views. Margaret dove under the water and jumped up. Rachel laughed and splashed Margaret. They laughed and played in the cool ocean tide. The crash of the waves was soothing.

Margaret plunged underwater and came up for air. A wave crashed into her, and it was then that memories started to creep back in. *Harry went under in the sea...* She shivered and started making her way back to the shore.

"Meg!" Rachel called out. "Where're you going?"

"I'm cold," Margaret called back and went to their spot where their things were. She huddled in her beach towel and dried off her hair.

"Are you ok?" Rachel asked as she joined her.

Margaret nodded. "I'll be fine. Want to go walk around the boardwalk?" She forced a smile and Rachel shrugged.

"Sure,"

They put shorts on over their bathing suits and kept their towels around their shoulders as they walked around the boardwalk and got something to eat. They followed the jazz music, which played out from a live band to the carnival attractions. There were more people the farther they got away from the windy beach. Women pushed baby carriages, men in suits walked here and there, children scampered under the feet of the adults, and G.I.'s on leave sauntered in groups.

"Aren't they spiffy in their uniforms?" Rachel whispered into Margaret's ear as they walked through the crowds to a ride. She giggled.

Margaret didn't reply. They only reminded her of Harry.

"Oh, Meg..." Rachel realized it as soon as she said it. "I'm sorry. That was terrible of me."

"It's alright, Rachel." Margaret replied. They walked closely next to each other. "It's so terribly hard, but life goes on whether we like it or not."

Rachel put her arm around her shoulder. "Come on; let's go on some of the rides. My treat," she offered encouragement.

They walked to the Island's Ferris wheel and bought two tickets. From their elevated spot on the large ride, they could see the entire beach and they finally spotted the live band down by the concessions stand that sold hotdogs.

The two girls had a grand time despite the heaviness of grief that seemed to hang over Margaret. They were starting to get hungry as they played small carnival games and went on a ride that resembled parachuting. They bought two hotdogs, wrapped them up, changed into dry clothes, and then hailed a taxi over to Breezy Point Tip, the beach to the south and east of Coney.

Once they were there, Margaret and Rachel saw there were hardly any people there. They asked their taxi to wait for them and started to have their picnic on one of the sandy dunes. Sparse oceanfront grass grew up out of the sand here and there and yet there were no trees as far as the eye could see. The beachfront lived up to its name, for it was more than breezy and the girls packed up their picnic blanket and the rest of their food early to race back to the taxi.

"Where next?" Margaret asked as they slid into the taxicab.

"Should we go to Little Italy and then walk back up to the park?" Rachel closed the car door.

"Let's go!" Margaret nodded.

"Onward, Paul! To Little Italy we shall go!" Rachel told their cab driver.

"Yes, ma'am!" The old taxi driver laughed. "I'm on it," the driver started the long drive back into the heart of the city as the girls finished their hotdogs.

The sun was high in the sky as they came into Manhattan. Once in the garland-clad streets of Little Italy, Margaret and Rachel paid their cab driver and then walked down the festive, people-filled alleys. Red canopies jutted out into the roads and men and women, young and old ate Italian food underneath them in the cafés. Margaret and Rachel got two servings of gelato and ate them in the shade of one of the buildings. They sat on a bench and listened to the Italian music coming from one of the cafés.

Margaret took a spoonful of gelato. "I wonder how Harry liked Italy... I'm sure he wasn't eating gelato, though." Margaret grew sad as she thought him.

"Oh no..." Rachel slumped her shoulders. "Meg!" She exclaimed. "I didn't even think!"

Margaret actually laughed.

"Oh, Meg, I'm such a terrible friend! I'm doing the worst possible job of cheering you up. First the ocean, then the soldiers, now Italy..." She shook her head. "I couldn't have even planned something as awful as this!"

Margaret shook her head and continued to eat. "Don't sweat it, Rach. It actually feels good." She looked around at the Italian flags and heard the Italian music drifting through the air.

Rachel squeezed her arm comfortingly and Margaret merely offered a weak smile as the song, 'Soli, Soli Nella Notte,' started playing from the café.

"Let's start heading back to the park." Rachel took off her light blue short-sleeved sweater. "It sure is sweltering now!"

The girls walked close to each other, happy to be in each other's company. It would take them an hour to get to the park, but it was a wonderful walk. They meandered all the way down Broadway and walked through Union Square Park, through the shady green, and by the monument of Admiral David Farragut. The girls stopped and looked up at the monument of the civil war admiral. Both tried to emulate the admiral who looked proudly over the park. They laughed and teased each other before they continued and gazed up at the Flatiron Building that was massive, tall, and looked as thin as a pencil.

After that, they walked down the rest of Broadway and then turned up on 6ᵗʰ Avenue. They stopped at Bryant Park with its hedges and lawns. The green park was busy with men and women seeking the lush feel of grass and the rustle of the leaves in the breeze amongst the busy city. The girls sat in the park in front of the New York Public Library and watched people go by. By then it was 2 o'clock and they passed Rockefeller Center and Radio City Music Hall. They came upon Central Park at quarter-after and stopped at the Grand Army Plaza to throw a coin in the fountain. Margaret and Rachel walked hand-in-hand and comically skipped their way up 5ᵗʰ Avenue, singing 'Mairzy Doats.'

They ventured into the shady park and found a nice bench where they could sit. They watched people go here and there and finally headed home a little before 3 in the afternoon. However, on their way back to the house, they unexpectedly saw Gabriella coming to meet them. Margaret saw the look on her mother's face. She understood instantly; either she had very good news, or really bad news. Either way, she looked like she was about to cry as she went right up to Margaret without saying anything and hugged her.

"Mum, what is it?" Margaret grew anxious. "Mum?!"

Gabriella sniffed and stepped back, putting her hands on either side of Margaret's face. "The Cavanaugh's called. He's alive." Tears were gathering in the corners of her eyes.

Margaret gasped and hugged her mother back. "What did they say?!"

"His plane went down, but he survived. He was found near Corsica! Oh my dear!" Gabriella hugged her daughter again. "I'm so relieved."

"Oh, Mum! Harry's alive!" Tears of joy were streaming down her face. "I have to go and call them!" Margaret stepped back.

Rachel gave her a huge hug and smiled in happiness. "I'm so glad, Meg." She squeezed her so tightly.

"Thank you, God, he's alive." Margaret prayed.

Together, they all walked home as fast as they could.

Margaret nearly collided into several people, as she wasn't paying attention to anything else. She nearly walked out into traffic too and would have if her mother hadn't stopped her. So full of relief and happiness, Margaret dashed into the house and to the telephone where she rang

Harry's parents. She didn't care what it cost; she'd cover any expenses. Nothing could have kept her from calling; it was a day to celebrate.

After she called the Cavanaughs and rejoiced with them, she called her father. His sweet, deep voice was music to her ears. The world seemed lighter around her as if life itself was dancing for joy in her midst.

# Chapter 35

Harry closed his eyes as he lay on the cot in the transport plane. He thought of his friends he had left behind to recover in Corsica. The hardest goodbye he had said was to Val. They had been by one another's sides for three years. They had fought together in England, Algeria, Tunisia, Libya, Malta, Sicily, Italy, and lastly, the Ligurian Sea. Harry might have lost Evan during the war, but he had gained Val as a brother. Harry had sworn they would meet again in England. And sadly, neither of them would ever be back in a Beaufighter cockpit. The thought was more terrifying to Harry than anything. His Beau had been his home during the entire war and to leave it behind for good? He couldn't quite face the harsh reality just yet. The prognosis for his leg would never allow him to fly again. Val was also too injured to return to fighting. His eyesight on the side of his face that was burned was very poor. He had been told he might not regain full sight in his right eye. However, they were alive; of that, they could not be more thankful.

The Douglas C-47 Skytrain rumbled over Rome and Harry glanced out his window in the compact fuselage of the transport plane. He saw the other transports gliding onto the Roman airfields just outside the ancient city. Once they landed, Harry would be taken into the city by an ambulance at the airfield. They would go directly to the hospital from there and the next morning Harry would receive his operation. He prayed fervently that it would work, and he'd be able to walk again.

"Good morning, lieutenant!" A Scottish voice called out as the Skytrain's main door was opened.

The pilots started to carry Harry out by the cot that doubled as a stretcher.

Harry shook the man's hand as the men set down his stretcher.

"I'm Squadron Leader Meyers; it's nice to meet you, Lieutenant Cavanaugh. I've heard some incredible things about your squadron, Praetor Sescentos."

"Thank you, Meyers, I appreciate that." Harry yelled over the drone of the aircraft that was behind him.

"Let's get you to your hospital. Officer Penry will be driving you and a few others there." The squadron leader called over a few of the ground crew and together they carried Harry over to the ambulance that was waiting.

It was going to be a long next couple of days.

Harry was at the back of the ambulance and as they drove through Rome, he never thought he had seen anything more beautiful and fascinating. Flying Officer Penry squatted in the back of the Jeep-turned-ambulance and gave them a few explanations about the things they were passing. They drove past the Arch of Constantine and the Roman Coliseum. Harry was lost for words. He couldn't believe the buildings were so old and were in such remarkable condition. They drove through beautiful tree-lined medians and around courts and cobblestone courtyards. Perhaps someday he'd return with Margaret, and they could see Rome in its true glory, not as a recently surrendered military post.

The sun was setting, casting orange rays through the Sacred City. Finally, the ambulance rolled to a stop right in front of an old hospital. It was a sandstone building and had a large, full tree in front of it.

"I assure you, gentlemen, there are no more Germans in *this* city." Penry jumped out of the back of the Jeep and undid the tailgate. "They've been out of the city for a month."

Harry was closest to the edge, so he was taken inside to the cool, quiet hospital first.

The day passed by in a flurry. Harry got settled in and wasn't surprised to see that the hospital was full to the brim. The doctors made their rounds, and Harry was introduced to Surgeon D'Ortona who would be operating on his leg in the morning.

"Get your sleep, lieutenant. We shall see you to your feet before long."

The only thing Harry remembered in the morning was being wheeled into an operating room. He was hooked up to machines and felt his stomach churn as the anaesthesia took control of him. He remembered his eyes fluttering and seeing the faces of the nurses and the doctor looking down at him. Then he lost all sense of where he was, what was happening, and why he was in the room as the surgery began.

---

It was the middle of July and Margaret sat in the studio alone.

Samuel was working, Rachel was taking a lesson from Miss Archer at the school, Grubbs and Pitcher had gone to a baseball game in the park with Mr. Ackerman, and Gabriella was outside in the garden watering everything.

Margaret practiced a new piece she had learned. The piece was Beethoven's Cello Sonata No. 4. Her cello, Fiore, was shining from the polish and her bow had new rosin applied.

With news of Harry's safety, her passion for music had returned. Although, it wasn't quite what it was when she was younger. Margaret didn't know if it was because she was simply growing up, or because there were other things that vied for her attention, but she wasn't as driven as she had been. Perhaps her passion would return more as time went on and the shocks of the last year grew less painful.

Nonetheless, Margaret set to work playing the piece. She practiced and practiced and it gave her mind a welcome respite from the worries of the past few weeks. The piece called for a piano and cello duet, but Margaret had no one to play a duet with, for everyone was out. As she played the sad tune, an idea suddenly popped into her mind. She put Fiore on the stand and ran to one of the back windows of the studio.

"Mum?!" She called down to her mother once she had opened the window.

Gabriella looked up with her sunhat on. "What's wrong?"

"Nothing. Could you come upstairs?"

"You want me to walk up six flights of stairs?" She asked incredulously.

"I have a favour to ask you!" Margaret called back.

"Alright," Gabriella sighed and then muttered under her breath. "Six flights of stairs... What does she think I'm made of? Steel?"

Margaret smiled to herself and closed the window. Louis came trotting into the studio and flopped down. His little legs stuck out from his chubby body. He was no longer the cute little puppy he had been when Margaret had first come to the house. He was now quite a hefty boy and had an attitude Margaret never imagined a dog could have. A few minutes later, Gabriella entered the studio, still with her gardening apron on.

"So, what is this favour you want to ask of me?" Gabriella approached Margaret who was sitting behind her beautiful cello.

"I picked up this piece out of my Beethoven book. Do you know it?" Margaret handed her mother the piano part of the duet.

Gabriella nodded with a far-away expression, as though she was looking at something she had seen before, many years ago.

"Could you play it?" Margaret asked meekly. "Could we play it together?"

Her mother had never brought up playing unless she was teaching someone. But now that they didn't have many students, she almost never sat in front of the grand piano.

A few seconds passed before Gabriella responded. "I'm not sure I could play it," she handed the sheet music back to Margaret and rubbed the back of her neck. "I have to finish watering the beans." She started to leave the studio.

Margaret bit her lip and looked at the sheet music her mother had rejected. "Please?" She asked

Gabriella stopped.

"If I can do it... then you can do it too. I know my desire to play music vanished when I thought Harry was gone. But it's back now. Do you think you can play again too? I promise we don't have to play the whole thing, just the first bit? It would sound so much better..." Margaret pleaded.

Gabriella barely turned around. "I'm sorry, Meg," her voice was so quiet, Margaret could hardly hear her. "I can't."

She left Margaret in the studio alone, wondering why she had refused to play for so many years. Although, Margaret could slightly relate. Her own little world was back to peace and happiness and her dear Harry was back. Gabriella's world was still missing something... she was missing her husband.

The next day the entire brigade went back out into the park. Simone and Grace joined them again and the kind sisters who had been studying at the house brought along their twin violins. Margaret always brought her violin with her now, for she didn't want anything to happen to Fiore.

They formed a semi-circle underneath the shade of a tree on the green lawn in front of a busy walk. It had been ages since they had all played in the park. The trees sighed in the breeze and the squirrels chattered noisily to each other in the treetops. Margaret stood beside Grace and Simone. Rachel stood to their right with her flute and Grubbs stood next to her with his oboe. Pitcher was on the drums and had a small part in the song they were about to play together. Gabriella stood to the side watching. Samuel was working, so it was up to the musicians to stay on the melody and rhythm.

"One, two, three," Margaret counted up to the beginning of *'How Great Thou Art.'*

Simone played the main melody as Margaret and Grace played the harmonies with Rachel and Grubbs. Simone played very well and Margaret only wished she had the lower tones of the cello adding depth to the hymn. But they played it excellently and a crowd began to form.

Next, they played *'Amazing Grace.'* Grace, the short blonde-haired young girl played the main melody low on her violin. Simone and Margaret added layers to the song. Rachel and Grubbs picked up the melody in the next verse and the three violins played together. As they came upon the chorus, Pitcher kept the beat with his snare drum. Whenever Margaret heard the rat-tat-tat, she thought of a Revolutionary War march. The picture that came to her mind was a silent battlefield with redcoats and patriots quiet on either side. Tension could be seen and felt, but no one dared to stir.

Margaret's imagination was broken as the song ended with the three violins playing quietly. The musicians all took deep breaths as they saw that their crowd had grown to about thirty people. The audience clapped as the final note of *'Amazing Grace'* faded in the park.

"What shall we play next?" Margaret looked to her friends. They had a list of hymns they had been practicing.

"How about *'Nearer My God to Thee?'*" Simone spoke up.

Grace nodded enthusiastically. "That's a good one! I've been practicing it." She looked up expectantly to the older girls.

Margaret looked to Rachel and Grubbs and Pitcher who all nodded.

"Alright," she counted to three and started up the first few notes of the glorifying hymn.

Grace started playing as well and once they got to the chorus, Simone added a harmony. Grubbs and Rachel played the same notes as Simone, just lower. Pitcher punctuated with his drums. Then the song came to a close and the audience that had now grown to forty clapped and applauded the young musicians. The musicians all smiled and looked to each other with joy. Their time off from playing in the park had paid off. They were all more accomplished with their music and the public seemed to appreciate their music more and more.

As they packed up for the day, Margaret noticed a lady talking to her mother. She closed the lid of her case, locked it, double checked that she had, and then went over to her mother.

"Mum? Who was that?" She inquired.

"A lady that works for a newspaper. She wants to take our picture and write an article about us. I was just going to ask everyone if they would mind. What do you think?"

"I'm alright with it," Margaret shrugged. "What newspaper does she work for?"

"She didn't say. Also, she wants to interview me after she takes the picture. Be a dear and stop Pitcher from climbing that tree." Gabriella went to Simone and Grace and spoke to them about the idea while Margaret persuaded Pitcher to come down and get his picture taken.

In the end, the lady took a picture of the group of young musicians, asked Gabriella a few questions, and was on her way, still scribbling down things in her notebook. The family returned to the house, Simone and Grace returned to their family's apartment, and they settled down for a quiet evening.

Several days later, Margaret excitedly tore open a letter from Harry. She had another one from her father which had arrived on the same day. Margaret began to read Harry's after glancing at the return address that said Rome, Italy.

*'Dearest Meg,*

*What an adventure this has been, and it is all coming to an end. By the time you get this letter, I will be packing for England. That's right, I'm going home. The doctors here in Rome were able to improve the condition of my leg and are optimistic that I just might be able to use it. However, that is far off, and I still have a monster of a cast on my leg and a long road of recovery ahead.*

*When I land in England, I'm not quite sure how I will react. There is still a war going on and my friends will be fighting in it while I sit and recuperate. I know what you will say, 'be thankful you're alive.' And I am. I am so thankful that I will be able to see my family, my country, and finally, I will soon see you. Once I am able to hobble across a room, I will put my strength and skill to use and do my part to help end this war. The end can't be far off. Remain strong and be of good courage.*

*Please send your reply to my parents; they will be able to hand it to me in the very near future.*

    *Yours ever,*

    *Harry.*

    *P.S. I hope you know how much I love you.'*

Margaret reread the letter several times then opened her father's letter and was pleased to hear that he was doing well and the church was staying full. However, Lily's End was not completely unaltered. The pews had been changed out and the altar had been repainted. The lilies were blooming, the trees in Regent's were full, and yet the Reverend said that his home hadn't been the same since Margaret left. He said as soon as the war was over, he would do anything he could to bring her back to London. The thought made her smile. She longed to see and live in London once more. *It has been so long... I miss them all so much.*

That afternoon, as they all worked in the garden, lounged in the cool rooms of the house, and practiced their music, Mr. Ackerman paid them a surprise visit. Usually during Saturdays, he had errands to run and calls to make.

"You won't believe it, Gabriella!" He said as he quickly entered the house and met her in the kitchen. He tossed off his fedora and Margaret came bounding down the stairs with Louis in hot pursuit.

"What is it?" She asked as he planted a newspaper on the table in the middle of the kitchen.

All the children congregated in the kitchen and they saw the paper was the New York Times. They all gasped when they saw who was on the front cover. It was a picture of them!

"It can't be!" Gabriella couldn't believe it.

"My telephone has been ringing off the hook all morning. Everyone wants lessons from *'New York's finest,'* as the reporter called us. Here," he picked up the paper and went to the article.

Everyone read it quickly and hugged each other and the boys jumped up and down. They were famous!

The article mentioned everyone, their age, and their instrument. It also included the two teachers who had been present, Gabriella Sutton and Mr. Ackerman, the former Juilliard professor. Something deep down inside of Margaret realized that their financial worries her mother had mentioned, were over. There was no way this school was going to close as long as they still had instruments to play and an audience eager to hear the encouraging harmonies that came from their hearts.

That day, the phone rang a dozen times. Everyone was beyond excited. Mr. Ackerman returned to his apartment to return his calls and fix music lessons that everyone in New York City was clamouring to get for their children. The house was busy with people who stopped by to say congratulations, donate a sum to the school, or set up music lessons with Gabriella, the esteemed pianist that was once part of the London Symphony Orchestra.

The possibilities were endless.

And the future was brightening.

---

The final landing.

Harry lay on his cot in the back of the Skytrain with the other soldiers that were returning home. They had flown over battling France and Harry was thankful the Allies had full air control. Soon, France would be completely liberated and after that, it would be a steady path to victory. The English Channel passed by underneath the formations of Skytrains that were bringing the wounded back to England. They would land at the RAF base in Odiham, just southwest of London. Then they would be transferred by Red Cross ambulances to hospitals in London and the surrounding towns. Harry didn't know where he would go, but he didn't care so long as he was home.

And soon he would see his parents.

The last time Harry had flown over the English Channel he and his squadron had been leaving Portreath, Cornwall for Blida, Algeria. That had been in November 1942. Now the chilly waters passed beneath them, indifferent to all else.

No one was firing at them.

No one was chasing them.

They weren't racing the clock to get back in time before their fuel ran out and they weren't trying to get to friendly territory before they crash-landed. It was a feeling Harry had been foreign to for years.

It was the feeling of peace.

The mix-matched, green-quilted landscape of England showed up ahead. Harry was facing the front of the plane and looked far out the cockpit's window.

They were nearing home.

Not long after, the planes touched down and the brakes were heavily applied. Nothing exciting happened until Harry's ambulance took the five men that were with him to the hospital they would be staying at. Harry looked out the ambulance's window and felt queasy.

They were in London.

The streets looked like they had years ago. However, there were patches of rubble here and there that had once been homes and houses. Harry swallowed hard and felt like he was watching things happen outside of himself. He couldn't quite grasp the fact that he was home. They drove through the streets to a hospital north of the city by Belsize Park. The ambulance parked and the British Red Cross volunteers, most of them women in white uniforms, proceeded to unload the men and help them out of the ambulance. Most of them had broken bones, bullet wounds, shrapnel injuries, and the like. It took two men to lift Harry out of the ambulance and carry him inside. He was in a large room with scores of beds amassed in it. He was set on a bed in a corner, and a clipboard was put at the foot of his bed to let the doctors know who he was and what his injuries were.

About an hour passed as all the men were unloaded and looked after. Harry found it extremely comforting to be around fellow Brits. Some were Americans, but most of them were all Englishmen in an English hospital. The thought put Harry's mind at ease. And yet he wondered where his fellow survivors were. Were they transferred to England? Were they somewhere else entirely? He hoped they were home where there was no more danger and no more shooting. Harry closed his eyes, thinking. He could still hear the Hercules engines of his Beaufighter. He could hear the gunfire and the machine guns strafing their targets. He could feel the cockpit shudder as explosions went off far below him. It was something he would never forget and something that would stay in his mind for the rest of his life.

"Harry?" A voice woke him up.

Harry opened his eyes to see that the hospital room was dark, save for the small lamps that were lit on nightstands here and there.

There they were.

His parents.

"Oh my dear boy!" Mrs. Cavanaugh rushed to his side as a nurse who had escorted them in left them alone. The men in the room didn't seem to notice, they all knew what it felt like to be reunited after such terrible times.

"Mum!" Harry hugged his mother as she sat on his bedside and embraced him.

He felt like a child again. He held tightly to her, and she cried. Her off-white cardigan smelled of home. It made Harry weep, and he never wanted to let go.

It was over.

And it all came crashing down on Harry in that instant... everything he had endured, everything he had seen, it was all over.

He was home.

He buried his head in his mother's shoulder as they both trembled in between sobs.

"It's alright, my darling. You're safe now. You're home." Mrs. Cavanaugh reassured her son, petting his hair between his head's bandages.

Harry could feel his father sit beside them and put his arms around them both. Happy tears in his eyes, thankful that their youngest had returned to them safely and soundly.

*Home.*

Harry closed his eyes as he held on as though his parents were his anchor to reality.

*Home, home, home.* Harry breathed in the word and let it settle deep down in his soul as his mind grasped the fact. *Home.*

It was over.

# Chapter 36

As the weeks passed, Harry wrote and read letters to and from Margaret. He wrote about everything that had happened in Rome. He wrote about his homecoming and how good it felt to be back in England. He still couldn't write about being adrift at sea. He couldn't go there yet, nor could he think about many of the things that he'd gone through. But she seemed happy for the news he could tell her and genuinely concerned about him and his recovery. They talked about what they would do after the war. Harry had thought about what he would do as a profession in the past weeks, something he had never dared to do during his sorties overseas. The men had believed if they thought such things, or if they planned for the future, they would tempt fate. But now Harry had time on his hands and as the doctors examined his left leg every week, he found himself thinking more about life after the war. It was an odd sensation, for he had truly believed if he came out of the fighting alive, he would always be a pilot. Of course, now that had changed with his prognosis.

Margaret wrote about how she planned to finish her schooling in Juilliard and get her four-year degree. After that, her possibilities were endless, and she honestly said she couldn't be more excited for what lay ahead.

One chilly day in September, Harry heard some good news that he desperately needed to cheer him up. The rain was pouring down outside and yet in the hospital everything was warm and calm. The radio played snappy tunes and the nurse that Harry had come to know, Nora, was doing her rounds.

She tapped Harry on the shoulder and said, "Lieutenant Cavanagh? Doctor Redding will be coming around this morning, he told me to leave these here for you." She leaned a pair of crutches against the wall and then went to the next chap who was recovering from some sort of lung damage from an explosion.

Harry watched her go and then looked back to the crutches as a smile spread across his face. He wanted desperately to get up, move around with the other men who were recovering, and feel the ground beneath his feet. And crutches meant being released from the hospital. One thing was for sure; Harry's parents would be thrilled to hear the news. They came by every day and checked in on how he was doing. He was still being monitored because of the deep wound on his head and the fragile condition of his leg; otherwise, he would have been released weeks ago. However, his parents were diligent in visiting him and they brought news with them every time. Once they talked about the reverend's latest sermon, another time his father brought news of Richard. From what their eldest son had said, he was in France helping the wounded. Still, he was with Dr. Wells, the medical professor from Oxford. Their Rich was still in one piece and doing well. He sent his love, said that he hoped he would be home soon, and told Harry to get better.

Harry fell asleep every night thinking of his friends, and of course, Margaret. He thought of Val and wondered where he had gone to next. He wouldn't be flying again, that was for sure. Harry prayed for them and only wished that he had his Bible with him, the one item of his that was still in Voltone, Italy.

---

September slipped into October, New York City's Central Park was engulfed in the colours of autumn and all about the world, people could feel something stirring in the air. Perhaps their loved ones would be home for Christmas... Maybe, just maybe, the war would be over by then.

As October's fall leaves gave way to November's bare branches, the New York Youth Orchestra became more popular amongst the men and women on the home front. They played weekends at Carnegie's Chamber Music Hall and on this Saturday, they were traveling out of town. They had received a special request from West Point Military Academy to give a special concert to the soldiers that were training there. Needless to say, they accepted.

So, on November 18th, the children who included Margaret, Samuel, Rachel, Cassie, Simone, Grace, Grubbs, and Pitcher, found themselves being driven north out of New York City. It was a welcome respite for them all, for they had been in the city for years and they were excited for the diversion. The songs they had decided to play were encouraging, heartening, and patriotic. They would play 'America the Beautiful,' and 'Nearer My God to Thee,' and 'The Battle Hymn of the

*Republic,'* and *'New York, New York.'* They had the sheet music, they had the talent, and now it was time to put it all to use to encourage the men who trained to fight for their country.

The bus driver that was transporting the children, Betty and Ted, Mr. Ackerman, Gabriella, and all the instruments to West Point, stopped in front of the stately and prodigious military academy. *Here we go!* Margaret thought to herself as the instruments were unloaded. She grasped Fiore's case tightly as they were greeted by a man in an army uniform. The man in the brownish green uniform shook Mr. Ackerman's hand and led them to the hall they would play in that evening.

"This is the Mess Hall." The man explained. He was obviously in charge, for the few men that were in the Mess saluted him.

Margaret gazed around and stayed close to Rachel.

"Will the stage have enough room for you all?" He asked Mr. Ackerman.

"It will, thank you." Mr. Ackerman took off his fedora and inclined his head to the man.

"I'll bring some men back with me so they can give you a personal tour before the concert." Then he left. His many badges and bars clinked together on his brown uniform.

"Alright, let's set up." Gabriella walked with Mr. Ackerman to the back of the room.

There were banners and buntings that were red, white, and blue hanging everywhere and flags from different divisions and units were hanging up on the high ceilings. The Mess was very large and very clean. Tables were everywhere and at the far end, where they would set up, there was a stage. Margaret and Rachel walked up the steps and arranged the chairs they would sit on into a semicircle. Betty and Gabriella, in their best dresses, helped arrange the chairs while Mr. Ackerman and Ted, in his old Navy uniform, wheeled the upright piano to its appropriate place. It wasn't a Steinway, but Cassie would have to make do.

Next, they tuned their instruments, did a rehearsal, and as they finished practicing the last song, a group of three G.I.s came into the Mess.

"Hello," Mr. Ackerman shook their hands.

"Hello, sir." They greeted Mr. Ackerman and then nodded their heads to each one of the musicians while the professor introduced them.

Margaret heard Rachel giggle to herself and since Margaret was standing right next to her, she hit her leg with her foot and gave her a sidelong glance to keep her quiet. Rachel merely smiled in reply.

The soldiers took them on a quick tour of the massive campus. They mainly stayed by the large buildings and looked at some of the statues. Ted fit right in with them and they had a great deal to talk about, for they had all served in the Pacific Theater. The children gazed at the statues of great generals and militia men with awe and Grubbs and Pitcher seemed to relish the moment. Their breath came out in big white billows, but none of them seemed to mind the cold. Personnel, all in matching uniforms, marched here and there in perfect, neat rows. Margaret watched them and couldn't help but think of Harry. In so many countries troops marched the streets, whether to protect or to invade. Margaret was thankful that America had not seen any battles on their mainland shores. She couldn't even imagine troops fighting off the coast of the Carolinas, or enemy bombers bombing central cities in the States, or destroyers patrolling the Hudson... The war seemed far away, but it was happening nonetheless... And it was happening in a way that made victory imminent. It was just a matter of when.

The concert started around 5 o'clock, or 1700 hours, military time. The men gathered in the Mess, eagerly awaiting the concert before dinner. Margaret sat in her place across from the twin violins. Samuel entered the stage and a spotlight was put on him. They had received attention and fame before, but nothing as important as this. Samuel stood in front of the chamber orchestra and gave them a faint smile which seemed to put them all at ease. He tapped his wand on the music stand and then motioned for them to start playing the first song, the National Anthem. All of the musicians stood up, as did the military men who were gathered in the Mess. Pitcher started up with a militia-style rat-tat-tat. Then a violin picked up the solo melody while Margaret and the other musicians put their hands over their hearts and looked to the American flag that was being raised behind them. It was a beautiful violin and drum version of the Star Spangled Banner and the audience of personnel clapped heartily when it was over. They had all been standing in salute as the American flag was raised behind the musicians.

They played the other songs with emotion and feeling and no one slipped up during the entire performance. To finish off the evening, they played 'America the Beautiful,' and again, the men rose to their feet in reverence for their country and the things that came to mind when the song played. Margaret thought of Harry as the lyrics ran through her mind, *'Oh beautiful for spacious skies!'* The men sang the song along with the orchestra, which added to the feel of the song immensely. Margaret even found herself getting choked up. America had become her second home and she felt the American's passion for their heritage, their freedom, and their country. It was a night that Margaret would never forget as a deafening round of applause rang through the vaulted ceilings of West Point's Mess Hall. The G.I.s gave the small New York Youth Orchestra a standing ovation. The musicians heartened the soldiers before they transferred overseas. Dinner was served shortly after and the family sat around one of the tables eating, drinking, and talking happily.

Margaret watched them quietly, feeling contentment wash over her. In between dinner and desert, she snuck out of the Mess through one of the side doors. Her black heels clacked on the cold sidewalk once she was outside and she huddled her arms around herself to keep warm, for she had left her jacket inside and she wore only an off-the-shoulder purple dress.

She breathed in the cold air and looked up at the sky that was full of stars.

"Thank you, God." She felt relief well up inside of her. "Thank you that this is almost over."

Her Harry was safe at home. Soon, they would be reunited. The war was nearing an end. Allied victories were announced on the front page of the Times almost every day. She could see her breath as she breathed a sigh of relief. "Thank you that we've been spared so much when others have lost everything..." She smiled to herself as a few snowflakes began to fall. "How did we deserve a grace such as this?"

---

Harry sat at his desk in the front room, looking out onto the street and their front yard.

He was writing a letter to Margaret, telling her about how good it was to be home again. He described the transition from hospital to home and the doctor's diagnosis. There was nothing more they could do. After taking Harry's cast off, examining his leg, and scrutinizing the x-rays, the doctors had determined that his bones and multiple breaks and fractures had healed, but he would have to work very hard following his recovery to regain his range of motion and ability to walk normally. Harry sat at the desk, watching passers-by walk here and there, going on errands or walks in the park. It made him slightly envious, but not very much. At least he wasn't paralysed, he had all his limbs, and his body was healthier than ever, despite his weak leg. He could have been dealt a much worse hand.

In the letter, he also told her how they had turned the back office into his new bedroom, as he couldn't manage the stairs. They had moved all his furniture downstairs, and he got around on the first floor with ease. It had taken some getting used to, but he reiterated just how fortunate he was to be home safe and sound.

Harry looked up from writing and saw a postman walk up the front path that led to their front door. His mother was in the kitchen washing dishes listening to the radio, so he swung over on his crutches to the front door just as the doorbell rang. He opened it and greeted the postman who handed him a small parcel and had him sign for it.

"Harry?" Mrs. Cavanaugh met him in the foyer, drying her hands off with a towel. "Who was it?"

Harry told her as he opened the package that had a return address of Voltone, Italy. He was breathless.

Inside were his things he'd left behind after he'd gone down. He reached in and pulled out his Bible.

"Oh, Harry!"

"I can't believe it." He turned through the pages that still had all his letters nestled safely in between. "They're all still here. I didn't think I'd ever see this again."

His mother watched with tears in her eyes. Harry handed her his Bible and pulled out what was underneath it. It was Bruno Russo's revolver. Harry was truly amazed. He thought his things would be split between his remaining comrades in the 600, especially such an old, expensive firearm.

"What's that from?" Mrs. Cavanaugh asked after the gun.

"It was a friend's." Harry thought of all the memories that came along with holding the gun's grip again.

He set it on his lap and pulled out a note that was at the bottom of the box.

'I hope these things make it to you safely. I'm sorry it took so long to get them to you. I hear you're recovering well, and I hope you continue to regain your strength every day.'

The note was from Will. Harry was amazed and glad that the lieutenant had made it out of that fight over the sea that had doomed so many of them.

'We're doing well here. Rearming ourselves with new aircraft and we'll be moving to a new base soon. Feel better, kid. We miss you and hope to see you soon once the war is over.

Godspeed,

Flying Lieutenant William Branch.'

Harry finished the note and retreated to his room with his things while his mother went back to the kitchen. He sat looking out his window and missed the purpose and routine of the RAF bases.

Outside, a robin flitted up to his window.

Out of everything, though, he wished he could see Margaret and learn his friends' whereabouts. Harry watched as the robin flew off on swift, sure wings into the grey sky above.

# Chapter 37

*The ground rushed up to Harry. He was falling. Flaming debris fell from above him. The cold night wind whipped around him. He crashed through the canopy of the trees and fell. A sickening snap sounded as he collided with the ground.*

Harry gasped for air, and his eyes flew open. He leaned over the side of the bed, thinking he was going to be sick.

*Where am I?*

He clenched his sheets in his hands. His heart was racing, and he tried to catch his breath through gritted teeth.

*I'm home. I'm home. I'm home.* He repeated it to himself and leaned back against his pillows.

He swung his legs out of bed, trying to get some air. Covered in sweat, he panted and put his head in his hands.

He had been dreaming again.

"Harry?" A quiet voice came from the other side of his door and a gentle knock sounded.

"I'm alright, Mum." Harry took a deep breath and wiped his forehead.

His mother opened the door and peeked in.

"I'm alright, really." Harry laid back down and turned away from the door, pulling the sheets back up despite the sweat that dripped down his back.

---

Reverend Frank Sutton had just returned from sending off a letter to his daughter and was writing up a sermon. Margaret had written to him just that week and he had sent out a reply that morning. The chilly air was enveloping London, yet no one seemed to mind. This Christmas they just might have sons and fathers back home near their hearths and hearts. It was sure to be their last lonely Christmas. The reverend smiled when he thought of that. *Perhaps my last Christmas without Margaret...* He could hardly believe it. It had been a lonesome past few years. However, he had met many new people during his war volunteer service and often he was invited to dinner or teatime to sit and chat with the kind, middle-aged men and their families.

In times like these, Reverend Sutton could not help but think of his wife. When the war was over, he could not imagine what would happen. Would they see each other? Would she return to London? Would he want to risk everything and live in New York just to be with her again? It had been twenty years since he had seen her and yet Margaret had grown to love Gabriella. They were family. But how could he mend his still-broken heart? Whenever he played the old records on his gramophone, he remembered the beautiful woman he had fallen in love with. She had such talent and simply soared when she was behind a Steinway. She had been kind, earnest, and determined and strong. But would she even want to see him again? The reverend battled with those questions, yet he turned to the scriptures for his answers and for his comfort. From there, he always uncovered wonderful truths and beautiful promises.

As the reverend turned to Philippians, he saw the verse he had read so many times.

*'Finally, brethren, whatever things are true,*
*whatever things are noble, whatever things are just,*
*whatever things are pure, whatever things are lovely,*
*whatever things are of good report,*
*if there is any virtue and if there is anything praiseworthy,*
*meditate on these things.'*

And he did as the scriptures said as best he could.

Suddenly, a knock sounded on his door.

He got up with a groan and answered it, surprised to see Harry on his crutches at his front door.

"Harry Cavanaugh, it's good to see you." He let him in. "I'm glad you've come to visit. I so enjoyed dinner the other night at your parents' place. Please thank them again for me."

"I will, of course, Reverend Sutton." Harry hobbled over to the couch and sat down with a relieved breath.

The reverend sat down as well in one of the chairs. Both were silent for a moment.

"It feels like forever ago Meg and I sat here talking the night before she left." Harry looked around the room that held so many memories. He felt like a completely different person than the boy who had sat there five years ago.

"Feels like another lifetime." The reverend agreed. They were silent for a minute. "I don't think you came here to reminisce, though. You were never the nostalgic type unless war's made you so." He chuckled.

Harry grinned. Margaret's father knew him well.

"You're right, of course." He collected his thoughts. "I wanted to come and ask for your advice. I've been having nightmares. I hear my... I hear my friends..." He paused, unable to meet the reverend's gaze. "And I see their faces." He looked down to his hands. "During the day, I'm alright. Sometimes things bring up memories... like when the washing machine starts banging... I think they're gunshots. Or I'll hear kids yelling outside and think..." he trailed off. "At night it's the worst. I want to sleep, but even if I can fall asleep, it's not the kind that leaves you feeling rested." He finished and looked to the reverend who was listening thoughtfully. "Perhaps I should go to a doctor... but Mum encouraged me to come here first. I don't know what you or a doctor could do to help, but maybe there's something."

The reverend put up his hand to stop Harry from going on. He leaned forward in his chair, resting his elbows on his knees.

"Harry," he spoke slowly, "you've been through a nightmare and back. You've seen things some of us can't even dream about."

"I see it all the time." Harry choked out.

"You can expect to be shaken up, to have nightmares, and feel doom all around you. I can tell you to pray hard, as a good reverend would do, and God *can* take this away from you through prayer. There also comes a time when you just have to wait on time to heal. Too often we want to rush our healing, whether mentally or physically." He motioned to Harry's leg. "Find your joy again. But don't cover up your wounds with busyness. Walk through them. Feel them keenly again and open up to someone you trust who can relate. Share your worries and your thoughts with them. It will help you more than you can imagine. Of course, pray and spend time reading your Bible. God can do what no man can even possibly attempt on his own. There's a point where our strength runs out and we must let Him be enough for us."

Harry thought about what he had said and nodded.

"Does that help?"

Harry said that it did. "I'll get in touch with some of the fellow pilots who've returned. And maybe I'll look in to going to work with my dad. It'd give me something to do."

"I think that's very wise. Know that Jesus Christ also suffered and endured unimaginable pain. But, *'our light affliction, which is but for a moment, is working for us a far more exceeding and eternal weight of glory.'*" The reverend said and let the words settle for a few moments.

He then ventured into sensitive territory. "How are things between you and my daughter?"

Harry smiled and met his gaze. "Thank you for letting me pursue her. She makes me happier than anything."

"I'm glad to hear it. Treat her well." The reverend stood up.

"I will, sir," Harry stood up as well and the reverend handed him his crutches. "You needn't worry about that." He shook his hand.

---

A snowstorm blew through on Christmas Eve day. On Christmas morning, the flakes were still falling gently from the sky. It was the perfect winter wonderland. All bundled up, Margaret, Rachel, Grubbs, Pitcher, and Samuel all went down to Central Park with toboggans and sleds in tow. They trudged through the snowy streets in their black and brown coats, hats, gloves, and boots. Margaret pulled Pitcher on a sled and Samuel pulled Grubbs.

"You just keep getting heavier and heavier!" Samuel exclaimed comically. No longer was he a shy boy. He was a strapping young man who now chatted away fearlessly.

"Onwards Dancer, Dasher, Donner, and Blixen! Cupid, and Comet, and Donner and Blitzen!" Grubbs shouted and pretended he was flicking a whip.

"That's not how it goes!" Rachel laughed.

Grubbs stuck his tongue out at her.

Margaret's breath puffed out in big white billows. She was breathing hard, but it felt good to be outside huffing and puffing. It was a wonderful day to be alive! The snowflakes were falling and the sun promised to come out later. Central Park was quiet, so they trudged deep into the wonderland. It felt like they were in a fairy or make-believe world.

The two younger boys sledded down some of the steep hills and then cruised as they reached flat ground. Then they would trudge back up the hill with ruddy cheeks and the others would have a go. Margaret hooted and hollered as she went sailing down the hill on the toboggan. Rachel was sitting behind her on the same sled and laughed as snow sprayed their joyful faces. The sled skidded to a halt and tumbled over. Margaret and Rachel rolled over and were covered in snow. They laughed hysterically as the chilly air blew around them. Grubbs and Pitcher ran down the hill, racing each other. Grubbs fell over and toppled onto the girls who started laughing even harder.

After they sledded, they had a snowball fight and played a rousing game of sardines. It was Margaret's turn to hide and she found a nice place underneath a stone bridge. She stood in the corner and blew in her mittens to warm them. In a matter of minutes, Samuel found her and they hid together, giggling as Grubbs whined and complained on the bridge above them.

"Come on! Tell me where you are! I know you're here somewhere!" His voice faded away as he continued on his search.

Next to join them was Pitcher. He crawled deeper under the bridge and whisked away their footprints in the deep drifts so it would be harder to find them.

Finally, Rachel found them and they all laughed as Grubbs passed by overhead again. This time, he peered underneath the massive stone bridge and yelled out in triumph.

"I found you! HA!" He laughed and jumped off the bridge and landed in a snow bank.

"You lost!" Pitcher ran over to him and tackled him.

"I did not! I found you, didn't I?" Grubbs jumped to his feet, but Pitcher was faster than him.

"After an hour," Pitcher teased and pulled Grubbs' hat down over his head, running off towards the north of the park.

The children frolicked all morning and only took a break when they reached Bethesda's Fountain. They sat around the frozen fountain and caught their breath. The angel, with her wings covered in snow, looked down at them. Margaret looked back up to her and was amazed at how beautiful the statue was. She smiled and then shivered against the cold.

Suddenly, the children all heard a dog barking.

"Louis!" Grubbs called out as the corgi ran all the way from the Mall to the fountain. His little legs worked furiously against the snow and he jumped over the high snow drifts.

Coming down from the steps of the Mall, Margaret could see her mother in her familiar dark brown coat, tan hat, and curly brown hair. Margaret couldn't help but think how similar they looked.

"How's my Louis boy?" Grubbs picked up the dog and then crashed into the snow and played with him as he sprawled around in the snow.

Louis growled playfully and Pitcher scooped him up.

"No, Louis doesn't like that!" Grubbs exclaimed as Pitcher held him on his back in his arms.

The dog wiggled to get free and Margaret, Rachel, and Samuel all laughed.

"How was your adventure?" Gabriella asked as she approached them with her hands deep in her pockets to keep them warm.

"We had fun," Margaret replied and smiled widely. She was more than happy for the respite from school and the joy that Christmas brought. It was truly her favorite holiday.

That afternoon, Margaret got a surprise. The phone rang. Either it was her father or Harry. And the thought made her run all the way into the hallway. Her white socks made her skid across the smooth wood floor, her red and grey and white plaid skirt swished as she skidded to a stop and picked up the phone quickly.

"Hello?" She spoke into the earpiece.

Margaret could almost hear him smile.

"Hello, Meg." The voice was Harry's.

"HARRY!" Margaret jumped up and down and twirled in the hallway. She leaned against the wall and twirled the phone cord in her hand. "How are you? How was your Christmas? I haven't heard your voice in years! Oh, Harry!" Margaret was beyond excited; her smile spread from ear to ear.

"I'm fine. Christmas at home was wonderful." His reply came in over the phone, crackling with static. "It's so good to hear you again, Meg. I hope we can see each other soon."

"How I would love that!" Margaret exclaimed. "What did you do for

Christmas? Oh, Harry, you have no idea..." She trailed off, at a loss for words. Her feelings were too great to even speak about.

"I know exactly how you feel," Harry responded quietly and then took a deep breath. "Your dad came over for dinner last night and this morning we all sat around and told stories. I can't tell you what it's like to be home for Christmas... It almost makes the war feel like a dream I've just woken up from. Although, I wish you were home."

"Maybe soon I *can* come home." She smiled fondly. "Maybe soon this war will be over. It's dragged on long enough..." She chuckled.

Harry laughed as well. "So, when does your next semester start?"

"In a week and a half." Margaret sighed. "I never thought that *I'd* be a college graduate."

"Is work going well?" Harry asked.

"It is," Margaret nodded. "I enjoy the work and yet it's slowed down some. What about you? You said in your last letter you were thinking about working for your father?"

"For the time being," he replied. "I have my eye on a few other jobs, but for now, this'll do."

There was a moment of content silence before Margaret asked carefully, "how's your leg?"

Harry sighed. "It's doing alright. I have to wear a brace on it, but I have a doctor's appointment soon and we'll see how it's healing and if there's any progress. At least I don't have to wear the crutches all the time."

"I'm glad, Harry. God knows, I'm so glad for you... I'm so thankful you made it through alright; that you're alive and well." Margaret closed her eyes in contentment and thanked the Lord that he was safe.

"Thank you, Meg." Harry sounded truly grateful. "Thank you for everything."

Margaret smiled. "You mean more to me than you can possibly imagine. I'll be praying for you and for your leg to heal."

"I love you," Harry said, his voice quiet with tenderness.

Margaret smiled. It was the first time she had ever heard him say it to her. "I love you too." She beamed. "And Happy Christmas, Harry."

"Happy Christmas, my love."

Then the phone clicked off.

# Chapter 38

1945.

The end of the war was forthcoming with the German retreat from the Ardennes, the Soviets capturing Warsaw and Auschwitz, the Japanese withdrawal to the Chinese coast, The Yalta Conference, the U.S. landing at Iwo Jima, the U.S. encircling the Germans in the Ruhr, and the complete liberation of France.

Harry read about these happenings in the newspapers and heard about them on the radio from their little cottage next door to Lily's End. He went to work with his father and didn't mind the quiet lawyers' offices of Claude, Baker & Cavanaugh. He liked the work, but he felt like he could do more. He'd often find himself staring out the window of his second-story office... looking for planes on the horizon.

"Dad?" Harry knocked on his father's office door.

Mr. Cavanaugh looked up and motioned for his son to enter.

Harry hobbled in, using a crutch to help support some of his weight. "Can I talk to you for a moment?"

"I'm all ears," Mr. Cavanaugh motioned to the door and Harry closed it. "Is it about the Weston's case?"

Harry shook his head. "It's about the work, more in general. You know I enjoy it here, but I think it comes as no surprise to either of us that I don't want to work here forever. This is your speciality. I still can't get flying out of my head."

Mr. Cavanaugh shook his head disapprovingly. "They won't let you rejoin your squadron."

"I know."

"And you know you can't fly, son... at all, I'm sorry to say."

"I know, I know," Harry checked himself from growing defensive. "But there must be something. I've thought about aircraft engineering... or working at one of the RAF bases. I know I can't be a mechanic anymore, but maybe... the doctor said my leg was looking better."

"Harry, you can't risk that." His father leaned forward on his desk and clasped his hands on the tabletop. "What if you were to reinjure it?"

"What if I don't reinjure it? I can't live my life in fear of reinjury and... cease to *live*. I could be running my own repair shop, or working on manufactural engineering, or better yet, returning to the Air Force."

"You keep mentioning engineering," his father paused. "But you have no university education yet." He said it as gently as he could.

"No," Harry leaned back in the chair. "I don't. But I have experience that not a lot of men have. I've been a mechanic and worked on almost every type plane from Spitfires to Harvards. And I have over six thousand hours of flight time. That's got to count for something."

Mr Cavanaugh thought for a moment. "You can work here until you find something else, of course. If this is what you want to do, you know your mother and I will support you. Just Harry," his face looked pained. "Please be careful."

Harry knew what his father was trying to say by his few words. "I will. I just want you to know, I'm going to start looking for something. But know I'll be careful, Dad. You needn't worry."

They couldn't lose another son.


That chilly Wednesday, Harry was limping down the sidewalk with a mission. He had the address scribbled on a note in his hand and he had a folded-up envelope in the pocket of his jacket. He crossed several streets, limped over the Thames, and started down a quiet street in the middle of London. He checked the address again and then knocked on the door. Holding his breath, Harry hoped that he had gotten the right house. The street was quiet, and no one was about, save for a few children playing hopscotch down the street.

The door opened and a young woman with a child on her hip stood in the threshold.

"Hello. Can I help you?" She eyed Harry over and the little boy sucked his thumb.

"I am sorry to bother you, ma'am, but are you Claudie Neff?" He asked, his gaze lingering on the little boy.

The lady nodded her head. "Yes, why?"

"My name's Harry Cavanaugh. I know you don't know me, but I knew your husband, Guy. I have something that belongs to you. He gave it to me years ago and wanted you to have it." Harry forced a grin.

"Oh?" She adjusted her son on her hip.

Harry looked at the little boy who had jet black hair. He looked so much like Guy. "Is this John?" Harry couldn't help but remember that his comrade had wanted his son to be named John after his father.

Claudie nodded again. "Yes, and he's quite the little rascal, aren't you, Johnnie?" She moved his black bangs off his little forehead.

"I served in England, North Africa, and Malta with your husband." Harry swallowed hard.

Claudie bit her lip as painful memories washed over her too. "Would you like to come inside, Mr. Cavanaugh? I can offer you a cup of tea."

"Thank you, ma'am, but I just came to deliver this." Harry pulled out the letter that Guy had told him to take care of.

Putting her hands delicately to her lips in amazement and sadness, Claudie took the envelope with her faded and worn address on the front. She fingered the lettering and almost started to cry.

"How can I ever thank you, Mr. Cavanaugh? This means more to me than..." She trailed off and wiped a tear from her eye. She looked to her son and put on a sad smile. "This letter's from Daddy," she bounced John on her hip and tried to stop the tears from coming.

"Daddy," the tot sucked on his fist and repeated what his mother had said.

"Yes, Daddy!" She smiled as John giggled, yet she wiped another tear from her eye.

Harry found himself also getting choked up. He had lost some of the closest friends he had ever had.

"He was the best pilot I knew, Mrs. Neff. He fought bravely. He told me all about you and how excited he was to meet his son or daughter. He spoke of little John and how, if it was a girl, you wanted to name her Susan."

Claudie smiled. "He was so sure it was a boy..." She said through her tears. "He was right about everything." She sighed and took a shaky breath.

Harry tried to smile as well. He patted her on the shoulder and touched John's little arm. "I hope you find comfort in his words. Rest assured, time does heal the grief." He started down the stairs, bidding her farewell.

"Thank you, Mr. Cavanaugh. Thank you very much." Then she looked to her son. "Let's go and read Daddy's letter... shall we?"

Margaret sat on the rooftop and watched the sun sink below the horizon. It was a sad day. America was mourning the death of their beloved president. President Franklin Delano Roosevelt had died the day before, April 12th, 1945. He had been president for more than twelve years and it had come as a shock to the public. Roosevelt had seen America through its darkest times and now with the impending defeat of Germany and the looming defeat of Japan as well, it was gut-wrenching that he did not live to see his country celebrate victory.

The next day, the 13th, Margaret walked to school with her hands deep in the pockets of her light brown trench coat. She wore her khaki skirt, light blue blouse, and her Mary Jane's. She briskly made her way across the 65th Street Traverse, under the bridges, and to Lincoln Center where her school was. It was another day in the City That Never Sleeps. It was another day closer to the end of the war.

When Margaret got home that early afternoon to an empty house, for all the children were in school, Gabriella had run out on errands, and Samuel was working, she sat in the living room and read a letter from her father before she headed off to work.

*'My dear girl,*

*Happy 21st Birthday. I wish I could be there to celebrate with you as you turn into an adult. No matter how old you are, you will always be my little girl. I hope that you were able to celebrate and enjoy your birthday immensely. However, I must apologize at not sending this letter sooner. The mail has been rather slow here lately.*

*Everything at Lily's End has remained the same. The lilies will soon be blooming and you will never guess what news I have to share with you. Bess sent me a letter and said that she is in Leeds! I cannot remember the last time I heard from her. She said she is swamped with her WVS work. You should be proud of her. She says to send all of her love to you and she hopes to see us all very soon.*

*With the flowers blooming and the buds coming out all across at Regent's Park, one cannot help but feel that victory is close at hand. The air is full of it and it is on everyone's minds. Oh my dear girl, when victory is* ours, I will do everything in my power to bring you back home. Which reminds me to ask you…

What shall our plans be after the war? I do not expect an immediate answer, but please be thinking on it. If you would like to spend half your time with me and half your time with your mother, or if you would like to venture out on your own now that you're an adult, we will do anything to support you and help you so long as you are happy. I do not know how things stand with your mother and I, but I will do my part and ask her. I shall write a letter and enclose it here for you. Please give it to her when you receive this note. We must pray that we find a solution and maybe, just maybe, we can all be back together again.

How I miss you and look forward to seeing your shining face and your lovely laugh. Lily's End has been too quiet. Your cello is still on its stand right where you left it and the pianos have a thin layer of dust on them.

Oh, how my mind is racing! Harry is even worse…

We have our breakfasts together every day and we speak about what will happen after the war. A massive burden will be lifted off our shoulders. Harry is still the kind young man he always has been. He has so many plans. Just yesterday he was speaking about becoming a lead mechanic at an airfield, or going into engineering, or opening his own repair shop. He is set on doing something grand and I rather admire him for it. I assured him that if he ever wanted to join the church, he knew the man to talk to. He didn't seem too interested in that idea. But he is a good man, Meg. I couldn't have asked for anyone better for my girl to be pursued by. I pray for your relationship with him, that the Lord's will shall be done and you both walk wisely and in faith.

I love you so much.

That is all I have room to write, my girl.

Sending all my love, praying for you often, and hopefully we will be reunited again soon,

Your father'

Margaret finished reading the letter with a smile and pulled out the folded-up piece of paper that was addressed to her mother. Things were starting to mend and maybe after everything they had gone through, their family would be stitched back together again.

---

Harry was alone in his room thinking. He sat on the edge of his bed and looked out the little window to his left that overlooked the back garden. It was dark outside, but he could see the lights from the neighbouring houses. It was strange to see them, as they had been blacked out the last time Harry had lived at home. He stared out into the night and thought. He still hadn't reconnected with any of his old friends. He had sent a letter to Whitehall, inquiring as to Val's current location, but he hadn't heard anything yet. The military systems were too choked up at the moment. Harry knew he might never hear back from them. He looked up Val's family but couldn't find them either. Apparently, they had moved and hadn't left a forwarding address. Still, he didn't give up trying to find his whereabouts. He knew he just might have to pay a visit to Whitehall and he was planning to go down there in the morning to get some kind of an answer.

In the meantime, his mind was too busy to sleep. He thought of Dirk and wished he was still alive. He simply wished he could talk to him... or anyone who knew what doubts and fears and trauma raced through his head... someone who had gone through those things beside him. *It's hard to be the one left behind.* The dead received their peace. Those that were left in the aftermath of the war had to deal with the repercussions of it. The world wouldn't be the same when it was over.

Looking down to his leg, Harry considered the scars that ran along either side of it. He had taken his brace off for the night. Grabbing it from off the floor, he put it on either side of leg and secured the leather straps, fastening them as tight as he could bear. It went down his lower leg and around his ankle so it could barely move. He sat there and sighed. He would have to wear the brace for a set amount of time and depending on how he did, the doctor would let him walk without it at some point.

At his last doctor's appointment, they had said his leg was still very fragile, but his ankle had healed better than they had thought. Harry was glad for the good news. He flexed his ankle and it was extremely stiff and reached a point where it was painful. However, he kept up with walking on it with the brace and flexing his joints as often as he could. *I won't be a cripple for the rest of my life.* He thought with determination.

His dreams were pleasant that night. When he woke, he thanked God he hadn't heard any gunshots in his dreams, or seen his friends dying again. Both mind and body seemed like they were slowly starting to heal.

The cab stopped beside the busy intersection and let Harry out. He got out awkwardly and thanked the driver who left after he paid him. The large white buildings of the War Office were ancient and stately and abuzz with people going every which way. Harry checked in at the front desk and had to wait a few minutes before a secretary came and retrieved him, leading him to a quiet back office.

"You've inquired as to a missing person?" She asked.

"Yes, and I'm trying to track down a friend as well."

"I see," she motioned to the chair in her office.

Harry sat thankfully.

"What's the name?" She asked.

"The first is Sergent Michael Herschel of the U.S. Army Air Force. He went down near Monte Cassino and was taken as a prisoner of war. The other is Flying Lieutenant Valentine Grant Woodard." Harry said. "He should be back in England by now; he was convalescing in Corsica last I heard."

The middle-aged woman nodded and repeated the names. "I'll go see what I can find." She replied and left the room behind.

Harry sat patiently and waited for her to return. He leaned forward in the chair, resting his elbows on his knees. He tested his foot again while he sat, putting equal weight on either leg. *I hope she has good news.* He feared what she would come back with.

The woman returned, interrupting Harry's thoughts. "Here we are." She sat behind her desk and opened the file. "Flying Lieutenant Valentine Grant Woodard of the No. 600 Squadron, is that correct?"

"Yes, ma'am."

"Let's see..." She traced her finger along the pages. "Lieutenant Woodard was transferred from Corsica to Paris. He recovered in Paris before being sent home with other discharged soldiers to London. That was in December."

Harry was just glad he was alive. "Is there a current address?"

"Yes," the woman wrote down a copy of his address. "Here you go," she handed it to Harry who took it eagerly.

"He came back to England in December?" He spoke more to himself as he wondered why he hadn't gotten in touch.

"That's right," she closed the file. "Now, for Sergent Herschel... Unfortunately, we don't have many records of those that were in the USAAF, as you can imagine. But I'll contact those that do, and I'll be in touch. If you'd just give me your name and address, I'll let you know as soon as I hear from them."

Harry did as she asked, and she stood up once they were finished.

"Does that answer your questions?"

"Yes, thank you." Harry dipped his head to her in thanks and put Val's address in his pocket. They bid each other farewell.

Harry left the way he had come and wondered if he should just show up to Val's address or write first. He knew he should write. Perhaps something had happened and that's why Val hadn't gotten in touch.

Hailing a cab, he headed home and thought about what he would write during the whole drive.


Weeks passed and a reply never came from Val. Harry wondered why and he had grown impatient with waiting. So, he found himself taking a cab to the address that was just on the outskirts of London. The car rumbled to a stop before a small flat and Harry reread the number, making sure he had the right place.

He walked up to the first-floor flat and knocked on the door. Everything was quiet, then he heard the door unlock and it opened quickly.

Harry had never been so glad to see his friend.

"Val," Harry greeted him. But he didn't have time to say anything else.

Val stepped forward and greeted him in a tight hug. Harry hugged him back, glad to be reunited with his brother-in-arms. He noticed after a moment, that Val was crying.

"You alright?" Harry stepped back and kept his hand on his friend's shoulder for support.

"I'm alright." He wiped his eyes, embarrassed.

"Did you get my letter?" Harry asked, concerned for his friend.

"I did." He nodded. "I'm sorry I didn't reply. I've been going through it since I came home... I can hardly get a proper sleep." He pressed his eyes with the heels of his palms. "I've hardly left my flat since I moved out of my parents' house."

Harry took a deep breath and nodded. "I know. I know exactly what you're talking about."

"I feel awful – feel like I'm falling apart."

He *looked* like he was falling apart. His face was pale and drawn; the part that had been burned was scarred. His right eye was clouded over; it looked as though he had indeed lost sight in it. He had dark circles under his eyes, and it didn't look like he had gained any weight since returning from the front.

"Let me help, Val." Harry was moved with compassion. He tried to swallow past the lump in his own throat.

"Thanks, Harry." Val ran a hand over his pale, drawn face. "Everything's just a mess, ain't it?"

"Cheers to that." Harry replied as they went inside. "Let's hear the whole of it. I admit I'm a tad jealous you got to see Paris... just don't tell me there's a French wife of yours inside."

Val chuckled. "No chance of that for this ugly sod. No, I daresay there's no chance of *anything* like that now."


Victory came on the warm winds that blew across Europe on May 8th, 1945.

The war was over.

V-E Day.

Harry and Val were right in the middle of the crowd that had gathered to celebrate. They were lost in the masses on the streets of London. Grinning and celebrating sailors and soldiers walked here and there with pretty, young, smiling girls on their arms. Old couples with red, white, and blue paper hats walked happily down the streets, waving the Union Jack joyously. The storm that had passed through during the night gave way to a hot summer day that reminded Harry of something out of a piece of poetry. He limped along with his cane in and out of the dancing and cheering and flag-waving Londoners. It felt like a massive family picnic.

Piccadilly Circus was full to the brim with people celebrating and crowds travelled from Westminster to Piccadilly, to Buckingham Palace. Bands played and everyone from children to old men and women, and even dogs wore red, white, and blue. Harry had a bandana around his neck that had England's flag printed on it and he wore his RAF uniform that had been sent back to him from Italy just a few weeks prior. He and his parents had been separated near Regent's Park, but he knew they were there somewhere, in the massive crowds waving flags and trying to get a glimpse of the king and queen and Winston Churchill near Buckingham.

Just then, in late morning, Harry and Val were in front of Buckingham Palace with a host of other people cheering. King George and Queen Elizabeth had just made an appearance on the balcony with their two daughters. The crowd cheered themselves hoarse after chanting 'We want the king!' over and over again. However, when Churchill appeared, the crowd went from cheering, to roaring. The deep-throated roar of the crowds praised their Prime Minister who had gotten them through so much. Harry cheered until he couldn't hear himself anymore. Val clapped wildly.

As the king and queen and princesses and Churchill left the balcony, the crowd began to move about. Harry and Val started to head back to Piccadilly with the flow of the crowds. He marvelled at how well Val was doing. In just a few weeks, he seemed happier and not so panicked and afraid at every little thing. They had spent every evening together. After Harry finished work, he would drive over to Val's and they'd eat dinner together, reminiscing and talking about the war and recovering from it. A few times, Harry invited Val to the reverend's to join them for breakfast. Val took him up on his invitation and the reverend liked Val immensely, giving him some advice and counsel as well. It must have helped, because Val was almost back to his old self; steady, wise, witty, and curious. Harry was glad to see his brother improving.

From amongst the crowd, Harry caught sight of a familiar face.

"Well, well, well, I never thought I'd see you in a dress." Harry said as he approached his old-time friend and squeezed through the mass of people to get to her.

"I'm glad to see you didn't get yourself killed," Mitch smiled. Her ginger hair was down, and she had a pretty light green dress on that matched her eyes. She looked enthralled with the spectacles and was grinning from ear to ear. "Although I see you're a little banged up." She looked at the cane he was walking with.

Harry shrugged. "It could be worse. Mitch, this is Val," Harry introduced them.

"Nice to meet you," Mitch shook his hand.

Val looked impressed. "Nice to meet you, too. Is Mitch your full name?"

"Why do all you aces ask me that?" She rolled her eyes. "Michelle

Hugal's my name... But you..." She looked him over from head to toe dramatically. "...can call me whatever you like." She winked at Val.

Val swallowed hard.

Harry smiled, amused. He spoke up to end the awkward silence. "Walk with us?" Harry started through the crowds and Mitch and Val followed close behind.

"Where're you headed?" She asked as she and Val walked on either side of him.

"Want to go to Piccadilly?"

"Let's!" Mitch exclaimed. "I heard there's a conga line and everyone's dancing there!" She exclaimed. "So what did you do, sprain your ankle or something?" She asked in her flamboyant way.

"That's about the size of it," Harry smiled, not wanting to get into the whole story on such a happy day.

"What's your story, Mr. Serious?" She asked Val who was walking beside her.

"I was in the same squadron as Harry. We trained together." He explained.

"Poor chap's always been my shadow." Harry joked.

Val rolled his eyes.

"Well, I'm glad, otherwise we wouldn't have met." She simply continued talking. "Where do you work?"

"This upcoming semester I'm actually going to be teaching at a local school."

"What're you teaching?"

"Algebra." Val replied. "And how do *you* know Harry, again?"

"We were aircraft mechanics at Brize Norton together." She answered.

"What've you been doing since last I saw you, Mitch?" Harry asked her.

"Too much to cram into a short reply." She scoffed playfully. "Come *on*, or we'll miss the dancing!"

As they neared Piccadilly, the crowds grew thicker. Everyone was laughing and a few cars drove by with people sitting on the hoods, trunks, and roofs. They all waved flags and cheered, shouting *The war is over!* Harry couldn't remember such a thrilling time. He and Mitch and Val squeezed between the people that were everywhere and finally got into the throng of Piccadilly. Men and women had joined hands and were dancing in a massive circle, laughing and smiling as music played from somewhere.

"Come on!" Mitch was beyond excited.

She took Val's hand and pulled him into the dancing.

Harry laughed, watching his gangly friend try to keep up with the headstrong young woman and dance to the music.

The celebration lasted all day and all night. Having lost Val and Mitch in the dancing at Piccadilly, Harry found an unoccupied bench and merely lay down to take a nap. People dropped everywhere as they grew tired; on road curbs, underneath trees, on top of benches, on a house's front steps, at a pub's barstool... Then when they had gotten a little sleep, they would get up and start all over again. Once Harry had gotten a few winks, he ducked into one of the pubs. He ordered something to eat and drink and was refreshed. The pub was full of men laughing and talking and having a pint to celebrate. Some were drunk and laughed crazily. No one wore a frown that day.

He finished his quick meal and then went out into the warm afternoon air. Next, he made his way over to Westminster Abbey and Parliament Square. The crowds were still thick, so the going was slow. However, Harry managed to find a spot to sit underneath a tree. He sat and rested his leg, watching young couples dance in the square. Harry's eyes drifted to a couple dancing underneath a tree across the square. He laughed. His parents were holding hands and swaying with the music. 'Bless 'Em All' was playing boisterously from someone's loud gramophone they had brought along to the revelry and the couples were all singing along.

"There you are!" Mr. Cavanaugh smiled down to his son. He had spotted him sitting under the tree.

"We were beginning to wonder where you'd gotten to." His mother said.

"Not far," Harry laughed.

"Have you eaten today?" His mother asked as they stopped dancing and caught their breath.

Harry nodded. "I had a bite at the pub. Why don't you two go and dance?" He motioned to the dancing couples that were now boogying in the square.

Mrs. Cavanaugh shook her head modestly. "I'm afraid a slow

dance or waltz is all I'm good for these days. These young couples with their new dancing... it wears you out proper." She laughed.

"Come, dear... Harry has to learn to dance from someone." Mr. Cavanaugh took his wife's hand even when she weakly protested. They joined all the dancing couples, swing dancing slowly.

Harry chuckled and sang along with the song that came from the blaring gramophone. Everyone in the crowd was belting out the song and clapping along without a care as to how they sounded.

*"We're going to hang out the washing on the Siegfried Line!*
*Have you any dirty washing, mother dear? We're going to hang out the*
*washing on the Siegfried Line, 'cause the washing day is here!"*

He tapped his toes and was thankful to be alive. His mind wandered to Margaret and he thought about what she was doing, no doubt celebrating as well.

A young lady dashed up to him and even though they didn't know each other, she asked him to dance.

"Dance with me?" She didn't hide her admiration of his RAF uniform as he sat alone under the tree.

"Afraid I can't," Harry motioned to his cane and brace and the girl looked forlorn. "Sorry," Harry grinned as the young lady sagged her shoulders and apologized.

She disappeared back into the crowd and Harry smiled to himself. He was saving his next dance for a very special young lady.

---

The crowds in Times Square rivalled London. Waving American flags could be seen everywhere. The streets of New York were a sea of red, white, and blue. Margaret and Rachel and Samuel ran all the way down to Times Square to take part in the celebration that morning. Gabriella said she would be right behind them with Grubbs and Pitcher. No doubt, somewhere in the crowds, Mr. Ackerman and Betty and Ted were all waving flags and cheering. Jeeps and cars and buses went by with people on the roofs and people standing on the bumpers and sitting on the hoods. The three friends ran into the throng out of breath. *'Chattanooga Choo Choo'* was playing from somewhere and Margaret and Rachel took each other's hands and danced together. Samuel waved an American flag he had found. Even though Japan had not surrendered, it would not be long. All the Americans knew that the beginning of a new era was starting.

*The war in Europe is over!*

The sentence seemed to be painted all around the city.

*Our boys are coming home!*

People shouted it out, it was plastered on newspaper headlines, and the air was full of it.

Margaret and Rachel both wore matching blue and yellow and white sundresses. They danced and laughed and cheered as the music came from a live band nearby. Samuel was perched up on a lamppost cheering high above the crowds.

The celebration lasted the entire day. Navy men in starch white uniforms amassed together and cheered and revelled with their sweethearts on their arms. Older gentlemen and ladies clapped to the music and waved newspapers that bore the headlines that the war was over; Germany had surrendered. Families were clustered together, and children ran everywhere, winding through the crowds with American flags in their hands.

Margaret and Rachel and Samuel stayed together through the whole day. They never got hungry, and they never got tired. All about Times Square, there seemed to be a victory tune coming from one shop or another. They wove in and out of the crowds and ducked underneath the broad shoulders of the older people. Red, white, and blue was everywhere as people waved the flags, put out banners and buntings, and wore festive colours.

Margaret waved a flag and skipped along with Rachel as Samuel jogged to keep up behind them. Men waved their fedoras, tossed them high into the sky, and the crowd's cheer was almost deafening. Women waved scarves and newspapers as they celebrated the end of the war. Years of bloodshed and sacrifice were over. President Truman gave an address that day, declaring success in Germany.

It was the best of days in the worst of times.

One thing was sure, the war was over and the future was very bright indeed.

# Chapter 39

Harry was standing on his own two feet. His left leg was shaky, but he was determined. Looking across his room, he put his left foot forward. His brace was done tightly and he took a step. His knee buckled, but he brought his right foot forward quickly. He steadied himself. One step at a time, he crossed his room without his cane and opened his door. He limped his way into the kitchen and was rather proud of himself.

"I say, you're not going to need that brace before long."

It was the reverend's voice. Harry looked over his shoulder and saw that the reverend of Lily's End had just entered. Their families were so close they never really knocked when coming over.

"Morning, reverend." Harry grinned. He was glad his parents weren't home, or he wouldn't have attempted walking on his own.

"Is your leg healing that well?" The reverend asked as he entered the kitchen. There was a note of scepticism in his voice.

"It is. I've been doing a little every day. I'm taking my time... being *anxious for nothing*." He shared the inside joke.

The reverend sat down at their dining room table that was in the same room as the kitchen. "Took the liberty of bringing this in for you," he set the mail down on the table.

Harry thanked him and went through the different letters and papers.

"I had a letter from Bess yesterday. She's doing well; living in the city now and just started working at St. Clements as a housekeeper and organist for the father there."

The reverend was speaking, but Harry didn't hear much of what he was saying. His attention was fixed on the letter in his hand he had opened from the USAAF.

"Ill news?" The reverend inquired, obviously noticing Harry's concerned expression.

"I was hoping for good news." Harry folded the letter back up. "One of pilots I came to know during the war asked me to look up one of his crew that went missing. Unfortunately, they said he was transferred from Italy to Austria and... he died near Bretstein." He felt numb.

News was just coming out about how bad conditions in Europe

had been for Jews, Christians, prisoners of war, and those of other religions. The horrifying summaries coming through the papers were enough to make anyone sick to their stomach in deepest shock. Concentration camps and extermination camps had been widely used by the Nazis, killing millions. The numbers were still going up as they found more records and more camps liberated by the Allied armies. Harry could hardly believe it. He had assumed the worst on Hersch's condition after seeing the papers. Still, it was a hard blow.

The reverend respected the quiet Harry lapsed into.

"Would you pray with me? For Hersch?"

"I would be honoured." The reverend replied.

Harry nodded his thanks and folded his hands, respecting Dirk's final wish that he'd say a prayer for the lost member of his crew.

"Our great God..." Harry started. "We know that you're with Hersch's family. Give them a peace beyond understanding. I pray he knew You in the end." Harry could hardly form the words. "I pray that I get to meet him one day and that he's with Dirk now, reunited with the rest of his crew. I pray for all those who were killed in the camps... that they are with You now and know no more pain." Harry swallowed past the lump in his throat. "Amen."

"Amen," the reverend echoed.

Harry piled the mail up and took a deep breath.

"Too many good men have been lost." Reverend Sutton remarked, looking at the letter that still sat on the table between them. "But thank God they left us with a world we can still live and thrive in."

Harry couldn't help but agree. "It doesn't make the price seem so steep when you put it that way."

"No," the reverend smiled. "It certainly doesn't." His tone changed. "What news from your brother?"

Harry shook his head in admiration when he thought of Richard. "God bless him, he's finally been allowed to come home. He'd stay if it were up to him, but his superiors ordered him back to England. He'll be home in a few weeks." Harry finished, thinking with just a small bit of regret and worry that he might not see Rich before he acted on his own plans. If all went well, he might not be in England in two weeks.

As if reading his thoughts, the reverend spoke up. "Now that you're walking and now that victory is declared in Europe, do you have any plans to go to America?"

Harry nodded, wondering if his expression gave so much away. "How'd you know?"

"Just a hunch." He grinned amusedly.

Harry went into the kitchen.

"Would you like any breakfast?" He asked the reverend.

"No, but thank you." He replied and joined him, watching as Harry scrambled some eggs.

"Would you mind?" Harry asked.

The reverend looked amused and surprised. "Why would I mind if you went to America?"

"It'd mean I would see Meg. I know how much she means to you and how close you both are. It seems unfair that I could possibly get a flight there, having been in the RAF, before you get a chance to see her." Harry cleared his throat, trying to move on from the grief that had settled on his shoulders after getting the news about Herschel.

The reverend thought for a moment. "'To everything there is a season,'" he quoted Ecclesiastes. "Harry, nothing would make me happier than to know Meg had you in New York with her. Though I cannot go yet, I will wait and plan..." he looked sad as he sighed. "Perhaps you can bring her back." He smiled then. "Also, you will come to know as you age and have children, at some point you have to let them go."

Harry couldn't help but smile and he knew he needed to ask a very important question.

"Reverend?"

He met Harry's gaze.

"I need to ask you and I'm going to ask you quickly before I lose the courage." He paused for a second. "If I can get to America, I would like to ask Margaret to marry me, and I'd like your permission to do so. I would be honoured by your blessing."

The reverend sighed and leaned back in his chair.

Harry waited patiently for his answer, yet he still found himself holding his breath.

"I always wondered if this day would come." He looked amused that the day had finally come. "Harry, you're a good man. And I hope when you go to New York, you'll treat Margaret with the utmost respect and decorum and propriety she deserves."

Harry nodded. "Of course, and I plan to provide for her and make a home for her... I want to be the best husband I can be. She deserves..." his voice cracked. "God knows, she deserves so much. I would try and be worthy of her."

The reverend scrutinized the young man who sat eagerly before him. "I know you'll do all those things and more, Harry. Of course, I give my permission... and my blessing."

Harry stood up in excitement. "Sir, you're going to have to allow me shake your hand."

The revered stood as well, laughing, and shook Harry's hand heartily. "I'm proud of you, Harry. I'll be proud to have you as a son. I couldn't imagine anyone better for my daughter."

"Thank you," Harry clapped him on the shoulder. "I love her very much and I pray I'm worthy of her."

"You are, my boy; you most certainly are."


Harry had made plans, and he hoped they would be able to be carried out. He drove to the Northolt RAF Base on a drizzly day and entered the office room he had gone in to so many times before. There, sitting like an ever-fixed mark, was a man in a chair with a newspaper unfolded in front of him. Harry recognized the stout man.

"Hello, Fyfe. It's good to see you again." Harry grinned at the bald Scotsman.

The man quickly folded back his paper and peered out above it. "Well, well, well... if it isn't Harry Cavanaugh. Welcome home, lad. I didn't think I'd ever see you again."

"You'd be surprised," Harry shook his hand as Fyfe stood up. "I'm surprised you remember me."

"I remember everyone," he scoffed and laughed. "What can I do for you?" He asked as he looked down and saw Harry's cane

"I was wondering if you had any flights leaving for America this week or next?"

"Can't say we do... Why the States?" He furrowed his eyebrows in amicable interest.

"I want to get to New York City." Harry replied. It was true enough. "Any transports going soon?"

Fyfe scratched his head in thought. "You know civilian travel is still very limited..."

"That's good, because I'm not a civilian..." Harry cracked a grin.

"Hmm..." Fyfe squinted as he thought. "This is a personal trip?"

"I guess you could say that." Harry felt his hope draining.

"You're lucky I've gotten soft in my old age." Fyfe scratched his head. "You might have to go to Upwood. The States' Army Air Force is still stationed there. They're sure to have planes going through to New York. Planes going home... never thought I'd see the day." Fyfe offered what help he could.

"Thank you very much, sir, I'll look into it. Say, is Ed Marwick still out back?" He inquired.

Fyfe looked pained and shook his head. "Ed died two years ago during a bombing raid. The whole warehouse was destroyed. I'm sorry, lad."

Harry tightened his jaw and took a deep breath, taking in the news. "I'm sorry to hear that. He was a good man..." It seemed like all the people he ever knew were either dead or injured. This war's wound ran deep.

*But not everyone...* A little voice spoke in his mind.

Harry made his way north to Upwood. His parents didn't expect him home until the afternoon or evening, so he drove his father's car through the rain that never ceased its pestering drizzle. Once he was in front of the lonely barracks of the USAAF, he got out of the black car and made his way into a building that was the office and Ops Room. Behind the barracks, Harry could see many, many B-17s. Once inside, he saw a young man sitting behind a desk smoking a cigar.

"Good morning," Harry nodded his head to the man.

"Morning!" The young American man returned the nod and then kept smoking his cigar. "What's a fella like you doin' here at Upwood? Didn't you hear? The war's over!" He laughed at his own joke that Harry wasn't amused by and put the cigar back in his mouth as another man came into the room.

"Pull yourself together, Reynolds, or you'll be no use to us in the morning." The stern-looking man threw a towel at the laughing youngster. "I'm sorry about that," he turned to Harry. "How can I help you? I'm Master Sergeant Thompson." He strode forward and saluted.

"Flying Lieutenant Harry Cavanaugh." Harry returned the salute.

"At ease, lieutenant." The sergeant dipped his head.

Harry relaxed. "Well, I'm afraid I have a bit of a favour to ask you."

"Shoot," the sergeant nodded his head for Harry to continue.

"I was wondering if your squadron was heading back to the States any time soon? Perhaps you'd have room for an extra man in those B-17s that were parked out back." Harry waited for the sergeant to reply.

"What do you think, Reynolds? Do you think we could squeeze him into one of the gun turrets? In the tail perhaps?" The Master Sergeant looked to the young man who blew out smoke dramatically.

"Hey now, that's my spot. Besides, there ain't much room back there." Reynolds shrugged. "This one's a tall Brit."

"I wouldn't take up much space." Harry assured them.

"Why do you want to go to the States? I assume it's not on government business as I've had no orders to transport a lieutenant." The sergeant sat down at the desk after playfully smacking Reynolds on the head and shooing him out of his chair.

"I'd like to get there to see... well she's not family, but..." Harry replied.

Thompson raised his eyebrows in silent challenge.

Harry hesitated.

"This about a girl? It's written all over your face, son." He smiled in what appeared to be amusement.

"I... well, yes. I'm hoping to propose to her when..."

The master sergeant laughed. "Well, what was this all for if not for a love-struck lieutenant to fly across the ocean to reunite with his sweetheart? Are you fit to go?" He eyed the cane and the lack of weight Harry was putting on his left leg.

"I am, sir."

Thompson thought for a moment. "What's your status?"

"Medically discharged, sir." Harry replied, wondering if that would help or hinder him.

The older man sighed. "Well, you'll need, what is it, Reynolds... passport, visa, your discharge papers, and... I'm not sure if you still need it, but your exit permit. I'd look into it, could take a few weeks to months."

"Done," Harry nodded. He pulled the packet of papers out of the inside of his coat pocket. He set them on the table.

Thompson raised his eyebrows, obviously impressed. "Well, looks like this Limey has a fire lit under his ass." He thumbed through the papers. "You're lucky I want to get back to the States as much as it seems you do." Thompson continued. "One of my bombardiers had a last minute transfer. Figure you can take his spot. We'll be flying into Hancock Field tomorrow night. Be here and be ready at 0700 hours, it'll be a long flight."

"Sir, I can assure you," Harry took the papers as he handed them back to him. "I'm properly used to long flights."

---

It was a lovely spring day as Margaret hurried home from her last day of school. She jogged with her cello at her side through the still-busy city streets and was excited to get home. That night, they were having a concert in Central Park to celebrate V-E Day. She was thankful she didn't have to work that day, for Grumman had cancelled production so everyone could celebrate the momentous occasion. Even though there was still fighting going on in the Pacific, they *had* to celebrate. Germany had surrendered and that was a miracle in itself. Margaret skipped stairs as she ran up to the giant double doors of their house and unlocked it. She rushed inside, put her cello by the stairs in the foyer, and dashed through the kitchen to the dining room. Louis barked at her and ran after her.

"What can I do?!" She exclaimed as she shrugged off her sweater and threw it on a chair.

Mr. Ackerman, Gabriella, Betty, Ted, Grubbs, Pitcher, Samuel, Rachel, Simone, Grace, Elizabeth, and Cassie were all in an assembly-line fashion. They were making up flyers for their concert that night. The streets still had some sparse crowds, for it was only two days after V-E Day. Therefore, they would go out that afternoon and hand out flyers to anyone they came across. They were hoping it would be a large concert, their largest to date. They would play their favourite pieces and include patriotic compositions. Margaret was so excited.

"Help us stack these up," Betty handed Margaret a pile of papers that she tidied up.

"How was school?" Gabriella asked.

"It was lovely. My final tests went well. I can't believe I'm done for the semester." Margaret replied as she read a flyer.

*'The New York Youth Orchestra*
*Proudly Presents the Concert in the Park*
*Where: Bethesda's Fountain, The Mall, Central Park*
*When: 7pm – 9pm*
*Why: To celebrate Victory in Europe*
*Please attend our free concert and come celebrate our victory and give*
*thanks to all the men and women who gave their lives for freedom.'*

All the children had a line to write, and they made up hundreds with paper Mr. Ackerman had brought over from his apartment.

It was going to be a busy day.

Everyone split up. Rachel, Margaret, and the two younger boys started towards Times Square where there were revelling groups here and there, not to mention the busy commuters walking every which way. Simone, Grace, and Gabriella had gone to Central Park. Cassie, Samuel, Elizabeth, and Betty had gone south to cover as much of that area as they could. For the whole afternoon, they passed out invitations and were greeted with many friendly smiles and happy faces that assured them they would come. When they ran out of flyers, they made their way back to the house and took more from Mr. Ackerman and Ted who had stayed behind to make them. Then they went to Central Park and distributed the rest of their flyers to vendors, commuters, and pedestrians. They hoped it would be a large turnout.

Late in the afternoon, when dusk was soon approaching, the house had a knock on its door.

Margaret ran to get it, as the others were finishing up the last hundred flyers.

She opened it to see Miss Dorothy Archer standing at the threshold.

"Miss Archer!" She said in amazement. "What a lovely surprise."

"It's good to see you, Margaret. Is your mother or Mr. Ackerman home?"

"Everyone's home, actually." Margaret stepped aside so she could enter. "We've all been rather busy today."

"Is that because of the concert?"

"Yes, are you able to come? It's not until seven tonight."

"Well, I actually wanted to talk with you all about that. You see, I have an idea..." She smiled with mischief and excitement.

And what an idea it was.


The afternoon faded fast and soon, night enveloped the city. The girls all had their best dresses on. Margaret had put on her beautiful, purple, knee-length dress that she had never worn before. She had been saving it for a special occasional. It was too expensive and too beautiful for words. It was shimmery and had a purple tulle skirt and soft, silky fabric on the bodice.

"Oh Meg!" Rachel exclaimed as they got ready together. "You look like a princess!" She finished putting in her earrings.

Margaret looked at her reflection. "Just once, doesn't every girl want to feel like a princess?"

Rachel wore a dress that was like Margaret's but it was pink.

"You look like a ballerina!" Margaret remarked as they twirled together.

"Alas, I have found my new calling!" Rachel laughed. "Forget the flute. I shall be a ballerina!"

"And what a splendid ballerina you would be!" Margaret took her hands and they danced together, laughing at each other's silliness.

"Come on, Meg! Rachel!" Pitcher poked his head into their room. "Betty says it's time to go!"

"Don't you look spiffy, Mr. Potter Watson." Margaret was taken aback by how old he looked in his little suit.

He stuck his tongue out at the dancing girls and disappeared.

"Charming," Rachel chuckled and together, they left Margaret's room and started down the stairs.

They all walked to Central Park together, carrying their instruments and music stands. The adults carried the foldable chairs and stools and they started down the stairs of the Mall. The fountain was lit up and there was a hush in the peaceful air, only broken by the sound of the fountain splashing amid the terrace. It was six o'clock and they started setting up and their instruments and tuning them.

It was then that Dorothy Archer's idea went underway.

From the stairs came the New York Philharmonic.

Margaret couldn't help but smile as they all came carrying their instruments in black cases. How regal and professional and important they looked in their fancy black suits and dresses. Miss Dorothy Archer's idea had been a splendid one. Everyone would still play from their small orchestra, but the philharmonic would play with them and Samuel would conduct them all.

As the hour passed, the philharmonic set up along the front of the fountain. Interspersed here and there were the young people of the New York Youth Orchestra. The gathering audience had grown from ten to one hundred. It kept growing and as the time came for them to start playing, there was a radio broadcaster also asking if he could broadcast the concert to local stations of New York City.

Margaret was flattered and excited and nervous. She knew everyone else was feeling the same way by what their faces gave away.

The stairs were full. It looked like there were now over two hundred people watching and listening, eager to hear the celebratory music come from the combined orchestras.

Margaret took a moment and looked around her.

Samuel was setting up at the front of the orchestra, ready to conduct, adjusting here and there meticulously, as he had just finished handing out all the sheet music. Grubbs was talking excitedly with the adult oboists from the philharmonic. Pitcher was talking with the other drummer and laughing about something, though his eyes kept darting to the crowd with big eyes full of wonder. Simone and Grace were practicing quietly with the other violinists. Cassie was sitting at the piano the philharmonic had brought for her looking amazed that such a feat could have been pulled off. Elizabeth sat next to Margaret, swinging her feet back and forth in anticipation, looking at the other cellists behind them and talking to them enthusiastically. Lastly, Rachel met Margaret's eyes from where she sat with the flutists and gave her a wide smile as if to say, *look how far we've come.*

Margaret returned her smile and dipped her head to her. *How far indeed!* She marvelled as she sat amongst the world-renown musicians of the philharmonic.

And so, they started.

Samuel stepped up to the wooden box he conducted from and cleared his throat.

A hush settled.

"Take us away, Sam." Margaret said quietly enough so that only he could hear her from where she sat in the front row.

He smiled at her and lifted his hands.

The first song they played was 'The Star Spangled Banner.' It was a violin solo and Grace did the honors. The crowd went silent and one could hear a pin drop. She played it beautifully with heartfelt passion. A flag was raised by Ted in his Navy Uniform on a small flagpole that had been brought out especially for the occasion. The audience put their hands on their hearts and took off their hats, showing the utmost respect for their country and those who had died during the war. The national anthem then faded and Pitcher picked up a rat-tat-tat militia beat on his snare drum. The trumpets came in next, playing the first verse of 'When Johnny Comes Marching Home.' Margaret got goosebumps at the power of the orchestra she felt behind her. Margaret picked up her bow and the orchestra started playing. The violins played a fast undertone as the woodwinds picked up the melody of the fast, courageous song. The brass was powerful and beautiful as they played. They ended the song with a triumphant crescendo and the crowd cheered for the orchestra's first performance, waving American flags they had kept from V-E Day.

The orchestra grew still and silent as Samuel turned the pages of sheet music. The musicians did as well. Most of them did not even look at the notes; they knew the melodies they had played for years by heart. Even the philharmonic seemed to know every note instinctively. Next up was Spring by Vivaldi. The strings had the spotlight, but so it was with many of the famous compositions. They played the familiar tune effortlessly with feeling and liveliness. It was a happy song that was amplified by the breeze coming down and into the Mall. Bethesda's fountain was aglow and trickled and splashed and added a beautiful undertone that could only be produced by nature. The sunset was beautiful and Margaret looked to her right. She gazed at it for inspiration as she played along with the fast tunes of the composition Simone and Grace effortlessly produced. The red bricks of the Mall radiated off heat from the warm sun that had beat down on the city all day. Margaret closed her eyes as the song ended softly and passionately.

The next song to play was a selection of Mozart's Piano Concerto. The composition had many different parts to it that all came together with a single melody and feeling. Cassie was in the spotlight and the woodwinds and strings took up the additional notes and added feeling and punctuation and harmony where needed. Margaret, as she played a long vibrato, looked to Samuel who was conducting them with a gentle face and a happy expression. *He's going to be famous someday...* She thought to herself. The song progressed and Rachel's flute added more notes and additional rhythms and dynamics to it. When a few minutes elapsed and the composition came to a close, everyone took deep breaths and turned to their next piece.

The audience waited patiently for the next song to start. To change things up, they played Vera Lynn's *'White Cliffs of Dover.'* Margaret played the main melody that normally would have been sung by the lovely singer. It sounded beautiful on her cello and was turned from a popular sensation to a classical composition. As the song radiated from Margaret's cello, she heard the front row of people start to sing it. She smiled as the entire crowd began to sing. They couldn't help it. The war was over! They needed to celebrate as well. Instead of just standing and watching an orchestra play, they interacted with them and felt the music as though they were playing it as well. That was the real treasure Margaret loved about music; how they were inspiring people and lifting their spirits, just as the LSO in the Royal Albert Hall had done for her so many years ago.

> *"There'll be bluebirds over*
> *The white cliffs of Dover*
> *Tomorrow, just you wait and see."*

The woodwinds played an interlude as the verse was played.

> *"There'll be love and laughter*
> *And peace ever after*
> *Tomorrow, when the world is free.*
> *There'll be bluebirds over*
> *The white cliffs of Dover*
> *Tomorrow, just you wait and see"*

The last lyric faded into the night and the musicians flipped their sheet music to their next song, *'Amazing Grace,'* as the crowd cheered and clapped. Grubbs and Simone and Cassie were the stars of this song. Grubbs' cheeks blew out comically as he played the lovely hymn on his oboe along with all the other woodwinds. Simone, Cassie, and the adult violinists accompanied him. The other instruments all added depth to the song.

They played many other songs as well. *'Abide with Me'* was played and they turned to another hymn, *'Agnus Dei.'*

The song brought back a vivid memory to Margaret. She closed her eyes and felt herself grow emotional as the strings played a long vibrato. She had never felt such music around her. It was as though she was living in it as the others accompanied her. She pictured herself standing on the prow of the *Aquitania* with her violin from her father on her shoulder. She could almost feel the salty air, the cool April breeze, the sound of the waves hitting the prow... She started to cry silently as the song grew to the crescendo.

Margaret had been just a girl; just a little girl. She had ventured into the unknown equipped only with the love that her father had given her and taught her to cling to. How much she had accomplished since then! She had met her mother and had come to love her so dearly. Now Margaret couldn't imagine her life without her mother at her side. As the song continued to the next verse, she lost all sense of awareness. According to her, she was the only person in the whole world. It was just her and her cello and the music that came from the depths of her heart. Margaret thought of her Saviour and how He loved her more than anything. So much so, that He had died for her and was the embodiment of truth, mercy, grace, and love. He would never leave her, nor forsake her. Margaret played the chorus that was still making tears fall down her cheeks. She played the final few measures alone. The entire audience was silent and the only sound that could be heard was the splashing of the fountain and her cello.

Margaret took a deep breath as she finished the song and silence gave way. Not long was it until the crowd clapped and applauded her, they too had felt the passion and praise in the hymn.

The next half hour saw the orchestra play many songs that the audience clapped and cheered for every time. The hour that was waning brought forth the stars in the dark blue sky. The lampposts had been turned on and it gave the concert a whole new feel. The Angel of the Waters looked down on them from the top of the fountain and her face was the picture of serenity. She held flowers down to her side in her left hand and her right was outstretched, as if gently touching a child's head. The audience filled Bethesda's Terrace, their faces lit up from the lampposts. The underground chamber beneath the Mall was also lit up and reminded Margaret of a grand hall in one of the esteemed houses in England. It was a beautiful night, one of the most beautiful nights Margaret could ever remember. She only wished that her dear Harry was there to see it.

The musicians played many more songs as the hour drew on. They played more Mozart and then turned to Bach and played Pachelbel's *Canon in D*.

Margaret picked up the first few bars and notes that were so familiar, it was like having a conversation with an old, old friend. The violins picked up the higher melodies. Margaret gazed down at Fiore, her dark mahogany cello that she was so grateful to have. Margaret's purple dress looked pretty against the wood of her cello and she took a deep breath as she continued the low, melodic notes as the violins played the high notes expertly and precisely. Elizabeth was doing remarkably well from where she sat next to Margaret. She gave her a smile in encouragement. Elizabeth beamed. It was a beautiful piece and they played it as well as the professionals.

The hour grew old and the last few songs of the night came up. Beethoven's '*Moonlight Sonata*'. Cassie started up the lonely tune and played it with the passion and feeling it required. Margaret played her cello's low, deep, resonating tones and scanned the crowd. Her eyes settled on Mr. Seymour who was standing beside her mother. They, along with Betty, Ted, and Mr. Acker were watching with tears in the eyes, proud of their little New York Youth Orchestra. It made Margaret smile as she turned her attention back to the music. The six-minute song ended quietly and mysteriously, and then it was time for the last two songs of the night... something to lift everyone's spirits.

Boccherini's happy Minuet was played by the strings and the piano and the woodwinds and Pitcher even threw in a few surprise beats with his drum; he didn't want to be left out. Samuel gave Pitcher a stern and angry look as he continued to keep time and conduct the large orchestra. Margaret laughed and it showed in her music. The other musicians made the song even happier and joyous now that they had something to laugh about. Samuel rarely got angry, unless it concerned his music.

The last song they played for the finale was, '*When you Wish Upon a Star.'* Cassie started up the piano intro and then the violins started the lyrical melody. By the end of the song, they were all playing together and the audience was singing with them. It was the most beautiful thing Margaret had ever heard. It was as though they had been playing it for years. No one could tell that there were such young people playing with the philharmonic. They all sounded like professionals. Margaret looked up to the sky and saw a single star. She put her heart into her music and prayed, *God, if I could just see Harry this year...* She wished and prayed as the song ended and the audience gave a tremendous cheer. They clapped whole-heartedly and wove their flags. It was a beautiful end to a beautiful day. The war was over and the concert seemed to solidify that into everyone's minds and hearts. Six years of violence were finished and the ones that died would never be forgotten and the ones that lived would live on as heroes to their fellow countrymen. When words could not express everyone's relief and joy that the war was over, and their sadness and despair that sons and fathers would not be coming home, music had come to say what could not be said.

# Chapter 40

The crowd began to disperse, and the musicians started to pack up. Margaret put Fiore in its padded case and shook hands with the other cellists, thanking them and receiving many much-too-generous compliments. She couldn't believe they had just played with the New York Philharmonic. Her heart was still soaring. She watched as countless members from the audience stayed about to enjoy the cool evening and congratulate the teachers and the musicians that had played so well. Margaret stood up. It felt good to move about after sitting behind her cello for two hours. She looked about the terrace and spotted someone going against the current of the people who were walking up the steps to leave. Margaret's heart stopped and then it started to race. *Could it be?* Her face instantly grew red and warm. But she had only caught a glimpse...

She made her way through the tight crowds and squeezed in between people, excusing herself as she went. She had lost sight of the stairs now, but she was making her way towards them as she moved with the crowd.

"Meg? Where are you going?" Rachel called to her.

Margaret couldn't reply. The person reached the base of the stairs leaning on a cane. Margaret put her hands to her mouth and stood there... staring at the man whom she had grown to love.

She was shocked.

She started to cry and laugh and smile all at the same time.

Harry had his RAF uniform on and his navy cap atop his head. Margaret took a step as her heart fluttered. She watched him stand there with such a huge, pleased smile on his face. She took another step closer and then ran to him.

They didn't say anything. They didn't need to. They hugged each other tight, and Margaret cried. Harry held her and had dropped his cane. Margaret's feet barely touched the ground, but he held her up. She never wanted to let go.

"Oh Harry!" She cried.

"It's ok," he was crying as well. "I'm here. I'm here now..."

She held on tighter and wept into his shoulder. She couldn't believe it. *How is he here?* After so many years apart, her best friend and the love of her life had come for her and now held her. She had never thought this day would come and she knew in that instant that she loved him more than she ever could have imagined. He was her home. He was her safe place; his, the only presence that mattered. Their hearts were tied together and she never wanted to be apart from him ever again.

Neither of them moved for what felt like hours. Margaret finally let go and he lowered her to the ground. Harry wiped the tears from her cheeks. She wiped off his shoulder that was wet from her tears.

"I got your uniform all wet." She laughed, her tears still coming. Her fingers grazed the many badges and medals on his uniform in wonder and awe and admiration.

"You're so beautiful, Meg." His voice cracked.

"Oh, Harry!" She bit her lip and hugged him again.

"It feels like I haven't seen you in a lifetime." Harry stepped back and held her shoulders gently. "There were days I thought I'd never see you again."

"Harry..." It was Margaret's turn to wipe the tears from his face. She was surprised that he had stubble. Last they saw each other, he didn't. She smiled at the realization. "You look so much older." More tears slid down her cheeks as she realized what the war had done to him.

He had darker circles under his eyes, and his face was more drawn. He didn't have the full, lively face he had as a teenager. He was a man now; a man who had seen and done so much... things she could never imagine. Her shoulders trembled and shook as she cried, realizing it.

"You look so beautiful," he rasped out, his voice hoarse.

"How did you get here?" She couldn't believe that he was standing in front of her. She held him tighter as though he might disappear at any moment.

"I had help from some Americans... turns out they're not too bad."

"Oh, yeah?" Margaret playfully teased, smiling through her tears.

"Oh yes... not bad at all." He held her gaze.

Margaret could have melted under his blue-eyed gaze that sparkled with tears of happiness.

"Oh, Meg, I have so much to tell you. So much I haven't told..." Harry took her hands and kissed them.

Margaret was aware of her mother approaching them.

"Harry," Margaret started and stepped back, wiping tears from her eyes. "This is my mother, Gabriella, and this is Rachel, my best friend." She introduced her family as they approached.

"It's a pleasure to meet you, ma'am." Harry shook Gabriella's and Rachel's hands. "I've heard many great things about you two." Harry smiled, not able to wipe the grin off his face.

"I'm assuming you know this gentleman, Meg? Could this be the famous Harry Cavanaugh we've heard so much about?" Gabriella asked with a pleased smile on her face.

"Mum, Rachel, this is Harry." Margaret introduced them.

"To be honest, we weren't expecting you." Gabriella stepped forward and hugged him, wiping a few happy tears from her eyes as well.

"No," Harry chuckled. "I'm sorry about that. I wanted it to be a surprise. We only got in this morning." He explained.

"Oh, it's so romantic!" Rachel exclaimed and wiped tears from her eyes. She hugged Harry. "It's so good to finally meet you!"

Margaret laughed.

"I think this calls for a celebration!" Rachel added. She called over to Simone and Grace who were just starting to go up the stairs to leave. "Will you two play a nice waltz for our two lovebirds?" Rachel made Margaret blush, and Harry couldn't help but laugh.

"A waltz, eh?" Simone took out her violin when she joined them. "I know a few waltzes..." She whispered in Grace's ear. The young girl nodded enthusiastically and smiled as she took out her violin.

Harry looked down to Margaret and thought that she was more beautiful than anything in the whole world. He reached out his hand.

"Dance with me?" He smiled.

Margaret blushed again and took his hand. "I'd be my pleasure, lieutenant."

He started leading her to the covered terrace that sat beneath the Mall. The arched columns were lit up and created contrasting shadows in the dark corners of the hall.

"Your cane," Margaret hesitated. "Don't you need it?"

Harry thought her concern completely endearing.

"Not when you're with me," he smiled that smile Margaret knew so well.

The violinists moved into the covered area and started to play.

Margaret and Harry bowed to each other. He took her left hand and put his other on her waist; her other hand went on his shoulder. She smiled and they started to waltz to the three-beat composition that Margaret had never heard before. As they waltzed around the terrace, Margaret felt Harry falter every other step.

"Are you alright?" She asked quietly.

"I couldn't be better." He twirled her around and they took up the waltz again.

As they waltzed around the terrace, Margaret studied his face. He looked so much older, yet he was the same. His hair was still blond and messy, and his blue eyes were eager and kind... however, they carried a depth and sadness that hadn't been there before. He had a few scars here and there and a large one on his forehead that hadn't been there before. Yet it didn't seem to matter... he was still the same old Harry on the inside.

"Where did you learn to waltz so well?" She teased him.

"You taught me, remember?" He looked amused.

Margaret tilted her head to the side in question.

"You were nine. We were in your kitchen, and you insisted. Rich teased me for a week."

"I don't remember that," she chuckled.

"I do," Harry held her a little closer. "I remember it perfectly."

As the waltz moved into a beautiful chorus, Betty and Ted joined them and many other couples who had lingered about all started to dance as well to the lovely waltz. Rachel and Cassie waltzed together comically and Margaret laughed from pure joy. She truly felt like a princess.

Harry smiled down at her and he could not take his eyes off hers. She was so beautiful... She had grown into a remarkable young woman. Always she had been gentle and sweet and funny, and those traits only seemed to grow with her age. Her brown eyes were warm and wise. According to him, she was the only woman in the whole world.

The waltz slowed and softly ended as the couples who had been dancing came to a stop like a fading breath of wind. Margaret gazed up at Harry. She still couldn't believe that he was there... right in front of her.

"I'm so glad you're here," Margaret hugged Harry tight once more and he sighed.

"So am I, Meg. So am I." He replied as he kissed her forehead, so thankful to the Lord for bringing them together after so long.

Over the next few weeks, Harry became another member of the family. He stayed down in one of the rooms next to Samuel's. In the evenings, he would tell tales about England during the war and North Africa and Malta and Italy and Corsica. Margaret would watch with pride and admiration as the man she called hers told story after story with maturity and wisdom and an occasional joke thrown in here or there. He never went terribly deep with his stories, but she didn't mind. That would come with time, and she felt privileged that he might only share those things with her.

Adding Harry to the family made everything change. Betty and Ted came almost every day. Ted and Harry became close friends, for they had many things in common. Ted was planning on becoming an engineer after the war with Japan was over, for he despised his job at the library and wanted to do something that required more of him. Harry thought the idea of being an engineer was brilliant, as he had been thinking of that for a great deal of time. So they spoke often about the job prospects and what it would require of them. The boys, Pitcher and Grubbs, looked up to Harry immensely. Pitcher taught Harry the in's and out's of baseball so he could play with him and Harry showed Grubbs how to tinker with and fix things that were broken in the house. Margaret watched him interact with the family she loved and it made her smile and her heart glow. He was so kind and funny and thoughtful. He hadn't changed a bit.

Towards the end of May, Margaret and Harry and Rachel were all taking a walk through Central Park. Margaret and Harry were hand in hand and Rachel kept glancing at them as though they were some marvel at a circus. Finally, Margaret rolled her eyes and spoke up.

"Heaven's sakes, Rachel! What do you keep staring at?" She chuckled.

"Oh nothing," Rachel smiled to herself. "You two are just so cute together." She skipped ahead

Harry laughed. Margaret looked up to him. "So, out of all your stories, none of them seem that frightening. I'm sure there were times though..." She trailed off. "Well, times that were much harder, I can tell."

Harry looked down to Meg and stopped walking. There was

sadness in his eyes. "Well, you're not wrong." He admired her for noticing and told her so. "There were definitely challenges and days were I absolutely feared for my life."

Margaret looked distraught. "Oh Harry... I'm so sorry. I can't even begin to imagine."

"Don't be," Harry replied and took her hand. "It's hard to think back to those times... But it's getting easier to talk about them." Harry admitted. "When I think of Guy or Dirk and their families who are mourning, I can't help but remember every single detail of the time we spent together. Every conversation, every fight we fought together... I can still hear it and see it as if it were yesterday." Harry closed his eyes and Margaret gave his hand a squeeze.

She touched his cheek gently.

Harry took a deep breath and thought for a moment. "I promise, I'll tell you everything. Every single detail. I wasn't able to during the war, but I will, soon. I can't now," his voice broke. "But I promise. I'll go through each day and tell you everything I remember, everything I feared and did. I'll tell you all about Guy and Dirk and Val and our squadron leaders and every sortie we went on. We can talk for hours, just the two of us."

"I'd like that, Harry. God knows, I'm so sorry you went through all that you did." She huffed. "Sometimes I feel so helpless and silly... I was sent away from all the suffering and have no way of sympathizing with what you went through. I feel so ignorant and... it makes me feel ashamed I was spared what everyone else went through."

"Don't talk like that." He shook his head. "It makes me happier than I can ever say that you didn't have to go through any of that. The things I saw, Meg," he cursed silently, unable to continue.

She watched him compose himself.

"We went through all of that Over There so you and millions others didn't have to. It's the greatest gift we could give. Don't feel ignorant and don't you dare feel ashamed. You had many trials to walk through here as well. Trust me; I didn't want to be in your place when you were sent away. I could think of nothing more terrifying than getting on a boat and sailing to a country with people I didn't know. That took more bravery than I'd have been able to muster, believe me. You *are* brave. Don't let anyone tell you otherwise."

Margaret listened in amazement, wondering who the wise man

who stood before her was. She had never heard Harry speak so.

"Well then," she smiled. "There's no arguing with that."

"Good," Harry took her arm and they continued after Rachel who had left them far behind.

Harry grinned and decided to change the subject. "The most terrifying night I went through, though, was the night before we left Cornwall." He said playfully.

"Oh?" Margaret raised her eyebrows.

"It was right before you sent me your letter that responded to mine... the letter in which I poured out my feelings." He teased.

Margaret smiled and looked down to the ground for a moment. "I still feel terrible about forgetting your letter... and turns out it was the most important one of all. Did I really cause you that much worry?"

"You have no idea," Harry responded, his voice fading away. He looked at Margaret for a long moment.

He kissed her hand and they kept walking.

"You kept me grounded through the war and you keep me grounded after."

Margaret smiled up at him.

"Would you like to go on a date with me? Tonight? You could show me that place you said has excellent pizza."

Margaret raised her eyebrows. "Mm, a date? I suppose I can clear my schedule."

"As ever, I am in your debt, lady."

They wound their way lazily through Central Park, just as they had done countless times at Regent's Park in London. But how long ago that seemed!

A few days passed before Margaret got a letter from her father which made her laugh. She sat in her room writing a reply at her desk. She glanced at the letter and smiled again.

*'My girl, Meg,*

*I am writing to you in such a state! To think that Harry is there in New York and I am not... Soon I shall be though, my girl, soon I shall be. I have been looking at the ships coming into and leaving Southampton and none are bound for the New York harbor yet. When one comes though, I shall be on the first ship that sails for America. I thought I would have to wait until Harry brought you back here. Turns out I was wrong. I shall come to you and I cannot wait.*

*This must be a quick letter, for this is the only piece of paper that I could find and it is very small indeed. Just know that I am thinking of you and soon we shall be together again. I love you, my girl.*

*God be with you,*

*Your father.'*

Margaret had never heard her father be impatient before. It made her smile as she wrote that she couldn't wait to see him and even her mother had said she was looking forward to it.

A knock sounded on the door and Margaret turned to see Harry in the threshold.

"Your mum wants to know whether or not you want to help her make some bread." Harry relayed the message with an amused voice as he gazed about the room.

"Oh, yes! I'll be right down! I'm just writing a reply to Dad." She explained. She added with a chuckle when Harry hesitated on the threshold, "you can come in."

Harry entered her room and looked around. His gaze was caught on the map on the wall at the far end.

"What's this?" He asked.

Margaret grinned and got up to join him by the map with the blue ribbon. "That's the map I tracked your location with. Clever, isn't it?" Margaret went back to her desk and sealed up her letter while Harry looked at the map of Europe and the Mediterranean.

The blue ribbon and the pins went from Portreath, England to Blida, Algeria. From Blida to Maison Blanche. From Maison Blanche to Setif and then Luqa, Malta. From there, it went to Cassibile, Sicily. Then it went to Montecorvino, Italy and from there, it tracked up to Marcianise, Italy. That was when he had gone down. What it didn't say on the map was that the 600 Squadron had gone to Pomigliano while he had been recovering with the Russo's before going back to Marcianise. *I travelled that far!* Harry couldn't quite believe it now that he was looking at it. The blue ribbon went from the city north of Rome to Calvi, Corsica before it went back across the Tyrrhenian Sea to Italy's capital. Harry was touched.

"You did all this?" He was amazed.

Margaret nodded, re-joining him at the wall with the letter in her hand. "I wanted to see where you were. And every time I saw it, I prayed for you. Where did you go after Rome?"

"Back to England." Harry replied as though she should have known that.

"Right; back to England." Margaret nodded and sighed. "I like the sound of that."

She took a pin and put it on London. However, she paused.

"Would you like to do the honors?" She held the pin out to him.

He took it with a bow and she held the blue ribbon as he pinned it down right where it should have ended... London, England.

Harry still couldn't take it all in. "You must really like this chap, eh?" He turned to her and she hugged him around his middle.

"Just a little. Oh!" She stepped back. "Guess what! Dad says he's coming. He'll get the first liner from Southampton to New York. Could be a week, could be a month thought."

"I'm glad. You need to see him."

They went down the stairs together and Margaret held Harry's hand to support him. He had left his cane downstairs.

"When do you think *we'll* be able to go back to England?" He asked as they reached the bottom of the stairs.

"I don't know." Margaret shrugged and let go of his hand as she handed him his cane. "I have to finish at Julliard."

They went into the kitchen together and she put on her apron, joining her mother by the oven.

"Yes, she does have to finish her school." Gabriella commented. "She's gone almost entirely on scholarships!" She boasted and Margaret smiled, embarrassed at her mother's praise.

"So I heard," Harry sat on the single stool against the kitchen wall to rest his leg. "Seems like yesterday I was sitting outside Lily's End listening to her play Bach's Unaccompanied Cello Suite."

Gabriella threw Harry an impressed glance. "I'm surprised you know what that is. He's a keeper, Meg!" She joked and threw him a towel. "Would you mind drying and putting those dishes away, lieutenant?"

"Not at all," Harry laughed in reply.

"What did the doctor say about your leg before you left?" Margaret asked, watching him limp over to the sink.

Harry took a deep breath in frustration. "He said the brace can come off next week. Then I can walk on it with just my cane 'as tolerated,' he said. I have a few more appointments in London scheduled for when I get back, so we'll see how it goes."

Margaret offered him an encouraging smile. She was simply glad he was in one piece and with her now... they would figure the rest out later.

# Chapter 41

The reverend was meeting the next month with a rather anxious outlook. He had just finished giving a sermon about giving thanks and was taking a stroll through Regent's Park with Mr. Cavanaugh. The two middle-aged men had their nice black suits on and both of them had their walking sticks. Eugene was contemplating his son's position and possible profession.

"I know he wants to be a mechanic or engineer, he told me so when he left." Mr. Cavanaugh stated with a glum expression.

"There *are* worse professions." The reverend pointed out. "If he ever wants to get into the church, I'll put in a good word for him."

"That is generous of you," Mr. Cavanaugh stated with reflection. "But, I believe Harry thinks it too tame. Ever since he came home he has been quite determined and busy. He's always on the go."

The reverend scoffed. "Can you blame him?'

"I suppose not." Mr. Eugene Cavanaugh chuckled as he swung his walking stick lazily at his side.

After a moment's repose, the reverend inquired, "what do you think of my daughter and your son?"

Mr. Cavanaugh walked forward a few paces before he replied. "I think they do very well together. But how can we tell when they're across the ocean? It's been six years since I've seen Margaret last." He stated with validity.

"True, but from what she writes in her letters, it sounds as though she does like him very much. She is just reserved in showing how she feels." The reverend contemplated.

"Nonetheless, they will get married. There's no doubt about that." Mr. Cavanaugh said confidently.

The reverend nodded thoughtfully. "He asked for my permission before he left."

"Well, that's something." Mr. Cavanaugh commented. "He also asked Mary and I if he could have his grandmother's ring before he left." He started walking again and the reverend meandered beside him. "Harry was always to inherit Mary's mum's ring and Richard will have my grandmum's ring. Poor Evan, he vowed he'd never get married and turns out he was right... Bless the lad." Mr. Cavanaugh sighed with sadness.

The reverend pondered what his friend had said. "They'll make a good match, I believe. They're both quite steady and even-tempered. I daresay, they're so similar, almost like the same person in two different people."

Mr. Cavanaugh nodded. "Yes, they'll be good together."

Though the topic was a happy one, the reverend was rather anxious. He was very protective of his daughter, for he hadn't seen her in so long and she was so very far away. If he was honest, he just wanted to see her again as his daughter, not an engaged young woman. Not yet. The reverend just prayed that soon he would be able to make the voyage to America.

Most thankfully, the reverend's prayers were answered the next morning. A knock on the door sounded and he went slowly from the kitchen to get it. His kettle started singing as he opened the door.

"Bess!" He exclaimed with surprise.

The short, rotund, ginger maid that had helped him raise his little girl was standing in the doorway. However, she looked so much different. She looked older, a great deal thinner, and much more prim and proper with her red hair in a bun and a hat on top of her head.

"Good morning, reverend. It's been a long time since I had the pleasure of looking upon Lily's End. I'm glad to see that it's unchanged and its keeper is just the same!" She smiled.

"How happy this makes me, Bess! Come in!" He stood aside. "I was just making some tea." He asked if she would like some as she entered the little parish and went into the kitchen with the reverend.

"Yes, thank you!" She sat down at the little table that had been hers for so long. "Any news from Meg? I'm sorry I haven't responded to your letter, I've been so busy. My new job keeps me active as does my WVS work."

"That's grand! I'm glad for you, Bess." The reverend said as he poured the tea. "Meg sends her love, as always. Harry took a skip across the pond to be with her about a month ago."

"Did he? Does he still fancy her? But then again, I knew he always carried a torch for her."

The reverend chuckled and put the tea on the table. "Indeed, Bess. In fact, I believe he intends to propose soon."

Bess looked surprised as she sipped her tea. "My goodness! What news! Are you planning on making the journey to America as well?"

"No tickets yet despite the fact I have my paperwork in order... No ships leaving the harbor bound for New York either." The reverend shrugged. "Something will come up though." The reverend took a sip of tea. "It's good to have you back, Bess." The reverend said truthfully.

"It's good to be back in this little kitchen again. Even though it looks like the faucet still drips and I know that oven goes out too often and that window still has a cracked pane of glass." She gazed about the kitchen and all the fond memories it held.

She had cooked with rationing books, spilled soups on the floor, and had hidden during air raids in the little kitchen. It would always remind her of those ten glorious years that she worked for the reverend and his beautiful daughter.

"Yes..." the reverend looked around the room, too. "I daresay it's not the same without you, Bess. But I'm glad you've found a purpose and a place."

Bess smiled. "I'm glad too, reverend." She sighed in contented ease. "I couldn't have done it without your family. Know, too, I'll always be here for you and Meg. That girl is like a daughter to me, always has been. Thank you..." she truly meant every word. "Thank you for being my family."

---

"Are you sure you want me to stay?" Margaret asked Harry.

"You don't have to if you don't want to." Harry replied as he sat on the doctor's table.

Margaret sat down in one of the chairs in the little examination room after taking Harry's cane for him. He had called to make an appointment at Tisch Hospital.

After dinner a few weeks ago, he had stood up without his cane and even walked to the kitchen by himself... with Margaret watching in concern. He had stumbled slightly, but caught himself. However, ever since his leg had been swelling and there was more pain than usual.

The doctor entered and greeted both he and Margaret.

"Alright Harry, tell me a little about your history... I see you had multiple surgeries; one in Rome after your accident, is that correct?" The doctor looked over the medical file the nurse had started on Harry.

"Well, I landed on it after having to drop out of my chute that was stuck in a tree."

Margaret listened, hearing the details of the story for the first time.

"The ankle broke, I'm not sure which bones. Long story short, a doctor was able to set the leg, but not perform an operation. I opted out of that, as I couldn't be admitted to a hospital. After that, several months later, my plane went done. We crashed nose first into the sea and I don't know, it must have been the impact, but it felt like my leg was..." he motioned the flat of his hands together. "Compressed, I guess? It wasn't able to be looked at by a doctor for about a week. It was set, then it was operated on maybe four or five days later? It's hard to say exactly, I can't remember the exact dates." He continued to explain what the doctors had told him overseas and tried to relay as much of the information as he could.

"Let me take a look."

Harry put his legs on the examination table and rolled up his left khaki pant leg. Margaret saw two long scars going down either side. The doctor felt along his leg and took several notes.

"Alright, come with me and we'll take some x-rays." He motioned for Harry to follow him.

Margaret handed him his cane and he offered a kind smile. She took a deep breath, praying that the news would be good. She knew how important his mobility was to his pride and his future job choices. *Please God, let it have healed. Please let it not be reinjured.*

The doctor returned with Harry behind him and they sat in the room talking for almost an hour. During that time, the doctor told Harry how his bones had gotten stronger and his breaks were not in any imminent danger of regression, in his opinion. He said his ankle would always be weak, but not so weak that it couldn't hold up his weight. He recommended that he continue using his cane and transition out of the brace by the end of the month. The recent pain and swelling was likely due to a muscle strain, as the muscles had a great deal of scar tissue in the calf and around the ankle joint.

"You will never run a marathon, rest assured, or possibly never run at all... but there's no reason why you shouldn't have a normal job, a normal life, and simply a normal limp." The doctor gave his prognosis. "Movement will be tight and at times, painful. In the future, that will be something to keep an eye on. Arthritis will most likely start to set in early, but it's not something I would worry about now. Overall, you seem like a determined young man. I have the greatest confidence it won't slow you beyond what is expected."

"Thank you," Harry got down from the table.

"Thank *you*, lieutenant, for your service and sacrifice."

Margaret stood up as they prepared to leave.

The doctor continued. " *'Never in the course of human history was so much owed by so many to so few.'* " The doctor smiled and shook Harry's hand.

"Churchill said that," Margaret grinned.

"Indeed he did." The doctor opened the door for them. "He is a great man. I hope you two have a wonderful day." He bid them farewell as they left and wished him a good day as well.

Harry took Margaret's hand and they walked out together.

"You're so wonderful," Margaret said as they walked closely to each other out on New York's busy streets, leaving the hospital behind.

Harry chuckled. "Why do you say that?"

"You just are," Margaret squeezed his hand, lacing her fingers in between his. "You fought so bravely and for so long. I can't even imagine bombs going off and gunfire and seeing London attacked during the Blitzkrieg. Did you ever give up hope?" She looked up to him, surprised again by how tall he had gotten.

Harry was silent for a moment. "Plenty of times." He looked down to her. "I'm amazed God still wants me after how many times I wanted to give up."

"His grace is made perfect in our weakness." She assured him.

Smiling, Harry kissed her on the head. "What did I do to deserve you?"

Margaret merely laughed and led him into the drugstore they were passing.

"What're we doing here?" Harry asked as the bell rang over the entrance of the shop they entered.

The storekeeper told them if they needed any help, to ask. It smelled of carbolic soap, mothballs, and rubbing alcohol and the shelves were starting to fill up again... a lovely sight for rationed civilians.

"I just needed to pick up a few things." Margaret replied and went to the aisle with the soap. She took a few shampoo bottles off the shelf and smelled them, picking out a scent she liked.

Harry looked over the shelves, his cane knocking on the wood with every other step.

"How long do you plan to stay here?" She asked, somewhat afraid to ask the question.

Since Harry had come, she had thought many times as she was falling asleep what their plans would be. Soon, she'd be able to travel home, too, and Harry couldn't stay forever with his current travel documents.

Harry joined her in the aisle. "I had to purchase a return ticket when I put my papers in order. It'll be in September, before winter sets in."

Margaret nodded, picking out a bottle of lavender-scented shampoo. "I wish I could come, too. But once I'm done at Julliard... I could get a ticket as soon as I could."

Harry nodded. "We could plan on that."

She smiled at the idea of returning to England and went to another aisle to get a few toiletries before checking out.

"Allow me," Harry got out his wallet as Margaret fished for hers in her purse.

"Thank you, love. You don't need to."

"It's alright," to the cashier, "cheers, mate," as he took the bag and they went back outside.

"So, I'd like to talk to you about something."

"Oh?" Margaret was intrigued.

"I don't think we've ever officially said we're 'going steady.' I'd like to make it official, I suppose." He stopped so he could see her as he said the following words. "Margaret, I want to spend time with you and get to know you again. I feel like a different person than when we were kids and I think you feel the same way. Would you like to see, with me, whether or not this could work? If it does work, I'd like to be with you for the rest of my life. If it doesn't, if you feel like you'd rather go somewhere else or be with someone else, I want you to know you can always tell me the truth and not worry about how I feel about it. I guess what I'm saying is..." he took a deep breath. "I want to see if this works, if *we* work, so maybe we can form a strong marriage and a strong family."

Margaret thought over his words and was glad he was being forthcoming about what they were doing and where they were going.

She nodded. "I want that, too." She chuckled. "I can't really find the words, but yes."

"Good," Harry felt relieved. He would have rather been in a foxhole than having a conversation about his feelings, but he steeled himself and they continued walking. "I want to be clear about my intentions and maybe we'll have some discussions about more practical things... what a life together would look like or what our expectations are. I wouldn't want you to be disappointed." He winked.

Margaret rolled her eyes. "You know I'm *always* disappointed in you."

"Oh, for shame." He laughed.

Margaret got home from work that night and was exhausted. She was thankful she was on summer break and didn't have classes on top of her already busy week. It was past midnight and she hung up her purse and went up the many flights of stairs to her room. However, before she entered, she saw that the door was open to the last flight that went up to the roof. She grabbed a sweater from her room before heading up to the roof.

It was windy outside. Margaret looked around, wondering if someone was out or if the door had just been left open. She could see the many buildings and skyscrapers that filled Manhattan, lit up in the dark night. Then she spotted Harry sitting by the edge of the house. There was a wide wall that went around the rooftop area and came up a little past Margaret's hip.

"What are you doing up?" Margaret joined him, noticing he was watching something out in the direction of the Hudson.

"Just thinking." He replied and then met her gaze. "Waiting for you."

Margaret hopped up onto the wall. Harry quickly held her arm to make sure she wouldn't go falling off the other side.

She smiled. "Thank you. We come up here every Independence Day to watch the fireworks. But Mum never lets us sit on the wall."

Harry still looked worried.

"It's alright, I won't fall. Besides, you're sitting on it too."

He released his grip and relaxed.

"What were you thinking about?"

"How was work?"

"I asked you first. Don't avoid the question." She teased playfully.

Harry grinned. "Just thinking... I got a letter from Rich. He's home safe and sound. He'll stay at my parents for a few weeks before returning to Oxford to resume his studies. I'm sorry I missed seeing him before I left. It would have been nice."

"That's good news that he's back." Margaret shivered against the chill wind. "And don't worry; we'll all have plenty of time to catch up..."

"I know," Harry grinned. "Your turn; you didn't answer my question."

"Work was well..." Margaret trailed off. "Until our line was laid off."

"Really?"

"It's alright," Margaret shrugged half-heartedly. "We knew we would be let go sooner than later. With all the G.I.'s coming home, they're returning to work and they're laying off many of the women that stepped up during wartime."

"What'll Emily and Heather do?" Harry asked, for he knew of Margaret's friends there.

"Well, they both won't need to work. Heather's husband should be returning from the Pacific soon. And Emily's engaged, her fiancé just came home yesterday from France." Margaret replied.

"And what about you?" Harry asked quietly.

Margaret pulled her sweater tighter around her shoulders. "What about me..." she mused over the question. "I'll find work somewhere. I could work in a shop or something until I graduate. I could be a shopgirl." She smiled to herself.

"What if you didn't have to?"

Margaret eyed him. "What do you mean?"

He smiled mischievously at her.

"What are you saying, Harry Cavanaugh?" Margaret couldn't help but notice the spark in his eyes and how the wind tousled his dark sandy hair.

He smiled. "What I'm saying is," he spoke slowly, "I'm not going anywhere, Margaret Jane Sutton."

They exchanged a knowing look. Margaret knew exactly what he was talking about. It hit her so quickly and all at once, she hardly had time to process it or grasp it. She looked back out over the city, unable to hold his blue-eyed gaze. They both grew quiet, looking out at the view. Cars honked and subways rumbled, a ship's horn signalled its arrival. Far away, Margaret thought she even heard a lone accordion playing. The air was cool and the wind refreshing after being in the factory all afternoon. Margaret sighed.

"Why would... I mean..." She stuttered, thinking how she could talk so openly about this subject. "Harry..."

"What is it?" He tried to catch her eye, though she was looking out over the distance, the corners of her eyes glistening.

"Why *me*?" Finally, she met his gaze and bit her bottom lip nervously. "How did your... our... feelings go from such a close friendship to this?"

Harry's eyebrows rose and knit together. "I think I always loved you. It just took time and maturity to realize it." He paused, thinking. "You were always by my side. As we grew up, I knew I couldn't lose you. There was no one else I'd want by my side other than you." He leaned into her playfully. "You can't really decide who you fall in love with anyway, I think."

Margaret could feel her pulse quicken and the heat rise in her cheeks. She leaned back into him and put her head on his shoulder.

"I love you, Meg." He put his arm around her.

"I love you too, Harry." She breathed out, her blush finally ebbing.

They lapsed into silence, looking out over the rooftops, listening to the city around them.

"I want to go home." She spoke so quietly, Harry could hardly hear her.

He gave her a squeeze. "Me too."

"Blast this last year at Julliard." Margaret chewed the inside of her cheek, thinking over the last year she had ahead... constantly, she wondered if she needed to finish her schooling. The draw for home grew stronger every day.

They were silent for several long moments before Harry spoke. "You're not going to stay, are you?"

Margaret straightened up and sat on her hands, trying to get them warm as she thought of her answer.

"I think your hesitancy says enough." Harry remarked. "It sounds like you've already decided, you just..."

"Alright," Margaret put her hand up to stop him. She didn't mean to be curt, and he didn't take it that way. But he knew her well. She merely wanted to be the one to ultimately speak her thoughts.

It took her a moment to get the words out. "I think I may go home with you."

Harry nodded. "No one would blame you. But make sure this is really what you want. Once you leave Julliard and your scholarships, there's no going back."

"I thought I cared about that... I really did. I do. It gave me a purpose while I was here. But now that it's possible for me to go home... to be with you and spend more time together..." She trailed off. "I wouldn't want to go back to letter-writing. If we're going to try and make this work, I think we need to *be* together. Not simply write letters."

"I don't disagree with you. Just make sure this is really what you want first. Just say the word, though, and I'll buy you the ticket. Trust me, *I* want you to come too, but," he looked into her eyes. "I want what's best for you more than what I selfishly want."

Margaret smiled. Harry surprised her by leaning down and gently kissing her.

The color rose in her cheeks at the gentle kiss, and she smiled as they parted. His blue eyes seemed to sparkle and he put his arm back around her.

"How did you get up here?" Margaret asked.

Harry chuckled at the sudden change of topic. "Very slowly."

"Well," she hopped down from the wall. "It's a bit chilly up here and it's late... I should get to bed."

Harry followed suit, aware he landed somewhat lopsided and heavier on his right side. She held his upper arm to steady him.

"Thank you," he said as they left the peaceful midnight behind.

"Goodnight, Harry," Margaret stood on the stairs as they parted.

"Goodnight, Meg," he kissed her again and she hugged him goodnight.

They parted ways and she retreated to her room, collapsing on the bed with the biggest smile on her face.

# Chapter 42

Margaret wound her way through the kitchen as she put her lunch dishes in the sink. She passed Grubbs and Pitcher who were debating the latest sports games they watched. Margaret never paid it much mind. But she ruffled Pitcher's hair as she passed, and he protested and swatted at her hand.

She laughed and he stuck his tongue out at her. She did the same and hurried up the steps, Louis trotting after her. The little corgi was somewhat slower now and halfway up to the studio, Margaret took pity on the little guy and carried him the rest of the way.

He eagerly jumped from her arms when they entered the room and he saw Gabriella by the piano, putting away music books from her latest lesson.

"How'd it go?" Margaret asked her.

Her mother had started with a new student that afternoon and had been excited for the advanced newcomer.

"Very well, I think." Gabriella seemed pleased. "He has great talent, and I think with some polishing, he'll be ready for his recital."

Margaret was glad to hear it. She watched her mother close the lid to the piano and wipe it off, there was a small layer of dust on the top.

"What is it?" Gabriella asked after the lapse.

Margaret shrugged, not really knowing what to say or how to say it. "Do you like Harry?"

Gabriella looked at the wall for a second, caught off guard by the question. "I think you know I do. He's a great lad. A proper gentleman. I see no fault, my dear, which perhaps is a fault, as none of us are perfect," she chuckled. "But... I guess I just hope you two have your feet on the ground. That's the only thing I can think of. Reality hits hard and I'm not saying you're not being realistic, but... you're an idealist and I think Harry is too. It's not a fault, but something to keep in mind, I suppose."

Margaret nodded, understanding completely what her mother meant. She knew she often had her head in the clouds, and she knew she had to work on keeping her feet on the ground. However, it made what she really wanted to talk about even harder.

"I'm glad you like him. I don't want you to worry, either. We're working hard at making a plan and he keeps me grounded." Margaret added with a smile. "Yesterday we talked about what our expectations would be at home if we were to get married. Things as silly as if we'd make the bed and as serious as working and providing for ourselves. We have much more to discuss, but we're trying to visualize what all of that could look like."

Gabriella stood at the piano and Margaret sat down behind the keys, looking at the wooden grain of the lid.

"I wanted to see how you felt about an idea I had, too."

Gabriella listened, already guessing at the topic, as most mothers do.

"Harry will be leaving this fall." She met her mother's gaze. "I was... well, I was planning on going back too."

The news settled and Gabriella contemplated the idea. She finally replied, "you're an adult, my dear. If you want to go back to London, as I *completely* understand, you should. You'd be giving up your degree, though, but I'm sure you've thought about that."

Margaret nodded. "I have. Getting the degree doesn't make me any less of a musician. It may impact what sort of a job I could get, but," she thought for a moment. "I don't really know if I *want* a job in music. I want to play and play well and even perform when I can, but if Harry and I *do* marry... if we have children... I want to spend every moment enjoying them and raising them as well as I can. Harry and I have talked and he's going to enrol in university when we return. He wants to be an aircraft engineer, and I think he'll be jolly well good at it." Margaret noticed the look of bittersweet pride on her mother's face. "I can't bear the thought of leaving here, but I miss being *home*."

"Then, my dear, you must go." Gabriella looked like she was about to cry.

"But what about you?" Margaret asked.

Gabriella laughed and wiped away a tear. "My darling daughter, I have been on my own for quite some time. I will steady the buffs."

Margaret was more terrified than anything to ask the next question. "Would you come? Would you come home with us?"

Her words made her mother lose more tears. "Oh, Meg." They embraced and Gabriella held her tight. "I want to. I would want to try and mend things, if possible, with your father. I daresay I don't deserve his forgiveness though. But Samuel, Rachel, Pitcher, and Andrew..." She stepped back. "They would have nowhere to go. Trust me, I've thought on this, too." She straightened up and wiped away her tears. "If you are truly going back in September, I will start looking into what we can do. Samuel is almost off on his own. But the others, I could look into being their legal guardians. It would be a very difficult and long process, but I won't leave them."

"No, I wouldn't want you to." Margaret added. The last thing she'd ever want would be for her near brothers and sister to be sent to an orphanage or foster home system who knew where. Mr. Ackerman was aging and not in much state to raise the children and Betty and Ted couldn't take them in as they weren't at the halfway house anymore and not legally allowed to take them on. They'd have nowhere to go.

"This will take time, but maybe we'll be able to get this sorted and I can bring them, too. I *wish* I could come, Meg. I wish I could hop on the boat with you, but we'll get there... I truly believe we will get there in time."

Margaret hugged her mother again, tears now forming in her eyes. She couldn't stop repeating in her mind that her mother wanted to come *home* too. The thought was sweeter to her than honey.

The sun was shining, the air was warm, and there was a heady wind that blew in off the ocean.

"I'll race you!" Pitcher challenged Grubbs as they kicked off their shoes and took off their shirts to race to the waves.

"You're on!" Grubbs took off unfairly first and Pitcher shouted about it the whole way across the beach.

Following behind the energetic boys, Margaret, Harry, and Rachel made their way down the boardwalk steps towards the beach. Margaret picked up the boys' shirts and shoes and went back to holding Harry's hand.

"Be careful!" Margaret called to the boys who were tackling each other in the water.

They didn't pay her any attention.

"They're always beating each other up," Margaret remarked impatiently as she sat down beside Harry on the towel they had spread out on the sand.

"That's what boys do," Rachel scoffed. She had her swimming suit on under her clothes and tossed them Margaret's way before heading out into the ocean to swim amongst the crashing waves.

Margaret asked Harry. "Is that all boys do is tackle each other?"

He laughed and shook his head. "Depends on your level of maturity."

"I'd have to argue with that. I saw you and Ted wrestling that one time in the living room." Margaret smiled and leaned back, looking up at the clear, blue sky. It was a beautiful day.

"That was different; we were showing Pitcher and Andrew how to fight." Harry sniffed and replied defensively.

Margaret shook her head and chuckled. "Do you want to go swimming?" She asked him.

"I didn't dress for it," Harry replied, motioning to the khakis and light blue button-down he wore, keeping the real reason to himself. "You go on."

Margaret hesitated. "I'd rather stay here with you,"

Harry couldn't help but grin. "Go on, Rachel needs your help keeping those two from killing each other. And besides... I would rather like the view."

Margaret gaped at him playfully, throwing a towel at him. She watched Pitcher and Grubbs wade out farther from the shore and Rachel walk through the knee-high surf. She looked back to Harry and noticed he looked a little pale.

"Are you alright?" She asked.

"Couldn't be better." He assured her and motioned to the ocean. "Go on, go have fun."

Margaret obeyed. She kissed his cheek quickly and got up. She had her dark green swimming costume on under her clothes. She took off her skirt and blouse and started towards the ocean. She heard Harry catcall her and it made her blush and laugh. She waved her hand at him as if to shoo him off and ran the rest of the way to the water. Diving into the foamy waves, she made her way to where Rachel was.

Harry watched her go and wished he could join them. He didn't like the ocean much anymore and his reasons were understandable, he thought. He closed his eyes and took a deep breath. The previous night he had a nightmare for the first time since coming to America. He needed something to do. True, he loved spending time with Margaret's friends and family; he had gotten along well with Ted, but he only saw him occasionally on the weekends. No, when he returned home, he'd start researching jobs and universities again. He had to start somewhere so he could earn a living and then, hopefully, support Margaret.

She had become his home... his whole world. They'd figure out the future together. He pulled the small box out of his pocket and opened it. His gran's ring shimmered in the sunlight. It was simple yet stunning... much like his dear Meg.

He hoped she'd say yes.

The group ate lunch together on the boardwalk, sitting at one of the picnic tables. They had hotdogs and the boys talked Harry into buying them cotton candy for dessert.

"Can we play some games?" Grubbs asked, stuffing the blue cotton candy into his mouth, his lips already completely blue.

Margaret shook her head and laughed. "Haven't you two had enough fun for one afternoon?"

"Please!" Pitcher folded his hands and begged comically.

"Come on, I'll take you two." Harry stood up from where he was sitting beside Margaret.

"You're spoiling them." She teased.

"No, please, take them." Rachel laughed.

"Boys, let's go. Uncle Harry will pay, but only two games each."

"We love you, Uncle Harry!" Grubbs jumped up excitedly.

Margaret and Rachel followed, wanting to join in on the fun and watch.

Harry paid for a few tickets and handed them to the boys. They played a game that they, unfortunately, lost. They had to toss a ring around a middle bottle that was surrounded by several other bottles and both missed all three tries.

"Let's do this one!" Pitcher ran up to one carnival game that had little handguns attached to the counter they sat at and had to shoot cans along the back wall. Grubbs joined him and begged Harry to let them try it.

"Alright," he handed them the tickets, and the boys started shooting the guns that shot out small pellet-sized balls. They hit loudly against the back wall.

Margaret and Rachel encouraged the boys and watched with smiles on their faces. There was quite a cacophony in this area of the attractions. A ride was almost directly above them and people were screaming as it flipped them upside down and around in circles.

However, Margaret noticed Harry. *He looks... antsy?*

She approached him. "Is everything ok?"

He jumped, acting much more startled than he should have. He was pale again and was rubbing the back of his neck.

"Harry?" Margaret was worried.

It was as though he saw her, but he didn't *see* her.

"Need a minute," his clipped voice managed to say. He started to limp away from the game and back towards the beach, his cane thudding on the boardwalk with every other step.

"Rachel?" Margaret got her attention. "Watch the boys for a minute?"

She nodded, seeing Harry go and putting two and two together that something wasn't right. "Of course."

Margaret jogged to catch up with Harry. He didn't stop until he got to the edge of the boardwalk and put both hands on the railing, leaning against it. His knuckles were white as he gripped the rough wooden rail. Margaret joined him and looked up to him. She didn't know what to say.

Margaret put her hand on his back reassuringly. "What do you need?"

"Just give me a second." He grit his teeth and looked out over the beach. The waves crashed. He suddenly felt more trapped. He took Margaret's hand and together they walked quickly down the boardwalk and he pulled her into a small changing tent. He sat down on the bench and put his head in his hands.

Margaret didn't know what to do, so she sat next to him and rubbed his back.

He wanted to tell her everything... about hearing those events and seeing them over and over as though they just happened. He wished he could get away from whatever *this* was. His hands were numb and cold and he felt like he was going to pass out. *Am I having a heart attack?* He thought and leaned back against the tiny bench and looked up, taking in the red and white tent's stripes.

"It's alright, Harry. You're safe." Margaret took his hand and squeezed it reassuringly.

It seemed to ground him. He finally looked at her, taking her in, and his breathing started to level out.

"I'm sorry." He rasped out.

"It's alright." She assured him. "I just wish there was something I could do. Is it... from everything you went through?"

He nodded.

To Margaret, he was starting to look more collected and less pale.

"I'm alright. Let's join the others, they'll wonder where we went."

He got up and took her hand as they left the small tent and walked back towards where their group was.

"Let's just enjoy the rest of the day." Harry said and took a deep breath. "I saw there was a dance here later. There was a poster for it. Would you go to it with me?"

Margaret was touched. "If you're sure you're up for it." She said with uncertainty. "Is there anything I can do?"

He shook his head and gave her hand a squeeze. "You help me more than you know just by being here for me. Thank you. I'm working on it, I promise. Just sometimes it's worse at times than others." Harry looked around as the noise and screams and shouts and cacophony surrounded them once more. He swallowed his panic and put on a brave face... he kept reminding himself he was *safe.*

The afternoon waned and after the boys swam some more, Rachel took them home with her. Harry and Margaret stayed and sat on the beach, watching as the evening grew quiet and the sun sank far away on the horizon to their right. As they sat and watched the colors of the sky change, Margaret told Harry everything she and her mother had talked about the other day. Harry seemed pleased and was glad Margaret had discussed their plans with her. It mattered to him deeply that her mother approved of him. From what he had seen of her, she seemed much like Margaret, but instead of an open, optimistic heart, she had a very guarded, reserved one. She was always kind to him but never looked completely trusting. Harry wondered at it, however he was relieved that she and Margaret had formed such a close bond over the past several years.

"Shall we?" Harry inclined his head to where the live band on the boardwalk was playing *'Dream A Little Dream of Me,'* and couples swayed to the music. Margaret nodded and they joined the soiree.

A cool breeze came up from the ocean and onto the deck.

Margaret shivered, mentally scolding herself for forgetting to bring a sweater to wear over her blouse and swimming costume.

"Are you cold?" Harry asked quietly, holding her close to him.

"A little," she replied.

Gentlemanly, he gave her his sweater he had put on over his short-sleeved shirt.

"Won't you be cold?" She asked, pulling the maroon sweater on.

He shook his head, his eyes resting on hers. Harry was almost weak in the knees he loved her so much. "Blimey, you're beautiful."

Margaret blushed.

The night was growing darker. The stars were coming out one by one and the moon was rising over the crashing waves. Lights had been strung up and they cast a serene light on the dance floor. Men in their Navy suits and G.I.'s in their khaki uniforms danced with their sweethearts. The band changed up the tune and played 'You're my Everything' by Al Bowlly. The slow, swinging tune was touching and calming and Margaret rested her head on Harry's shoulder. They played other songs like 'The Very Thought of You,' and 'It's Been a Long, Long Time.' To Margaret, it was one of the most wonderful nights of her life. She could have danced the whole night away with him.

"Can I ask you a favour?" Harry asked quietly as they swayed to 'Midnight, the Stars, and You.'

"Of course," Margaret replied, her eyes closed.

"Could you not step on my bad foot?"

Margaret gaped. "Did I?!"

Harry chuckled.

Margaret caught on and punched him in the shoulder.

"Ouch," he spun her on the dance floor.

"That didn't hurt."

"Maybe it did."

Margaret rolled her eyes. "So much for a romantic moment."

Harry held her tight again as they swayed to the music. He spoke softly in her ear. "In all seriousness, would it be possible to leave before the fireworks?"

It was the Fourth of July after all.

She looked up at him and nodded, thankful he was asking her and being open about what he could and couldn't handle.

"Of course. Let's go," she stopped dancing, and they went back to collect their things.

Thankfully, they got a cab and were being driven back to Manhattan before the fireworks started going off.

Harry started to apologize in the cab. "I'm sorry, I-"

Margaret stopped him short. "Don't apologize. Please. You never need to apologize for things like this."

Harry nodded. "Very well. In that case, thank you." He took her hand.

"You're welcome. Do you want your sweater back?" She asked.

He shook his head.

Margaret smiled selfishly; she liked wearing it. It smelled like him.

They pulled up to the house and Harry paid the driver even though Margaret offered. They walked up the steps together.

"Wait a moment," Harry stopped at the threshold before Margaret opened the door.

Margaret looked to him curiously.

"Before we go in and join the others," he stepped closer to her.

She thought he looked nervous.

"I have something I want to ask you."

Margaret, completely unaware, nodded. "What is it?"

Harry thought her innocent modesty endearing. He put his hand in his pocket and felt the small box that was there.

"Meg," he started.

"Harry," she echoed and made him laugh.

"I love you. I've loved you for as long as I can remember and..." He paused and swallowed hard. "So, it'll come as no surprise if I ask you this,"

"Ask me what?" She was still confused.

However, he knelt and pulled out the ring box and opened it up.

His voice cracked. "Will you do me the honour of becoming my wife?"

Margaret put her hands to her chest in shock. "Harry!" She burst out in tears and smiles. She couldn't describe her feelings; they were soaring so. "Yes!" She took his head in her hands and kissed him, quite forgetting the ring. "Yes! Of course!"

He stood up and wrapped his arms around her, lifting her off the ground. In the distance, they could hear the fireworks going off over the Hudson... but none of that seemed to matter.

Margaret burst into the house, only to find it empty and all the lights off.

"Maybe they're all upstairs watching the fireworks?" Harry offered.

Together, they climbed the stairs, Margaret supporting Harry on his left side all the way up.

Once they climbed up to the rooftop, Margaret was surprised to see it empty as well.

"Where could everyone be?" She thought out loud.

Suddenly, everyone jumped out from behind furniture and planters and stored odds and ends.

"Surprise!" They all shouted. "Congratulations!"

Margaret was beyond surprised. She looked to Harry who was beaming.

"Did you plan this?" She asked him.

He smiled and gave her a wink.

Gabriella and Rachel congratulated her, looking at the ring she now wore. They hugged her tight and couldn't believe she was engaged. Mr. Ackerman was there too and of course Pitcher and Grubbs. Betty and Ted congratulated the couple and had their own exciting news to share with the family. Betty was expecting and was due in six months.

Margaret couldn't have been happier. She looked around at her family. Everyone she loved was there... well, everyone except one very important person; one of the *most* important.

That night she phoned her father and told him the good news. He was ecstatic and so proud of she and Harry both. However, she left out the good news that she was returning with Harry in just a few short months... *that* she wanted to be a true surprise.

# Chapter 43

Any day, any hour, any minute President Truman could announce the U.S.'s victory over Japan. The air was wrought with it. The month passed by like any another; the only news to be had was quite distressing. A B-25 plane had crashed into the Empire State Building on the 28th of July. Everyone in the house heard the explosion and the crash. The news that played that night over the radio assured everyone that it had been a terrible mistake, for the fog had been heavy and the pilot had been flying too low. The news affected Harry, and he grieved the loss of the pilot.

He sat at the dining room table reading a letter.

"Who's that from?" Margaret asked as she entered carrying her breakfast of tea and toast.

"Val," Harry responded. He and his old friend had started writing to each other. He laughed in amazement. "He's engaged now as well!"

Margaret brightened up. "Really? That's wonderful! To who?"

Harry looked amused. "To Mitch."

Margaret's mouth dropped open in shock. "The young lady you used to work with?"

"One and the same. I introduced them on VE-Day and lost track of them near Piccadilly. I guess they got on rather well." He laughed and folded the letter back up.

"Well, that's terrific. Good for them!" Margaret finished her breakfast, deep in thought.

Harry was reading the paper. The boys were chatting noisily at the far end of the table. Rachel wasn't up yet, and Gabriella was off on errands already that morning.

"I want to get married…" Margaret said, still deep in thought.

"We *are* going to get married." Harry didn't look up.

"I want to get married at home."

Harry met her eyes and half-folded the paper closed. "I figured we would." They hadn't talked about the specifics yet. However, Margaret had told everyone recently that she would be leaving in September.

The boys tried to hide how disappointed they were. But Rachel was almost inconsolable. She didn't speak to Margaret for a whole day, and finally came around to the news when Gabriella gave her there was some hope that they may be able to go, too, down the road.

Together, the newly engaged couple left the house behind and meandered down to the park, hand in hand. They had started to make these walks a habit. Harry would go through some of his memories at the different bases he'd been stationed at, and Margaret would listen and write them down for him in a journal. They had started all the way back when he was at Brize Norton. Patiently, Margaret had listened to all of the bombings Harry had survived and endured. She listened as Harry described how smoke had filled the London sky for weeks and months on end as neighbourhoods burned and bombs were extinguished. Then Harry told her about his training and Jim and Donald and Val and all the drills they had to do and textbooks they had read and flying hours they had logged. Margaret was more than interested. She hadn't known any of the details as they had been happening, as Harry hadn't been able to tell her. She was amazed at the full story and she felt even more thankful he had made it through alive.

From training, Harry told her about joining up with the 600 Squadron and how he, Guy, and Val had become close friends.

Now, they were talking about Africa and the missions he had gone on there.

Margaret and Harry sat on a bench in the quiet park. Harry looked out over the green that led down to a pond where happy ducks swam underneath the drooping branches of weeping willows. Margaret could almost imagine they were back in Regent's.

"We flew night fighter raids mostly in Algeria and aerial cover for transport ships."

He looked like he was searching for something in a file cabinet of memories.

"It was peaceful out there at night. I don't know what it was, but there was an untamed beauty to Africa I'd love to see again. We flew over sand dunes on our way to the aerodromes, but there were only a few towns in the north Sahara. The people were friendly when we ran into them. But they mostly kept their distance. And we flew low," he shook his head in amazement. "I can't believe how low we flew some raids. I'm surprised we stayed aloft." He looked at his fiancée and she smiled in encouragement.

"Where you scared?" She asked.

Harry took a deep breath. "I first started feeling it there... even when I wasn't flying, I felt anxious. I spoke to the chaplain, and he helped some... not as much as your father has. He just said it was normal and to not worry about it. I just felt like things were slipping out of control."

Margaret took his hand and followed his gaze out to the pond. "I'm glad you made it through. God saw to your safety and brought you through it."

Harry nodded half-heartedly. "But not all of us made it back."

They were silent for several minutes. Margaret gave him the time to think. Harry fished an envelope out of his pocket.

"What's that?" Margaret asked, looking at the address.

"It's for Dirk's family." Harry replied, his voice low. "It's his dog tag... and a letter I wrote to his parents. I was going to send it off on our walk home. Is there a post office nearby?"

Margaret nodded. "There is. Loretta will be thrilled."

He blinked in confusion.

"I'll explain later," she chuckled.

"So... on to Malta." He took another deep breath.

"That's it for Maison Blanche?" Margaret asked, writing in the journal.

Harry nodded.

"So, what about Malta?" She looked up from her writing.

"I'm sorry, Meg, for the language, but Malta was hell." He continued, for she didn't look surprised. "It was hot, and it was dry and during a bombing raid, Guy's plane went down. He, Val, and I were some of the few pilots to get in the air during the raid. The Stukas and Messerschmitts were coming in thick. Guy had one close on his tail and I tried to get him off," He shook his head and leaned forward, putting his head in his hands. "I don't know how I missed. But I missed the perfect shot and because of it, Guy was shot down. No chute let out. He was gone."

Gently, she put her hand on his back. "It wasn't your fault." Though she noticed, as she said it, that he gritted his teeth.

"Of course it was."

"If Guy was here, he would tell you the same thing." She insisted.

"I missed! And because of that, Claudie has to live without her husband and John has to grow up never knowing his *father!*" His shoulders shook with emotion. He breathed out in frustration, his nostrils flaring.

Margaret didn't quite know what to say. She hadn't walked that path. She could hardly imagine the weight of fear and responsibility and guilt that tore through Harry. If it was her, if she had made a mistake and it had cost Rachel her life, how would she feel? She imagined she'd feel the same way... solely responsible.

"Bad things happen, Harry." She started slowly. "Mistakes are made... sometimes the consequences are unbearable. It was a chance Guy took when he got into that plane... every time you flew, it was a risk *you* took as well. There's nothing else you could have done. You must get that right in your head, Harry, or that lie will always haunt you. How would you feel if you were shot down and killed and Guy spent the rest of his life tearing himself apart with guilt?"

Harry found himself glaring at her and he didn't want to. He leaned back and composed himself. "I'd tell him he was being a sentimental sod and to get on with his life..." He took an exasperated sigh. "Alright," he gave in slightly, rubbing his face as though he could rub the memories from where they always surfaced behind his closed eyes.

Margaret watched him for a moment, waiting for him to continue.

"I see what you're saying. But I can't say I believe it right now, but... I understand. I'm sorry." He apologized and she accepted before he went on. "We moved to Sicily the next day. Val and I joined the Desert Air Force shortly after."

"Do you want to stop there for today?" Margaret asked, thinking they had covered enough territory.

Harry didn't hear her. He was looking out at the pond. "I thought I went deaf in Luqa."

Margaret listened with interest. She hadn't heard this story before. She put her pen down.

"We were bombed, and Val and I were nearly hit. Our foxholes collapsed and planes were exploding around us. The ground was heaving like it was alive... like it was breathing."

He went very still as he recollected the memory.

"The impact of the bombs sucked the air from my lungs and took my hearing. I thought I had gone deaf." Harry met her eyes. "The man we were with... I can't even remember his name, but he took a hit to the chest." He looked down to his hands and flexed them. "There was blood everywhere."

Margaret's eyes pricked with tears, but she blinked them away. She put her hand on Harry's knee and scooted closer. They stayed still for several minutes, watching a boy point and laugh at the ducks while his mother watched on.

Once they passed, Harry reached into his pocket and pulled out a small bag with the ends of an old loaf of bread. He handed it to her.

"Where'd you get that?" She asked with surprise.

He shrugged. "I found it in the rubbish bin."

She smiled at his thoughtfulness and took the ends from him. Together, they went down to the pond, throwing pieces of bread to the mallards that swam in circles in front of them, gobbling up the treat.


"Good morning, Harry! Andrew!" Margaret leaned against the doorway and greeted them, using Grubbs' first name.

He had spoken up the night before at dinner and said he didn't want to be called Grubbs anymore. Margaret and her mother had exchanged knowing glances. The boys were growing up.

Harry and the boy who was nearly a teenager were sitting at the table; their breakfast dishes pushed aside and were arm wrestling. Harry was doing his best to let Andrew feel like he was doing well when he could easily overpower him.

"Morning!" They both said at once, not even looking up from their tournament of arms.

Margaret chuckled to herself and made a quick breakfast of toast and eggs. She ate it while she looked over the latest newspaper with the headlines, *'JAPAN SURRENDERS!'* Margaret could hardly believe her eyes.

Everyone filtered downstairs one by one as the news of the day started to fill the air.

Once again, Times Square was filled with confetti, tickertapes, waving flags, kissing couples, children shouting triumphantly, bands playing songs, and G.I.'s and Navy personnel cramming the streets.

America had hoped for victory since the first few hours of the day that lived in infamy. Now they were finally celebrating in the crowded streets of New York City. Everyone from the house went to celebrate. They wove their flags and celebrated the victorious day that marked the official end of the war.

The day felt like it had no start and no end. Everyone celebrated for hours and cheered and wove their flags, shouting, "Victory for America!" and "The Japs surrendered!" There were people everywhere, and just like how it had been in London for V-E Day, people celebrated the end of the dark days of war together... their homes were safe.

Today in the Pacific, the guns were silent.

After several hours of joining the excitement, Margaret and Rachel walked back to the house while Harry stayed with the boys who still wanted to galivant around the city and celebrate. They walked arm-in-arm as the hot August sun glared down on them.

"So," Rachel started. "I guess we're just down to six weeks now, right?" She asked, the topic of Margaret returning to London never really leaving her mind.

"I can't believe how fast it's gone." Margaret replied, looking around the street at the brownstones she had come to love so much. "Mum told you a bit of her plan, right?"

Rachel nodded. "I hope it works. Thankfully, I'm eighteen now, so it'll be a simpler process for myself. But Pitcher's only fifteen and Andrew's a year younger." She sighed. "I guess we'll have to wait and see."

Margaret squeezed her arm. "I'm sorry... I wish I could scoop all of us up and take us back to England."

"You don't have to apologize, Meg. I'm sorry I flipped my wig when you first told me. I guess I've just come to think of you as my sister. I've gotten used to having you around." She chuckled.

Margaret smiled, she had gotten used to having a sister, too.

After they walked another block, letting go of each other's arms because they were starting to get sweaty, Rachel questioned, "are you glad you came?"

The question hit Margaret harder than she thought it would. They stopped in front of their house, and she looked up at it admiringly. She remembered the day she came like it was yesterday. It had been warm, quiet, sunny... she was so young and so naïve, so full of trepidation. She answered Rachel's question with a fondness in her tone.

"I am." And she truly was utterly thankful everything had happened the way it had. "I'll always be glad."

On the first day of October, Margaret found herself standing somewhere she had stood once before. The wind rushed about her. The waves broke beneath her. The prow of the ship glided on the water far below. She watched as New York passed her by and they headed out to open sea.

How time had changed her.

"Thought I'd find you here," Harry came up behind her and wrapped his arms around her.

Margaret laughed and tried to get away playfully. "Stop it,"

He kissed her cheek and released her, putting his arm around her shoulder. "Are you alright?"

She nodded. "It's just so bittersweet. My heart's split in two by a proper ocean now."

"Mm," Harry agreed sadly. "I'm sorry, my love."

"What about you?" Margaret looked up to him, admiring him for everything he was and all she saw in him.

He grinned down at her. "I was thinking about how beautiful of a bride you'll be."

Margaret blushed.

Harry kissed her.

In that moment, he couldn't help but think that this was what he had fought for... This was what his comrades had died for. The crisp, free air whipped around them on the deck of the ship, carrying a promise of peace, unfettered possibilities, and most importantly, undying, undaunted hope.

---

Margaret gazed upon a familiar cobblestone path.

"Are you coming?" She looked over her shoulder at Harry.

He shook his head and rested against the fence. "You go ahead, love."

A plane droned by overhead.

Margaret smiled and started up the leaf-strewn path. Excitement hastened her steps under the sunshine that was, for once, shining down on

London. Without a moment to lose, she opened the door.

"Dad?!"

She stepped over the threshold of her home and left the din of the plane and the noise of the outdoors behind.

*The End*

*"Our debt to the heroic men and valiant women in the service of our country can never be repaid. They have earned our undying gratitude. America will never forget their sacrifices."*

*President Harry S. Truman*

*Three Beaufighter Mark IF night fighters of No. 600 Squadron RAF flying in starboard echelon formation near Colerne, Wiltshire.*

## The No. 600 Squadron

The 600 Squadron was a real squadron of the Royal Air Force that fought during WWII. They were a night fighter squadron that fought valiantly during the Battle of Britain and in many places including France, North Africa, Sicily, Italy, Salerno, Anzio, Netunno, and at the Gustav and Gothic Line.

During the war they almost exclusively flew the Bristol Beaufighter.

While Harry and his comrades are fictional, many of the stories of the night fighter raids are true – taken from first-hand accounts and real missions, following the path the 600 Squadron took during World War II. Their journey started in Northolt, Middlesex at the beginning of the war and ended in northern Italy at the end of the war. During that time, they made a massive difference providing night cover for Allied bases and transport shipping. In Italy, they flew many intruder missions and eventually the Beaufighters were replaced with Mosquitoes. On August 21st 1945, the No. 600 Squadron was disbanded.

It was the highest-scoring night fighter squadron in the RAF.

# More Books By Lea:

*The Sacred Rose*

*The Rolling Thunder*

*Percival Annum & the Spinning Clocks*

*The Guardians of Brinheim Trilogy:*

*The Dragon's Seal*

*Uniting the Realm*

*The Golden King*

*The Realm of Ice and Fire:*

*Frost*

*Fire*

*Fierce*

*The Legacy Series:*

*Lady Knight*

*The Valiant Heart*

*A Royal Accord*

*The Forgotten Lands*

*The Great Deliverance*

*Beckoned*

*Secret of the North*

**Available at Barnes & Noble, Amazon,
Amazon Kindle, and bookstores near you!**

## About the Author:

Lea Henze has been a passionate writer since she was young. She has written 20 books which genres range from medieval fantasy, action & adventure, and historical fiction. As a dedicated Christ-follower, Lea strives to weave the truths of the Bible into every one of her books, holding fast to her Christian principles and morals to encourage, inspire, and uplift the reader. She grew up on a small horse farm in rural Northern Illinois, spent many wonderful years in Kentucky, and currently resides in Ohio with her husband.